Treas... JADE

For Sharyn—
Thank you for
your continued
interest—

11-11-06

Treasure Coast JADE

Paul E. McElroy

Treasure Coast Mysteries,
43 Kindred St., Stuart, FL. 34994

www.TreasureCoastMysteries.com

Printed in United States of America

Publication date January 2006
1   3   5   7   9   10   8   6   4   2
Copyright © 2005 by Paul E. McElroy
All rights reserved.

Publisher
Treasure Coast Mysteries, Inc.
43 Kindred Street
Stuart, FL 34994
772-288-1066

LIBRARY OF CONGRESS CATALOGING-IN-PUBLICATION DATA:
McElroy, Paul E.
Treasure Coast JADE/ by Paul E. McElroy
476 Pages   6" x 9"
Trade paperback

ISBN 0-9715136-5-1

1. McCray, James – (Mack) Fictitious character – Fiction.
2. Undercover agents – Florida - Fiction
3. Florida – Fiction   I. Title.
PS-------   T --------------- ------------------

Dedication

For my mother and father who instilled my ideals and values.

For Michi who stood by my side and supported me in the good times and the bad, through sickness and health and all of those times when she knew that I had to do something because I just had to do it regardless of the outcome - like this one.

Florida's 'Treasure Coast'

Appropriately named for the twelve ship *Spanish Plate Fleet* that sank along it's shores on July 30, 1715 Florida's *Treasure Coast* stretches along the Atlantic coast from Jupiter to Sebastian sixty miles to the north. Tucked in between Highway 1 and the Atlantic Ocean the *Treasure Coast* ambles along luring visitors to its Gulf Stream kissed beaches of fine sand.

Amateur treasure hunters strolling along the sandy beaches with metal detectors in hand attempt to appear disinterested in the trinkets that they scoop up from the sand in wire-meshed baskets.

The *Cartagena* and *Vera Cruz* Spanish treasure fleets arrived in Havana in May 1715 on their way back to Spain. They planned to replenish their meager stores and sail a few days later. The captain of the *Vera Cruz Fleet* had 1,000 chests of silver in the cabin beneath his own and had stuffed the holds of his other ships with gold bullion and silver ingots. The *Cartagena Fleet* was loaded with silver and gold coins from the mints in Columbia, gold jewelry from Peru and 166 chests of Columbian emeralds.

The combined ships, now named the *Plate Fleet* departed Havana the morning of July 24, 1715 to enter the Gulf Stream and proceed northward along the Florida coast. However, on July 30 a hurricane struck the fleet. All but one of the ships had its bottom ripped out on coral reefs and sank resulting in the death of more than 1,000 Spaniards and the scattering of treasure from *Sebastian* to *Stuart*. Historical records indicate that much of the treasure was salvaged, but the *Urca de Lima* has yet to be found.

Hopeful treasure hunters from around the world come to the *Treasure Coast* to try their luck. Why don't you visit us too? You might catch sight of Rat, Mack or Tina and can even wet a line in hopes of catching a record setting *'cat-snapper'*.

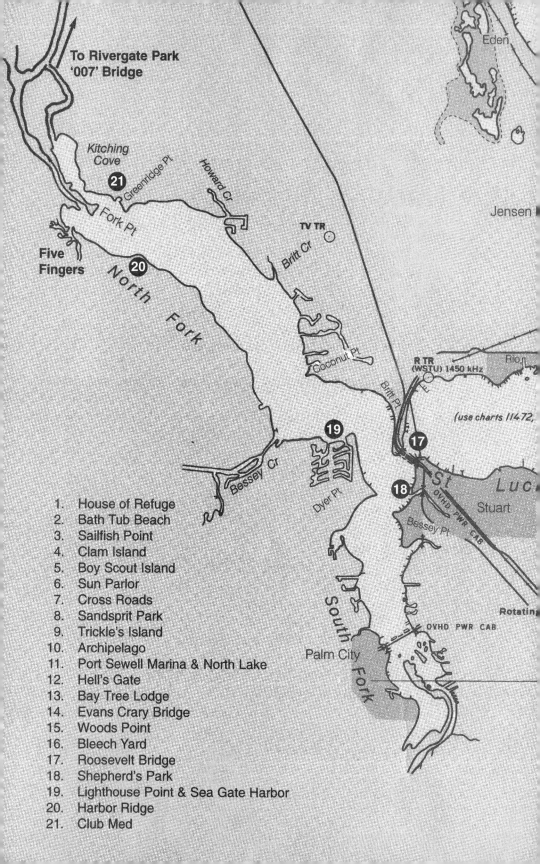

To Rivergate Park
'007' Bridge

Eden

Kitching
Cove

21

Greenridge Pt

Howard Cr

Jensen

Fork Pt

TV TR

Britt Cr

Five
Fingers

20

North Fork

Coconut Pt

R TR
(WSTU) 1450 kHz

Rio

Britt Pt

(use charts 11472,

19

Bessey Cr

Dyer Pt

17

St Luc

18

OVHD PWR CAB

Bessey Pt

Stuart

1.   House of Refuge
2.   Bath Tub Beach
3.   Sailfish Point
4.   Clam Island
5.   Boy Scout Island
6.   Sun Parlor
7.   Cross Roads
8.   Sandsprit Park
9.   Trickle's Island
10. Archipelago
11. Port Sewell Marina & North Lake
12. Hell's Gate
13. Bay Tree Lodge
14. Evans Crary Bridge
15. Woods Point
16. Bleech Yard
17. Roosevelt Bridge
18. Shepherd's Park
19. Lighthouse Point & Sea Gate Harbor
20. Harbor Ridge
21. Club Med

South Fork

Palm City

OVHD PWR CAB

Rotating

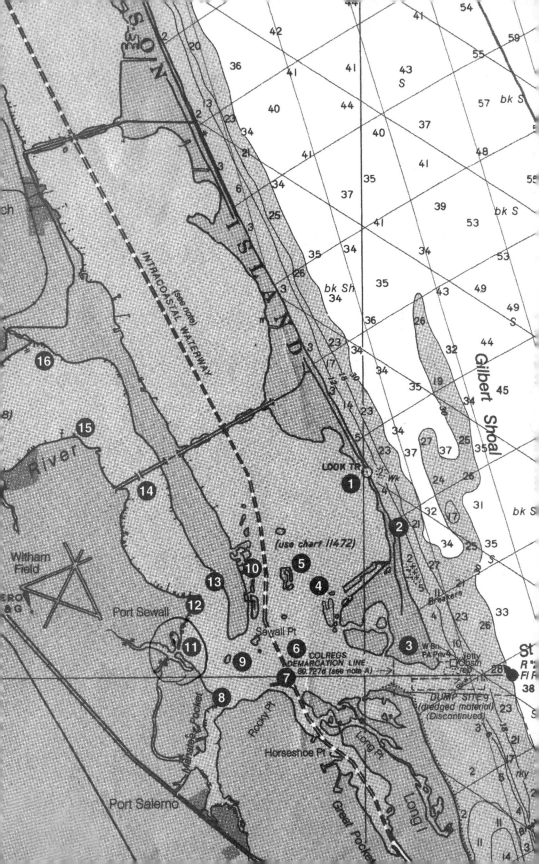

Also by Paul E. McElroy

Treasure Coast DECEIT
ISBN 0-9715136-0-0
January 2002

Treasure Coast Archipelago
ISBN 0-9715136-1-9
March 2003

Treasure Coast GOLD
ISBN 0-9715136-2-7
January 2004

Treasure Coast ENIGMA
ISBN 0-9715136-3-5
December 2004

SPIRIT CHASER
ISBN 0-9715136-4-3
June 2005

Prologue

It has been said by men far wiser than I, that evil often lurks in the minds of men. Strange ideas appear in the idle human mind, quickly disappear and reappear overnight. Mind control, brain washing, psycho synthesis, or whatever else you may choose to call it has been the lure of despots and possibly even democratically elected leaders.

JADE leaped into my mind like a raptor leaping from the darkness of a primeval jungle trail. It burrowed into my mind and tenaciously clung onto my conscious thought patterns during my waking hours and ravaged my subconscious mind during many restless periods of sleep. I could not rest until I committed the saga to paper.

How much of what you read between these pages is truth and how much is fiction? There is more of the former than the latter. Many people strongly suggested that I not broach the topic of government mind control experiments, but I couldn't stop.

Unfortunately, we live in an imperfect world filled with people who would control, and even destroy, our minds in the name of peace. That terrifies me. This is such a tale.

While perusing these pages imagine that you are traveling down a dark country road at night, without the benefit of a map or headlights, as the plot jogs here and there. Where does it all come together? For me it was at the end of the road, but I didn't know where it was until I finally got there.

I hope that you enjoy the many twists and turns of *JADE*.

Paul McElroy

Chapter 1

Wednesday evening came early for Mack McCray. He was bushed from guiding Tina Louise McShay's 48-foot sailboat from its berth in Port Sewall Marina up the picturesque St. Lucie River and down the Okeechobee Waterway to the Indiantown Marina. They left Port Sewall Marina at 9:15 Wednesday morning and the thirty-plus mile trip took twelve boring hours because Mack had to fight an outgoing six-knot tidal current all the way from Port Sewall Marina to the St. Lucie Locks. The sailboat's ancient gas kicker chattered in protest the entire way and the best it could make on a good day under full power was only eight knots. The boat's effective speed over ground was two knots and it took four hours to reach the Palm City Bridge about eight miles from the marina.

Upon arrival at the Indiantown Marina, Fred, the aged dockmaster, helped Mack guide the sailboat into a quiet slip on the west wall. Tina left Mack alone to check out a noisy rocker arm in the ancient engine while she checked into the Seminole Inn. It was almost nine-thirty by the time Mack took a shower and cleaned up. Tina was waiting for him outside the cabin door. When he emerged she directed him into a waiting taxi before he could utter a protest. The taxi dropped the non-talking duo off in front of the Silver Saddle Bar.

Mack contemplated attacking the last two slices of a large sausage pizza while Tina played with the remains of a Rueben sandwich. He was drinking draft Bud while she swilled down *Absolut'* vodka martinis. About a dozen Guatemalan day laborers dressed in blue jeans, cowboy boots and white cowboy hats wagered over a lively game of 'horse' played with a leather cup and a pair of dice. They cheered and cursed in Spanish when the red plastic dice rolled across the top of the pool table and came to a stop. Large amounts of money changed hands with each roll of the dice.

Mack noticed that the bare incandescent light bulbs overhead pulsated in time with the raucous county music blasting out of the ancient jukebox in the corner. He decided to open the conversation

"It looks like those guys are having a good time," he offered. "Isn't gambling illegal?"

"I wouldn't worry about it," Tina dryly responded. "This is the only fun those guys have. Most of them will lose all of their money and go back to the migrant camp broke. They'll be back tomorrow night with their day's wages to try again."

"Shouldn't someone stop them?"

"Why? They're having fun."

"Is the game fixed?"

"Of course. Carlos keeps it that way. He always wins."

"Which one's Carlos?"

"He's the guy behind the bar. He owns the place. His right-hand man Pedro controls the dice. He slips a loaded pair of dice in and out of the game as it goes along."

"Don't those guys know that they can't win?"

"They suspect it, but Pedro lets one or two of them win a little bit of money every night. That way they all keep their hopes up and keep coming back to play night after night. Tomorrow night tonight's losers will win and tonight's winners will lose. It balances out in the end. Let's change the subject."

"Fine with me. I was just trying to make conversation. Did Joy tell you about Ralph's sex pheromone business?"

"What? Sex pheromones! What does Ralph know about pheromones much less about sex?"

"He told me that when he is on the beach digging up sand fleas to sell for fishing bait that women stop and talk to him. He figures that they're attracted by the sex pheromones in his sweat."

"Ralph smells like a wet goat when he sweats! No woman would ever be attracted to him!"

"I'm just relating what he told me. Don't take it out on the messenger."

"Duck!"

Tina shoved Mack's head down onto the table. His face met the pizza pan as a glass beer bottle sailed over his head from the direction of the pool table where the day laborers were gambling. The beer bottle smashed against the ancient jukebox and it skipped over a complete chord of Roy Orbison crooning *Pretty Woman*.

"What the hell was that for?" Mack sputtered as he peeled tomato paste off his left cheek.

"One of the Guats threw a beer bottle in this direction," Tina softly whispered. "Keep your head down. I think that all hell's going to break loose in a minute."

"Why?"

"One of the Guats lost all of his money and he's upset about it. He's accusing Pedro of cheating"

"You said that they all know that the game's crooked and they accept it."

"He's a new guy. I haven't seen him in here before. He doesn't know the rules."

"What do you mean you haven't seen him in here before? How often do you come over here?"

"That's really none of your concern is it? I come over here whenever I feel like it."

"What's happening? I can't see a thing. I've got tomato paste in my eye."

"It's time to head for the back door."

"Why?"

"The straight razors are coming out and this is going to get real nasty real fast! I hope that Carlos called the Sheriff's department."

"How long will it take them to get here?"

"A couple of minutes. There're two deputies on duty out here every night."

"Duck! Here's come another beer bottle!"

Mack voluntarily obliged as an empty *Corona* bottle sailed six inches over his head and crashed into the jukebox. Roy Orbison skipped another chord of *Pretty Woman*.

"Here come the cops. You can get up now." Tina whispered as she lifted her hand off of the back Mack's head. "It's Elmo! Watch how he handles the Guats! He doesn't take any crap from them."

Mack obliged and lifted his head out of the pizza pan. A piece of crust was wedged in his right ear.

"What's he going to do?"

"He'll hit them all with pepper spray and then he'll zap the rowdy one with his Taser gun. It'll be all over before you can count to five."

Tina's prediction of Deputy Elmo's actions to quell the disturbance was right on. Elmo held a large can of pressurized pepper spray in his left hand and a plastic Taser gun in his right. An immense cloud of pepper spray enveloped the terrified men who huddled together for protection. Several of them bolted for the door and Elmo zapped the last one in the back with the dual metal darts from the Taser gun. The man screamed and ripped off his white cowboy hat as he fell to the floor writhing in pain.

"He got the right guy," Tina dryly remarked. "He seems to have a sixth sense when it comes to picking out the guilty party in a crowd."

"Should we let him know that we're in here? We can be

witnesses if it goes to trial."

"No! That's the last thing we should do. I didn't see anything. Did you?"

"No! You shoved my face into the pizza pan. I couldn't see anything."

"Then you can't be a witness. Just sit there and keep your mouth shut. You didn't see anything."

"What about the illegal gambling and the loaded dice?"

"I don't know anything about it."

"You told me that they were gambling and that Pedro was using loaded dice!"

"Did I? I don't remember saying that? Maybe you've had too much to drink."

"I distinctly remember you saying it."

"I don't. It's your word against mine and I win."

"What do you mean you win?"

"I'm female and in court the judge always takes the word of a woman over that of a man."

"I should've known. Okay. I'll forget that I saw or heard anything."

"That's better. Now sit there, sip on your beer and keep your mouth shut while Elmo drags that Guat out of here. I don't want Elmo to know that we're here."

"Why not?"

"Because. That's why. It would be uncomfortable for him and also for us."

"Why?"

"If it goes to trial I could wind up as the prosecuting attorney and I would have to disqualify myself. It would be difficult to explain to the judge why I was here. Just keep your big mouth shut! "

"I didn't say anything!"

"You were thinking about it. If you open your big mouth you could be called as a material witness and you would have to disqualify yourself too."

"Why would I have to disqualify myself?"

"Because Elmo's a friend of yours and you'd be biased in his favor."

"Oh. Now what?"

"Just sit here, sip your beer and don't look over there. Elmo might see us."

"What about after he leaves? Then what?"

"You're going to sit here and watch me get smashed. I need to relax."

"It's after midnight and I'm beat. Why don't we catch a cab back to the marina and sack out?"

"We're going to walk back!"

"Why?"

"The cab stops running at midnight."

"What do you mean by the cab?"

"There's only one. The driver starts at noon and goes home at midnight. He needs to sleep too."

"It's a long way back to the marina!"

"Waking is good exercise and you can use some. You're getting a paunch over your belt."

"I don't have any paunch and I'm beat!"

"It's not even a quarter mile."

"If it's so close why did you have a cab waiting at the marina when I came out of the cabin?"

"It was easier that way. I knew that you'd throw a hissy fit if you had to walk a couple of blocks."

"I was tired."

"So was I. Now shut up and drink your beer. You're going to need your energy later."

"Why?"

"Why what?"

"Why will I need my energy?"

"I plan to be very smashed and you'll probably have to carry me back to the Seminole Inn."

"Why am I going to have to carry you back to the hotel?"

"Because I won't be able to walk by myself and you're not going to drag me back by my hair."

"What if I just leave you here and walk back to the marina by myself?"

"I'd kill you. You're not going to leave me here with all of these migrant workers!"

"Why not? You seem to be on a first name basis with all of them and the bartender."

"Because I plan on being very drunk and I don't want to be groped by some sweaty migrant worker and his buddies!"

"It might be good for you. They say that variety's the spice of life."

Mack didn't see the blow coming. Tina's right fist caught him on the left cheekbone and the force knocked him off the edge of his chair. He landed straddle legged on the sawdust covered wooden floor.

"What was that for?" Mack shook his head as he rubbed his stinging cheek. "That's assault. I want to press charges."

"Shut up and sit down! You're making a big fool out of yourself."

"I didn't do anything. I was just sitting here minding my own business and you clobbered me in the face."

"You insulted me and you deserved to have your face slapped!"

"I was giving you a tongue in cheek compliment and that was no slap. You hit me with your closed fist! It hurt!"

"I intended to hurt you and you deserved much more than what you got."

Tina slammed back another vodka gimlet and pushed the empty glass away as she reached for another full glass. Apparently Carlos was aware of her drinking habits and served her three drinks at a time. She motioned for him to bring her another round.

It was 2:13 A.M. when Tina finally passed out, slipped out of her chair and landed with a soft 'plop' on the wooden floor. Mack scooped her up, tossed her limp body over his right shoulder and looked across the smoky room towards the bar. Carlos gave Mack a 'thumbs up' signal and pointed at the front door.

A Guatemalan bouncer held the door open and pointed at the Seminole Inn across the street.

"Senorita Tina always stays over there when she drinks too much," the Guatemalan said in slow, halting English. "They know her very well."

"*Gracias*," Mack responded as he slipped out the door.

Three passed out Guatemalans were sprawled face down on the sidewalk in front of the Silver Saddle. Mack carefully navigated around them and headed for the Seminole Inn.

"It makes me wonder just how much time she spends out here," Mack thought. *"The bartender knows what she drinks and the waiter knows where she stays when she passes out. I wonder what other surprises she has in store for me?"*

Chapter 2

"Mack! Are you going to sleep all day?" Tina's sharp voice rang out of the darkness.

Mack sat straight up in the narrow bunk and smacked his head on the tongue and groove polished Brazilian mahogany ceiling. He tried to focus his eyes on the shapeless figure standing motionless in the sailboat's narrow hatchway.

"Well? Are you going to sleep all day? It's almost nine o'clock and we have places to go and people to see. Drag your hairy butt out of that bunk and get yourself cleaned up."

"Why?" He managed to stutter. The inside of his mouth felt like the inside of a chicken feather pillow. "I don't have any plans for today."

"I do! Now get out of there and get yourself cleaned up. We

have to get over to the Silver Saddle!"

"Why? Didn't you have enough to drink last night? We didn't leave the place until almost two-thirty this morning."

"You forgot to pick up my cell phone when you unceremoniously dragged me out of there over your shoulder like a bag of flour. My belly button still hurts from your bony shoulder."

"How else was I supposed to get you back? You couldn't walk and Carlos didn't offer to loan me his stock room dolly."

"You could have scooped me up in your arms and carried me that way. That's the way a real gentleman would have done it."

"I wasn't carrying you across the threshold of the bridal suite. I was just trying to get you back to the hotel before you puked all over yourself."

"I don't get sick when I drink. I just pass out. Why did you leave me all alone in the hotel room last night?"

"What makes you think that I left you all by yourself? There were three Guats lined up outside your door when I left. Two of them were holding guitars and one of them was shaking a pair of gourd maracas. They told me that Carlos sent them over to serenade you to sleep."

"What! I didn't see any Guats when I woke up this morning! I was alone."

"They had to go to work in the fields at six-thirty this morning. They're day laborers and they can't sleep all day. They have to work for a living."

"You lying bastard!" Tina screamed as she slammed the hatch cover closed. The small cabin went black.

"I guess she'll leave me alone now," Mack chuckled to himself as he rolled over and pulled the pillow over his head. He should have known better.

The metal prongs of the electrified cattle prod caught him just below the left side of his *gluteus maximus*. The 10,000-volt jolt of electricity ran up his leg, through his hip and straight along his backbone. His brain knew that something was wrong and the intense pain hurt really badly!

Mack leaped up, his forehead smacked into the mahogany and knocked one of the custom-made tongue and groove boards loose from its perch. It flew across the tiny cabin and slammed into the metal sink. His brain reeled in pain and he babbled incoherently as he attempted to regain his senses.

"Is that all you can say? I can't understand anything you're saying!" Tina sang out as she waved the electric cattle prod over her head in a slow menacing circle. "Are you going to get up now?"

Mack rolled out of the bunk and forgot that he was buck-ass naked.

Tina took full advantage of his weakness and reached out with the cattle prod toward his maleness. He shoved it away with his left hand and dove for the safety of the galley center island. She caught him in the rear end with the cattle prod and got in another 'lick' as his buttocks cleared the bunk.

He screamed in pain. "Woman! What the hell are you doing? That thing's designed for cows not people!"

"I forgot that it was so strong. I apologize," Tina gushed as she swung the cattle prod behind her back. "I promise not to do it again. I was just trying to be funny."

"It wasn't one bit funny! It hurt! You could've killed me with that thing!"

"I don't think so. Carlos told me to put the switch on 'low power' so that it would only sting."

"What do you mean Carlos told you to put it on low power? When did he give that thing to you? You were passed out cold when I dragged your butt out of his place this morning."

"I'm not talking about Carlos at the Silver Saddle. I meant the Carlos that's the foreman on my uncle's cattle ranch. He stopped by the hotel this morning and joined me for breakfast."

"Why did he give that thing to you? Doesn't he know that you have a sadistic streak?"

"I saw it on the seat of his truck and asked him if I could borrow it because I wanted to play a joke on you. He's waiting for me on the dock."

"It wasn't very funny! I've got a big red welt on my butt. Look!" Mack swung around and bent over so that Tina could get a full view of his *gluteus maximus*.

"Yuk! I don't need to look at your hairy butt!" Tina screamed as she turned and dashed up the narrow hatchway. She smacked her head on the wooden hatch cover.

"Crap!" She bellowed. "That hurt!"

"Serves you right," Mack responded as he rubbed the sore red welts on his *gluteus maximus*.

"I'll get even with you later!" Tina snottily responded as she swung open the hatch cover and skipped out onto the deck of the sailboat. She slammed the hatch cover shut and Mack heard the stainless steel hasp slip into place with a soft metallic 'click."

"I guess that I don't have to be in any hurry now," he muttered. "She's locked me in here."

"You've got five minutes to get cleaned up and out here," Tina's voice echoed through the deck-mounted standpipe used as a ventilator.

"But you locked me in. I can't get out."

"I'll be waiting up here for you. Knock on the hatch cover when you're ready to go."

"Then what are you going to do? Smack me with the boomvang when I stick my head up?"

"No. It's lashed down. I won't do anything to you. Just hurry up. We've got to get over to the Silver Saddle and get my cell phone before some Guat takes off with it."

"Why the hurry? It's only eight forty-five. What time does Carlos open up the place?"

"When he hears me beating on the front door he'll open up damn quick."

"Okay. Give me a few minutes to shave and take a shower."

"Hurry up. I want to get started back to Stuart by noon. It'll take us at least six hours to get back and I have to get ready for a court hearing in West Palm Beach at one-thirty tomorrow afternoon."

"Yes ma'am. I'll hurry as best I can considering that I'm severely injured," Mack shouted up the standpipe ventilator shaft. "I can't move very fast with these wounds."

"You don't know what injured means! If your butt isn't up here on the deck in five minutes I'm going to sink this boat right at the dock and you'll go down with the ship."

"I'm not the captain. It's your boat."

"Don't play with words. Just get yourself cleaned up and up here fast!"

"Yes ma'am," Mack cordially responded as he rubbed the red welt on his behind.

He shaved and showered as fast as he could in the cold water because he forgot to plug in the dock's shore power outlet when they docked the night before.

Mack rapped three times on the overhead hatchway door and ducked in anticipation of a swinging, fully charged cattle prod as it opened.

"You don't have to duck," Tina hissed. "I'm not going to zap you with the cattle prod. I don't have it anymore."

"Where is it?"

"Carlos came over and picked it up while you were playing with yourself in the shower."

"What are you blabbering about? I wasn't playing with myself!"

"Then why were you moaning?"

"There isn't any hot water because I forgot to plug in the shore power last night. I was groaning not moaning. There's a big difference."

"Moaning, groaning, whatever. I don't really care. Are you finally ready to go?"

"I suppose. Where are we going?"

"I already told you! We're going to the Silver Saddle to pick up my cell phone. You forgot to pick it up when you threw me over your bony shoulder and dragged me out of there like a side of beef. You must think that you're some kind of caveman."

"I threw you over my shoulder because you were easier to carry that way. It's a long way from the Silver Saddle to the Seminole Inn. But of course you didn't notice."

"What do you say we pace off the exact number of steps? I'll bet that it's less than one hundred yards."

"I don't really care how far it is over there. Why don't you go over there by yourself, pick up your cell phone and zip back over here? I can have the boat engine warmed up and ready to go by the time you get back here."

"The engine doesn't require any warm up time and I don't

want to walk all the way over there all by myself."

"All the way over there? Didn't you just say that it was less than one hundred yards?"

"The exact distance isn't the point."

"Then what is the point?"

"I don't want to walk over there by myself. You never know who might be hanging around. I might get mugged!"

"Mugged at nine o'clock in the morning? I don't think so. But if someone that you put in jail recognizes you they might run over you with their truck."

"That could be true as well. Now come on and let's go. The sooner we get over there and get my cell phone the sooner we can leave for Stuart."

"I'm not in any hurry," Mack responded with a sly smirk. "I don't have any pressing matters on my plate today."

"Yes do you!"

"What?"

"You have to get me back to Stuart by six o'clock tonight so I can drive back to West Palm and get a good night's sleep. I have an important court hearing at one-thirty tomorrow afternoon."

"Yes ma'am. I understand and I'll do my best to get you back by six o'clock. Keep in mind that one of the pushrods was knocking pretty badly on the way over here."

"Didn't you add some oil like I told you to do?"

"Yes I did and it seemed to help some. I'm just saying that we should take it easy on the engine on the way back."

"Fine. Let's go!" Tina slapped Mack on the left shoulder and gestured towards the dock with her thumb. "We don't have all day."

"I thought we did." Mack responded as he ducked in anticipation of a blow.

The walk from the Indiantown Marina to the Silver Saddle took Mack and Tina less than ten minutes. The front door was locked and a handmade sign read, "Open at noon for the Kiwanis luncheon."

"I'll get him out of there," Tina barked as she picked up an empty Budweiser long neck beer bottle from the dusty ground.

"What are you going to do with that?" Mack asked.

"I'm going to beat on the door with it. Carlos will hear it and he'll drag his fat butt out here to find out what's going on. Duck when the door opens."

"Why?"

"He might come out shooting."

"What! Let's get out of here now!"

"What's the matter? Are you afraid of getting shot? He only uses number-eight birdshot in his shotgun. It won't kill you. It'll just sting a little bit when the doctor digs them out of your ass."

"A shotgun? I've shot quail with loads of low-power number eight shot and it kills them!"

"Don't worry about it. I'm sure that he'll look out the security peephole before he shoots."

"What if he doesn't?"

"Then you'd better be ready to duck because he usually doesn't ask questions first. He gets real cranky if he gets woke up before noon."

"That's real comforting. Can't you call him on the telephone and tell him that we're out here?"

"How can I? You left my cell phone in there when you dragged me out last night."

"You seem to forget that it wasn't last night! It was almost two-thirty this morning."

"Let's not quibble over the exact time. The point is that you forgot to pick up my cell phone."

"I didn't know that I was in charge of it. You didn't tell me that I was until fifteen minutes ago."

"There you go with that smart Yankee mouth again."

Tina spun around and began beating a tattoo on the sheet metal covered door with the bottom of the beer bottle. She paused, switched the bottle to her left hand and began the process over again.

"The metal vibrates through the bottle and all the way up my arm," she offered. "It hurts."

The metal door suddenly swung open without warning and Mack dove for the sparse dirt of the flowerbeds. Dust flew in all directions and filled Mack's eyes and nostrils. He couldn't see and he couldn't breathe.

"What'cha do that for?" Growled a deep male voice with a heavy Hispanic accent. "I wasn't going to shoot ya'll. We're civilized over here in Indiantown. We haven't had a gun fight in the old rodeo coral on Second Street for almost three years."

"Tina said that you shoot first and ask questions later. I wasn't taking any chances," Mack sputtered through the dust cloud surrounding his head.

"I knew it was you guys." Carlos offered as he swung the door open. "I didn't even bring my shotgun."

"How did you know it was us?" Mack asked. "I didn't see you looking through the peep hole."

"There's a closed circuit TV camera mounted under the eave right above your head."

"Oh. I didn't see it."

"Come on in anyway. What brings ya'll by so early in the morning? We don't open for lunch until eleven-thirty."

"This bozo forgot to pick up my cell phone when he dragged me out of here last night."

"Yeah. We found it on the floor when we were sweeping up. I stuck it behind the bar."

A young Hispanic girl draped in a blue terry cloth towel dashed out from behind the bar and ran in the direction of the kitchen.

"Who's that?" Tina quipped with a smirk. "Is she your niece or your cousin? You got in trouble for messing around with young stuff once before. Didn't you learn your lesson?"

"She's my niece. She stopped by this morning to take a shower before going to school. They don't have running water in their trailer. I told her that I'd look over her homework before she catches the school bus."

"It's kind of late for a school bus." Tina grinned. "Why doesn't her family have running water?"

"Her mother didn't pay the water bill last month. Her boyfriend blew her welfare check on booze."

"Are you sure that he didn't gamble it away in here?"

"Maybe he lost a little bit. I try to keep my eye on him when he comes in here, but I can't watch him every minute."

"I'll bet."

"What's that thing behind the bar?" Tina inquired as she pointed at a green stone face peering out from the mirrored wall behind the bar. "It looks like a mask!"

"That Guat that Elmo dragged out of here in handcuffs last night brought it in here a couple of days ago to pay off his bar tab. He tried to pay it off in chickens but they were all spoiled. When I cleaned them they all had black meat and black bones. He told me that they were Chinese chickens from Guatemala and were supposed to be that way. I figured that they were the losers in one of the cockfights the Guats hold in the woods out by the Naked Lady Ranch. I tossed him out on his ear and told him to bring me in cash. The next day he brought in that stupid looking green stone mask. He said that it is part of his family treasure and is very valuable. I think he bought it at Wal-Mart."

"It's very pretty. Is it worth anything?"

"I doubt it. He has a fantasy that he comes from Mayan royalty, but he's a troublemaker. Elmo's dragged him out of here a couple of times before. When he drinks three *cervazas* he gets smashed. He has zero tolerance for alcohol. The Guats lack the enzyme in their blood that converts the alcohol in booze to sugar. They're the same as Indians and Eskimos. They get crocked on two *cervazas*."

"What's the guy's name?"

"Octavio. At least that's what he told me, but you know how those Guats lie."

"Did you call Elmo over here to arrest him last night? I didn't see him do anything wrong."

"There wasn't any of their special music playin' on the juke box last night and that made the Guats nervous. The music keeps them calmed down. Music soothes the savage beast and Guats."

"Why would the music keep them calmed down?" Mack interjected.

"I don't know but it always seems that if their special music isn't on and playing loud enough to blast the ear drums out of a goat that they drink too much *cervaza*, get rowdy and cause trouble."

"Why does the juke box pulsate?" Mack followed up. "It seems to have a beat of it's own."

"I don't know. It's been doing that for about a month. I hate those damn guitars, but I put up with it because the music makes them drink more beer. They gotta' have their damn guitar music blaring all the time."

"I noticed that Hispanic music is coming out of loudspeakers mounted on the light poles. Why?"

"The Guats would riot if they didn't have their damn music all day long. A Guatemalan radio station is piped in over a satellite and a DJ passes along messages and announcements. These peoples' ancestors believed in human sacrifices on alters on top of stone temples. They cut their victims' hearts out with a stone knife and drank their blood. I saw a bunch of Guats building an altar out of sod pallets in the woods next to the Naked Lady Ranch on Martin Grade Highway last week. I don't want my heart cut out and my head cut off! These Guats can get real nasty when they get drunk."

"I think that you're overreacting," Tina quipped. "Migrant workers are normally docile people."

"You haven't been here to see them on a Friday night after they've been paid and slopped down a half dozen *cervazas*. They can get real nasty."

"How much will you take for the stone mask," Tina inquired as she reached for her purse.

"It's not for sale. I kinda' like it up there, plus the Guats are afraid of it."

"What makes you think that they're afraid of the mask?" Mack asked.

The bartender turned to face Mack as he responded.

"They look down at the floor when they walk past the bar on their way to the head. They can't look directly at it. The Guat that conned me into taking it told me that it's supposed to represent a Mayan God. He couldn't look the mask directly in the face either."

"I think that it's a cheap replica turned out by the dozens for sale in tourist traps," Tina offered as she waved a fifty-dollar bill in front of the bartender's nose. " I'll give you fifty bucks for it."

"I already told you that it's not for sale."

"What's that weird-looking stone thing beside the mask," Tina asked as she pointed at an off-white stone statue about six inches high. "It looks like a dog smoking a pipe."

"I don't know what that is," Carlos responded with a shrug of his shoulders.

"Did Octavio give it to you?" Mack interjected.

"No," Carlos replied. "That young Guat girl that cleans up for me around here stuck it up there."

"I'm going take a picture of the mask if you don't mind," Tina stated as she removed a digital camera from her purse, focused it on the mask and snapped the shutter.

"Now, if you're both happy why don't you take your camera and cell phone and get out of here?" Carlos snapped.

"Don't get so testy about it," Tina snapped as she snatched her cell phone off the bar and spun on her heel. "If you decide to get rid of the mask give me a call," she quipped over her shoulder.

"Mack! Are you coming or are you sniffing around his niece? She's young – even for a letch like you."

"I'm coming," replied Mack as he winked at Carlos and gave him a 'thumbs up' salute. Carlos returned the salute with an accompanying grin and a sly wink. Mack turned and headed for the door. Tina waited for him in the open doorway.

"It's going to a long trip back to Stuart," Mack thought.

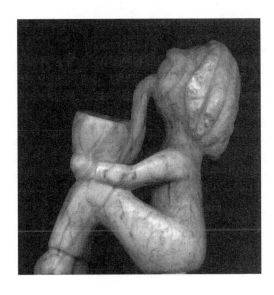

Chapter
3

Tina snored contentedly in the aft cabin. Her deep, almost comatose, condition was the result of downing a pint of *Absolut'* vodka mixed with frozen orange juice concentrate. She passed out cold about 4:30 P.M. as Mack was holding west of the St. Lucie Locks waiting for the lockmaster to whistle him clearance and guide the clumsy sailboat into the empty lock chamber.

Mack pondered his situation as he navigated the sluggish sailboat northward up the winding south fork of the St. Lucie River towards the Roosevelt Bridge.

"What the hell am I going to do with this broad?" He thought as the sailboat's keel scraped the top of an oyster bar jutting out from the mangrove-lined shoreline. *"She raises hell with everyone, drinks like a fish, passes out cold and conveniently*

forgets everything when she wakes up."

Mack passed the green day marker marking the shoal that jutted out from shore close aboard on his starboard side as he passed Hell's Gate made a sharp right turn and headed towards the mouth of Willoughby Creek and North Lake Lagoon to the east. It was 8:27 P.M. and the thirty-mile trip from Indiantown Marina took significantly longer than Mack had expected. They were held up for almost thirty minutes at the St. Lucie Locks while the Corps of Engineers lockmaster allowed a westbound towboat pushing three open hopper barges filled with scrap metal pass-through on its way to Lake Okeechobee and Fort Myers on the West Coast.

Mack tenderly guided the 48-foot sailboat into its slip at Port Sewall Marina and the port side rubber bow rub rail gently kissed the rubber bumper of the wooden dock. When Mack slipped the balky transmission into reverse, the right hand propeller reversed it and pulled the stern gently into the dock. He made the stern line fast with a round turn, followed by three figure eights and a half hitch, and made his way forward towards the bow so that he could loop the bow line around the metal cleat mounted in the solid planking of the wooden dock.

"Hey Mack! Toss that line over here and I'll wrap her on there for ya'," barked a twangy voice from the darkness. "I've been waitin' here for you to pull in since just about dark. I shoulda' figured she be passed out," rasped the voice from the darkness.

"Rat! What are you doing here?"

"I saw you pass by the sailboat anchorage at Shepherd's Park about seven o'clock. I hollered at ya', but apparently you were thinking about something else and didn't wave back at me. I rowed my dingy over to Shepherd's Park and rode my *Vespa* down here. I've been waitin' for ya' almost half an hour."

"There wasn't much I could do about it because the tide had turned and was coming back in when I passed under the Stuart Causeway Bridge. This old engine can barely make six knots on a good day. I had a piston rod knocking when I pulled into Indiantown Marina. I dumped a can of heavyweight oil over the tappets to keep them quiet."

"What are you going to do with Tina?"

"I'm going to leave her in there and let her sleep it off. I'm bushed. She kept me up in the Silver Saddle until almost two-thirty this morning and I had to carry her back to the Seminole Inn over my shoulder like a sack of wheat. She showed her gratitude by shoving an electric cattle prod half up my ass this morning to wake me up. I've just about had it with her."

"You've just about had it with whom Yankee Boy?" The high-pitched female voice echoed upward from the narrow passageway from the cabin below. "It wasn't for my navigating you'd never had made it through the St. Lucie Locks."

"The dead speaks," Rat rasped.

"What did you say you mangy excuse for a human being?" Tina screamed as her head popped in to view. "I should ring your scrawny neck and feed you to the buzzards! Get off of my dock before I really get mad!" Tina made an attempt at a round house right in Rats general direction, lost her balance and fell to the deck. "Now you did it! I broke my leg!" Tina rolled on the wooden deck and held her right leg to her chest. "If I could walk I'd chase your mangy butt all the way back to that ugly rat trap sailboat you call home!"

"I didn't do nothin'!" Rat rasped. I just came down here to help Mack tie up your boat."

"I don't care! Get off my property right now!"

"Okay. Don't have a hissy fit. I'm leavin'. Next time Mack can tie up your boat all by hisself." Rat slunk away in the darkness. "Mack, watch out for her. Female black widow spiders eat their mates after they're done with 'em."

"Are you calling me a black widow spider you little worm?"

There was no response from the dark shadows along the boat dock.

"How did you expect him to act after you treated him like that?" Mack offered. "He's a human being and he has feelings too."

"You call that mangy maggot a human being? A Cro-Magnon man is a gentleman compared to him. Now help me get up from here before my leg cramps up." Tina beckoned Mack to her side with the motion of her right index finger. "I have to get back to West Palm Beach tonight because I have to be in court tomorrow afternoon at one-thirty sharp."

"You aren't in any shape to drive a car. You might get stopped and arrested for DUI."

"I don't think so. A pint of vodka isn't enough booze to have any effect on me."

"But you passed out in the cabin before we got to the St. Lucie Locks!"

"I wasn't passed out. I was just taking a nap. Don't you remember that I didn't get to bed until after two-thirty this morning and I was up and at 'em two hours before you got your mangy butt out of the sack."

"You looked passed out to me. You were snoring like a hibernating bear."

"I have a nasal polyp that restricts my breathing. Besides how do you know what a hibernating bear sounds like when it's snoring?"

"I spent two nights in a black bear's cave during survival training in the Smokey Mountains of North Carolina."

"Are you going to help me up or not?" Tina raised her outstretched right hand in Mack's direction. "I'm hurt and I can't get up by myself."

"I suppose I can. You're not going to bite me are you?"

"I'll whack you between the legs with my foot if you don't help me up! I'll make sure that you never father children!"

"I understand." Mack reached for Tina's right hand, gave it a jerk and she practically flew up off the deck into his arms. "How's that?"

. "You smell like an oil tanker!" Tina screamed as she shoved Mack away. "Go take a bath!"

"I had to work on the engine on the way over from Indiantown."

"I don't care." Tina stepped across the boat deck onto the wooden boat dock. "I'm leaving. I expect that you'll wash down my boat before you do anything else?"

"You distinctly told me to go take a bath."

"Don't be silly. Do that after you wash down my boat and put things away. I'll call and check on you tomorrow when I get a break from court," Tina barked over her right shoulder as she headed for the narrow wooden stairway leading up to the marina parking lot above. "I think you have a visitor up here," she shouted as she disappeared over the top of the stairs.

"Who?"

There was no response from Tina.

"It's me Elmo," whispered a hesitant male voice from beneath the dark stairway. "Is she gone?"

"Elmo! Why are you hiding under the stairs? How long have you been there?"

"I pulled in while she was chewing your ass. I met Rat just as he was pulling out of the parking lot. He told me to hide out under here until she was gone. He hauled his butt out of the parking lot on that old blue Vespa of his like a tom cat with turpentine on his ass!"

"How did you know that we were back from Indiantown?"

"My cousin's the lock operator at the St. Lucie Lock. He called me on my cell phone when he locked you through a couple of hours ago. I figured that with the incoming tide it would take you about three hours to get here and it did."

"What can I do for you?"

"What happened to Tina? She had a stick up her butt when she ran up the steps."

"She got smashed at the Silver Saddle last night and I dragged her out of there about two-thirty this morning. To get back at me she stuck an electric cattle prod half up my butt to get me out of bed this morning. What brings you by here this time of night?"

"I saw you and Tina in the Silver Saddle last night and I wanted to explain what was going on. I didn't want the Guats out there to know that I knew you."

"Why not?"

"I'm kinda the bad guy over there. I help Carlos and the grove owners keep the Guats in line."

"So, you're a paid thug in a Martin County Sheriff department's uniform?"

"No! I'm not a paid thug! I'm a professional, highly-trained law enforcement officer and I'm paid to keep the peace over there."

"Carlos already told us about you. You're his enforcer and you threw the Guat out because Carlos told you to do it. He was in there to get something back from Carlos that belongs to him."

"What you mean something that belongs to him?"

"He brought in a carved stone mask to pay off his bar bill and Carlos refused to accept it as payment, but Carlos kept the mask. He has it displayed behind the bar. The Guat wanted it back because it's a family heirloom."

"Carlos didn't tell me anything about that. When he called me on my cell phone he told me that the Guat was getting carried away and the other ones were getting restless because their Mexican music wasn't playing on the jukebox. Oops!"

Elmo stood up and glanced at his pager.

"I just got beeped and I've gotta' go," Elmo added.

"There's something going on in the Red Coconut Bar in Port Salerno. I've gotta' get down there and check it out," Elmo quipped as he raised his right hand in a mock salute, turned and raced towards the wooden stairway and the parking lot above.

"I'll catch you later gator," he shouted over his right shoulder as he reached the top of the stairs and headed for his patrol car.

"Nobody, including me, knows what the hell is going on around this place," Mack mumbled under his breath. *"It's time for me to go inside, pour myself a tall glass of warm Merlot and try to forget what's going on in the world. I'll wash her boat down in the morning. She won't know any different."*

Mack tossed the nylon mooring lines in a pile on the dock, rather than coiling them in neatly flemished coils, turned and walked towards the stairway alongside the boathouse. His day was finally over.

Chapter 4

Time and a lack of sleep can play tricks on a sleeping man. Mack's semiconscious knew that it was time for him to wake up and crawl out of bed. However, heavy curtains blocked out the vicious rays of the morning sun and allowed him to remain oblivious to his surroundings.

The Brittany spaniel resting on the foot of the bed knew that it was much too late for Mack to be in bed. He hadn't been out to pee since Mack turned in about midnight and his full bladder was about to pop. Plus, there were fat squirrels to be chased out of the bird feeder. The dog decided to test his luck and slowly inched his way up the bed until his muzzle was directly along Mack's exposed right cheek. Without a second's hesitation his moist tongue made a pass at Mack's face and connected!

Mack wiped his cheek with the back of his right hand, shook his head and rolled over to face the other side of the bed. The dog, not offended over his master's rebuff of his good intentions, rolled over on his back and stared at the ceiling. He couldn't crawl over Mack's wide shoulders to reach his face.

"Mack! Wake up!" Ralph was yelling directly in Mack's face. "Mack! Wake up! It's almost ten o'clock!"

Mack, stirred into consciousness by Ralph's persistent bellowing, opened his eyes and rolled over to face his tormentor. "What do you want? Can't you see that I'm sleeping?"

"When did you get back from Indiantown?"

"About eight-thirty last night. Why weren't you here to meet us? Everyone else in Stuart was."

"Joy dragged me off to 'Jammin' Jensen' in Jensen Beach. We didn't get back home until about ten-thirty and I just plopped my butt into bed."

"What's 'Jammin' Jensen'?"

"A local radio station sets up a live broadcast and local merchants set up tables all along the main drag. People walk along the street and buy things. We went over a little bit early and ate dinner at Maple Street. By the time we finished dinner and got out to Jensen Beach it was real hard to find a parking place. I would've rather been here to help you dock the boat when you got in last night."

"Rat was waiting when we pulled in and he helped me tie the boat up to the dock. Tina jumped all over his case and made him mad so he left in a snit."

Where is she?"

"She was drunk as a skunk and passed out in the cabin before we got to the St. Lucie Locks yesterday afternoon. The last time I saw her last night she was tearing up the stairs towards the parking lot and hollered down to tell me that I had a visitor."

"Who was it?"

"Elmo."

"Why was Elmo down here?"

"He wanted to explain his side of something that happened at the Silver Saddle Wednesday night."

"What were you doing in the Silver Saddle? When I saw you

and Tina leave in her boat Wednesday mornin' I figured that you took her on a romantic overnight cruise up to Vero Beach."

"The last thing you will ever see me doing is taking Tina on a romantic cruise anywhere. She got a bug up her butt and insisted that we take her boat over to Indiantown. We got over there late Wednesday night and as soon as we tied up at the marina she wanted to go to the Silver Saddle. She swilled down *Absolut'* vodka martinis until she passed out about two-thirty yesterday morning. I had to tote her sorry butt across the street to the Seminole Inn and tuck her in bed. She showed her appreciation by jamming an electric cattle prod up my butt yesterday morning to get me out of bed."

"Why would she want to go the Silver Saddle on a weeknight?"

"She said that she wanted to get away."

"What was Elmo doing there?"

"He dragged a Guatemalan migrant worker out of the bar in handcuffs because he was giving Carlos the bartender a hard time. Elmo's the law over there. He takes care of things in Carlos' bar when the Guatemalans get plastered and start acting up."

"Carlos's an easy going guy. I can't imagine him having Elmo throw somebody out of his bar unless the guy did something really bad."

"The Guatemalan owed him a bar tab and he brought in a carved stone mask to pay it off, but Carlos wouldn't accept it. That's why Carlos had Elmo throw him out."

"I can't make heads or tails out of what you're trying to say."

"That's okay. It's not really important. What's been going on around here? Have you been digging up the marina parking lot looking for buried pirate treasure?"

"I'm over that treasure hunting stuff. My sand flea business is doin' real good now."

"How about the sex pheromones project? Did you find a way to bottle your sweat?"

"Joy nixed the whole idea. She said that I when I sweat I smell like an Iowa hog on a hot July day. She didn't think that it was a very good idea."

"Mack! You bastard! Why didn't you come down to the boat and wake me up? You knew that I have to be in court this afternoon!" Tina's shrill voice echoed throughout the cottage from the front door. "Don't you care what happens to me? I could've been kidnapped by a gang of Guatemalans and sold to a white slave ring for prostitution at fifty bucks a pop!"

"I forgot to tell you that Tina's Beamer's parked out front," Ralph stammered. "I'm sorry."

"Don't worry about it. I can handle her. Watch this." Mack cupped his hands around his mouth. "The Guat pimp would go broke at fifty bucks a week," Mack responded with a grin.

Ralph sensed the impending danger and decided to take off for the beach to catch sand fleas. He dashed out of the bedroom toward the small living area with the terrified dog right behind him. Ralph saw Tina standing in front of the door, made a head fake to the right, cut to the left and made it out the door without a scratch He didn't bother to acknowledge Tina's presence and she couldn't let it rest.

"Ralph! You bastard! Come back here right now!"

Mack realized that it was futile for him to remain in bed even though his head pounded like a ten-pound sledgehammer ringing true on a steel railroad spike. He wrapped a sheet around himself and 'schlepped' out of the bedroom into the living area. Tina blocked the front door and glared at him with smoldering emerald-green eyes that could melt stainless steel.

"Why didn't you come down to the boat and wake me up?" She shouted at him. Her hands were on her hips and her right foot beat a nervous tattoo on the wooden floor. "You knew that I have to be in court this afternoon!"

"I didn't know that you were here. The last I saw of you last night you were you taking off up the stairs towards the parking lot like a scalded duck."

"When I got to Indian Street, I realized that I shouldn't be driving and couldn't risk a DUI charge. I doubled back, parked my car outside, went down to my boat and fell asleep. When I got back here you were already passed out, Ralph knew that my Beamer was out there and he should have told you."

"If he had thought that it was important he would've said

something to me about it."

Mack sat down in the overstuffed green recliner and drew out the padded footrest.

"I wish that I could stay here and argue with you all day, but I have to get down to West Palm Beach for a one-thirty court hearing. When I get out of court I'll run back up here and we'll go out to dinner tonight. I certainly hope that you plan on washing down my boat before you take off this afternoon." Tina spun on her heel and slammed the screen door behind her.

Mack listened to the 'click, click, click' of her high heels on the wooden porch as she made her way to the parking lot.

"That woman never ceases to amaze me," he thought. *"How come whatever I do is always wrong and whatever she does is always right? I think I'll take a shower, stop at the Queen Conch for breakfast, make a trip down to the Blake Library and do some research. I have a sneaky suspicion that there's more to this stone mask story than an unpaid bar tab."*

Chapter 5

James 'Mack' McCray had arrived in Stuart, Florida in March of this year. He was fingered as an inside informer by the Chicago outfit and ordered to leave Chicago by his Federal handlers. He found himself in the Federal witness protection program and assigned to a feisty, redheaded, green-eyed female handler appropriately named Tina Louise McShay.

Tina is a prosecuting attorney in the felony division of the West Palm Beach Office of the Florida Attorney General. She doesn't have to work because her parents left her with a generous General Motors stock trust fund after they died in a terrible car accident a few years earlier.

Tina also inherited what was left of the Port Sewall Marina located on Northlake just off of Willoughby Creek in an area called Port Sewall. The main house burned down years ago and its location is marked by a pair of classical Greek urns on each side of the cracked concrete sidewalk that originally led to the main house.

A weathered, gray cottage is supported in what seems to be mid-air by creosoted black timbers, is perched above the boathouse. The twenty-eight by twenty-eight foot cottage, about 800 square feet in all, consists a front porch, a small living area, a kitchenette, two bedrooms and a single bathroom down a short hallway between the bedrooms. Four wooden steps rise up from the sidewalk to the front porch that opens directly into the small living room. The spare bedroom is filled with complex electronic equipment that appears to be directly out of a Star Wars movie.

A stand-alone home entertainment center equipped with a twenty-four inch color television set and a CD player with speakers at least four feet high dominates the northeast corner of the living room wall. A fake brick fireplace, with a wooden mantle, is framed between two windows on the east side of the living area.

Above the mantle hangs a painting of a white-haired man wearing a straw hat, long sleeved blue cotton shirt and khaki shorts. He is standing up in a green wooden skiff and the open cast that is leaving his outstretched arms hovers in a perfect circle over school of panicked silver mullet. The walls of the cottage are paneled in ancient knotty pine.

A continuous floor to ceiling bookcase constructed of richly grained dark wood, probably rare Brazilian mahogany, frames the right side of the tiny room and runs from the southwest corner to the short hallway leading to the bathroom and two bedrooms. The bookcase rises gallantly upward from the bare pine floor to the vaulted ceiling ten feet above.

A green, round throw rug forms the centerpiece of the floor. Two pea-green fabric covered recliners and an oblong glass-topped coffee table mounted on spindly legged, gray driftwood base completed the living room's sparse furnishings. The recliners form a divider between the living room and kitchenette.

There were no air-conditioner ducts or wall-mounted units in sight. A solitary ceiling-mounted, slow moving brass fan equipped with four wooden paddle blades stirred the stale, humid air around the tiny room.

An avocado-green refrigerator stands as a silent sentinel in the corner next to the short hallway. Next to it is an avocado-green electric range, followed by three feet of green, plastic-covered countertop that leads to the corner and meets an avocado green ceramic sink. The white microwave oven snuggled in the corner niche between the sink and the range looks out of place.

The kitchenette faces south and features a sliding glass door that opens onto a small wooden deck that overlooks Northlake Lagoon and the St. Lucie River to the east. A mid-1950's vintage chrome-legged, plastic-topped oblong dinette table and four matching plastic-covered chrome-legged chairs completed the spare furnishings.

High definition television cameras mounted in each outside corner of the cottage provide a 'real-time' view of the cottage, the marina and the open parking lot.

Two huge rhombic, high frequency receiving antennas facing east to west, and north to south, are anchored by one-inch steel cables to four giant Australian pine trees that form the outer boundary of the marina parking lot. Several VHF and UHF antennas sprouted from the roof of the cottage.

A ten-foot diameter parabolic dish antenna mounted on a concrete slab quietly stands behind a ten-foot high chain link fence enclosure. Mack told inquisitive visitors that it was a satellite-receiving antenna for the cottage's television system. In reality it served that purpose too along with a few other things.

Immediately upon his arrival six months earlier Mack quickly realized that Tina, the red-aired, green-eyed assistant state attorney had him firmly under her control. They have little in common because they are exact opposites, however she is able to completely dominate him with the tone of her voice and a few well-chosen words. Her husband disappeared during a covert military operation in Laos in the 1960's. Mack served in the same obscure black unit that consisted of four eight-man teams which were identified only by a number stamped in a particular location on the front side of a South African One Rand coin.

Mack's six months in south Florida had its ups and downs and it's pluses and minuses. He obtained his Coast Guard captain's license and had established himself as a local fishing guide with a good reputation for entertaining his customers. During an evening snook fishing outing under the old Roosevelt Bridge Mack met Rat who was there fishing for cat snappers, a catfish red snapper hybrid.

Rat is a slightly mentally deranged Vietnam tunnel rat who lives on a broken down sailboat anchored off of Shepherd's Park and survived by collecting fresh road kill from his blue Vespa motor scooter. Rat's wife left him several years before for a lesbian hairdresser in Key West. After that traumatic event Rat became a local recluse. Rat shared his life story with Mack during their first chance meeting.

Rat was captured by North Vietnam Army regulars who tortured him for several days by hanging him head down by wires secured to his big toes over a pen of wild jungle hogs. When his toes pulled loose from their sockets and ripped out of the flesh he fell head first into the hog pen much to delight of his captors. Rat killed one of the hogs with his bare hands and as retribution the Vietnamese commander drilled holes in his toe bones, laced wire through them and hung the two toes from Rat's neck. From that day forward Rat proudly wore those two toe bones around his neck as a symbol of his mental courage.

Rat's given name was Rodney William Mathers and he was born in Turkey Foot, Kentucky, a small town located deep in the Daniel Boone National Forest.

During his teenage years Rat spent many solitary days prowling deep in the mountains. That experience provided him with the basic skills he needed for survival when he was lost in the deep Laotian jungle.

Rat was perceived as being 'different' from his teenaged peers and they tended to avoid him. His dark black hair and copper complexion didn't fit in with the blue-eyed, fair-skinned complexion considered 'normal' for white folks.

His grandmother still lives in a wooden cabin equipped with a single-hole outhouse located high up on High Knob Ridge. She told Rat that his ancestors were Portuguese sailors who were stranded on Ocacroke Island in the 1500's and made their way west across the coastal plains and settled deep in the Smokey Mountains.

The men married Cherokee Indian squaws and their children were often called 'copper ankles' because their high pant legs allowed the summer sun to reach their ankles and turn them into a deep copper color. Rat's fifth grade teacher told him that his father was a *Melungeon* and he was not considered to be the same as the rest of the kids. To this day his grandmother, and many of the locals, calls a wristwatch a *swatz*, which is the Swiss word for the wrist-worn timepiece.

Rat always seems to pop-up when Mack needs his friendship the most and Mack looks at him as a true, but quirky friend.

Went Rat retuned home from his second tour in Viet Nam he spent four months recuperating in the Veterans Administration Hospital in West Palm Beach. During his hospital stay Rat's wife ran away to the Florida Keys with a lesbian hairdresser

Rat went to Florida State University on the GI Bill, earned a Masters Degree in Criminology, and worked for ten years as an undercover narcotic agent in the Florida Keys for the Florida Department of Law Enforcement. He gave it up because he was fingered as a 'narc' and migrated to Stuart in his twenty-five foot sailboat in 1992 right when Hurricane Andrew was approaching Miami.

When Rat was passing under the Evans Crary Bridge a discarded plastic bread wrapper clogged up his engine's water intake, the engine overheated and burned up. When he passed under the Roosevelt drawbridge under sail the bridge tender lowered the draw span to soon and snapped off his sailboat's delicate mast. Rat towed his disabled sailboat to the city anchorage at Shepherd's Park behind his green rubber kayak and tied up inside the jetties. After Hurricane Andrew passed Rat removed the inoperative engine, tossed it overboard and uses it as an anchor. His mildew splotched sailboat has been anchored just outside the boundary of the Stuart Anchorage ever since.

Rat survives on a VA disability pension and a check from Social Security. But, although he has no money worries Rat serves as a counselor and mentor for the many homeless Viet Nam era veterans who aimlessly hang around Shepherd's Park.

He uses his blue Vespa motorbike to collect fresh road kill along Federal Highway, from Stuart to Bridge Road in Hobe Sound, and prepares giant pots of stew for his homeless associates. He prefers not to tell them what type of meat is in the stewpot and advocates that 'meat is meat once it's cooked' it shouldn't matter what it is.

Deputy Elmo, a Martin County Sheriff's Department Deputy, has been on the force for twelve years and is also Tina's cousin. His shift assignments alternate between road patrol duty on Kanner Highway from Stuart to Indiantown some twenty-plus miles to the west and the marine unit. He prefers the marine unit because he can spend Saturday and Sunday afternoon ogling the scantily clad teenage girls sunning themselves on the Clam Island sandbar located directly across from Sailfish Point.

Elmo doesn't always have his act together and finds it difficult to connect the obvious dots and solve the puzzle. Mack often uses that weakness to his advantage without damaging his close personal relationship with Elmo.

Ralph and his wife Joy live on Inlet Harbor Drive located within walking distance of Port Sewall Marina. Ralph has lived in Martin County all of his life and comes from a long line of commercial fishermen.

When the gill net ban in Florida waters took effect in 1995 Ralph had to find another source of income although quite often he sells a boatload of pompano, silver mullet and Spanish mackerel at the Port Salerno Fish House that seem to have net marks on them. When questioned about net marks on the fish Ralph will insist that he caught them in a cast net which is legal.

His wife Joy has a Masters Degree in Egyptology from Wellesley College and tolerates Ralph's antics. His latest venture is collecting sand fleas and selling them to local bait shops. Ralph felt that because women seemed attracted to him when he is digging for sand fleas in the surf along Stuart Beach he considered bottling his sweat and marketing it as sex pheromones. Joy nixed the idea gently informing him that he smells like an Iowa hog when he perspires.

Mack often finds himself involved in controversial events that cerate turmoil in his life. Although officially out of government service he is often called upon to solve unique problems that require his training and expertise. Chicago was his last base of operations and his handlers know that he can fit in places that most agents would find uncomfortable.

His background in investigative work makes him curious and he utilizes the resources of the Blake Library in Stuart to research things before he gets completely embroiled in them.

Today's sojourn to the library wasn't necessary to solve any great mystery, but only to satisfy his curiosity about Guatemalan migrant workers and the stone mask. He was in for a surprise!

Chapter
6

It was 11:32 A.M. when Mack pulled out of Port Sewall Marina and headed up Old Port St. Lucie Boulevard towards the Blake Library. It was easy for him find a parking place because most of the employees in the Martin County Administration building next door to the library had already left for lunch. Tina's digital camera rested beside him on the truck seat. On a hunch Mack had 'borrowed' Tina's digital camera when she was passed out in the sailboat cabin on the way back from Indiantown.

When Mack entered the double glass doors he turned left towards the reference desk in the center of the library. Janet, a reference librarian who knew Mack well, gave him a slight wave of recognition from behind the reference desk. He approached the desk, rested his elbows on the granite counter and whispered across to Janet so that no one close by could hear.

"What do you know about carved Mexican stone masks?"

"What makes you interested in carved Mexican stone masks? It seems to be out of your normal range of interests."

"Take a look at the image in the viewing screen of this digital camera," Mack replied as he held Tina's digital camera so that Janet could see the green stone image. "I saw this mask in a bar in Indiantown yesterday and I'm curious as to its origin."

"What were you doing in a bar in Indiantown yesterday?" Janet responded with a grin. "I thought that you knew better than to hang around in bars. Aren't you behaving yourself?" She added with a knowing wink.

"The places I go and the things I'm required to do are out of my control. I just do what I'm told to do."

"This mask could very well be a rare archeological artifact."

"The bartender at the Silver Saddle Bar in Indiantown took it as partial payment for a bar tab that had been run up by a Guatemalan migrant worker. He claims that he's descended from Guatemalan royalty and that the mask is an heirloom that has been handed down from generation to generation."

"It might be a fake," Janet replied. "A lot of stuff like this is sold in Mexican open-air markets to naïve tourists who think that it's genuine and smuggle it across the border. The customs agents laugh at them, but they don't spoil their dream. It's a game with them."

"I have a gut feeling that this one isn't a fake and there's an interesting story behind it. Have you ever seen anything like it?"

"It looks Mayan to me and you said that the guy was Guatemalan. Guatemala's the homeland of the Mayan civilization."

"So I've been told. Do you have any way of identifying the origin of the mask? Is this the kind of thing you'd expect to find in Mexican museums?"

"I think the best thing to do is to contact the Mayan museum in Miami and ask them for their opinion. When I was in college I went on an archeological expedition to Guatemala Mexico and I have a feeling that this mask is Olmec and predates the Mayans by one thousand years."

"It re-dates the Mayans?"

"Do you see the V-shaped shape that runs above the of top of the nose?"

"Of course! It's obvious."

"The heavy brow vee is a characteristic of Olmec facial sculptures. I think this is an *Olmec* king's funeral mask. If it's genuine it's extremely rare and very valuable. The only ones I ever saw were in the Smithsonian Institute in Washington and the Princeton Museum. When you get back to the marina download the photograph and e-mail it to me. I'll forward it to the reference librarian at the Smithsonian and see what I can find out about it."

"Okay. I'll e-mail it to you this afternoon. Do you think this thing has any value?"

"The *Olmec* civilization died out about five hundred B.C. and predates the Mayas by almost one-thousand years. If I remember my history there were thirteen Olmec kings and only twelve of their funeral masks have been found and they are in private collections and museums around the country."

"Would you check around for books on the Olmecs in other libraries?"

"Of course I will. If I can find one I'll order it for you via an interlibrary loan. The front desk will call you when it comes in. Is there anything else that I can do for you today?"

"No. I don't think so. But if I think of something I'll be back. You've already told me more than I knew when I walked in. Oh! Can you do some research for me on the Internet on the *Olmec* civilization so I can discuss it somewhat intelligently?"

"Of course. I'll *GOOGLE* the Olmecs on my computer and I'll printout the articles that I find. When will you get back with me?"

"After I leave here I'm going to stop for lunch at The Taste of Italy in downtown Stuart in the Publix Shopping Center. After lunch I have some running around to do. I'll get back with you on Monday. Thanks for your help." Mack rapped the granite counter three times with the knuckles of his left-hand and turned towards the front door.

"I'm working this weekend," Janet's soft voiced echoed throughout the library. "Stop by if you have time."

Mack nodded in acknowledgement, turned headed for the entrance of the Blake Library.

"If that mask pre-dates the Mayan civilization by almost one thousand years it must be valuable," he thought to himself. *"I think that it's made out of jade and the eyes have an Oriental look. It could have some Chinese influence. I remember reading a book a few years ago that talked about how Chinese sailors made their way to Central America and the Yucatan Peninsula. Possibly that has something to do with thee black chickens that Carlos was talking about. When I was in Laos and Vietnam I saw black chickens running around rice farmer's hooch's. There's something's going on that doesn't seem quite right to me"*

Mack drove down East Ocean Boulevard towards Confusion Corner and downtown Stuart. He was almost oblivious to the traffic around him because he was deep in thought over the many possibilities of the stone mask. He swung around Confusion Corner, headed down Colorado Avenue towards U.S. Highway 1, the Publix Shopping Center and The Taste of Italy. His watch read 12:47 P.M.

Mack crossed Federal Highway, turned right into the shopping center and headed towards the far end and The Taste of Italy. He heard a loud 'blat' from behind him, glanced into the rearview mirror and saw a Martin County Sheriff's Department green and white patrol cruiser behind him with its rooftop-mounted red and blue lights flashing.

"What the hell does he want? I didn't run the red light and I used my turn signal. I'll pull into a parking place and find out what this clown wants."

Mack made a hard right turned and slipped into a parking place in front of the Sake House Restaurant. The sheriff's car pulled in behind Mack and blocked his exit from the parking space. The patrol car's driver's side door opened and out slipped Deputy Elmo. He was grinning from ear-to-ear.

"Hey there Mack. Are you on your way to lunch?"

"Elmo! You scared the hell out of me! Why did you blast that thing off behind me? I didn't run the red light!"

"I was leaving the Martin County Courthouse on my way to lunch when you drove past. I pulled out and followed you down

East Ocean Avenue, to Confusion Corner and down Colorado Avenue. You never looked in your rearview mirror and I could give you a traffic citation for that."

"Get off my back Elmo! I wasn't speeding, I didn't run any red lights and I used my turn signal."

"What'cha doing for lunch?"

"I was heading for The Taste of Italy."

"Want some company? I ate breakfast at the Queen Conch real early this mornin' and I'm starving."

"I'm not certain if I do after what you just pulled. It wasn't funny! But I guess I'd better say yes or you'll give me a ticket for doing something stupid. I'll meet you down there."

"Okay."

After lunch mixed with some idle conversation Mack said 'goodbye' to Elmo, pulled out of the Publix Shopping Center onto Federal Highway and headed south towards Colorado Avenue.

"Why does Elmo always show up when I'm on my way to or coming back from somewhere? If I didn't know better I'd think that he planted a GPS transmitter in my truck so he could track me where ever I go," Mack muttered under his breath.

Mack turned left onto Colorado Avenue and headed towards Confusion Corner. He didn't catch the red lights at Kindred Street, or Martin Luther King Boulevard, and at the Confusion Corner traffic circle he turned onto East Ocean Boulevard. It was 1:52 P.M.

"I might as well stop at the library and check with Janet. She might have found something by now."

Mack pulled into an open parking place at the Blake Library and headed for the double glass doors. He turned left and headed for the reference desk. When Janet saw him she almost flew out of her chair and began waving at him with both hands.

"I found it! I found it!" Janet blurted out as Mack neared the reference desk. "I found it!"

"What did you find?" Mack responded. "Hold your voice down because this is a library and somebody might 'shush' you."

"I found some stuff about that mask! It's definitely Olmec and it's between twenty-five and thirty-five hundred years old! It could be the missing thirteenth mask! You need to get it examined and authenticated by an archeologist. If it's authentic it could be worth thousands of dollars! I checked the Sotheby's website and they sold an Olmec mask similar to this one, except it wasn't in nearly as good condition, five years ago for seventy-five thousand bucks!"

"Hold your horses! It isn't mine and I don't have the right to sell it. I'm just trying to find out some background on it and if it's worth anything. What else did you find out?"

"I researched the Smithsonian Institute in Washington and the Princeton University Museum. Just as I thought twelve of these stone masks are known to exist. Most of them are in private collections, but some of them are in museums. There was a color catalog of the known Olmec masks published by the Smithsonian a few years ago. I ordered a copy for you via an interlibrary loan. Tell me again. How did that bartender get his hands on it?"

"A Guatemalan migrant worker asked him to take it in exchange for his bar tab. If it's worth as much as you seem to think it is Carlos should take it as payment for the Guatemalan's bar tab, shut down the Silver Saddle for good and retire."

"That wouldn't be fair to the Guatemalan!"

"Life isn't fair."

"You'd better tell that bartender that he has something real valuable on his hands."

"Officially it doesn't belong to the bartender because he refused to take it as payment for the Guat's bar tab. The next time I get over there I'll mention it to him."

"What did you mean when you used the term Guat? It sounds offensive to me."

"It's short for Guatemalan. It's a common term used by the locals in Indiantown."

"It is offensive! The Guatemalans are proud people. Do they know that people called them Guats?"

"They don't care what they're called as long as they get paid."

"That's obscene."

"Whatever. Why don't you slip this digital photo cartridge in your computer and download it? Then you can print out a photo of the mask and e-mail it to whomever."

"We don't have a connection on our computers which allows us to download photographs from digital imaging cards. You'll have to e-mail it to me."

"Okay. I'll do it when I get back to the marina. Give me a call when the book comes in so I can do my homework."

"No problem. I'll be here all weekend if you want to stop by and check on what else I found out about the mask"

"If I get a chance I'll drop by. Have a good weekend."

Mack turned and headed for the front door of the library. It was 2:47 P.M.

"I'd better get back to the marina and wash down Tina's sailboat before she shows up this afternoon or they'll be hell to pay," Mack muttered as he walked toward the parking lot. *"It'll be just my luck that red-headed broad wants to take her boat to Indiantown tonight. I have a gut feeling that she wants to get her hands on that mask. It wouldn't surprise me one bit if the ignition coil is shorted out and the stupid sailboat's engine won't start."*

Mack smiled as he headed towards his blue Ford F-150 pickup truck snuggled in a parking place under a carrotwood tree in the Martin County Administration Building's parking lot.

Chapter
7

It was a lazy Friday afternoon and Mack saw no reason to hurry back to Port Sewall Marina. Tina had a 1:00 P.M. court appearance and she'd be tied up until at least four o'clock. Mack didn't expect her to show up until after 6:00 P.M. so he decided to dawdle on his way back to the marina.

He pulled into the Finest Kind Marina in the Manatee Pocket to check on the charterboat fleet and rap with the captains about the day's fishing. Most of the charterboats had docked, the mates were preparing baits for the next day's charter and the captains were in the tackle shop swapping fish stories.

Mack was enjoying the good-natured ribbing the seasoned captains poked at the 'rookie' captain and glanced at the clock on the wall above the bait freezer. It read 5:17 P.M. Mack knew that he'd better get back to the marina and wash down Tina's boat before she arrived from West Palm Beach. He still had to short out the ignition coil so that the sailboat's engine wouldn't start just in case she decided to make a trip to Indiantown that evening.

Mack pulled into the Port Sewall Marina parking lot at 5:36 P.M. and Tina's silver-blue BMW Z-3 convertible was already there. Before he turned off the truck's ignition Tina dashed out of the cottage waving her arms in the air and screaming at the top of her lungs.

"Where the hell have you been the last two hours?" Tiny bubbles of froth formed in the corners of her mouth as she screamed. "I got out of court at two-thirty and I'm been waiting here for you since three-thirty! What good excuse do you have for not being here?" Tina barked as she took all three steps off front porch in one leap, slipped in the loose pea-gravel and fell flat on her face in the parking lot.

Mack held back a smile, slowly slipped out of the truck cab and closed the door. He only had to take two steps to reach Tina's face down prone position.

"You certainly picked an impressive way to greet me. Give me your right hand and I'll help you up. What was all that fussing and cussing about? I had a few places to go this afternoon. On the way back here I stopped by the Finest Kind Marina to talk with the charterboat captains. Why do you have a hair up your butt? You didn't tell me to expect you back early."

Mack helped Tina regain her footing, led her onto the front porch and gingerly guided her into a wooden, ladder-back rocking chair. She wiped three pieces of pea-gravel off of her forehead, dusted off her skirt and took a deep breath before she said a word.

"I got out of court early because the bad guys took a plea bargain. I drove back to my condo, threw some clean clothes in my overnight bag and got up here as quickly as I could. I figured after the hell I put you through in Indiantown that you deserved a home cooked meal. I've been waiting for you so we could go to Publix on Cove Road together, pickup some prime New York Strip steaks, a couple of Idaho potatoes and a bottle of imported

French wine. I was planning on a quiet weekend here with you and you spoiled it!"

"How was I supposed to know that? When you left here this morning you were ready to eat me alive and spit me out in pieces for not waking you up. I never know where I stand around here. When you left this morning you said that you wanted to go out to dinner. When did you change your mind?"

"It's my prerogative. I decided that it would be more fun to stay in tonight and I thought that you would appreciate my concern for you. Men never understand the way women feel."

Mack was caught between a very large rock and a hard spot. He knew that if he said anything that it would be wrong and she would light into him with both feet. He decided to remain mum. That was a mistake.

"Well? Aren't you going to say anything?" Tina sat straight up in the rocking chair and glowered at him. "You must have something to say in your own defense."

"What do you want me to say?"

"That you appreciate all of the things I do for you."

"Okay. I appreciate all of the things you do for me."

"Is that it?"

"That's what you told me to say."

"If I told you to jump off a bridge would you do it?"

"I guess I would. You're my boss."

"You don't have any backbone do you? Can't you stand up for yourself?"

"*What the hell am I supposed to say?*" Mack thought. "*If I agree with her she'll take it the wrong way and if I disagree with her she'll keep yapping at me like a mongrel dog.*"

Before he could form a neutral response in his mind Tina answered for him.

"I suppose you can't. Let's get going to Publix and pick up those steaks before the best ones are gone." She motioned towards her BMW. "I'll drive."

"Okay."

Tina made it to the Publix Shopping Plaza on Cove Road in record time and slid into a parking place almost directly in front of the store entrance. When they entered the store she pointed at a pale green vinyl-covered bench seat next to the wall. Mack snatched a yellow legal pad off the kitchenette table on his way out of the cottage so he could make a few notes about what things still had to be done at the marina that weekend so he could explain why he couldn't go to Indiantown.

"Sit over there and wait for me. I'll be out in a few minutes. I know exactly what I want to pick up."

Mack dutifully slid onto the bench seat and immediately noticed a thin young woman hawking the *Palm Beach Post* a few feet away. She was gesturing at a middle-aged woman entering the door pushing a shopping cart in front of her.

"Hello ma'am!" The newspaper saleswoman yelled out in the direction of the female customer passing directly in front of her on her way to the dairy case. "Do you read the *Palm Beach Post?*"

The disinterested female customer pushed her cart towards the dairy case and pretended that she didn't hear the rude salutation. The shopper's lack of interest didn't faze the newspaper subscription hawker in hailing the next shopper who passed through the door.

"Sir!" The newspaper hawker's nasal voice rang out towards an elderly white-haired man on his way to buy a lottery ticket at Customer Service. "Sir! I'm talking to you! Do you read the *Palm Beach Post?*"

He paused in his step and that was a big mistake! She sensed his momentary weakness and immediately pounced on him. He was fresh meat and available for the taking!

"Excuse me sir. Do you read the *Palm Beach Post?*" She was unrelenting in her sales pitch and made a hand gesture in the disinterested man's direction. Momentarily distracted, but not persuaded he continued towards the Customer Service counter. She turned her attention to the next prospect heading towards the dairy case. "Excuse me ma'am. Do you read the *Palm Beach Post?*"

Her intended prey smiled in polite recognition and paused. That's all it took for the newspaper peddler to pounce on her with an offer she couldn't refuse. Something for free!

"Ma'am! Please give me just a minute of your time. It won't

cost you anything to talk to me and I'll help you fill out an application form for a free drawing for a one-hundred dollar Publix gift certificate."

"Do I have to subscribe to your newspaper to register for the free drawing?"

"Of course not! Come on over!"

That's all it took to convince the aged female shopper to shuffle backwards like she was doing the 'Moon Walk.' She accepted the ballpoint pen offered by the savvy newspaper peddler and began filling out the free drawing application form. The newspaper peddler waited until her prey was concentrating on properly filling out the registration form for the free gift certificate to set the hook.

"Ma'am would you like try a sample subscription to the weekend edition of the *Palm Beach Post* for only one dollar and ninety-eight cents per week?" She didn't wait for a positive response and slid a blank newspaper subscription authorization form towards her victim.

The patsy didn't hesitate as the newspaper hawker slid the trial subscription form in front of her and began filling it out as she was directed.

"You don't have to pay me anything. We'll begin delivering the newspaper to you next Saturday and Sunday and you'll receive a bill in the mail from our accounting department. Thank you very much for your interest in the *Palm Beach Post* and I hope that you'll win the free one-hundred dollar gift certificate." The newspaper hawker carefully removed the ballpoint pen from her prey's fingers and slid the completed newspaper trial subscription form into the center drawer of her table.

Realizing that she had just been 'had' the shopper repositioned herself behind her shopping cart and continued towards the dairy case. She knew that the incident wouldn't cost her anything because she would call the newspaper office on Monday and cancel the trial weekend subscription. However, she was pleased with herself because for the mere cost of a few minutes of her time she was able to register for the free $100 gift certificate

A fresh, potential elderly male victim aided by an aluminum walker shuffled through the glass door.

"Excuse me sir! Do you read the *Palm Beach Post*?"

The white-haired man ignored her and hustled towards the Customer Service counter to purchase a lottery ticket for that evening's drawing. A smiling young couple was the next prospective victims through the door.

"Excuse me. Do the two of you read the *Palm Beach Post*?"

The young couple exchanged knowing smiles and continued on their way toward the dairy case.

"Excuse me sir." She directed her salutation at Mack and carefully emphasized the 'sir'. "I asked you if you read the *Palm Beach Post*?"

Mack stood up and she acknowledged his presence by bending down from the waist to allow the top of her cotton sundress to fall open thus exposing her small, but unfettered breasts.

"I haven't subscribed to a newspaper for almost a year."

"Why not?" She pretended to challenge Mack's intellect and knowledge of current events. "You must be very far behind on what's going on the world."

"Everything I see on the six o'clock news appears in the next day's newspaper. It's a waste of time to read yesterday's news."

"Oh," she replied as she groped for a suitable comeback. "I'm sorry that you feel that way."

"Don't be sorry. Can I register for the free one hundred dollar shopping gift certificate?"

"Are you shopping in the store today?"

"No. I'm here with a friend."

"Then you can't register for the drawing. It's only for people who are shopping here."

"That sounds like discrimination to me," Mack replied with a smirk. "Free drawings should be open anyone who comes in the front door. They shouldn't have to buy anything. Do you require them to subscribe to the newspaper before you let them fill out the registration form for the free drawing?"

"Of course not! First they fill out the registration for the free drawing then they can choose to accept our offer of a trial subscription."

"I'm only interested in the free drawing and I don't want to subscribe to the newspaper."

"I can't allow you to fill out an application form for the free drawing because you're not shopping in the store. I'm very sorry."

"Thanks anyway. I'm going back to my seat and take a few notes while I'm waiting for my friend to finish her shopping spree," Mack responded and started to turn away.

She touched his arm to get his attention. "What are you going take notes about?"

"I'm thinking about writing a book and you'd make a great character."

"What! Me? A character in a book! What kind of books do you write? I've never met an author before."

"You still haven't. I'm not an author yet. I'm just thinking about writing a book. I haven't done it yet."

Mack turned and headed back towards his vinyl-covered bench seat. Fortunately there was no one there to bother him. He sat down, placed the yellow legal pad on his right knee, cocked his leg up and started to take notes about the newspaper sales woman, her customers and her unique display.

Her sales kiosk was constructed of one-inch white PVC pipe that made it very light and portable A plastic Publix bag filled with small slips of white paper dangled from one corner. When the sales woman looked up at him Mack hailed her.

"What's in that plastic bag hanging from the corner of your table?"

"Those are the entry slips for people who registered to win the free shopping spree."

"Do you use them as prospect slips to call people who didn't take you up on your offer for a trial subscription?"

"No. That wouldn't be right! We pull out one name and destroy the rest of them."

Mack continued taking notes on the young saleswoman.

She wore a light gray sundress decorated with white hibiscus flowers. The dress was held in place by small spaghetti straps and it was obvious that she was not wearing a bra underneath. Her tiny breasts bobbed up and down each time she stood up to make her sales pitch. Mack noted that she bobbed up and down on her toes when she was addressing a male prospect.

She wore brown leather sandals and her stringy brown hair was pulled back into a makeshift ponytail. White plastic whelk shell earrings dangled from her ears. Her harsh, 'no nonsense' tone indicated that she had recently moved to South Florida from the New York metropolitan area.

When things slowed down she strolled over to Mack, stood in front of him and bobbed up and down on her toes to get his undivided attention.

"What're you taking notes about?" She inquired as she attempted to read Mack's indecipherable scribbling.

"A few notes about you. Your sales pitch is very unique. You don't miss a prospect and you don't take 'no' for an answer."

"I know from experience that only two of every ten people who walk through that door will come over and talk to me. The more people I talk to the better the chance I have of making a sale. I can make real good money on a good day."

"I noticed that sometimes you walk out from behind your table and almost block people from going past you. Aren't you concerned that you might offend someone?"

"Sometimes I have to slow people down in order to get their attention."

"Did you see me head off that woman who was heading for the dairy case? I just walked in front of her shopping cart and she couldn't go any farther. She had to stop and talk to me."

"Yes. I saw that slick maneuver. You were darn lucky that she didn't run over you."

"She couldn't resist me. She filled out an application for the free drawing and a form for a trial weekend subscription."

"My guess is that she filled out the subscription form to make certain that her application for the free drawing was put in the plastic bag. She'll probably call the subscription department on Monday morning and cancel the subscription. She just wanted a shot at the free drawing."

"It doesn't matter if she cancels because I get paid based on the number of people who fill out the subscription application. It's up to somebody else to follow-up and maintain the sale."

A fresh, elderly male prospect shuffled through the door and walked within earshot.

"Excuse me sir!" She yelled at the elderly man slowly shuffling towards her table. Do you read the *Palm Beach Post*?"

He seemed to ignore her and was busy watching where he placed his feet.

She raised herself up on the balls of her feet and bobbed up and down to get his attention. When he paused to look at her bobbing breasts she sensed weakness and pounced.

"Excuse me sir. Do you read the *Palm Beach Post*?"

The old man smiled, perhaps thinking of conquests of his youth, and continued on his way. Apparently he had a much more important mission on his mind.

"Can you make a living doing this?" Mack asked.

"Not completely. That's why I own my own business."

"What kind of business?"

"I was hoping you'd ask," She softly replied as she pulled a white business card out from somewhere deep in her open-necked blouse and offered it to Mack. "Here look for yourself."

He retrieved it from her hand.

"It appears that your other business has something to do with health food and home remedies. I don't take any vitamins, or medications, and I'm perfectly healthy."

"That's a typical male attitude! You're in full-blown denial. You don't know if you have something or not! You should be taking something to increase the level of antioxidants in your blood and fight off cancer. It's very important to take antioxidants to counteract the chemical additives in commercially grown foods. The antioxidants have been bred out of fruits and vegetables and replaced by man-made chemicals."

"If commercially grown foods are so dangerous why are you working in this store?"

"I just sell newspaper subscriptions here. I don't eat their food. I grow my own organic vegetables in my backyard and I don't eat meat of any kind."

"How do you survive on only vegetables? The human body needs meat for protein!"

"I get all the protein my body needs from soy bean oil and *tofu*."

"*Tofu*? Isn't that a form of curd made from soy beans?"

"Yes and it's very good for you. I eat *tofu* three times a day and have regular bowel movements three times a day."

"That's more information than I need to know. Don't you have to get back to hawking newspaper subscriptions?"

"Nope. I'm done for today. I'm going home and fix myself some *tofu* salad."

She flounced her dress, pirouetted on her toes and skipped over to her kiosk. It took her les than a minute to disassemble the PVC table, stuff the pieces into a green laundry bag along with her other paraphernalia and head for the door. On her way out she paused in front of Mack and bobbed up and down on her toes several times to make certain that she had his undivided attention before she spoke.

"See ya' around big guy," she whispered.

Then, she was gone and Mack went back to making notes on his yellow legal pad.

An old man, perhaps all of five foot, four inches tall and wearing a cream colored T-shirt with 'Chicago' emblazoned in Navy blue block letters across the front shuffled across the tile floor, stopped in front of Mack and pointed his bony, arthritis-crippled right index finger at an open space on the bench seat.

"Is this seat taken?" The old man hesitantly asked.

"There might be an open seat if you can behave yourself," Mack replied with a grin. "It'll cost you a dollar. Do you have a buck in your pocket?"

"No. You'll have to trust me. Give me your address and I'll mail it to you when I get home."

"That's okay. I'll let you get away with it this time."

"Is she a hooker?" The old man quipped as he slid in alongside Mack.

"Is who a hooker?"

"That sexy broad that was talking to you."

"No. She hawks newspaper subscriptions and sells health food and vitamin supplements."

The old man craned his neck towards Mack's legal pad in an attempt to read his writing.

"Can I help you with something?" Mack playfully asked.

"I was looking to see if you jotted down her phone number.

"She gave me her business card. Here, you take it and call her sometime. She might like that."

"Oh no! Gertrude would kill me if she found that card in my wallet. You keep it."

"Suit yourself." Mack crumpled the card and tossed it into the trash container on his right.

"Your wife must be in here shopping and she stuck you here in husband hell,"

"Husband hell?" Mack asked. "What do you mean by that?"

"Don't you know?"

"No."

"The women come in here to buy groceries and make their husbands sit here while they do their impulsive searching and gathering. Usually there're a couple of real old guys parked here. You look kinda' young to be stuck here. Is your wife in there doing her thing?"

"I'm not married. I'm waiting for my boss."

"Your boss must be a woman. Right?"

"What makes you think so?"

"You're sitting here in husband hell with me. If your boss were a man you'd be in there huntin' with him. Men want to get in and get out of a grocery store as fast as they can."

The old man attempted to force his cataract-scarred eyes to look at the notes Mack was making on the yellow legal pad.

"Are you taking notes on how to sell newspapers?"

"I'm thinking about writing a book and I take notes about people I meet. My notes will form the basis for the characters in my novel," Mack replied. "I like interesting people and that gal who just left was hawking the *Palm Beach Post* to everyone who walked through the front door. She has a very aggressive marketing style and might make a good character in my book."

"How about me? I'm interesting too. Do you want to know something about me?"

"I can pretty well sum you up," Mack replied. "You're a retired engineer. However I don't know if you were a mechanical or electrical engineer, you're left-brained in your thought process and probably come from Chicago."

"Two of those are right on the button. I'm very left-brained and an aeronautical engineer. But, I'm not from Chicago."

"If you're not from Chicago why are you wearing a shirt with Chicago across the front?"

"My wife picks up my clothes from thrift shops and garage sales. Where you think I'm from?"

"You're not from New York because you don't have the right accent or attitude. You're most likely from a midwestern state because you don't have an accent."

"I lost it a long time ago. I was born in Springfield, Massachusetts and lived there until I joined the Army. I spent thirty years at the White Sands, New Mexico missile testing facility. After I retired from White Sands I moved back to Springfield, but I couldn't take the winters after living in the desert for thirty years. My wife and I moved down here twelve years ago to get away from the cold weather."

"Did you work for the Army when you were at White Sands?"

"Doesn't everybody? I was a civilian and the company I worked for did research and design work on prototype rocket engines for the Army. It was all top-secret stuff. My specialty was rocket fuel systems. There were a few other projects that I can't talk about."

"How did you get involved with rocket engines?"

"When I was a kid I was fascinated by space movies and rockets. When I was a teenager my mother got me a book about rockets that was written in England. There weren't any textbooks available on how to build rocket engines, but my brother and I used the book as a guide for building one of our own. We used gasoline for fuel and the spark to ignite it was generated from a metal striker that we attached to a rotating photograph record player table."

"You're damn lucky that you didn't kill yourselves! The flash point of gasoline is only one hundred and ten degrees Fahrenheit!"

"That's correct. One day we had a fuel spill and my brother got burned pretty badly. After that we changed to kerosene because it has a slightly higher ignition temperature."

"What college did you attend? I'd guess MIT because you're from Massachusetts."

"I never went past the fourth grade. I dropped out of school during the Depression and worked odd jobs to help support my family. When I turned sixteen I enlisted in the Army and the Army sent me to aeronautical school because I got a score of ninety-seven percentile on the mechanical portion of their aptitude test."

"How could you become an aeronautical engineer without a college education?"

"It's not a very long story. I can start telling it to you right now."

"I'd love to hear it, but I can't stay any longer. My boss is coming through the checkout line. She's at the number three register right now."

"Wow! She's a redhead and a real looker too! Does she treat you right?"

"She feeds me bread and water and beats me with a split bamboo whip every Friday night."

"Tonight's Friday! What's she shopping for?"

"Fresh bread and bottled water."

"Mack! Are you going to sit there and yammer all day or are you going to help me load these grocery bags into my car?" Tina was standing in front of Mack and the old man.

The old man's jaw dropped when she swished past him and he got a whiff of her *White Diamonds* perfume.

Mack patted the old man on the shoulder and grinned as he stood up and dutifully fell in line behind the teenaged bagboy.

Chapter
8

As one ages time flies by ever more quickly. Day and night become almost indistinguishable from day-to-day. Pleasurable dreams appear to be reality until one opens their eyes and faces the reality of stark consciousness. It was Monday morning and sunlight streamed through the bedroom window.

Mack rolled over expecting to find a soft, warm female body curled up against his. With his eyes closed he groped with his left arm on the other side of the bed. There was no one there. He cautiously opened his eyes expecting to find his red-headed dream goddess standing at the foot of the bed with her hands on her hips glaring at him for sleeping so late on a workday. There was no one there.

His mind went into 'rewind' mode. On Friday afternoon he had accompanied Tina to the Publix grocery store on Cove Road where she bought several bottles of imported French wine along with a pair of thick prime New York strip steaks. However, Mack had no recollection of the weekend. Here it was already Monday morning and he had a thousand things to do around the marina. His dog wasn't there and it was no sign of the black and white 'tuxedo' cat that would normally be yelling at the top of his lungs for his breakfast. Mack swung his legs over the side of the narrow bed and allowed his bare feet to touch the polished hardwood floor. It wasn't cold. He sat upright and headed for the small hallway that led to the bathroom. He took two steps into the hallway and felt a presence to the right and behind him and swung around to face whomever was there.

"Well sleepy head it's certainly time that you got your butt out of bed," purred Tina in a deep, sultry voice. "Did you have a pleasant dream?" Tina leaned against the counter in front of the kitchen sink.

"Tina! What are you doing here?

"Let me remind you that I own this marina and I can be here anytime I want."

"I thought you were supposed to be in West Palm Beach this morning for court?"

"It's only a quarter after seven and I don't have to be in court until ten o'clock. The judge has a full docket of first appearances to get out of the way before he starts hearing motions for the trials scheduled this week. I beat you up by almost an hour, showered and threw my overnight bag in the car. I'm ready to leave. I was waiting for you to wake up so I could tell you what a good time I had this weekend."

"What do you mean the good time you had this weekend? The last thing I remember is walking out of Publix store behind you and a pimple-faced bag boy."

"Well! That's not a good recommendation for me is it?"

"What do you mean not a good recommendation for you?"

"Normally a lady worries that her paramour won't respect her in the morning or call her the next day to ask how she's feeling. However, apparently you don't remember anything that happened the last two days so I shouldn't expect a call from you later this afternoon should I?"

"What happened? I don't remember anything after we left Publix."

"It's not important. If you don't have any recollection then I suppose nothing happened. However, I will soothe your feeble mind and tell you that we didn't make a trip to Indiantown and my sailboat is still moored at the dock. Perhaps you had better make an appointment with a doctor and have your cerebral functions thoroughly checked. I think that your short-term memory synapses are failing."

"What did you do to me?"

"I don't recall doing anything to you. I spent the weekend on my boat preparing for this week's trials. You spent Saturday and Sunday sacked out in bed. I suppose that you might have some flashbacks later on today, but I doubt that they will be very significant."

Tina slowly took the last sip of coffee from her cup, rinsed it under running tap water, turned it upside down and placed it in the sink.

"Now that you're up I can head for West Palm Beach and get ready for court. I have to be in the courtroom by nine o'clock." She blew Mack a soft kiss off the fingers of her extended left hand and headed for the front door.

"Aren't you going to tell me what you did to me this weekend? You must've slipped me something Friday night that put me out of it" Mack started towards the front door and realized that he was wearing only his jockey shorts.

"I didn't do anything to you and your short-term memory must be failing. If anything did happen it must not have been a very significant experience for you," Tina sniffed.

She took three long strides steps across the small living area, swung open the screen door with her right hand and stepped out onto the front porch. She paused, made a slight run to the left towards the door and shot back a terse parting remark.

"I left a full pot of hot coffee on the kitchen counter. Enjoy your own company."

She turned and headed for her BMW convertible.

"*I spend far too much time worrying about what that woman*

does to me. It'll be just my luck that she had a camera and I can expect to see naked pictures of myself on the Internet by noon. She's seriously disturbed. She must've had a very bad childhood and has a definite hatred towards men," Mack thought as he turned and headed for the bathroom.

"I'm going to take a hot shower and wash this weekend's memories off my body. After that I'll go to the Queen Conch and have an undisturbed breakfast that I'll remember an hour later."

Mack stepped into the bathtub and turned on the water. The hot water rushing out of the chrome-plated showerhead felt good. He closed his eye, held his head in the pulsating stream and tapped his foot to the soothing tattoo of the water rivulets. His relaxation was not to last for long because an unexpected visitor was on his way through the front door.

"Mack! Are you up? I was waitin' down the road for Tina to leave. When she pulled out onto Federal Highway I knew it'd be safe to stop by to see you. Are you alive?"

It was Elmo and the last person Mack wanted to see this morning. But he knew better than to ignore him.

"Come on in Elmo! I'm in the shower. There's a hot pot of coffee on the kitchen counter. Pour yourself a cup and take a seat. I'll be out of the shower in a few minutes."

"That's exactly what I had in mind. I brought in your newspaper and I'll catch up on the sports scores while you're making yourself beautiful."

"It must be someone else's! I don't take any newspapers!"

"It's the *Palm Beach Post*. Maybe they're doin' some kinda' promotion."

It only took Mack a matter of minutes to shower, shave and dress. Afterwards he walked out of the bedroom, through the short hallway and turned right into the kitchenette. Elmo was sitting at the table doing the crossword puzzle. A full, steaming cup of black coffee sat on the table in front of him.

"Did you feel a need for intellectual stimulation this morning?" Mack quipped as he headed for the kitchen counter and the coffee pot. "Elmo, I thought you wanted some coffee?"

"Not really. I got up at five o'clock and I already had five cups of coffee at the Queen Conch."

"What brings you by this morning? Why didn't you stop by and visit with Tina before she left?"

"No thanks. I don't want her to know that I stopped by to see you this morning."

"Why not?"

"We had a big problem in Indiantown Saturday night and I wanted to stop by and tell you about it."

"A major problem in Indiantown? Did Tina drag me over there again?"

"No. I didn't see either one of you Saturday night." Elmo lifted the cup of coffee to his lips, took a sip and sighed. "Don't go to Indiantown until things cool down."

"What does anything in Indiantown have to do with me?" Mack responded as he slipped into the chair directly opposite Elmo. "I didn't lose anything over there."

"Do you remember seeing me drag a Guat out of the Silver Saddle in handcuffs Wednesday night?"

"I vaguely remember seeing you come into the Silver Saddle, but that's all. Why?"

"The Guat I dragged out Wednesday night is new in town and the grove owners don't like him. They figure him to be a troublemaker because he's trying to organize the Guats. He pulled a knife on Carlos Saturday night and threatened to cut his throat if he didn't give him back that stupid green mask. Carlos pushed his 'emergency' button and I got there as quick as I could. The Guat was drunk as a skunk and had Carlos backed up in a corner of the bar with a kitchen knife at his throat. He was babblin' something in Spanish that I didn't understand. Carlos did and he was scared as hell."

"Why would he go after Carlos?"

"Carlos told me that the guy had too much to drink and got smashed. When Carlos asked him to pay his bar tab he refused, pulled a knife on him and went for the mask behind the bar. I had to Mace him twice before I got him under control and got cuffs on him."

"What's the guy's name?"

"His first name's Octavio. I can't pronounce his last name."

"Where is he now?"

"He's been locked up the Martin County Jail with no bond since I booked him in about two o'clock Sunday morning. His first court appearance is in front of Judge Greg Melton at nine o'clock this morning and I've gotta' be there to testify. I'm sure that Judge Melton will continue holding him without bail because he's charged with assault with a deadly weapon and attempted grand theft for trying to steal the mask. That boy's gonna' be locked up for a long time."

"It was his mask!"

"Technically maybe it is, but he gave it to Carlos to cover part of his bar tab."

"Carlos said that he wouldn't accept it as payment!"

"That may be true, but the mask was in Carlos' possession and possession is nine points of the law."

"Tina said that he was a new guy in town."

"He's only been in town for couple weeks. The grove owners and vegetable farmers consider him to be a real troublemaker."

"Why?"

"He's been trying to organize the migrant workers into a labor union and the grove owners don't like it one bit! He claims to have a couple of degrees from universities in Mexico and he's too book smart for his own good. He's lucky that they didn't take him for a ride out towards Fort Drum. If they do he won't come back. Now he's out of their hair and it's all legal. Mack, you'd better stay away from Indiantown for a while because the migrant workers are all riled up. Carlos closed down the Silver Saddle until Friday. He hopes that the situation will cool down by then."

"Why should I be worried about what's going over there?"

"Carlos and I think it's a good idea because the Guat's attorney, no doubt a nerdy public defender right out of law school, will call you as a witness because you were there when I jerked him out of there Wednesday night. They'll claim police brutality, discrimination and crap like that."

"How do they know who I am?"

"Carlos' niece was in the bar when Tina came back to get her cell phone Thursday. She saw you."

"Tina told me that I didn't see anything."

"I didn't see you either."

"But, when we got back here Thursday night you said that you came down here to explain why you arrested the guy Wednesday night."

"I never told you any such thing and I didn't see you at the Silver Saddle Wednesday night either. Plus, the conversation we're having right now never happened. Do you understand?"

"I suppose I do. I've had the same lecture before about other things that never happened. So, what do you want me to do?"

"Keep your eyes open for the next couple of days. If you see a Martin County Sheriff's Department patrol car pull into the driveway be sure that it's me before you come to the door. Our processor server drives a car just like mine. If he doesn't see you he can't serve papers on you to appear in court. Why don't you go to the Keys for a few days until this blows over?"

"Why?

"Tina's going to raise hell if you're called as a material witness and get involved in the case. It could be a career-ender for her. Her uncle's the judge that he's appearing in front of this morning. If they don't have a witness they don't have a case."

"I'll think about it, but I have a lot of things to get done around here."

"Think about it real hard. You don't have a lot of time," Elmo responded as he pushed his coffee cup across the table and stood up. "Would you mind dumping this cup in the sink for me?"

"No problem. When can I expect to hear from you again?"

"When you come back from your vacation in the Keys." Elmo turned, headed for the front door and his patrol car without turning around.

Mack shrugged his shoulders, turned towards the kitchen sink and froze. A tall, white-haired man was standing on the wooden deck outside the kitchen window. He smiled and motioned for Mack to come outside.

Mack nodded in acknowledgement, placed his and Elmo's coffee cups in the sink and headed for the sliding glass door that led out onto the open deck on the south side of the cottage. Mack's visitor greeted him with an outstretched right hand. His voice was deep and demanding, but this wasn't CNN.

"Mr. McCray, I realize that we told you that you would live

here undisturbed by the agency, but the time has come that we need your expertise. Will you help us?"

"Do I have a choice?"

"I'd prefer not to answer that question if you don't mind. We don't have much time and your plane leaves West Palm Beach at twelve-thirty this afternoon."

"Leaves for where? Who said that I was going anywhere?"

"The agency needs you and you have no choice except to go."

"What if I don't?"

"You would not care for the alternative. Please think carefully before you make any further rash negative statements. Look towards the Willoughby Creek entrance. What do you see?"

"There're a couple of guys fishing. It looks like they're working the shoreline for snook. So what?"

"Look a little closer. Do you see a man lying on his stomach in that tiny bunch of mangroves on the point? He's wearing a camouflaged jumpsuit and has a high-powered rifle pointed at your head. It won't make any noise because the barrel is equipped with a Russian sniper's silencer. Do you see him?"

"You're bluffing."

"Am I?" The man raised the little finger of his right hand. "Mr. McCray look above your head."

A hole immediately appeared in the wooden eave directly above Mack's head.

"Mr. McCray I don't bluff. I am prepared to carry out my assignment if you stupidly choose not to accept yours. You're on Delta Flight fourteen eighty-four out of West Palm Beach to Atlanta at twelve-thirty. Be on it! Your ticket is on the front seat of that ratty vehicle you call a truck."

"Where am I going?"

"Logan."

"Logan? Where's that?"

"Logan Airport in Boston. There's a rental car reserved in your name at *Enterprise*. Catch their shuttle bus outside of the baggage claim area. You will not be required to fill out any forms or sign anything. Just take the keys and go."

"Go where?'

"You are full of questions today. Didn't that sheriff's deputy tell you to take a few days off so you wouldn't be around to be subpoenaed as a witness?"

"Yes, but I was planning on going to the Keys for a few days."

"That makes this assignment even better. He will think that you are in the Keys and if anyone tries to find you there they won't. That makes it a win-win situation for everyone involved."

"When do I come back?"

"It depends on how long they want to keep you there."

"Who's the 'they' in this equation?"

"Naval Intelligence. That's really an oxymoron isn't it? I used Navy and intelligence in the same sentence."

"Why the Navy?"

"Did you ever spend any time on a nuclear attack sub?"

"No, and I don't want to either!"

Mack's visitor raised the little finger of his right hand and another hole appeared in the wooden eave directly in line with the first one.

"Mr. McCray, are you certain about that?"

"There's a first time for everything. Where do I go in Boston?"

"Actually you aren't to spend any time in Boston except for the time it takes you to get out of town. You're going to Springfield and you have to be there by six o'clock."

"Isn't Springfield about one hundred miles west of Boston?'

"Yes and you'll like it. It's a quaint little town."

"Is someone meeting me there?"

"You'll be picked up at your hotel tomorrow morning at exactly seven o'clock. Expect to see a black Chevrolet Tahoe in the parking lot outside of your room. Open the back door, get in and don't try to start a conversation with the driver. He is under orders not to speak to you or answer any of your inane questions. He will take you to where you are going and he may ask you to put a black scarf over your eyes. Do what he tells you to do without question."

"Where am I staying?"

"The Red Roof Inn. Take Exit Thirteen B off of Interstate ninety-one north.

"Is there a restaurant near the hotel?"

"There's an Outback Steak House on the east side of the Interstate, but I recommend the *Oishi Sushi* right down the street from the hotel. It's fairly new, but they have great sushi. I recommend the California Roll and the broiled eel."

"When were you there?"

"The night before last. I had to check out the accommodations for you. I always look out for my people. You know that. Did I ever let you down in the past?"

"No. I suppose not. What am I supposed to do there?"

"The Navy needs your expertise in electronics."

"I haven't been involved in electronics for years and I don't have any experience in nuclear submarines!"

"That's true, but you do have experience with Extremely Low Frequency radio transmissions."

"ELF? The Navy already uses it for communicating with their submarines. There's a series of ELF antennas buried in the ground in Minnesota and also between Cape Henry and Currituck Beach, Virginia. Don't forget the CIA's Project HAARP in Gakona, Alaska. They don't need me!"

"Maybe the Navy doesn't need you, but they think they do."

"What makes them think that I can help them with anything?"

"We told them you could. They think that you spent time working at the Russian attack submarine base at *Berdyans'k* in the Ukraine."

"I did, but I was working for the agency!"

"That's also true and that's what we told the Navy. Mack the project is deeper than what it seems to be on the surface. The agency needs detailed information and specs on the type of ELF system the Navy has under development."

"What are you talking about?"

"The Navy is up to something. We aren't certain what it is and how they plan on using it. It's buried in the Black Operations section of their budget and the Senate Armed Forces Oversight Committee hasn't been briefed about it. The committee staff suspects that there's a rogue element in Naval Intelligence and they want us to check it out. Plus, we might be able to tap into it and use it ourselves."

"What is it?"

"Mr. McCray, can you keep a secret?"

"The last I knew my top-secret security clearance was still good."

"Let's go inside so we can't be monitored. Have you swept the place for bugs?"

"The pest control people were here last week."

"I'm not talking about roaches and ants! What about electronic bugs! Have you had the place swept recently?"

"There's an automatic real time scanner in operation twenty-four seven. The place is clean."

"Okay. Let's go inside and I'll tell you what I can." The white-haired man responded.

Immediately as he gestured towards the glass door with his right hand a third round hole appeared in the wooden eave above Mack's head.

"That dumb ass can't remember the proper signal for ten minutes," the white-haired man blurted out. He was obviously irritated. "Waving my right arm for a 'hit' was last week's signal. Excuse me for a minute while I call off the United States Calvary."

The white-haired man turned around so that Mack couldn't hear him, whispered into his right sleeve and gestured for Mack to go back into the cottage. Once the two men were seated at the kitchenette table with a cup of hot coffee in front of them the white-haired man took the lead.

"Mr. McCray, please excuse my behavior. I had to make it look good out there. This is annual evaluation time for me and my boss was one of the guys in the fishing boat. He was watching every move I made."

"What about the guy with the sniper rifle?"

"He was serious about shooting you if I gave the signal. He transferred over from the FBI last week. He was trained as a sniper in hostage-taking situations and he likes to shoot people."

"So, what am I supposed to do?"

"When you arrive at Logan Airport take Interstate ninety west, drive out to Springfield, have a good dinner on the agency and get a good night's sleep. You'll need it. Be on time when they pick you up and keep your mouth shut except to ask intelligent questions. Take as many notes as you can and snatch whatever things they leave laying around. When they finish briefing you ask for a tour of the facility and a block diagram of the project, a flow chart if you can get it, would be perfect. When they're done explaining everything tell them that it's above your level of expertise and get the hell out of there!"

"What if they don't believe me and won't let me leave?"

"That's when you'll know that you have a real problem."

"What's the name of the project?"

"The Navy calls it 'The Big Boomer' project."

"That's a fancy name? Is it a form of explosive?"

"No. It's an Extremely Low Frequency electronic signal transmitted from a transducer mounted in the bottom of a Navy destroyer or the torpedo barrel of a nuclear attack submarine. The Russians installed it on all of their Akula class nuclear attack subs based in *Berdyans'k*."

"What makes you think that?"

"The Navy pulled up a Russian Akula sub off the coast of Africa two years ago."

"Didn't the Russians complain?"

"There's a series of metal submarine nets around our sub base in the Azores that can be raised up from the ocean floor with the push of a button. There're there to keep the Russians from getting too close. One of their Akula class subs got caught in the net and the Navy disabled it by dropping concussion bombs around it. When they pulled it up the crew was dead and the Navy towed the sub to their AUTEC base in the Bahamas. They discovered the electronic boomer and reverse engineered it."

"Did they make it work?"

"We think so. That's why we're sending you to Springfield. But, maybe they didn't and that's why they asked for you."

"I never heard of that project when I was at *Berdyans'k*."

"I don't doubt that a bit, but the Navy doesn't know that."

"Then why do they want me?"

"Because we told them that you worked on the project."

"But, I didn't!"

"That's a minor detail and you'll have to convince them that you did or you might not leave Springfield ever."

"How can I convince them if I don't know anything about it?"

"I'm going to brief you right now."

"How do you know anything about it?"

"I spent the last three days in Springfield. How do you think I know about the *Oishi Sushi*?"

"I'll be in big trouble if the Navy figures out what I'm doing there!"

"Maybe, but let's try to work though it together. Shall we begin?"

"Should I take notes?"

"No! Keep it all in your head!"

"Okay. Fill me in big man."

"The Navy's been experimenting with a SONAR system that uses an Electro Magnetic Pulse generator and a transducer mounted in the bottom of a barge towed behind a ship to transmit extremely low frequency sound waves at one hundred and ninety decibels. They call it a Low Frequency Towed Array. The sound penetrates a sub's hull and kills the crew."

"An interesting concept," Mack remarked.

"They can't risk using depth charges because modern subs carry nuclear power plants. They piggyback a modulated ELF signal on the EMP carrier wave that travels through the sub's internal power grid into and transmits an ELF message to the crew. The signal causes an extreme fear reaction among the crew, causes them to panic and makes them want to surface immediately. They've been testing the system at the AUTEC submarine testing facility in the Bahamas, off of Jacksonville Naval Station, Charleston, Norfolk, Pensacola and Hawaii. They've killed a lot of dolphins and whales."

"Is that why so many dolphins and whales have been washing up on the beaches?"

"Exactly. Do you recall when a pod of Atlantic rough toothed dolphins came ashore south of Fort Pierce a few months ago?"

"Of course. The media played it up that they all had some form of ear parasite that caused so much pain that they beached themselves and subsequently died."

"The ear parasites were the cover story. Their eardrums were blown out by the Navy's Big Boomer when they ran a test from a

Virginia class attack sub about thirty miles off of West Palm Beach. They gave themselves away because Atlantic rough toothed dolphins rarely come closer than thirty miles to shore."

"Can the Navy also transmit the signal from an airplane and disable surface ship crews?"

"Without a doubt. EMP generators weigh about twenty thousand pounds and that's a light load for a C-130. The signal is transmitted straight down via an acoustic coupler. It is very effective."

"What kind of signal are they using to affect the crew?"

"Are you aware that the earth has a normal pulsation cycle of seven point eight three Hertz?"

"Yes. So what?"

"People who meditate get in harmony with the earth's pulsation rate by consciously making their Alpha brain waves stabilize at seven point eight three Hertz. They claim that puts them in tune with the earth. Now, on the other side of the spectrum, if a human's Alpha brain waves are artificially forced to rise above ten point eight Hertz they become agitated and go into a panic mode. That's also what happened to the dolphins that recently beached themselves."

"Why is the agency interested in what the Navy's doing?"

"We've been using a form of ELF for years. A college physics professor in Macon, Georgia originally developed it and we tested it at Georgia Tech football games on the teams and the crowd. We proved that it causes anxiety and panic attacks, plus deep fear. If the ELF signal is transmitted at six point six Hertz it causes lethargy and mental depression."

"Can't that be dangerous if it's used on unsuspecting people?"

"Naw. It was fun to watch the football teams change from aggressive to complacent behavior. Plus, we picked up a few bucks in college football pools. Now we use it for crowd control at demonstrations. We tested it on recruits at the Federal Training Center in Brunswick, Georgia for five years before we put it to use in the field. Plus, it's marketed commercially as a relaxation tool via mail order CDs. They call it 'Transcranial Magnetic Stimulation.' We track the purchasers and measure their reaction to the ELF messages we installed in the Operating System."

"That sounds like mind control to me."

"It is. So what?"

"It doesn't sound right."

"Did I ask you for your opinion?"

"No."

"Then don't offer it. Let's get back to what we think the Navy's doing and how we can use it."

"Okay."

"The Navy's developed an electronic countermeasure to the Boomer that scans the ELF frequency spectrum with a phase array antenna, locates the transmitter's frequency, absorbs the signal into an electronic pad, runs it through an amplifier to double the power output and directs the EMP beam back at the transmitting source. Boom! It disables the sub, wipes out the crew and the sub sinks to the bottom without exposing the nuclear reactor. We want it! That's your assignment Mr. McCray."

"That's all?"

"That's all."

Chapter 9

"Mr. McCray, please wake up," the soft feminine voice cooed in Mack's left ear and overrode the soft hum of the giant Rolls Royce jet engines powering the massive Boeing 737. "Mr. McCray the captain wishes to speak with you in the cockpit immediately."

"Huh? What?" Mack's response was less than enthusiastic as he attempted to comprehend where he was at that time. "Who wants me where?"

"The captain wishes to speak with you in the cockpit immediately."

"Why? What did I do?"

"I'm not privy to that information. I was just told to wake you up and direct you to the cockpit. That is exactly what I am doing.

Please hurry. I don't want my butt chewed out."

"Yes ma'am. I'm on the way," Mack replied as he unsnapped his seat belt and stood up. "Point me where you want me to go."

The flight attendant gleefully slid her right hand into the waistband of his pants in the small of his back and pushed him towards the cockpit. Fortunately Mack had managed to get an aisle seat in the bulkhead row so that he had room for his long legs.

"Please do not look at or acknowledge any passengers on the way to and from the cockpit. We do not want to alarm anyone. They might think that you are a Federal sky marshal and that the plane is being hijacked."

"I understand. Can you move your fingers?"

"Of course I can. Why?"

"Then move your hand slightly up and to the right and wiggle your fingers."

"Why?"

"Because my back itches in that spot. I can't reach to scratch it myself with your hand in my pants."

"Mr. McCray! You should be ashamed of yourself," the flight attendant stammered as she jerked her fingers out of his waistband. "I'm not your personal concubine!"

"I'll bet a dollar that you wish you were."

"Mr. McCray! Shame on you twice over!"

The flight attendant removed the handset from the cradle of a telephone set mounted on the bulkhead alongside the cockpit door and whispered into the microphone. She replaced the handset in its cradle, pushed a small chrome-plated button and an electronic locking mechanism 'buzzed' and the cockpit door swung open. The tall, middle-aged pilot stood in the doorway.

"Mr. McCray I believe?"

"That's me. What do you want to see me about?"

"Please come in and don't touch anything. The plane is on autopilot."

"I'll keep my hands in my pockets."

"That's not necessary. The autopilot controls are mounted on the overhead bulkhead, but it's possible that you might accidentally touch a switch. Just be careful where you put your hands. Don't grab anything if the plane decides to bounce up and down."

After Mack entered the tiny cockpit the pilot shut and locked the door behind him.

I'm Captain Harold Kaplan and this is my first officer Ray Strickland.

Mack nodded an acknowledgement to the first officer.

"Take a seat at the navigator's position," the pilot gestured towards a chair mounted in front of a panel filled with instruments, colored lights, switches, buttons and gauges.

"Where's the navigator? Doesn't he need his seat?"

"We haven't had navigators aboard commercial aircraft for at least five years. We do the navigating ourselves with electronic charts and GPS."

"The passengers might be surprised to learn that."

"Don't tell them. It'll be our secret."

Mack slid into the navigator's chair, pulled the seat belt firmly around his waist and 'clicked' the chrome lock into position.

The pilot sat in the port side seat and turned his head to the right so he could see Mack's face. "Mr. McCray put on those earphones and position the microphone directly in front of your lips."

"Why?"

"There's a special message coming in for you. It's encrypted and my first officer and myself won't be able to understand it. When you're ready press that little red button just below the word 'encrypted' on the console in front of you."

"Do I have to say anything?"

"That's up to you. Are you ready to receive your message?"

Mack nodded his head in the affirmative and the headphones crackled to life.

"*Mr. McCray are you there?*" The slightly garbled words echoed in his ears.

Mack turned to the pilot and shrugged his shoulders. The pilot made a mouthing motion with his fingers and formed circle with his right thumb and forefinger.

"Yes. I'm here," Mack responded. "Who are you and what do you want?"

"How could you forget me so soon after we enjoyed such a delicious cup of coffee at your kitchen table a couple of hours ago?"

"Oh. What do you want?"

"There's been a change of plans. Do not catch the connecting flight out of Atlanta to Boston. I repeat do not take the connecting flight to Boston."

"Why not?"

"Your assignment has been compromised and you are being re-routed for security reasons."

"What security reasons?"

"You don't need to know. Just don't take that flight to Boston!"

"I understand. What should I do when I get to Atlanta?"

"A Delta gate agent wearing a red blazer with a pink carnation in the lapel will hand you an envelope containing your ticket and instructions."

The earphones went dead. Mack swiveled around in the seat to face the pilot and he simultaneously signaled for Mack to remove the earphones.

"That's it Mr. McCray," the pilot stated. "Were you able to understand the message?"

"Yes. Everything went fine."

"I'm pleased. You must be a real important person."

"What makes you think that?"

"The call came over the same 'secure' radio frequency that's used by Air Force One for presidential radio communications."

"It must have been a mistake. I'm not anyone special."

"The Atlanta ground controller said that your message was very high priority. That's why the flight attendant brought you into the cockpit. She's on her way in here to escort you to your seat. Have a good day."

The cockpit door opened and the pilot turned back to face the instrument panel.

"Mr. McCray are you ready to go back to your seat? We'll be landing in Atlanta in fifteen minutes."

"Yes. I suppose so." Mack stood up. "I still have that itch on my back just above my waistband. Do you want to put your hand back in my pants?"

"I will if it'll give you a 'happy face' when you walk through the First Class Cabin. The passengers are concerned. I told them that you're a physician and had an emergency call from the hospital."

"I promise that I'll smile all the way back to my seat. Ouch! That hurt!"

"I'm sorry Mr. McCray. I didn't mean to do that. I got very excited when I felt the waistband of your under-shorts and I overreacted. I believe that is called a 'wedgie' by teenagers."

"Now I know what it feels like to wear a thong and it didn't feel good."

"I don't believe that you can actually empathize with how a woman feels when she's wearing a thong. It doesn't hurt and can actually be somewhat erotic depending on how far up it rides."

"Thank you for that tidbit of information, but it's more than I need to know."

"Here we are! Row ten and the bulkhead aisle seat. Have a good day Mr. McCray."

"I'll try my best, but it hurts to sit down."

"Don't worry about it. The pain will go away soon and it'll only be a pleasant memory of your flight." The flight attendant blew Mack a kiss from the open palm of her left hand, turned and headed for the first class cabin. She winked at him when she drew the blue curtain closed to separate the First Class passengers from the main cabin.

"My underwear's stuffed up the crack in my butt, I don't know where I'm going after I get to Atlanta and I'm hungry," He thought. *"I hope that gate agent gives me a First Class ticket to Acapulco and a thousand bucks spending cash. I deserve an all expenses paid vacation."*

The plane touched down in Atlanta at 2:14 P.M. and Mack received a plain white, number ten envelope from a gate agent clad in a red blazer with a pink carnation in the lapel when he stepped into the terminal. Mack opened the envelope while sitting on the toilet in the Men's Room. He had almost an hour to kill before his flight to Chicago's O'Hare Field at 3:18 P.M.

Chapter
10

Mack's flight pulled into Gate L-7 in Terminal 3 at 4:34 P.M. He hustled down the concourse towards the main terminal and the lower level baggage claim area to catch the shuttle to Enterprise Car Rentals on Manheim Road south of Irving Park Road. The hand-written note instructed him to pick up a pre-paid car and head for the Galaxy Motel on Grand Avenue three blocks east of Manheim Road.

The Bulgarian shuttle driver fumbled while trying to pronounce Mack's last name into his radio. Mack snatched the microphone out of the driver's hand, pressed the 'transmit' button and phonetically spelled his name.

"Roger Mr. McCray. We have your reservation on file," echoed back a voice from the radio's tinny speaker. *"We'll be*

waiting for you when the shuttle van pulls into our terminal."

"Thank you," Mack responded. "I think that I deserve a free upgrade because of this hassle."

"Yes sir. A free upgrade it is."

It was 5:17 P.M. when Mack pulled out of the Enterprise parking lot, turned left on Manheim Road and headed south toward Schiller Park.

"This is the same dump I stayed in the last time I was in Chicago," he thought. *"They don't care who stays there as long as they pay in cash."*

Mack pulled into the parking lot of the 'Galaxy Motel' and slipped into an empty parking slot in front of the seedy office. The hotel had seen better days. The outside sign advertised *karaoke* in the lounge with the 'Wolf Man' from 9:00 P.M. until 2:00 A.M.

"It hasn't changed a bit since last time," Mack muttered. *"I wonder if that young Pakistani hooker still works the parking lot when the Ford assembly plant changes shifts at ten o'clock?"*

Mack grabbed his canvas overnight bag, locked the car doors with the remote and headed for the hotel office. When he entered the dingy lobby there was no desk clerk in sight, but there was the sound of a female giggling coming from the tiny office behind the wall. Mack tapped on the counter with his knuckles to get some attention.

"Excuse me!" Mack bellowed. "Is there anyone here? I need a room."

"Do you have a reservation?" The bored Pakistani clerk asked as he strolled out from behind the back wall adjusting his zipper.

"Why would anyone need a reservation here? There aren't any cars in the parking lot!"

"I can give you a better room rate if you don't have a reservation," the desk clerk replied in broken English. "There's no paper record of the transaction."

"What's the rate for a single?"

"Are you by yourself?"

"Yes."

"Are you paying cash?"

"Yes."

"Fifty nine dollars. If you pay cash I'll throw in a girl for free. She's right behind the wall. Would you like to look her over? I can call her out here."

"No thanks. I need a single room for tonight only, without a girl, and I'm going to pay cash." Mack pulled a folded wad of bills out of his right front pocket.

"The rate is sixty-nine dollars." The clerk looked up from his computer and smiled. "Cash in advance please."

"No! A minute ago you told me that the rate was fifty-nine dollars if I paid cash!"

"That's only if you take the girl. She needs a place to sleep tonight. Sixty-nine dollars please."

Mack reached into his hip pocket, pulled out his wallet and flashed his gold 'Florida Special Agent' badge in front of the startled desk clerk's eyes. He winced.

"That's different sir. For you the rate is only forty-nine dollars and the girl is free."

"I'll take it. Give me a room as far away from the road as you can get. I need peace and quiet."

"Yes sir. I'll give you room one forty-five. It's in the back. No one will bother you there."

"That's fine. How about the girl?"

"She's waiting for you behind the wall. There's no charge for you."

"No! I don't want her. What room does she use when she's working? I want to be as far away from her as I can get."

"She uses room one twenty-six. She won't bother you sir. May I have forty-nine dollars please?"

"What about the tax?"

"For you sir no tax. Just a flat rate of forty-nine dollars."

"Here's fifty bucks," Mack tossed two twenties and a ten on the counter. "Keep the change and give me a key."

"Yes sir," the clerk responded as he snatched the bills off the counter and slipped them into his pocket. "Here's the key to room one forty-five. Go out the front door, turn to your right and go all the way down to the end of the building."

"Fine. Is the lounge open? I'm thirsty and need a beer."

"Yes sir. They open every day at four o'clock. Tonight is

karaoke night and they will be very busy later. Now is a good time to order food if you're hungry. They have very good frozen pizza."

Mack briefly thought about heading for his room and decided that he needed a beer first.

"I'll stop in the lounge and have a couple of beers before I go looking for a place to eat dinner," he thought. *"It's only a little past five-thirty and I have lots of time to kill."*

Mack opened the door, entered the dimly lit bar and the smell of stale beer hit him in the face. There were no customers in the bar and he took a seat at the end of the bar.

The young female very blonde bartender scooted over to him. "What would you like to drink sir?" She gushed in English flavored by an obvious Russian accent.

"How about a bottle of Bud with a frosted glass?"

"Yes sir. Weren't you in here last month? You look very familiar."

"I don't think so. I have a very common face and people often confuse me with someone else."

"No! You're pulling my leg. I remember because you're from Florida! You told me that you know Mickey Mouse. I never forget that!"

"I guess that maybe it was me and I forgot that I was here. I travel to many places and I can't remember everywhere I go. Does the Wolf Man still sing karaoke here?"

"Of course! Didn't you see his name on the sign outside? He'll be here at nine o'clock tonight. Why don't you come back and see him tonight? He's resting in the back room right now."

"I just might. Now how about that cold Budweiser in a frosted glass?"

"Yes sir! Coming right up sir. Would you like something to eat?"

"What do you have?"

"We only have frozen pizza. We warm it up in the microwave. It's good!"

"No thanks. I don't like frozen pizza. I'm going out to find someplace to eat later on. Are there any good Italian restaurants in this area?"

"The Sorrento Garden is a couple blocks south of here on Manheim Road. My girlfriend from the Ukraine is a waitress there. I can call her and tell her that you're coming. She'll take good care of you."

"I recommend the Capri on North Avenue," boomed a deep male voice from the right and behind Mack. "It's a block east of Manheim on the right side of the road. It's my favorite restaurant."

Mack turned around on the bar stool to locate the source of the deep voice and a huge man swung onto the bar stool alongside him.

"Do you mind if I sit here?" The big man asked. "It's my regular seat."

"It's all yours. I'm just passing through."

"Thanks."

"Johnny!" Shrieked the blonde bartender as she raced behind the bar towards the newcomer and slid Mack's beer in front of him. "Tonight's your party and you're early. It doesn't start until ten o'clock!"

"I just came back from court and I'm tired. The traffic out here on the Eisenhower Expressway from downtown was terrible! I need a drink."

"What would you like? Everything is on the house for you tonight."

"How about a Black Russian? Do you know how to make one?"

"Of course I do!" The petite bartender replied with a big smile.

"Where do you think I come from? My people invented it to keep warm in the winter."

"Okay. Let's see how well you do. I've had Black Russians in the best bars in Chicago."

"Okey dokey," she responded as she skipped down to the center section of the bar and pulled down a bottle of Russian vodka and a bottle of black *Kaluha* from a glass shelf behind the bar.

While the pair was exchanging information Mack took the opportunity to size up the newcomer. He was at least 6' 6" tall and must have weighed in excess of 300 pounds. Mack was 6' 4" and weighed 245 pounds and the man made him feel small. His new companion's coal black, somewhat thinning, black hair was slicked back with no part in a style reminiscent of the 1950's. Oddly enough he wore a black shirt and a white tie under his Navy blue jacket.

"This guy has wrist bones the size of baseball bat handles," Mack thought. *"And his face looks like it went through a concentrated case of bad acne when he was a teenager. This guy looks tough. He must be a criminal defense attorney."*

Mack decided to open a dialogue and turned in his seat to face the big man.

"So, they're throwing a big party for you tonight. Did you win a big case?"

"No. It's a going away party. I'm leaving town for awhile."

"Going to the Virgin Islands on vacation? I hear there's lot of young virgins there."

"No I'm not and there's no virgins left anywhere. Take it from me. What makes you so nosey?"

"I'm thinking about writing a book. I like to talk to people. I get ideas for characters that way."

"What kinda' book you writin'? I might want to read it. I'm going to have lots of time to read while I'm outa' town."

"It's going to be a mystery."

"What's it about?"

"I'm not certain yet."

"What's the title?"

"I don't know that either. It's too soon. I haven't written the book yet. What type of books do you like to read?"

"I've only read one book in my life and I really liked it."

"What book was it? *The Old man and the Sea* by Ernest Hemingway is one of my favorites!"

"The Godfather. I can relate to the characters. "

"Oh. Is that because you're a criminal defense attorney?"

"Johnny! Here's your Black Russian," the bubbling Ukrainian waitress carefully set a large drink in front of the huge man. "Taste it and tell me if you like it."

"Thank you Olga It must be good if you made it and I'll savor it."

"What does 'savor it' mean? I never heard that word before."

"It means that I will value how good it tastes forever."

"Oh Johnny! You're so sweet," she gushed, leaned across the bar and lightly kissed him on the forehead. "I'll miss you."

"Leave us alone for awhile. I'm talking serious stuff with this writer guy. I'll call you when I need another drink."

"Okey dokey! I'll be right down there in the middle of the bar." She skipped away like a teenaged girl celebrating her first kiss.

"I'm not really a writer," Mack offered. "I'm just thinking about writing a book some day."

"That's okay. I might just make a good character for you. Do you have some time?"

"I'm not going anywhere for awhile. I'll skip out and get some dinner in a half hour or so. For you I'll make time. "

"Okay. Let me break your heart. I'm not an attorney."

"I distinctly heard you say that you just came back from court in downtown Chicago on the Eisenhower Expressway."

"I was in court because I was sentenced today. I'm going away for a while. The dumb-ass judge gave me fifteen years to make an example out of me because I was a copper."

"Why are you here? Don't they take a convicted person away right after the sentence is read?"

"The judge gave me seventy-two hours to get my affairs in order."

"Why would he do that? That sounds very unusual. You must have had a very good attorney."

"I did. He's the judge's son-in-law. The judge knows that I'm not going anywhere. I'm a dead man walking. I may not make it out of prison alive."

"What do you mean?"

"I was the assistant police chief in Stone Park and I won't last twenty-four hours in Joliet unless they keep me in solitary. The cons will find a way to get to me and shove a shiv in my back."

"What did you do to get fifteen years in prison?"

"A little bit here and a little bit there. And I got caught. I did some favors for a few people and kept my friends out of jail. I'm well known in the community and even own part of this bar. I put twenty grand in here ten years ago and helped them build the bar over several Saturday afternoons. Now it's all gone. Nobody wants anything to do with me."

"So, that's why the bartender mentioned a 'going away' party for you in here tonight. You're going to prison!"

"You finally figured it out didn't you? Good work Sherlock."

"What were you convicted of?"

"A big joke that's what! I helped out my friends and I took the rap for them!"

"What were you convicted of that got you fifteen years?"

"Embezzlement of city funds and extortion."

"How did you do that?"

"Did you ever get a speeding ticket?"

"Of course I have. I think almost everyone has at one time."

"Did you pay the ticket or go to court and try to beat it?"

"When I lived in Chicago I didn't worry about paying for tickets. I had friends and when I showed up in court they were always dismissed because the cop who gave me the ticket didn't show up."

"That's kinda' what I'm talking about. I helped out my friends, and a few strangers, with their tickets. I made a few bucks, some people got jealous and turned me in to Internal Affairs."

"What did you do that got you in trouble?" Mack innocently asked.

"I pulled their tickets when they got to my desk," the big man replied with a slight smile.

"So, is that worth fifteen years in prison?"

"That's not all I did," the big man grinned and took a big sip of his Black Russian.

"What else?"

"Are you a priest?"

"Of course not!" Mack exclaimed. "I'm sitting in a bar drinking a beer. Would a priest do that?"

"No, he wouldn't, but you make me feel like I'm confessing all of my sins and when I'm done you'll forgive me."

"If it'll make you feel better I'll forgive you, but I don't think it'll count for anything."

"Don't bother. It's too late for that. I dug myself a big hole and I couldn't get out. My girlfriend sold me out as state's evidence."

"What does your girlfriend have to do with you pulling tickets for your friends?" Mack asked. "Did she work in the police station too?"

"No. She worked in a currency exchange on North Avenue in Melrose Park."

"Is she still working there?"

"No. They fired her when they found out what she was doing. That's how we got caught. Her boss turned her in when she refused to split with him."

"This gets more interesting by the minute. What did she get caught doing?"

"Every day the parking and speeding tickets came across my desk with the checks attached to them. I reviewed and approved all of the tickets before they were sent in for processing and recording with the Illinois Secretary of State. If one of my friends got a ticket he'd call me. I'd pull it for him, destroy his check and he'd pay me in cash. It was a 'win-win' situation because he didn't get any points on his driving record, paid the same fee to me as he paid for the ticket. It worked fine and I made a couple thousand bucks a year in cash money."

"How did your girlfriend fit into this?"

"She worked in a currency exchange and could cash checks for me. I figured out that I could pull tickets for anyone, take the check to the currency exchange and she'd cash it for me. The person didn't get any points on their driving license, their check got cashed and they sure as hell weren't going to complain about it. I made an extra twenty grand a year and split it with her fifty-fifty."

"What happened" How did you get caught?"

"Olga!" Mack's new companion bellowed. "Make me another Black Russian pronto! Bring my friend another beer and put it on my tab!"

"Yes Johnny," the exuberant bar tender responded. "Did you savor the first one?"

"It was very good and I need to savor another one! Hurry up! I'm running out of time"

The huge man turned to face Mack and smirked. "Now where were we in my confession?"

"You had explained that your girlfriend was cashing the police department's checks for you and the two of you split the money fifty-fifty. Then I asked how you got caught. That's where we left off."

"Now I remember. That bitch was really stupid!"

"What do you mean? She couldn't be very dumb if she worked in a currency exchange. That's like working in a bank."

"Believe me she's a stupid broad!"

"What did she do?"

"She kept a set of books and recorded every check she cashed for me. She left the ledger in her desk over a weekend and her boss found it. I found out that she's a druggie and loves crack cocaine."

"He shouldn't have complained because he got his percentage for cashing the checks."

"He wanted more. He insisted on thirty percent in cash over and above the check cashing fee."

"What did you do?"

"He didn't know that I was involved until it all went down. I told her to give him twenty percent and get the ledger back from him."

"That should have been the end of the story. A win-win for everyone involved."

"He wouldn't give it back and insisted that she screw him in the back room every time he wanted some, plus give him thirty percent."

"What happened?"

"She gave him the thirty percent and he seemed to be happy with the fringe benefit she was giving him a couple times a week. After a couple of weeks he told her to forget the thirty percent and for her to keep all of it. I should've known that something was going on."

"Why did he do that?"

"He was under investigation by the State of Illinois for tax evasion. The auditors found her ledger in his safe and made him a deal if he'd turn state's evidence and help them catch me. They went after her and made her a deal if she ratted on me. She did and here I am."

"Wow! Where is she now?"

"The last time I saw her was when she testified against me in court last month. I think they put her in the witness protection program and shipped her out of state. They know that I've got some friends that would put her away for good if she stayed here."

"Johnny, here's your Black Russian." The blonde bar tender gushed. "I hope that you savor it."

"I'll remember it for a long time. At least fifteen years. How about my friend's beer."

"It's right here," she slid a cold Budweiser and frosted glass mug in Mack's direction. "I hope he savors it."

"I will. Thank you."

"How long are you going to hang around here?" The big man asked. "It's almost six o'clock and if you're going to try the 'Capri' down on North Avenue you'd better get going. The place fills up by seven o'clock and they don't take reservations."

"If you don't mind I'll take my beer with me. I still have to drop my bag off in my room."

"No problem. Will you be coming back here later? You're invited to my going away party and it starts at ten o'clock. You'll be my special guest."

"I'll try. I've been on an airplane most of the day and I'm pooped."

"You better come back mister!" The petite bar tender remarked. "The Wolf Man is expecting you to come in and hear him sing."

"How does he know that I'm here? You told me that he's sleeping in the back room."

"He got up to go pee about ten minutes ago and I told him. He has someone special for you to meet tonight. He's expecting you to be here after nine o'clock."

"I'll do my best, but I can't promise anything. I might fall asleep after dinner."

"I gave you a personal invitation to my going away party," the big man interjected. "If you don't show up I'll send a couple of people down to your room and drag you out."

"That's an offer I can't refuse. I'll see you at ten o'clock."

Mack slipped off the bar stool, balanced the full mug of beer in his right hand, lifted his overnight bag with his left hand and headed for the door.

"It's going to be a long night," Mack thought. *"I'll call Ben Brown out in Elgin and ask if he'll meet me for lunch tomorrow."*

Chapter
11

It was 9:32 P.M. when Mack made his way back into the karaoke lounge. The dim lighting left much to be desired and the forty-watt light bulbs mounted on the sides of the backlit mahogany bar mirrored themselves in the polished silver mirror behind the liquor bottles stacked on the clear glass shelves.

The soft voice of the Wolf Man crooning a Willie Nelson tune tumbled down from the ceiling-mounted speakers. The soft 'click, click, click' of pool balls making their way into leather-cupped pockets echoed across the smoke-filled room.

Two gigantic men clad in black golf shirts and black pants playing pool in the far corner glanced back and forth at Mack. They were obviously uncomfortable with his presence because they didn't know who he was or where he came from. They seemed anxious and ready for action.

An aging Italian man, five-foot five inches tall at most, watched Mack from his high perch atop a chrome-legged, plastic-topped stool at the bar. He slipped off of his lofty perch, walked across the room, pulled out the wooden chair across the table from Mack, sat down and lit up a non-filtered Camel cigarette

The old man didn't appear to be dangerous, at least outwardly, but Mack knew that he could order a hit on him with the nod of his head. He appeared to be in his late '60s, was balding on the top of his head and wore black plastic eyeglasses that framed his rotund, pockmarked face. His complexion had been deeply etched by acne in his teenage years and his pockmarked face added to his ambience. Gray chest hairs protruded through the neck opening of his blue and white short-sleeved cotton shirt.

The old man took a deep drag on his cigarette and opened the conversation.

"The Wolf Man told me that you write books. Maybe you'd like to write about me."

Mack didn't know what to say and hesitated before he spoke. "I don't write books. I told the bartender that I'd like to retire on an island and write books someday."

"Oh. I thought you were a published author."

"I might be someday."

"I think that my life is worth writing about. I'd like to write a book about it myself, but I don't have any formal education and don't know where to start."

"What makes you think that your life would be interesting to others?"

"You don't know who I am do you?"

"No. I don't. You just came over here and sat down. Should I know who you are?"

"You might. Do you live in Chicago?"

"I used to several years ago. Now I live in south Florida close to West Palm Beach."

"When you lived here did you ever hear of Charlie Mangini?"

"Of course. He was the mobster who was murdered in his kitchen while he was cooking sausages. He was going to testify before a Senate investigating committee and the mob wanted him out of the way. It was an inside job."

"No it wasn't. The outfit didn't do it. The Feds killed him because he was going to spill the beans on some of them and the payoffs they took. Charlie would've never beefed on the outfit."

"That's not how it read in the newspapers."

"That's correct. The Feds had to blame it on the outfit. One of his so-called Federal protectors shot Charlie in the back of the head while he was cooking sausages for dinner."

"What makes you think that one of his bodyguards shot him?"

"He was cooking sausages for three people. His two Federal bodyguards claim that someone came in from the basement, snuck up the stairs and whacked Charlie while they were watching the fights on television set in the family room."

"How do you know that he was cooking for three people?"

"There were three plates on the kitchen table along with three silverware settings."

"Isn't it possible that someone could have come in from the basement?"

"No. The basement windows were locked from the inside and there isn't a door to the basement from the outside."

"You seem very convinced."

"I am. There were two Feds stationed outside the front of the house in cars and two more outside the back door. Nobody could get in or out without being seen by them."

"How did you know that?"

"I delivered the sausages to Charlie about an hour before he got whacked. I saw them."

"Why? Were you in the meat business?"

"Charlie and I were old friends. I ran a clothing outlet on North Avenue for him and Joey Bandalli in the seventies. We sold stuff for half of what it was worth and we made a killing."

"How could you afford to sell something for half of what it was worth?"

"The secret to retailing success isn't what you sell something for. It's what you paid for it in the first place. We didn't pay anything for the crap we sold."

"How could you get clothing to sell if you didn't pay for it?"

"We ordered stuff from the Jews at the Merchandise Mart and

never paid them for it. It was hot stuff from the New York garment district and they couldn't complain to the cops. Besides if they'd bitched they'd found themselves buried up to their necks in cow shit in an Indiana cornfield. Joey's uncle was a corn farmer and he could always use extra fertilizer."

"Didn't I see something about that in a movie?"

"Maybe you did if you saw *Casino* with Robert Dinero and Joe Pesci. I was in that movie too."

"What? You're an actor?"

"No. I wasn't actually an actor in the movie. One of the characters was based on me and some things I did."

"What? Which character?"

"Rent the movie when you get back to Florida and try to figure it out."

Stunned and concerned about what he'd gotten himself into Mack took a deep breath before he opened his mouth to speak. It was obvious that for some unknown reason the old man had taken Mack into his confidence.

"Okay. Tell me about yourself and what caused you to take the fork in the road that affected your life."

The old man winked at Mack with his right eye, leaned back in his chair, took a deep drag from his glowing cigarette, blew the smoke up and away from his face as he closed his eyes and recalled the old days.

"I grew up the hard way on the streets and in the back alleys of the Little Italy section of Chicago. It wasn't easy for a homeless kid in the early fifties. I did what I had to do to survive." He took another long drag on his unfiltered Camel and deliberately paused for effect as he made a sideways glance at Mack. "It was tough on the streets in those days."

Mack sensed that the ball was in his court and the old man expected him to stroke his ego by asking him a question to clarify what he meant by homeless.

"What did you mean by a homeless kid?"

"My father abandoned my mother and went to live with a cheap whore when I was eight years old. My mother worked as a factory cleaning woman until she caught a cold that turned into pneumonia."

"What happened to her?"

"She died. I was ten years old." The old man took a deep drag on his cigarette and turned his face away so Mack couldn't see the tear forming in the corner of his left eye. "It was my fault."

"It wasn't your fault! You couldn't treat pneumonia. How about her doctor or the hospital?"

"We didn't have any money for a doctor and there was no way to drive her to the hospital. I couldn't drive and we didn't own a car."

The old man blinked twice, rubbed his cigarette out in the flimsy tin ashtray and shook another cancer stick out of the soft paper pack. He tapped one end on the plastic imitation wood-grained tabletop, pulled it to his lips, flipped the top of his vintage Zippo lighter and spun the wheel with his left thumb. The flame jumped to life and the aged mobster lit the end of the cigarette dangling from his tightly pursed lips.

"How about a friend or a neighbor? Couldn't they drive her to the hospital?"

"You didn't hear me did you?"

"What do you mean?"

"We didn't have any money for a doctor or hospital. Plus, she didn't want our neighbors to know that she was sick."

"Why not? They might have been able to help her."

The old man stirred in his chair, looked down at his feet, slowly shook his head from side to side, pulled the cigarette to his lips, took a long drag, held the smoke in his lungs momentarily and blew it out over his right shoulder in a single large cloud.

"If the bums knew she was sick they'd come in, smother her with a pillow and clean the place out."

"What? They wouldn't have helped her?"

"You really don't understand do you?"

"I'm trying."

"The streets of Chicago were Hell in the fifties. If you showed any weakness the street punks would eat you alive and toss your broken bones in an alley."

The old man's eyes began to water and he turned away from Mack's astonished stare.

"What about your father? Did he know that your mother was sick and needed help?"

"He didn't care. Besides we didn't know where he lived."

"What did you do?"

"My mother was burning up with fever and she kept asking me for ice to cool her off."

"Didn't you have ice in the freezer?"

"You really lived a sheltered life didn't you? We didn't have a refrigerator. We had an icebox. The ice deliveryman delivered ice once a week to families who could afford it."

"Because you didn't have a refrigerator with a freezer you didn't have any ice?"

"It's about time you caught on. I followed the ice deliveryman around. When a piece of ice fell out of his metal ice tongs I scooped it up and threw it in a bucket. I had to watch out because he'd smack me alongside the head if he caught me doing it."

"Why would he care if you picked up the pieces of ice?"

"He sold them to the guys who made Italian ice cones on the street corners."

"Oh."

The old man, leaned back in his chair, looked at the ceiling and took a long drag on his cigarette. Mack saw that his eyes were misting up and a single tear had lodged on his left check where it met the edge of his nose. The ball was in Mack's court and he had to relieve the tension.

"What did you do with the ice you picked up off the street?"

"I took them home dumb ass! They were for my mother. I needed to cool her off."

"How did you use them to cool her off?"

"I put the pieces in a bread pan on the bedside table, sat a small fan on the table and it blew the cool air over her."

"That probably cooled her off, but it might have aggravated her condition."

"I know."

Giant tears formed in the mobster's eyes and ran down his cheeks. He pushed his chair away from the table, turned away from Mack and stood up. "I have to check something in the kitchen," the old mad croaked. "I'll be back in a minute. Wait right here for me."

"I will," Mack responded. "I'm not going anywhere. I'll be here when you get back."

The old man slid the chair back under the table and shuffled off in the direction of the kitchen area snuggled behind the mirrored bar wall. Mack sensed that he was not coming back and that the colorful interview had ended.

"I guess I got too close to the old man's soul," Mack thought to himself. *"It's obvious that he is full of hurt and anger and he took those emotions out on others around him."*

Mack glanced at the two large Italian men playing pool in the back corner of the bar. They seemed to be completely oblivious to his presence now that the old man had left.

"Hey you! I'm back!" The old man barked. "What are you doing? Sitting there daydreaming that you want to be a wise guy like those two punks in the corner playing pool? Forget about it! You're to old for that," the old man snapped as he slid into the chair across the table from Mack.

"I apologize," Mack responded. "I must have slipped off. I wasn't daydreaming."

"Are you ready to pick up where we left off?" The old man reached for another Camel with his right hand and for his chrome Zippo with his left. "It's almost ten o'clock and I'm waiting for somebody to deliver some stuff from Iraq." The old man motioned towards the lounge door with his left thumb. "What else you want to know about me?"

It was only then that Mack realized that the waist-high windows were actually one-way glass. The old man could see out into the hotel lobby, but anyone entering the hotel would only see what they perceived to be a mirror.

"I don't know what to ask because of the way you feel about your father and what happened to your mother. What would you like to tell me?"

"You're not much of a writer! You didn't even ask me what my name is. Don't you care?"

"I never thought about it. What is your name?"

"Guido Cameri! That's an Italian name. My grandparents came from Sicily." He tapped the ash of his cigarette into the tin ashtray, took another long drag, and looked directly into Mack's eyes as he pondered what he should say. "Let me take a few minutes and try to make you appreciate what I went through when I was growing up. Did I tell you that I was the youngest of four children?"

"No."

"I had two older sisters and an older brother. I was the youngest kid. After my mother died my grandmother on my father's side took my brothers and sisters to live with her."

"Why didn't she take you?"

"She raised that bastard father of mine and I wanted nothing to do with her. The priest in our church recommended that my brother and sisters go to live with my grandmother and that I be sent to an orphanage." He slowly exhaled cigarette smoke from his scarred lungs into the air above his head and paused for effect to test Mack's reaction.

"Why? That doesn't make any sense!"

"The priest considered me to be an incorrigible criminal and didn't want me to influence my brother and my sisters." He coughed as he exhaled smoke from his nose.

"Why would he think that?" Mack responded with a shocked look on his face.

"What did you do to him?"

"It might have something to do with what he did to me when I was eight years old. Or, that he found out my friends and me swiped candles off the altar and sold them on the street. He knew that I was already running around with a tough group and that I might have some influence on my sisters and my brother."

"I would have thought that your grandmother would have wanted to take care of you."

"No way," the old man responded. "She couldn't handle me and she knew it."

"How old were you when you were sent to the orphanage?"

"Ten. But I only stayed there for two days."

"Only two days? Who adopted you that quickly?"

"I wasn't adopted. A couple friends of mine busted me out. They jimmied the lock on the back door and I slipped out at two o'clock in the morning."

"Where did you go?"

"They hid me in the attic of a garage behind a gas station on North Avenue."

"Did the people from the orphanage come looking for you?"

"They tried for a couple of days and finally gave up. They had more important things to worry about than some Italian brat running around on the street."

"How did you survive?"

"I wasn't old enough to drive so I couldn't steal cars. I was working in a car wash for a buck an hour plus tips before my mother died. I just went back there."

"Weren't you're afraid that the priest or somebody from the orphanage would see you and take you back?"

"Naw."

"Did your brother and sisters know that you escaped from the orphanage?"

"Of course. I told them that I'd bust out. The garage was only two blocks from my grandmother's house and my sisters slipped peanut butter sandwiches and milk out of my grandmother's house and brought them to me at night."

"Did your grandmother know that you were working in the car wash and living in a garage?"

"I don't think so, but even if she did she could've cared less."

"You really had a rough childhood."

"You have no idea city boy. It was rough because all the neighborhood wise guys brought their cars to the car wash to be washed and waxed. It had to be done exactly right or they'd box my ears and slap me across the head."

"Why didn't you tell the owner or call the cops?"

"Call the cops? Are you kiddin' me? The cops wanted nothing to do with the wise guys. They counted on their bosses for a couple hundred bucks every week for lookin' the other way when somebody got roughed up or shot on the street. There was nothin' anybody could do about it and the wise guys knew it."

"Why didn't the car wash owner say something to them?"

"Because they would've burned down the car wash after they beat him half to death with baseball bats and threw him in the grease pit. Those were some pretty rough times."

"I just can't imagine anybody doing that to a ten year old kid."

"City boy you lived a sheltered life. Did you see the movie *The Godfather*?"

"Of course. Didn't everybody?"

"Some of the things that happened in the movie weren't even close to reality. Reality in those days was much more vicious and brutal. Only the strongest and fastest survived."

"You definitely have the instinct for survival and it seems to me that you're always one step ahead of everyone else. How far did you go in school?"

"I dropped out of the fifth grade after my mother died. I don't have any education, but that hasn't held me back in my business career. I make about one hundred and fifty G's a year and I don't pay income tax on any of it."

"Aren't you afraid that you'll get caught for tax evasion and go to prison like Al Capone?"

"Prison? Been there and done that. I'm not worried. Getting caught for income tax invasion is for punks and people who don't know anything about street life. I only deal in cash and I don't have a bank account. If you don't put money in a bank there's no way the IRS can track you down."

The old man leaned back in his chair as he extinguished his cigarette in the ashtray with his left-hand and simultaneously reached for the soft pack of Camels with his right. It was obvious that he was an addicted chain smoker. He pulled the cigarette to his lips with his right-hand, lit it with the chrome Zippo in his left, took a deep drag and blew the smoke over his right shoulder in a series of seven undulating blue smoke rings.

"Anything else you want to know about me?"

"I don't know what to ask you."

"Do you want to hear about the wise guy down on Cicero I called the ear man?"

"The ear man?"

"That's correct. I said the ear man. Do you want to hear about him or not?"

"Of course I do. Why did you call him the ear man?"

"One day when I was working at the car wash one of the wise guys pulled in drivin' a bright red Chrysler Imperial. It was a nineteen fifty-seven model with great big tail fins and a round chrome circle on the top of each of the taillights. He flipped me the keys and told me to wash and wax it. He said that he'd cut my ears off if he found one water spot on the finish when he came back to pick it up."

"Why would he threaten to cut your ears off?"

"You might want to clean the wax out of your own ears. You obviously don't hear very well.

"I hear okay. I don't understand why he threatened to cut your ears off."

"That's why they called him the ear man. If someone made him mad, or he had to collect a debt from someone he didn't like, rather than break their kneecaps with a baseball bat or lead pipe he'd slice off their ears with a straight razor. He told me to look on the front seat of his car and he held the door open for me so I could get in. He slapped me across the back of the head and the force of the wallop knocked me into the front seat. There was a glass mason jar with a tin cover, like a mayonnaise jar, on the floor. It was full of shriveled up things that looked like flat prunes."

"Why would he keep prunes in a glass jar in his car?"

"They weren't prunes. They were human ears and they really smelled bad. That's why they called him the ear man."

"What did you do then?"

"I did what he told me to do. I washed and waxed his car. When I vacuumed the interior I noticed that he had a small refrigerator plugged into a cigarette lighter. It was the perfect thing for my mother to keep cold water and fruit juice in and I asked him if he would sell it to me."

"Did he?"

"He told me that he would sell it to me for fifteen bucks, but I didn't have fifteen bucks. I only had three bucks in my pocket and he told me to ask my boss if he would loan me the money."

"Did your boss loan you the money?"

"He gave me five bucks and told me to ask the wise guy if I could pay him off on time or in exchange for car washes and wax jobs."

"Then what did you do?"

"I told the wise guy that I could give him eight bucks now and pay him off at two bucks a week."

"What did he say about that?"

"He said okay."

"How did the deal work out for you?"

"He gave me the portable refrigerator and told me that he wouldn't give me a tip for washing his car because he found two water spots on the left corner panel. That was okay because I got the refrigerator and I knew that it would make my mother feel better."

"Did your mother like the refrigerator?"

"She sure did. I kept it filled with fresh fruit juice so that she could drink cold juice any time she wanted during the day. My mother was really happy about having the portable refrigerator."

"You must have felt very good about helping your mother in her time of need."

"The big problem came up after that. That's what killed her."

"What kind of problem?"

"One day the wise guy brought his red Imperial into the carwash and the left front fender was crumpled. When I asked him about the crumpled fender he whacked me across the head and pulled on my left ear. It was a message for me to keep my mouth shut."

"Then what happened?"

"I couldn't wax the crumpled left front fender, but I did the best I could. When he came back he was raising hell that his insurance coverage had been canceled because he hadn't paid his premium. That meant that any repairs to his car had to come out of his own pocket. He was really steamed."

"Did he give you a tip for washing and waxing his car?"

"No. He asked me for three bucks as payment on the portable refrigerator."

"Did you give him the three bucks?"

"No. I didn't have it. I told him that since he started coming in there that the other wise guys in the neighborhood started bringing in their cars too. None of them tipped me."

"He said that was my tough luck and for me to get over it and grow up."

"That doesn't sound like the end of the story?"

"After the car wash closed that night I went home to check on my mother. She was dehydrated because she hadn't had any fruit juice to drink all afternoon. The portable refrigerator was gone."

"Who took it? Did a hoodlum sneak in from the street?"

"No. The wise guy knew where she lived. He came in through the front door and took back the portable refrigerator because I didn't pay him the three bucks. She died that night."

"It wasn't totally his fault. Your mother was very sick."

"Yes it was! If she'd had some cold fruit juice to drink that afternoon she wouldn't have become dehydrated and died."

"That's a very sad story."

"But I got even."

"How? What did you do?"

"He lived off of Harlem two blocks south of North Avenue. I had a friend with a car who knew where he lived and he didn't like him either. We filled up two five-gallon gas cans with high octane gas and drove to his neighborhood about three o'clock in the mornin'. I knew how much he loved his red Imperial and that his insurance was no good. We poured both of those five-gallon cans of gas into the front seat of his car and tossed in a match. We parked a hundred yards down the street and watched his fancy Imperial burn into a pile of melted metal. That's how I got my start in crime. It was easy."

"Did he know that you did it?"

"I don't think so. If he did I'd been dead the next day. He had a lot of enemies and they all knew how much he loved that car."

"Did you go back to the car wash?"

"For what?"

"To work."

"That would've been real smart wouldn't it? Not after I found out that I could've pulled in more cash money stealin' and torchin' cars for the insurance money."

"Insurance money? How could you make any money stealing and burning up cars for insurance money? You didn't own them."

"Don't you know what insurance is?" The old man smiled and took a drag from his Camel.

"Of course. I pay my insurance company to cover my car in

case of theft, fire or an accident. But I own the car. Or, rather I share it with the finance company."

"That's not the type of insurance the outfit sold. Ours was different."

"What do you mean different?"

"There were two types of insurance; business and personal. If you insured your business with the outfit we guaranteed that your business wouldn't be burned down or robbed by street punks."

"That's extortion! That's not legal!"

"So? Who cared? Back then the outfit controlled the coppers. If you didn't make your weekly insurance payment when our guy came around on Friday afternoon two other guys would come in and break your left kneecap with a lead pipe. Most guys paid up on time from then on. The outfit didn't believe in accounts receivable. Or bad debts."

"Didn't the business owners report it to the police?"

"If they did our contact in the police department called us before they sent a copper out to talk to him. Our guys stopped by for a friendly chat before the copper got there and the business owner usually came down with a case of forgetfulness. We never had any complaints after the follow up visit."

"What if the business owner got fed up with your extortion demands and filed a report with the police? The police had to investigate it."

"The business would have an unfortunate fire or an explosion in the basement. If there was no building there wasn't any business and nothing for them to beef about."

"Wow! You guys played rough in those days!"

"You did what you had to do to survive, but it's not much different today." The old man tilted his head to the right and blew five perfect smoke rings. "We still offer business insurance."

"What! That's illegal. It's extortion!"

"Maybe and maybe not. Our rates are cheaper than most commercial insurance companies because we don't have any losses and collect all of our premiums. Take this hotel for example. I have the insurance contract and they haven't had a fire, serious reportable accident or robbery in three years. Oops! I take that back. There was an incident with the manager a few months ago. He was a little late with his premium payment."

"What do you mean by a little late and what happened?"

"When Rocco stopped by to collect the insurance premium about three o'clock on a Friday afternoon the manager wasn't around. He told the desk clerk that he had to make a run downtown and told her to cover for him. He knew better than to try and fool Rocco. He was hiding in his room."

"How do you know that he was hiding in his room?"

"His car was parked in a parking space behind the hotel. Rocco dialed his room from the house phone in the lobby and hung up when he answered."

"Did Rocco ask him for the money?"

"Of course not. He had to be taught a lesson and I wanted the word to get out on the street."

"What happened?"

"Thought you'd never ask." The old man simultaneously rubbed out his cigarette in the tin ashtray with his let hand and pulled out another fresh Camel with his right hand. "He had to be trained."

"Trained? How?"

"Did you notice that the windows in this place are one-way glass? You can see everything that goes on out there in the lobby."

"Of course. I wondered why. I never saw one-way glass in a lounge before."

"There's probably a lot of things going on here that you never saw before. Do you want to hear what happened or do you want to keep on yammering? I don't have all night."

"Sure. Tell me."

"The night desk clerk called in sick and the hotel manager had to cover his shift for him. About two o'clock in the mornin' two black guys wearin' black ski masks ran through the front door, pointed pistols at the manager and demanded money. He refused to give them any money so one of the black guys jumped over the counter, beat the hell out of him with the butt of his pistol and cleaned out the cash drawer."

"He's lucky that he didn't get shot."

"They didn't want to kill him. They just wanted money."

"Did you see what was going on?"

"It's funny that you asked. I had just looked at my watch, saw that it was exactly two o'clock and glanced out the window towards the lobby. I saw the two black guys run in and it all happened so fast that by the time I could react they were gone. Besides I wouldn't have gone out there anyway. I might've gotten shot."

"Did they catch the black guys?"

"Naw. They had a car waitin' for them in the parkin' lot. They took off southbound on Mannheim Road towards Stone Park and were long gone by the time the coppers got here."

"Was the manager badly injured?"

"Mostly just his pride. He got a few bruises on his face, but nothin' serious."

"Did the hotel's insurance company cover the loss?"

"Of course not! He didn't pay the premium like I told you before."

"You did it!"

"I did what?"

"You had the place robbed because the manager refused to comply with your extortion attempt."

"I didn't do anything. The place was robbed by a couple of black guys. I'm Sicilian and we don't mix with the blacks. I wasn't involved, but I suppose that if he'd paid up his insurance premium that one of our boys might've been watchin' the front door that night. He didn't show up because his grandmother was sick and he had to stay at the hospital with her."

"I understand."

"You've gotta' leave in a few minutes."

"Why? I'm enjoying my conversation with you."

"Look out in the lobby. Do you see those two big guys at the front desk?"

Mack swiveled around in his chair so that he could se through the one-way glass into the lobby area. Two extremely large olive-skinned men who looked liked mirror images of Mr. Clean leaned on the front counter and looked toward the lounge. Their dark black handlebar mustaches curled up on each end and framed their large cheekbones.

"I see them. So what?"

"They're smugglers from Turkey. They bring me things from Saddam Hussein's palaces in Iraq that I fence on the north side of Chicago for big bucks." The old man reached into his right pants pocket, drew out two stacks of $50 bills in bank wrappers marked $5000, and flashed them at Mack. "There's two matching stacks in my left pocket." He smiled and slid the bills back into his pocket. "Usually they bring me diamonds, rubies and emeralds, but tonight they're bringing me something special." He grinned, took a drag of his cigarette and blew the smoke over his left shoulder.

"Smugglers! You can't be serious!"

"Of course I can. They're airline pilots. They don't get checked and can bring in almost anything they want. Tonight's delivery is very special."

"You're baiting me just so that I'll ask you what they brought you."

"Of course. Are you going to ask me or not? I don't have time to gab."

"Okay. What did they bring you?"

"Tonight they brought me a tapestry that hung in Saddam's personal bedroom in his main palace. I'm paying 'em ten grand for it and I already sold it for one hundred and fifty grand to a lawyer on the Gold Coast."

"That's illegal!"

"It's a living and nobody got hurt over the deal. Everyone's as happy as a clam."

"How do you know that you're not being scammed yourself?"

"I know. They can't scam me. I'm the best. Meet me down here tomorrow morning at eight o'clock. I'll show it to you and prove to you that it's authentic."

"Is the lounge open at eight o'clock in the morning? That's awfully early for people to start drinking."

"I own the place and my office is in the back. I'll be here. Don't be late." The old man smiled, rubbed out his cigarette in the tin ashtray, stood up and turned to leave. "Forget what you heard. What you hear here stays here."

"I thought you were giving me information for a book that I

might write someday?"

"Naw. I wanted to test your reaction. I'm a pretty good storyteller myself and I'm thinking about writing a book about my life. You were a good listener and ate it all up."

"What about your father? Did you ever see him again?"

"No! The night he died the funeral director called me and told me that he'd been whacked in an alley in Stone Park. I told him to cut his heart out of his body, run a knife through it and tell him that it was from his son. I gotta' go." The old mobster winked at Mack with his right eye as he turned towards the front door of the lounge.

The two Turkish smugglers broke into wide grins when the old man emerged from the lounge door, but nervously looked around as he approached them with his right hand outstretched.

"I wonder if they paid their insurance premiums before they started dealing with him," Mack thought to himself. He waited for the three men to exit the front door of the hotel before he finished his beer, pushed his chair away from the table and stood up to leave.

"Where do you think you're going?" Bellowed a deep male voice from behind Mack. "Come back in the corner and shoot a game of pool with us. The boss wants to be alone with his business partners."

Mack swung around to face the two large Italian men who had been playing pool in the back corner of the lounge the whole time that he had been talking with the old mobster. He knew that they had made him an offer he'd be smart not to refuse.

"Sure. Why not? I used to be pretty good in my younger years."

Chapter 12

Mack sensed the soft 'click' of the brass door latch of his hotel room and opened his eyes. He sensed that someone had been there and he had no recollection of the evening before.

He recalled having a lengthy discussion with a semi-retired mobster and shooting a few games of pool in the back room. Mack glanced at the bedside table and the cheap digital clock read 8:12 A.M. He turned his head so he could see the door. The brass safety chain was not secure and the dead bolt lock wasn't closed. The combination of those factors and the soft 'click' of the door closing seconds earlier were cause for alarm.

He turned slowly to his right. The pillow on the right side of the bed had a deep indentation as if someone had used it during the night. A slight indentation in the other side of the mattress indicated that someone had slept on that side of the bed. Mack slid the palm of his hand into the indentation and was surprised that it was warm to the touch. His eyes began to focus in the dim light and he saw three long, black hairs on the pillowcase.

"Who the hell was here last night?" He muttered as he shook his head. "Whoever it was I sure hope that it was a female."

Mack threw back the sheet and was surprised to find that he wasn't wearing underwear. He threw his legs over the side of the bed and as he sat up he saw his underwear on a chair across the room. His pants and shirt were neatly hung over the back of the chair. His head felt like it was spinning in a centrifuge.

"Someone was apparently very good to me last night," he mumbled. When he stood up, he suddenly became light-headed and grabbed the chair for support. When his head finally stabilized he reached for his underwear and slipped them on.

He paused to look at his profile in the wall-mounted dressing mirror and was forced to squint in order to focus his eyes. His hair was totally disheveled and his blood-shot eyes looked like two pieces of raw hamburger meat set in the bowels of an overripe pumpkin. His face was a light shade of pink and it looked as if it was coated in a light dusting of rouge.

Mack kept his burning eyes closed, staggered to the edge of the bathroom door and grasped the doorframe to keep from falling down.

"This isn't going to be a good day," he thought as he held back the urge to vomit.

He had to urinate very badly and felt a warm liquid dribble down his right leg. When he entered the bathroom he almost fell backwards in shock. The young Pakistani girl was brushing her long hair with a tortoise shell hairbrush!

"Have you slept with a Pakistani woman before?" She purred softly as she looked straight ahead into the mirror and continued to brush her hair. Her face displayed no emotion. "I'm very sorry if I woke you up when I went outside. I had to stop at the front desk to tell my brother that I am fine and that you were very good to me last night. I tried to be very quiet and not wake you."

Mack found it difficult to form words because his tongue felt like a cotton bale.

"You spent the night with me?" He managed to spit out. "I don't remember you being here."

"When you left the karaoke lounge you fell down in the lobby. You were very fortunate that I was there to catch you. My brother was working asked me if I would help you get to your room safely. After I got you undressed and into bed I decided to spend the night with you in case you needed someone."

She completed brushing her hair, gently put the hairbrush down on the plastic-topped lavatory and attempted to scrub her teeth with her forefinger after dipping it into the running water rushing from the open tap.

"I told your brother when I checked in that I didn't want you."

The young girl looked paralyzed with shock. She turned off the water and her dark eyes blazed with fire as if he had just slapped her across the face. Small tears formed of the corner of her eyes, she looked down at her bare feet and she slumped her shoulders as she attempted to voice a soft response.

"If I hadn't helped you get to your room last night you would have been mugged by the Mexican gang members that hang around outside the hotel when the lounge closes. I protected you from them and helped you get to your room. I am very sorry that you don't appreciate my efforts and I am also very ashamed of my behavior. However, you were in no shape whatsoever to find your room and I was concerned that you might fall and hurt yourself in the parking lot. If I have shamed you I am very sorry and I apologize. I shall go now and leave you to your important business."

The young girl slipped past Mack without raising her eyes from the floor or saying another word. She opened the door and slipped outside into the raw morning sun that was effortlessly attacking the hotel parking lot. The only sound Mack heard was a soft 'click' of the door latch as it closed behind her.

"*Now what the hell have I gotten myself into?*" Mack thought to himself as he shook his head slowly from side to side. His head felt like his brain was rolling from side to side inside his skull.

"*That no good bastard desk clerk has no compassion whatsoever for his sister. He would sell her for the price of a room and I believe he just did.*"

Mack shuffled towards the front door, threw the deadbolt in place, fastened the brass security chain in place and headed for the bathroom. He needed to pee, shave, shower and get ready to face the day's activities. He felt ashamed of himself for what he might have done to the young girl the night before and realized that it was part of her culture. She was probably fortunate that she spent the night with him rather than other conscienceless customers that might have found her in the dark.

"It was 8:15 A.M. when Mack slipped out of his room and headed for the lobby. He still had to get in touch with Ben Brown in Elgin and hoped that he would be able to join him for lunch.

As he approached the lobby Mack remembered that the semi-retired monster instructed him to meet him in the breakfast area so he could show him the tapestry from Saddam Hussein's master bedroom that he had purchased the night before. Mack seriously thought about turning around and going back to his room but he decided that the old man wasn't really serious about showing Mack anything much less a smuggled tapestry from Iraq.

Mack entered the lobby, walked directly up to the front desk and rapped his knuckles in a fast tattoo on the plastic counter to get the clerk's attention before he spoke.

"You scumbag! Don't you have any remorse for sending your sister to my room to spend the night with me?"

"I'm sorry if she caused you any displeasure. She's very young and is still learning how to properly please a man. However it was more of a safety issue for you. When you came out of the lounge about three-thirty this morning you were very drunk and fell on your face right over there by the stairway. My sister was kind enough to help you into your room and prevent you from getting mugged by the Mexican gang members that hang around the parking lot. She feels very badly that you didn't show any appreciation towards her."

"I don't remember anything about last night and if she helped me get to my room I certainly do appreciate it. I told you when I checked in this rat trap that I wanted nothing to do with your sister and you set me up with her anyway."

"Sir, it was not my choice. She had no place to stay last night and was sleeping on a couch right here in the lobby when she saw you come out of the lounge and fall down on your face. She helped you stand up and got you to your room safely. Did she steal your money?"

"No. It was all there."

"Then you should have shown her some appreciation."

"If that's what happened I appreciate it very much. Please pass my gratitude along to her when you see her."

"I will. Are you going to be spending another night with us?"

"I don't know yet. I'm going to meet someone for lunch and a call may come in for me while I'm gone. I'll check back with you after lunch and decide whether I'm spending another night. Most likely I will."

"Would you like the same room sir?"

"That'll be fine provided that I don't have to share it with your sister. Tell her that I appreciate her efforts but I don't need her company."

"Yes sir. I shall tell her. You can count on it." The desk clerk nodded towards the far corner of the hotel lobby. "I believe that gentleman wishes to speak with you."

Mack turned his head to look. Guido, the retired mobster, nodded his head at Mack. Alongside him stood a middle-aged, very rough looking Italian gentlemen wearing a well-worn black leather jacket. His demeanor and deeply pockmarked face made him appear like a character fresh out of *The Godfather* movie.

"*I wonder if that's the old man's muscle from the old days?*" Mack thought to himself as he nodded in recognition and slowly made his way across the hotel lobby towards his new friend. "*I hope he's not here to break my kneecaps for something I said or did last night.*"

""Mr. McCray I'm pleased that you could meet me here this morning," the old man offered Mack his open right hand. "I'm afraid that I can't show you the tapestry right now because it's far too dangerous in the daylight. I might be able to show it to you tonight, that is if you're still going to be here."

"I don't know if I'll be here or not."

"Just in case you're still here we'll be in the lounge enjoying karaoke about nine o'clock. You have a very good voice and can really carry a tune. Everyone enjoyed listening to you and the

Wolf Man singing that duet last night. You practically brought the house down with applause."

"I don't remember a thing about it."

"Maybe not but you had a good time. As a matter of fact you spent quite a bit of time talking with Rolf about his professional boxing days."

"Who's Rolf?"

"He's the old guy who owns the bar. He used to box professionally in the fifties and sixties all over the country. When his legs went south and he couldn't box anymore he went to breaking legs for me. He might not look like it now but he was a very rough dude."

"What do you mean breaking legs for you?"

He was my enforcer and collected the weekly premiums from my clients when I was in the insurance racket. We go back a long way together."

Mack couldn't take his eyes off the short, squat pockmarked face man in the leather jacket and felt that he had seen him someplace and the man noticed that Mack was staring at him."

"Hey you!" The obviously irritated man ordered in a deep gravely voice that smacked of the smoky bowels of Pittsburgh. "What're you looking at?"

"You look familiar to me. Did I meet you somewhere before?" Mack offered.

"I probably remind you of a character that you saw in *The Godfather*," the man offered with an accompanying grin. "I hear that a lot. It wasn't me because I was in the joint when they shot the movie. But I would've made a good character wouldn't I?" He chuckled as if he had just made a joke about himself.

"That's it! *The Godfather* movie."

"Rocco thinks he's a comedian. He's a good friend of mine and he got out of the joint a couple days ago. I'm going to take him under my wing for a few days and show him around town. He needs to learn where he can go and who he can trust."

"What do you mean he just got out of the joint?"

"I just got out from spending seven years standing on my head down in Joliet," the aging enforcer spat out. "I was innocent and someone set me up for a fall."

"What were you in for?" Mack innocently asked.

"Four charges of bank embezzlement, six charges of extortion and I broke a few too many kneecaps. They called it aggravated assault."

"I understand that you met Johnny Amorati in the bar yesterday afternoon. You were his special guest at his going away party last night," the old mobster offered with a broad smile. "He's a real piece of work! Did he tell you why the judge sent him up the river big time?"

"He didn't have a very good lawyer."

"He had a pretty lawyer. He's the judge's son-in-law. The judge did what he had to do. It was a political case. Johnny got greedy, turned into a bad copper and got caught. A crack-head broad turned on him."

"He told me that she was his girl friend."

"Sure she was. She was splitting the money with the old Jew who ran the currency exchange and screwing him in the backroom for money to buy crack."

"He mentioned that."

"Johnny won't last twenty-four hours in the joint. Some con will shove a shiv in his back on the way to the chow hall. His only chance to survive is if he slugs a guard and gets sent to maximum security where nobody can get to him. But the guards will rough him up pretty bad."

"Why would the guards rough him up?"

"He's a dirty cop. Do I have to draw you a picture?"

"The guards didn't mess with me," Rocco offered with a grin. "They knew better. The cons didn't either."

"You don't have to explain why. I understand. You don't have to draw me a picture."

"Me and Rocco are going downtown this morning. He has to meet a few new people and get his feet back on the ground. Are you going to be around here tonight?"

"I don't know. I'm waiting for a telephone call. After that I'm going to meet a friend from Elgin for lunch. I'll know this afternoon whether I'm going to stay over another night or fly back to Florida."

"If you're in town tonight stop by the lounge after nine

o'clock to watch me and my boys sing karaoke. You had a good time last night at Johnny's going away party."

"I don't have any recollection of what took place last night and from what I hear I might have made a fool of myself. I'll have to think twice before I go in there again."

"I'm inviting you to be my guest. If you don't show up that'll be an insult to me because you came for Johnny's going away party. You certainly aren't going to insult me in front of my friends are you?"

"This sounds like an offer I can't refuse."

"I suppose that you could look at it that way."

"If I'm still here tonight I'll stop in the lounge for a couple of beers. And if I have time I'm going to stop by a Border's store and pick up something for you."

"What's Borders?"

"It's a bookstore. If they have what I'm looking for I'll bring it by the lounge tonight."

"Okay, you do that. Rocco and me gotta' get going. We have a lot of places to go and a lot of people to meet. I've got to get him back in circulation and let people know that he's back in town. He's a man of many talents and I can put him to good use." The old man winked at Mack, turned and motioned for his husky friend to follow him through the lobby and out the front door of the hotel.

"What have I gotten myself into this time?" Mack thought. *"I never thought that I would be given an offer that I couldn't refuse. I'm somewhere between a rock and a hard place and I can't see any way of getting out of going back to the karaoke lounge tonight."*

He turned right towards the bank of pay telephones mounted on the wall so that he could place a call to Ben Brown in Elgin and ask if Ben could meet him for lunch. It was only 9:17 A.M. and Mack had some time on his hands.

"After I call Ben I'll explore a little and become acquainted with this part of town. Plus, I need to find a Borders store," Mack thought. *"And it wouldn't be a bad idea to find out if there's more than one exit out of the parking lot in case things get out of hand tonight."*

Chapter 13

Mack easily found the Border's store in Oak Park and bought the current edition of *Writers' Digest* for his new friend.

He reached Ben Brown on the telephone just as he was leaving to take his wife to O'Hare for a flight to Florida. Ben planned to drop her off at the airport and drive down Mannheim Road South and meet Mack for lunch at the Chinese restaurant on the northeast corner of Mannheim and North Avenue.

Mack pulled into the parking lot of the shopping center housing the *Long Dong* Chinese restaurant at 11:52 A.M. and decided to go inside and wait for Ben. He had the current edition of *Writers' Digest* with him and he could spend some time going through the classified ads searching for a local ghostwriter to assist his new friend Guido Cameri to write his book.

Mack entered the restaurant and the young Chinese hostess didn't wait for him to get completely inside the door, slipped a plastic-covered menu under her right arm and gestured for him to follow her to an open table.

Mack paused, bowed slightly from the waist and said, *Nee hao*, in his best Chinese accent.

"*Nee hao*," the surprised hostess answered as she beamed from ear to ear and led Mack towards the dining room.

"*Ni chi nar?*" Mack asked.

The hostess stopped in her tracks and responded. "You speak excellent Mandarin. For an American that is."

"*Wa boo hway shuo han-yu.*"

"Yes you do. Most Americans only know how to say hello, thank you and please. You just asked me where I was going. Where would you like to sit?"

"I prefer a booth against the wall. I'm meeting a friend for lunch and he should be here in a few minutes. Would you please bring another menu for him."

"*Dwee.* You may order from the menu if you wish. However, I highly recommend the buffet. We have a wide selection of many types of food on twelve steam tables. I'm certain that you will find something to your liking."

"*Fay charng gan shie*"

"You are very welcome."

"You speak excellent English. For a Chinese girl."

"*Shie shie.*"

Mack slid into the booth with his back towards the steam table so he could have a full view of the parking lot and see Ben when he drove in and parked his car.

A petite Chinese waitress wearing a perky ponytail on the top of her head approached Mack's table and stopped about a foot away from him."

"*Nee hao*," Mack offered with a nod of his head.

"*Nee hao*," she responded with a wide grin.

"*Nee hway shuo ying-yu ma?*" Mack asked.

"*Scha.* Of course I speak English. I was born in Hong Kong and attended San Diego State on a scholarship. I majored in American Literature."

"Oh." Mack realized that he was in over his head and hoped that she wouldn't test his Mandarin any further.

"What would you like to drink?' She asked.

"*Schoy schoy.*" Mack responded and held up two fingers.

"*Wo dong le,*" she responded and raised her eyebrows as if she was perplexed.

"I must have pronounced it wrong. I asked for two glasses of water."

"No you didn't. You pronounced *schoy schoy* perfectly. I was jerking your chain to see how you'd react. You take things to seriously. Would you like a pot of green tea too? It's called *cha* in Mandarin."

"*Scha.* I'd like some *cha.* Please bring a glass of water with a slice of lemon for myself and my friend. He'll be here in a few minutes."

"*Shing*, no problem."

"*Fay-charng gan shie,*" Mack responded with a smug grin.

"You are very welcome. I'll be right back with your two glasses of water with a slice of lemon in each one and a pot of green tea." The petite waitress spun around on her toes, her ponytail flew around her face in response and headed for the water station. Her lightly swinging hips caught Mack's attention.

"*I'm sure as hell glad that she didn't test my Mandarin any further. I'd flunked big time,*" Mack thought. "*She was beginning to tell me her life story and I was expecting her to ask me to meet her when she gets off work this afternoon.*"

Before Mack could contemplate what imaginative things he might do with a Chinese girl all afternoon Ben came through the front door, paused and looked around. Mack waved at him with his right-hand and signaled for him to join him. Ben spotted Mack and hustled towards the booth peeling off his light jacket on the way.

"It's certainly nice that you came back to see us poor folks in the Windy City," Ben quipped as he slid into the seat opposite Mack. "It seems like you were here just the other day."

"I haven't been here for over a month," Mack offered with a grin. "Did you get Barbara off on her airplane?"

"Her flight wasn't until twelve-fifteen and I dropped her off at the departure ramp about eleven-thirty. She insisted on carrying her own luggage aboard rather than checking it all the way through. She should have a good time carrying one hundred-fifty pounds of clothes and assorted crap onto the plane and stuffing it into an overhead bin."

"Where's she going?"

"She flying into West Palm Beach, renting a car and driving down to Boynton Beach. Her mom's owned a trailer down there for over thirty years and Barb wanted to check to be sure that there was no serious damage caused by the hurricanes that ripped through there last month. If there is she wants to get it repaired before her mother goes down for the winter."

"Is her mother there?"

"No. She doesn't go down until after Thanksgiving."

"When's Barbara coming back?"

"I'd like for her to stay there for five or six years but I'm not that lucky. She's coming back Friday. I've gotta' pick her up at O'Hare about five-thirty. How long are you going to be in town?"

"I might be flying out this afternoon if I get a phone call at the hotel. If I don't I'll be here at least until tomorrow. Do you have any plans for this afternoon?"

"I don't have anything to do now that she's out of my hair. I've just got the two Labrador Retrievers at home and I don't have to feed them until six o'clock. Do you want to go to Heavenly Bodies in Elk Grove Village and get a lap dance?"

"No! I don't want to go to Heavenly Bodies."

"Then what do you have on your mind?"

"Have you ever heard about something called Cranial Massage Stimulation?"

"The correct name is Transcranial Magnetic Stimulation."

"Yes! That's it! What do you know about it?"

In commercial applications it's used in therapy to stimulate Alpha brain waves by using a form of magnetic resonance imaging."

"Ben do you understand what you just said?"

"I think so. A colleague of mine in Norcross, Georgia stumbled across the concept when he was attempting to improve the learning methods of university students. Back in the old days, when you and I were in college, students listened to tape recordings of examination questions and answers through a pillow speaker all night long. Unfortunately that form of learning isn't very effective in cramming for exams because the brain needs twenty-four to thirty-six hours to absorb material."

"I studied Japanese using the pillow speaker system and an endless tape on my tape recorder," Mack offered. "It worked pretty well for me. One night I'd memorize nouns, the next night I'd memorize verbs and the next night I'd memorize conjunctions. The hardest part was stringing them altogether in an understandable sentence. Japanese sentence structure is exactly opposite from ours. I could string words together and be understood, but my Japanese grammar was terrible! However, the Japanese people are very polite and no one ever corrected me."

"That's wonderful. What do you want to know about TMS?"

"Can it be used for human mind control by transmitting thought patterns over Extremely Low Frequency radio transmissions?"

"Yes. It was a joint project of the CIA, NSA and ONR in Gakona, Alaska between nineteen ninety-five and nineteen ninety-seven. They called it the HAARP Project. They were trying to influence the thought patterns of Eskimos living on the remote islands. They transmitted subliminal messages over the local AM radio stations and also via ELF transmitters through thick wire antennas buried in the tundra just above the permafrost layer. They also used electromagnetic resonant induction via atmospheric phase-locked resonant UHF and VHF transmissions in the Giga-watt to Tera-watt range. They were looking for a mass behavior modification weapon and also to alter DNA codes in a population."

"Did they find it?"

"Yes."

"That's what I want to pick your brain about. Can you spend sometime with me this afternoon?"

"I can do better than that. I have a TMS lab set up in the high school science department. My students experiment using CDs as a means to transmit thought patterns into other students' minds. I use it primarily as a learning tool and I'll write a paper about the results next year. We got a hefty Pell Grant to study TMS. Every month I summarize the results of our trials and mail them to a post office box in Hanover Park."

"Who leases the post office box?"

"I don't know. Most likely a three letter government agency that should remain nameless."

"Do you follow current events in the suburbs?" Mack asked with a deliberate quizzical look on his face.

"What type of current events are you talking about? Sports?"

"Did you see something in the *Elgin Courier* recently about a Stone Park assistant police chief getting indicted for embezzlement?"

"Oh yeah! That was Johnny Amorati! He was an assistant police chief in Stone Park and he got caught stealing the checks that were sent in to pay for traffic tickets. He was tearing up the tickets and giving his girlfriend the checks. She cashed them in the currency exchange where she worked and they split the money. He was supposed to be sentenced this week."

"He was sentenced to fifteen years hard time in Joliet yesterday by a judge in downtown Chicago."

"How do you know that? Why are you asking about him?"

"I met him yesterday afternoon in the hotel lounge and he invited me to his going away party."

"What do you mean a going away party?"

"Some of his friends threw a going away party for him in the hotel lounge last night. I spent about an hour talking with him at the bar yesterday afternoon about how he got in his predicament and wound up being sent to Joliet for fifteen years. The judge made an example out of him because he was a dirty cop."

"You'd better be careful hanging around those kind of people. I'd hate for you to disappear and wind up planted up to your neck in cow crap in an Indiana cornfield."

"That stuff only happens in the movies."

"Don't count on it. This is Chicago. Did you see the movie *Casino*?"

"Sure did. I met one of the characters last night."

"Who'd you meet? Everybody in that movie was a mobster from Chicago."

"Guido Cameri."

"Guido Cameri! Where'd you meet him?"

"He was at the going away party. He sings karaoke in the hotel lounge. Come over to the hotel lounge tonight after nine o'clock and I'll introduce you to him."

"No thanks! Mack you'd better watch your step around those people. They can be real dangerous. Cameri's leg breaker and enforcer from the old days just got out of Joliet last week."

"Do you mean a guy who goes by the name Rocco?"

Yes! That's Rocco Pirelli! He's a very dangerous man. How do you know about him?"

"I met him this morning in the hotel lobby. Guido's taking him around town and introducing him to people today."

"Mack we've gotta talk about this before you get yourself in so far that you can't get out."

"Guido asked me to help him write a book about himself. I told him that I can't and I picked up this month's issue of *Writers' Digest* for him so he can look for a local ghost writer."

"Let's get out of here and drive out to Elgin. There's no school today and I'll take you through my physics lab and introduce you to TMA."

"Sounds good to me. Leave a couple of bucks on the table for the waitress as a tip. She's still working her way through college at San Diego State. She's majoring in American Literature and speaks excellent Mandarin."

"How do you know that?"

"She told me. She might make an interesting character for my book if I ever get around to writing one some day."

Mack paid the check at the cash register, nodded at the smiling hostess and said, "*Dsia jian*" on his way out the door.

"*Fay-charng gan shie*, " she responded with a smile and a slight nod of her head. "*Dsia jian.*"

"Mack! What'd she say to you?"

"She's going to meet me in the hotel lounge at ten o'clock and she's bringing a friend for you."

Chapter 14

Mack followed Ben to Elgin because he had to return to the hotel later that afternoon and didn't want to inconvenience him. Ben pulled his Chevrolet Suburban into a faculty-parking place and motioned for Mack to pull his rental car in alongside him.

"There's no problem with you parking in a faculty parking place today. School let out at noon for a teacher's planning day and everybody's gone. There won't be anyone here to bother us. Let's go inside and I'll show you around my lab," Ben offered as he put his right hand on Mack's left shoulder. "You're about to get a real eye opener when you see how far advanced today's high school physics students are compared to when you and I were sixteen years old."

"I gave up when it came to memorizing valences of hydrogen

atoms and the atomic weight table. The chemistry teacher was damn lucky that I didn't blow the place up, go Mack offered in response with a wide grin. "He told my parents that I should never be allowed near any form of chemicals."

"Where did you go to high school?"

"Lane Tech. Why?"

"Me too. What do you remember the most about Lane Tech?"

"It was an all boys school and there were no girls."

"Do you remember the name of the swimming coach?"

"I think it was Ross. That's right Coach Ross. Why?"

"He's in prison now."

"What for?"

"Child molestation and child pornography."

"I always thought he was kind of weird."

"What made you think that?"

"We all had to swim nude in his class."

"Bingo!"

Ben paused in front of a gray metal door marked 'Physics Lab-Keep Out' in large block letters, swung a large brass key ring off of his belt and fumbled for a few seconds before he located the key that fit the deadbolt lock. He pushed the door open and gestured for Mack to enter ahead of him.

"Go on in and turn on the lights. I'll be there in just a minute. The key is hung up in the lock. Remind me to oil it before we leave. The light switch is on the wall to the left of the door," Ben instructed.

"This is your place. You go in first and I'll close the door."

"Have it your way. Do you suspect that my students might have set a trap for their trusted teacher?"

"I used to do it and it drove Mr. Stevenson crazy. He got so paranoid that he'd flick the lights on with a yardstick from outside in the hallway."

"They wouldn't dare to try anything! They know that I'd make their lives miserable, plus I know where they live." Ben flipped the light switch and the twelve sets of ceiling-mounted four-foot long fluorescent tubes lights flashed on.

Mack scanned the room for obvious ceiling-mounted booby traps and saw none. It appeared to be a normal high school physics laboratory equipped with ceramic-topped worktables, built-in sinks and a chrome-fitting outlet for natural gas.

"What I'm going to show you use isn't out in the open. It's back there." Ben nodded towards the back of the laboratory and a small, enclosed corner room. "The administration would have my hide, and what's left of my scalp, if they had any idea of what goes on back there. They think that room's an experimental electronics lab and I want them to keep thinking that way."

Ben fumbled through the clump of keys haphazardly strung on his key ring, finally located the right one and unlocked the door.

"This room is electronically shielded from top to bottom with fine mesh copper screen and it's completely soundproofed by those foam rubber things that look like an egg cartons. When someone's in here I don't want them influenced by noise or electronic signals generated from an outside source. When we conduct Transcranial Magnetic Stimulation experiments, TMS for short, the subject must be completely free of any outside audio or electronic stimulation or interference. Take a seat in that dental chair and relax while I hook you up. You're going for a free ride on the wild side."

"You're not going to electrocute me are you? This stuff looks pretty dangerous. Especially that machine in the corner with all of those flashing colored lights and dials."

Mack gestured with his head towards an ominous gray box equipped with eight parallel rows of push buttons, toggle switches, meters and gauges.

"That's a harmonic frequency generator that we use to generate frequencies as low as one-tenth of a cycle per second all the way up into the Ultra High Frequency range. It's crystal-controlled and very accurate. I'm going to use it to generate ELF frequencies for your TMS experience this afternoon."

"Does it hurt?"

"No. It doesn't hurt at all. You might feel a slight cranial vibration or hear a slight 'buzz' in your ear, but that's all."

"How does this TMS thing work?"

"TMS is actually quite simple." Ben responded as he held up a white, plastic helmet with a Chicago Bears logo painted on each side above the ear holes

"I don't want to play for the Bears," Mack remarked as he eyed the helmet. "There's no plastic faceguard on that thing. I could get my teeth knocked out."

"I'm sorry to disappoint you, but this isn't a Chicago Bears helmet. One of our graduate student's girlfriends painted the logo as a joke. This helmet is a very sophisticated test instrument and was developed by NASA for measuring astronauts' brain impulses during launch and re-entry operations. Are you ready to get serious about this?"

"I suppose so."

"Electronic pulses from the frequency generator flow through small electromagnetic coils mounted in the helmet and they generate electromagnetic pulses which pass into your brain."

"How can it go through the bone of my skull?"

"Simple. The principle is the same as placing a steel nail on the top of a wooden table and using a powerful magnet under the table to move the nail from below. The wood is a form of electrical insulator, but it does not stop electromagnetic waves. The porous bone of your skull allows the ELF pulses to travel directly through and into your brain. Hopefully they won't get lost in there."

"Is there any possibility that you will burn my brain out with this thing if you turn the power up to high?"

"Don't be silly. The TMS procedure is perfectly safe. We've only electrocuted two students and that's because their hair gel shorted out the sensors. You're not using hair gel are you?"

"Of course not! There's not enough hair left to worry about. Before you wire me up to that thing give me some background so I'll know what's going to happen to me. I might want to change my mind about this."

"It's to late to change your mind."

"No it's not! I can leave right now."

"You might say that but you don't really mean it. You want to know what TMS is like and you won't be satisfied until you do."

"I hate it when you're right. So now tell me about it."

"No problem. Scientists have been studying the human brain for hundreds of years and in nineteen twenty-nine Hans Berger discovered that the brain puts out electrical pulses and a machine was developed to measure and record them."

"That's an electroencephalograph."

"That's correct. When there are no measurable brave waves doctors consider a patient brain dead and pull the plug."

"Researchers in Helsinki, Finland developed the 'SQUID' machine in nineteen seventy-two which when pointed at the cortex picks up the electrical waves generated by the brain. They discovered that the brain generates four distinct types of electrical waves depending whether is it awake or asleep."

"Four types of brain waves! I only heard of Alpha waves. What are the other three?"

"I thought you'd never ask. *Alpha* waves are the most common talked about because they are the strongest and the easiest to measure. They operate between eight and fourteen Hertz and are associated with a normal and alert state of mind. *Delta* waves range between one-third and four Hertz and occur during deep sleep and in some brain disorders. *Theta* waves range between four and seven Hertz and occur during various stages of sleep in normal adults and during emotional stresses. *Beta* waves on the other hand, range between fourteen and fifty Hertz and are associated with intense activation of the nervous system or extreme tension. We can generate all of those frequency ranges, individually or together, via our frequency generator and pass them into a human brain via this helmet."

"Can you directly change human behavior through external brain stimulation?"

"Not so much change behavior as to affect the state of mind from contentment to panic in a split second. Of course, one's mental state directly affects one's behavior and reaction to various stimuli."

"In the hands of the wrong people this technology could be used to make all of us into robots."

"That's an interesting concept and remember that you are the one who brought it up. Isn't the goal of the United Nations to achieve world peace?"

"That's their propaganda line. Why?"

"If the technology was perfected to enable TMS signals to be transmitted over local radio and television stations, broadcast from cell phone towers, satellites, etc. then some areas of the world could be stimulated to war while their neighbors could be made passive. Isn't that an interesting concept?"

"It's definitely scary, but it's practical for world domination."

"Isn't that the goal of the United Nations? No country borders, no individual currencies, no wars, no nationalism, a single world police force and a New World Order?"

"Now you have me terrified."

"It's not a new concept. In nineteen sixty-nine Dr. Jose' M. R. Delgado wrote *Physical Control of the Mind: Toward a Psychocivilized Society* in the forty-first volume of *World Perspectives*. His basic principle was that human beings are born without minds and the newborn brain is not capable of speech or symbolic understanding. Thus, shortly after birth the newborn's brain can be molded via what Delgado termed 'Electrical Stimulation of the Brain', ESB for short, to give the brain the desired perspective required by society."

"Holy crap!"

"He didn't stop there. Delgado postulated that the role of the human will is mainly to trigger previously established mental mechanisms which can be programmed via ESB, or what today we call TMS. Humans can be mentally programmed not to be aggressive towards others and vice versa."

"It sounds like something out of The *Manchurian Candidate*."

"It's much worse than that fictional movie concept. It's real and stated as a goal in the UNESCO Constitution. I can quote it. *Since war begins in the minds of men, it is in the minds of men that the defense of peace must be constructed.*"

"Now you really have me worried. Are we working on something like that?"

"It all depends on who the 'we' is. The Defense Advanced Research Projects Program Agency has a plan to implant microchips in soldiers so their actions can be directly controlled on the battlefield via signals transmitted by military satellites."

"How do you know that?"

"I'd rather not say. Let's go back to TMS. There's a problem with the concept that has to be solved before it can be effective for use on large populations with a high degree of effectiveness."

"What's that?"

"The brain is active and generates wave patterns even during sleep. The brain's internally generated electrical impulses are rhythmically paced by the thalamus and take precedence over externally generated signals. However, artificial brain waves can be introduced into the brain, and the natural brain waves entrained during the thalamic silent, or free-run period."

"What the hell is that mumbo jumbo? Did you just make that up to confuse me?"

"No. You're already confused enough. What it means is easy to comprehend even for you."

"Thanks for your confidence."

"You are most certainly welcome. Listen carefully and you might just learn something today. Current research indicates that during the 'free-run' periods, when the natural brain waves are not paced by the thalamus, the brain's waves can be entrained by external man-made or natural electrical and magnetic rhythms."

"What does entrained mean in real English?"

"The literal meaning would be to pull or drag the brain along. Think about it as making the brain come into sync with a stronger external force that then will drag the brain along with it in a pre-determined direction. An excellent example is the master-slave relationship of a LORAN transmitter and receiver. The Master station forces the vessel's onboard LORAN receiver to synchronize its periods of signal reception to the exact timing of the Master station's transmitted signal. For a biological rhythm the concept of entrainment is important. When two rhythms have nearly the same frequency they can become coupled to each other so they both have the same rhythm. Technically, entrainment means the 'mutual phase locking of two, or more oscillators. On an oscilloscope the display would show a circle when the two oscillators are in phase. Another, easily understood example, is that an infinite number of pendulum-driven clocks mounted on the same wall will eventually entrain so that all of the clock pendulums swing in a precise synchronized rhythm. The vibrations transmitted through the walls are what couples the pendulums together. Simple enough?"

"I understood the part about the phase-locked oscillators.

Phase-locking was used on the old LORAN A receivers to determine a ship's position at sea."

"Correct. When only one circle was on the viewing scope display the ship's receiver was in phase, or entrained, with the Master station's transmitted signal. If there were two circles on the viewing scope the transmitter and receiver were out of phase. They weren't entrained. Excellent grasshopper!"

"Let's not go there. It brings back bad memories. Tell me more about the silent period? Does that mean the brain's sleeping or in detention?"

"It's more like a 'time out' for an unruly kid. Calcium ions slowly leak into single thalamocortical neurons, which oscillate for one and a half to twenty-eight seconds, triggering and entraining the brain waves, which spread upward and throughout the brain. Eventually the thalamic oscillations stop all together because of the excess calcium build up. During this 'silent phase' of from five to twenty-five seconds the brain waves are said to 'free-run' and can be entrained by external electromagnetic fields."

"I knew that!"

"Of course you did. Then what can you tell me about microgenesis?"

"I remember the term from high school biology, but I can't put my finger on the definition at this moment. I guess I'm having a brain fart."

"Most likely you are. The concept of microgenesis was first published by Jason W. Brown of the New York University Medical Center in nineteen seventy-seven long after your high school biology classes. You must have been thinking about something else."

"With out a doubt my learned colleague. Please continue. This is very interesting."

"Microgenesis is a unified theory that brings together language, perception, learning, movement, feeling, time, awareness, and the nature of self. It describes a 'quantum unit' of consciousness in relation to the energy of the brain waves flowing through the nervous system."

"What is the length of a 'quantum unit' of consciousness?"

"My God!"

"Now what?"

"You actually understood what I was saying."

"Of course. I asked if you knew the length of a 'quantum unit' of consciousness. Do you?"

"It's about one tenth of a second, or the length of an average brain wave. And there's no such thing as a brain fart! That's a slang figure of speech."

"Do you really think so? Come over here and smell my ear."

"No way! Can we get back to the subject at hand?"

"What you said is that externally generated signals, or brain waves to the layperson, can be artificially induced into the human brain during the one and a half to twenty-eight second 'silent phase' caused by the excess calcium build up in the thalamus."

"That's correct."

"Why did you go through all of that crap to explain something so simple?"

"I thought that you wanted a scientific explanation."

"You could have significantly shortened your lecture and still maintained the basic concept. The next time I ask you for an explanation of anything make it short and simple. Did you ever hear of the KISS approach?"

"No. What's that?"

"It's short for Keep It Simple Stupid!"

"Oh."

"So, the emotional state of humans can be altered to levels of panic and hysteria right down the line to complete relaxation though the transmission of artificial brain wave signals. If an intelligence agency developed a microgenesis machine, and an appropriate transmission medium, they would be able to control individual people, a city or possibly an entire country. Mind control would be the 'ultimate solution' for population control because they would be able start and stop wars on a whim. Now I understand what he meant."

"Are you referring to me?"

"No. It was someone else. I was thinking out loud. Hook me up to your machine so I can get some first hand experience with microgenesis. I need to feel and taste it for myself."

"You won't feel or taste anything. It's all a mental state."

"I know Ben. It was a figure of speech and not well thought out."

"If you're finally ready slip that helmet on your fat head, pull the visor over your eyes so you can't see and just lay back in the chair and relax. You're in for the ride of your life! It's show time!"

Mack nodded, slipped the helmet over his head, pulled down the black plastic visor, rested his head against the soft gray leather headrest and closed his eyes.

Chapter 15

"Mack! Wake-up! Mack! Do you hear me?"

Ben stumbled over his words as he shook Mack's shoulder.

"Come on Mack! You have to get up. The experiments over."

It was 5:36 P.M. and Mack had been in the experimental lab chair for more than three hours. Ben ran a battery of tests and simultaneously recorded Mack's brain waves for later analysis. He decided that Mack was a very good test subject and that he would include the results of his tests when he filed his weekly Pell Grant report.

Mack stirred, started to sit up in the dental chair and fell backwards against the backrest.

"Ben! Is that you? I can't see anything through this visor. When are you going to get this thing started? I don't have all day," Mack uttered from behind the black plastic facemask. "I think that I fell asleep before you got this thing started. I'm ready to go if you are. Go ahead, push the fancy buttons on that fancy machine and do whatever you think is necessary."

"You've been here for almost three hours and I ran you through every test I have. It's all over. What do you remember about the experience?"

Mack reached up with his right hand, slid the black plastic visor up, grabbed both arm rests, pushed himself up into a sitting position, removed the helmet from his head and set it on his lap.

"What do you mean I've been here for almost three hours? What time is it?"

"It's a little past five-thirty. What do you remember?"

"I don't remember a thing."

"That's normal. Just sit there and relax for a minute." Ben pulled down a silver microphone from a ceiling-mounted base above the dental chair and shoved it in Mack's face. "Describe your emotional state and your physical feelings into this microphone. Can you do that?"

"Do what? Pull a microphone down from the ceiling? I could if there was another one up there."

"No! Can you describe how you feel?"

"Of course I can! I feel perfectly fine except that my right leg fell asleep."

"Are you certain that you don't feel something unusual? Just sit there and describe how you feel."

"Now that you mention it I feel a terrific headache coming on, I have some tightness in my chest and the palms of my hands are sweating excessively. That's never happened to me before. And suddenly I feel completely wiped out." Mack attempted to swing his legs over the side of the dental chair and almost fell out of the chair onto the floor.

"Those are normal symptoms for most subject's who participate in TSM laboratory experiments Sometimes the symptoms resemble the so-called weather sensitive complaints that some sensitive people feel before the arrival of a violent thunderstorm. The headache will peak in about a half-hour, taper off slowly and be totally gone in an hour. After it dissipates you'll experience a very strong feeling of fatigue."

"Why should I wait a half hour? I feel like hell right now!"

"You should get something in your stomach before you pass out."

"That sounds good to me," Mack responded as he placed the helmet on the dental chair and stood up. "Did you find out anything special about my brain waves? Am I completely nuts? Did you see any little animals or munchkins running around inside my head?"

Mack stood up and grabbed the laboratory table to steady himself.

"Disappointedly there was nothing unusual about your brain waves. I ran you through a special test utilizing a pulsating electromagnetic field ranging from eight to ten Hertz, ran some basic cognitive recognition tests and found that it slightly affected your reaction time. However when I repeated the tests at a slower oscillation rate of between two and three Hertz it significantly slowed down your action time. But that's a normal effect."

"How could you determine my reaction time if I was out of it the entire time?"

"You were fully conscious and followed my voice commands as I gave them to you."

"Did you make me bark like a dog and 'quack' like a duck?"

"Of course not! These tests were legitimate scientific experiments not carnival side show acts! Subjects who complete these tests very rarely remember anything about their experience. That's why the use of electromagnetic fields to cause changes in human brain waves is very effective. The subjects don't realize what was happening to them and even if they did they can't recall anything about it. The waves can be introduced in a dentist's chair, a doctor's office and many other places."

"Suddenly I'm very hungry."

"I can see why. It's almost six o'clock. Let's run over to the Assembly at the corner of Barrington and Hassell Roads and have a Bionic Burger and a couple of beers before you go back to your hotel. Oh, I almost forgot. Do you want me to go back to the hotel with you?"

"Why? I can find my way back without help. I've done it before. I'll jump on the Northwest Toll Way at Barrington Road and take it east to O'Hare and exit at Mannheim Road south."

"Didn't the Chinese girl at the restaurant tell you that she was going to bring a girlfriend for me?" Ben smiled and lightly jammed Mack in the abdomen with his elbow. "I've never been with a Chinese girl before. I'm very good with languages and I can learn a few basic words before we leave. Can you teach me how to say 'I love you' and 'oh baby that's good' in Chinese before we leave?"

"Ben, don't be silly. I was only joking. She said that I speak good Chinese and to come back again. I don't have any plans to meet her or anyone else. Come on. Let's go and get something to eat."

It was a short fifteen-minute drive from Elgin to the Assembly and neither man spoke on the way. When they arrived at the Assembly the hostess noticed their glumness and tactfully seated them in a corner booth away from the other customers. They both ordered Bionic Burgers topped with mozzarella cheese and extra sauce on the side. Ben ordered a glass of Merlot and Mack ordered a cold Budweiser in a frosted mug.

Neither man spoke for several minutes because each of them was immersed deep in his own thoughts and carefully considering what he dared say. Ben was cautious to ask Mack anything for fear of what he might remember and Mack was cautious to ask Ben anything for fear he might learn something he really didn't want to know about. He decided to approach the topic gingerly with an open-ended question.

"Well then Ben, what did you find out when you analyzed my brain waves?"

"Your Theta and Delta waves were perfectly normal. However, I am concerned over some spikes and frequency shifts that I observed in your Alpha and Beta waves when I shifted the oscillator frequency below eight point zero Hertz and maintained the interval past the twenty-five second 'free-run' period."

"What does that mean?"

"That your brain attempts to stay in sync with the normal pulsation rate of the earth and it gets very agitated if it loses sync with the earth's entrainment pattern."

"What the hell are you talking about?"

"Something called the Schumann Resonance."

"What's that?"

"Geomagnetic micro pulsations of the earth that form a natural resonance in all living things. It's like being in tune with Nature. I'll use a magnetic compass as an example. The magnetic field of the earth, called the geomagnetic field, causes the magnetic compass needle to point towards the magnetic North Pole. However, if you look carefully at a compass needle under a microscope, you will see that the end of the compass needle is not still – it moves back and forth in a variety of rhythms. Some of these rhythms are diurnal and occur over a twenty-four hour period, some are much slower, and others are quite fast and in the ELF range. Those rhythms are geomagnetic micro pulsations. The natural earth waves resulting from electrical activity in the atmosphere and geomagnetic micro pulsations register at about seven point eight Hertz and it's called the Schumann Resonance Is it clear now?"

"Of course, but could I get a little more clarification? I want to be sure that I understand it just in case I have to explain it to someone else."

"Of course. If your brain and body are in tune, like the single circle on the LORAN A display, with the natural resonant frequency of the earth you are in effect in harmony with Nature and experience a state of calmness and well being. Some believers call the effect the reclaiming of the life force."

"Does that mean that I should sit cross-legged on a Navaho Indian blanket, hum with my eyes closed and smoke pot until I find harmony with the earth?"

"Not necessarily, but it might help you with your attitude. Your brain is unusual compared to other test subjects because it fights to stay in resonance with the earth's natural frequency, or pulsation rate, of seven point eight Hertz. The average subject's brain becomes depressed at resonant frequencies below six point six Hertz and becomes agitated at frequencies above ten point eight Hertz. Your brain becomes extremely agitated when it is forced out of sync with the earth's natural pattern in either direction as evidenced in the change in both the amplitude and frequency of your Alpha and Beta brain waves at frequencies above and below seven point eight Hertz."

"Now it all makes sense to me! I can certainly explain that to a Pakistani taxi driver on the way back to O'Hare. Did you attempt to induce artificial brain waves into my system?"

"Of course. I completed the entire spectrum of tests at my disposal even though your brain fought me the entire way. It was certainly fortunate that I didn't have you connected to a bio feedback system."

"Why's that?"

"Because your brain waves are similar to those of Indian yogis and clairvoyants that can bend metal objects like spoons with their projected Alpha waves. Your brain would've blown my frequency generator up! It didn't like me messing with it."

"What types of waves did you attempt to introduce into my brain?"

"Let's refer to the method as entrainment, or forcing your brain to come in tune with the introduced signal, similar to the pendulums of the clocks on the wall."

"Okay. So what were they?"

"I used a variety of signals including waves crashing on the beach, the sound of a violent thunderstorm, a baby crying, a dog howling in pain, the soft sound of wind blowing through the tops of trees. I was very surprised when I used the sounds of a simulated battle zone."

"Why?"

"Rather than becoming agitated as most subjects experienced in combat would have your brain became extremely relaxed and you had a smile on your face. I double-checked my instruments and the input from the computer to be certain that I wasn't feeding you the brain impulses of an eunuch stationed in a harem in Saudi Arabia."

"Maybe that's when I saw God in my dream."

"You saw God?"

"That's right. I saw God at the entrance to Heaven."

"That's great! It worked! Hold on while I make a note on my napkin."

"Did I die and you brought me back?"

"No! I applied a 'Thomas Pulse' to the right hemisphere of your brain. I hadn't attempted it before."

"What's that?"

"It's a precisely timed, repetitive signal introduced at a high amplitude. According to the research I've seen many subjects experience encountering God. Some researchers think that naturally occurring electromagnetic fluctuations could be responsible for paranormal experiences like ghosts. Some argue that religion itself could be electromagnetic in origin and that transcendent experiences told by saints and mystics can be recreated with electromagnetic pulse in a laboratory. I have to try it again."

"Not on me thank you very much."

"I don't need to try it on you again."

"Can these signals be transmitted via AM or FM radio stations? I want you to be honest with me."

"Yes. The AM carrier frequency could be varied slightly up or down by eight Hertz in either direction to cause either a feeling of relaxation or hysteria in the listener's mind. They could feasibly do the same thing with an FM station, but most likely they would adjust the modulation of the carrier wave's amplitude to create the same effect."

"What would it sound like to the listener?"

"The AM radio listener might think the signal was slowly fading in and out and blame it on atmospheric conditions. But the overall effect would be almost negligible and I doubt that they would even notice it. In the case of an FM radio station a casual listener wouldn't notice any difference at all."

"Are you aware of any experiments done to induce artificial brain wave patterns in people?"

"There were hundreds, if not thousands, of studies done in the nineteen seventies and eighties to ascertain the relationship between flashing strobe lights and low frequency musical beats. It was determined that human brain wave patterns can be changed to match the sequence of a flashing strobe light and deep, high amplitude musical beats."

"It sounds like disco music."

"Where did you think disco music originated?"

"Motown?"

"No! The CIA and NSA pioneered the strobe light technique in the laboratory and tested it on disco patrons during that time frame. That was the purpose of the strobe lights flashing in time with the disco beat. It was the first 'real time' trial of mind control methodology."

They stopped it suddenly because many people actually became catatonic in discos and had to be taken away by ambulance. Many of them are still in government mental facilities."

"So much for Donna Summers."

"They also experimented with the transmission of Alpha and Beta brain waves on disco records. But to be effective they had to be played over a high fidelity loudspeaker system with woofers that could reproduce frequencies well below the normal human hearing range of fifteen Hertz."

"That's why the loud speakers in discos were so huge! They needed a very large surface to reproduce the low frequency sounds."

"That's correct."

"That also explains why so many people seemed to be zonked out during the disco era. They weren't all potheads. It was caused by the music."

"Don't forget the strobe lights."

"I never spent any time in disco's. The lousy music sucked, plus I didn't like bell bottomed pants, silk shirts and gold chains around my neck."

"There a few other things that you may want to know about."

"For example?"

"Do you remember the Russian power plant in Chernobyl that melted down a few years back?"

"How can I forget? It was a reactor core meltdown. Thousands of people died."

"Did you realize that it was out in the middle of nowhere? It wasn't there to power factories or military installations."

"No. I didn't pay attention where it was located. Why is that important?

"It was built by the Russians to power their experiments in mind control beginning in nineteen seventy-six. They used power from Chernobyl to power seven giant transmitters located in the Ukraine to pump a one hundred megawatt radio signal that contained a ten Hertz mind control carrier frequency at the West. The Soviet pulse covered the spectrum of human brain frequencies, could entrain the human brain and induce behavioral modification. A research scientist studied the radio wave and found that it fluctuated between twelve and six Hertz. A six point six five Hertz frequency causes depression and an eleven Hertz frequency causes manic and riotous behavior."

"So what?"

"The Russians discovered that their experiments with Extremely Low Frequency transmissions were effective in modifying human behavior."

"What is the scientific basis for your learned opinion?"

"What do you supposed initiated the war in the Balkans between the Serbs and Yugoslavia? What caused the people in Sudan who are normally peaceful to suddenly go to war with their neighbors? How about the riots in Haiti? I could go on and on."

"That's all conjecture!"

"Is it? A byproduct of the mind control experiment was that the Russians discovered that high-power ELF transmissions could change worldwide weather patterns by alerting the earth's natural rhythm of seven point eight Hertz."

"How do you figure that?"

"They caused droughts in Africa, which in turn increased the frequency of hurricanes in the Atlantic Ocean, increased typhoons in the western Pacific Ocean, earthquakes in Turkey and Afghanistan plus severe floods in the Midwest."

"What's the basis for the system's operation?"

"The Russians named their pet project 'Wood Pecker.' They buried underground antennas spread out from the center, like the spokes of a giant bicycle wheel, for hundreds of miles throughout the central Ukraine and Eastern Russia. The antennas are solid copper cables about the size of your arm and they're buried three feet below the ground where they can't be picked up by spy satellites."

"If we have that much information about what the Russians are doing I'd expect that our government would have a similar system to act as a counter-measure."

"We do, but it doesn't work very well. It's sporadic at best and virtually uncontrollable because the power output is not high enough. We don't have a nuclear power plant with the capability of Chernobyl and the environmentalist would raise holy hell if we built one."

"That's true I suppose."

"Have you noticed that in the past several years that hurricanes seem to target Florida and don't veer away as they did in past years? I made a comment to a colleague that the hurricane pattern over the past several years appears to be an experiment gone awry that attracted the hurricanes to Florida."

"No doubt you're talking about Hurricanes Charlie, Frances, Ivan and Jeanne."

"That's correct."

"Did you notice that they appeared to be actually sucked into Florida?"

"That was a fluke caused by abnormal weather patterns in the Pacific and Atlantic Oceans

"You can believe that option if you wish, although I think that it was caused by a malfunction in the National Weather Service's GWEN Network."

"GWEN?"

"Ground Wave Emergency Network. It is a series of radio transmitters placed two hundred miles apart across the USA. They operate in the Low Frequency range of between one hundred-fifty and one hundred seventy-five Kilohertz. The LF signals travel in waves that hug the ground rather than radiating into the atmosphere. The individual radio towers range between three and five hundred feet high. Three hundred foot-long wires spread out in a spoke-like fashion from the base of the tower so the signal can interact with the earth's magnetic field."

"It sounds like the Russian's "Pecker Wood' project."

"The correct name is 'Wood Pecker' not 'Pecker Wood.' 'Pecker Wood' is a derogatory red neck term. You are an educated man and should know better."

"I do, but it just slipped out. Tell me about GWEN. I think I dated a GWEN once."

"GWEN is similar, but very different from the installation at Chernobyl. The Russian transmitting system is fixed in one location and depends upon a series of radiating antennas going out from that single location, but the massive power output is concentrated. However, the GWEN System's transmitted frequencies and output power can be tailored to the geomagnetic field strength in that area allowing the earth's magnetic field to be altered. Of course you know that the geomagnetic field controls our weather patterns."

"Of course. Now what?"

"What do you suppose caused the meltdown at Chernobyl?"

"A defective temperature gauge in the cooling tower."

"The workers. When they found out that Chernobyl was being used to provide power for Russian's mind control project and affect the behavior of thousands, if not millions of people, they sabotaged it."

"Ben! How do you know that?"

"If I told you I'd have to kill you."

"Now you've really scared the hell out of me. Is there anything else?"

"Of course. Our government has been experimenting with ELF and mind control for years. What secondary purpose do you think the GWEN Project was designed to do?"

"Not mind control experiments!"

"That's the rumor on the street. Let's look at some historical facts. Back in the sixties and seventies the CIA experimented with LSD on students, convicts, military people and minorities. Mind control experimentation is not a recent development and shouldn't come as a shock to you. Electronic mind control can be used to incite people to violence and, perhaps even more important, make them completely submissive. Plus, induced brain waves don't show up blood or urine tests."

"What mind control projects are you aware of that our government's currently involved with?"

"History is important. The CIA began its mind control

experiments in the nineteen fifties and it was motivated by the Russian, Chinese and North Korean's use of mind control techniques. The program, operated by the Office of Security, was titled 'BLUEBIRD' and later changed to 'ARTICHOKE.' In April of nineteen fifty-three CIA Director Allen Dulles authorized the ultra-secret MK-ULTRA Program. Most the project's documents were destroyed in nineteen seventy-one and seventy-three for fear that the public would get hold of them."

"What was MK-ULTRA?"

"It was a LSD-based program run by Sidney Gottlieb, a Strangolian scientist with a PhD from Cal Tech, who lived on a goat farm with his wife. They grew Christmas trees on their farm and sold goat's milk at a roadside stand."

"What a great cover!"

"It wasn't a cover. That was him! He had a clubfoot, stuttered very badly and was an expert folk dancer. He supervised testing LSD on people in the Armed Forces, prison populations, mental patients and in brothels run by the CIA. They called it 'Operation Midnight Climax' and installed two-way mirrors and cameras in the rooms so they could observe the subject in action, or inaction."

"At least he had a humorous side."

"What other mind control projects was the CIA involved with?"

"Project Orion, pseudonym 'Dreamland' operated by the Air Force, came onboard in nineteen fifty-eight, and used ESB modulated at ELF frequencies and sent over microwave systems. It was sold under the purpose of briefing top security personnel to insure loyalty."

"That's a strange way to inspire loyalty in people. I was in Air Force from nineteen sixty to nineteen sixty-four and I remember seeing civilian contractors, they called themselves 'tech reps' installing 'top secret' modification kits to military radio transmitters and receivers. They told us not to touch them because they were testing a new encryption system."

"Bingo! You were in the Air Force at the right time to see 'Project Deep Sleep' whose sinister code name was MK-DELTA. Started in nineteen-sixty it was a spin off of MK-ULTRA.

Funded by the CIA MK-DELTA utilized Very High Frequency, High Frequency and Ultra High Frequency radio transmissions modulated at Extremely Low Frequency to program mood swings, behavior dysfunction and social criminality in designated populations. They wired the signal into the spring coils of mattresses and ran signals through sixty Hertz house wiring."

"I worked on all of those radio systems!"

"The sneakiest Air Force project took place in nineteen eighty-three in Montauk on Long Island. It was called 'Project Rainbow' or 'ZAP' depending on what level of information you received. They used Ultra High Frequency transmitters coupled to directional antennas to target select sensitized population groups for programming."

"I was never in Montauk!"

"Most people are familiar with the black helicopters of the nineteen nineties. The NSA project named 'TRIDENT' with the pseudonym 'Black Triad' was funded by FEMA, the Federal Emergency Management Agency. The black helicopters flew in a Triad formation of three and transmitted an Ultra High Frequency signal at one hundred thousand watts of power! The purpose of the project was to control large assembled groups of people and for riot control. It worked very well."

"Ben, why do you know so much about these things?"

"I'd rather not answer that question. Walls can have ears."

"I understand. Anything else?'

"The CIA initiated 'RF MEDIA' pseudonym 'Buzz Saw' in Boulder, Colorado in nineteen ninety. It provided multi-directional subliminal suggestion and programming to trigger behavioral desire, subversion of psychic abilities of the target population and preparatory processing for mass electromagnetic control via standard existing television and radio signals.

"Go ahead Ben, you're on a roll. What else?"

"A nineteen ninety CIA project dubbed 'TOWER' pseudonym 'Wedding Bells' imposed ELF modulated signals over the nationwide cellular network. The purpose was to test cross country subliminal programming and suggestion over cell phones. Unfortunately the government has complete control of the cellular telephone network."

"Go on Ben. I know you that you know more."

"We already discussed Project HAARP which was in nineteen ninety-five, The CIA used electromagnetic induction to test behavior modification on people in remote areas of Alaska. The transmitter power output was in the Giga-watt to Tera-watt range."

"I know that you were involved in mind control experiments. What was the last project that you worked on?"

"A joint project of the CIA and NSA called 'CLEAN SWEEP' that began in nineteen ninety-seven right here in Chicago. However, I'd rather not discuss it."

"Why not?"

"It's still active. I could get in a lot of trouble if I talked about it."

"You're well past that point. Tell me what you know."

"Clean Sweep is a nationwide program that utilizes super sensitive receivers to gather and record high emotion brain wave data from people at media events and sporting events – usually outdoor football games. Electromagnetic resonant induction sensors mounted in helicopters that fly around and over the stands are used to pick up the brain waves of the attendees. The recorded brain wave patterns can be rebroadcast over the GWEN network and also through cellular telephones from the national cell telephone node located in Boulder, Colorado."

"For what purpose?"

"To stimulate high emotional levels at recreational events. It's a form of mass behavior modification. You can compare it to the canned laugh track used on some television shows."

"When did you stop working on these government mind control projects? Be honest"

"November two thousand four. I couldn't take it any more. We were turning perfectly normal people in zombies and they didn't know it."

"What else can you tell me about transmitted ELF frequencies and the effect they have on people?"

"The earth's resonant frequency is seven point eight three Hertz. People who mediate through Yoga concentrate and force their Alpha brain waves to the earth's resonant frequency of seven point eight three Hertz. If your Alpha brain waves exactly match the earth's resonant frequency you are in harmony with the earth and everything is wonderful! People whose Alpha brain waves are artificially raised above ten Hertz become extremely agitated and riotous. People whose Alpha brain waves are lowered below seven Hertz become depressed. People have no defense against this technology."

"I understand."

"ELF frequencies are used to plant subliminal messages over broadcast and cable television and radio networks and through cell phones. The CIA and NSA have been using ELF technology for years to render people ineffective and there are no counter measures available to defend against it."

"What do you know about the Navy's Boomer Project for anti-submarine warfare?"

"How did you know about that? It's Top Secret!"

"Let's just say that a little bird told me about it. I was on my way to Springfield, Massachusetts for a briefing on the project when I was diverted to Chicago. Did you work on the project?"

"No. The same company that manufactures SONAR equipment, underwater pingers and acoustic listening equipment for the Navy developed it. It's about thirty miles west of Chicago."

"I had a good idea who it was and just you confirmed it. What do you know about 'Boomer'?"

"Not much except it uses a lot of power and can virtually wipe the electronics and propulsion system of a Russian Akula class nuclear submarine down as far down as one thousand feet."

"Ben! Be straight with me. You know that the 'Boomer' transmits an ELF signal that goes right through the sub's internal wiring and creates tension and fear in the crew. That's mind control!"

"The Navy picked up on some of the things we did, but I wasn't directly involved in the project."

"Where has the Navy been testing this thing?"

"They started in Hawaii, but they blew the eardrums out of so many dolphins and pilot whales that they moved the project to Norfolk. When the dolphins and pilot whales washed up on the beach at Honolulu the animal rights people went berserk. The Navy told the media that the animals had a virus in their inner ears that affected their internal navigation system and they got lost."

"What do you mean they blew the eardrums out of dolphins and pilot whales?"

"Dolphins and pilot whales use a form of SONAR for locating food. It's a form of whistles that hit a target and bounce back to the dolphin's receptors so they can home in on the their prey. Their eardrums and signal receptors are extremely sensitive because the returning sound is very weak. The 'Boomer' emits such a strong signal that any cetaceans within five miles of the transmitter are affected. Have there been any recent dolphin or pilot whale beachings where you live?"

"We had a massive beaching of a school of toothed Atlantic dolphins south of the Holiday Inn on Jensen Beach about a month ago."

"Hello! Wake up and smell the roses! The Navy's Top Secret AUTEC submarine testing base is in the Bahamas about fifty miles directly east of West Palm Beach! Toothed Atlantic dolphins don't get lost and beach themselves because they rarely come within thirty miles of shore."

"I understand. Where else has the Navy been testing it?'

"Norfolk, Virginia. They have an ELF transmitter in the abandoned lighthouse at Cape Henry and an antenna is buried in the sand dunes between Cape Henry and Carrituck Beach. You can tell when they're transmitting an ELF signal because a magnetic compass goes nuts! It'll swing back forth as much as six degrees from a normal reading because the ELF changes the electromagnetic field of the earth as far as seventeen miles out to sea. There's a note on the nautical chart indicating that a 'Local Magnetic Disturbance' exists in that area."

"I've seen it. Ben, look at the time! It's almost ten o'clock! I'd better get on my way back to the hotel. I'm supposed to meet someone in the lounge tonight."

"I remember. She told you that she was bringing a friend didn't she? My offer still goes. I can learn a few words of Chinese between here and Grand Avenue. How about it?"

"I'm not meeting the Chinese hostess. I'm supposed to meet Guido Cameri in the karaoke lounge."

"Mack are you sure you know what you're getting into? Those people play rough."

"I'll be okay. I'm going to give him some hints on writing. I might help him write his biography."

"You're into something really deep. You'd better find a way to excuse yourself and get out of it."

"I have to get going," Mack stood up, reached into his pants pocket, pulled out a roll of cash and tossed two twenty dollar bills on the table. "That should take care of my share. I'll call you tomorrow and let you know what happened."

Mack winked, turned and headed for the door without looking back. He had a thirty-minute drive ahead of him. He didn't know what to expect when he arrived at the Galaxy Hotel, but he decided to repeat a few Mandarin Chinese phrases over and over on the long drive back.

Chapter 16

Mack pulled into the hotel parking at 10:23 P.M. and realized that he had stood up Guido Cameri. That might have been a very big mistake! The young Pakistani hooker stood in the parking lot talking to a group of six young bikers. She looked very nervous and crooked her little finger at Mack.

"I wonder if she's signaling me to come over there and bail her out of trouble?" Mack thought. *"It's none of my business and she's been out here before."*

Mack ignored her, entered the hotel through a side entrance and headed for the lobby.

"Mister McCray," hailed the hooker's brother from behind the counter. "You've got a message," he barked as he held up a pink slip. "You're supposed to catch Delta flight fifteen forty-three to

West Palm Beach at nine seventeen tomorrow morning."

"Why didn't you just shout it out a little bit louder so everyone in the lobby and lounge could hear it? Mack retorted as he snatched the pink telephone message slip out of the desk clerk's hand. "Why do you know what it says?"

"I took the message." The desk clerk smiled smugly. "Did you see my little sister Maya on your way into the hotel?"

"She's standing out in the parking lot rapping with a gang of bikers. They looked very interested in what she has to offer."

"She's not going to do anything with them! They don't have any money and four of them are gay! They're hanging around out there waiting for a drunk to stagger out of the lounge and head for his car. Then they'll roll him for whatever they can get."

"Why don't you call the cops?"

"It's good business for the hotel. They keep the Mexican gangs out of here. Those bikers will just beat someone up and steal their money. The Mexicans will cut his throat and let him die. That's very messy. The police and ambulances come and we get bad publicity. It's not good for business."

"That's a nice concept. You certainly picked the lesser of two evils," Mack muttered under his breath as he walked away from the counter and headed for the lounge. "I need a cold beer."

Before Mack took his second step the lounge door few open and an old man wearing a long sleeved white turtle neck shirt popped out into the lobby.

"Hey you!"

"Are you talking to me?"

"Your name's Mack isn't it?" The old man barked.

"That's correct. Why?"

"Guido called and told me to keep an eye out for you. He said that he was supposed to meet you in the lounge at nine o'clock but he got tied up in a business meeting downtown and won't be here until after eleven o'clock. He wants you to wait for him and the drinks are on the house. He feels bad about standing you up."

"It's okay. I'm a little late myself."

"My name's Rolf," the old man grunted through his teeth as he extended his open right hand in greeting. He couldn't speak clearly because a three-inch black unlit cigar butt was clenched between his teeth. "Come in, sit down and relax. I own this joint. Guido told me that you're a writer."

"A writer maybe, but not an author yet. I'm going to write a book someday."

"Where do you get your ideas for characters?"

"From people I meet."

"Can I be a character in your book? I'm real interesting."

"Maybe, but I don't know anything about you. Tell me about yourself."

"Are you going to take notes? I've got a pad behind the bar."

"I don't need to take notes. I have a good memory," Mack slipped a white cocktail napkin out of its plastic holder. "I'll make notes on this napkin if you tell me something complicated."

"You're from West Palm Beach right?"

"Close to it. I'm from Stuart. That's about thirty miles north of West Palm Beach."

"I know where it is. I used to box professionally in West Palm Beach in the fifties and sixties, but I never made it up to Stuart."

"You were a professional boxer?"

"Yes! I said I was didn't I? Look at my ears and my nose. Do you think they got that way from me working in a flower shop?"

"There's some pretty tough flower shops in Florida."

"Don't get smart! I might look like an old man, but I can send you into next week with one punch."

"I bet you can. What name did you fight under?"

"Kid Melrose. I grew up in Melrose Park just a mile down Mannheim Road from here."

"Were you a heavyweight title contender?"

"No. I fought as a middleweight. I never made it to the big time. I always fought in the preliminary bouts to get the crowd warmed up. Me and my partner took turns taking a dive every other fight."

"I don't understand."

"What don't you understand? Is the English language difficult for you? How can you be a writer if you don't understand plain English?"

"What did you mean that you and your partner took turns taking a dive every other fight?"

"You don't get out into the real world much do you?"

"I suppose not. I never met a professional fighter until now."

"The crowd goes to a fight to see two men beat the hell out of each other in the middle of the ring. It doesn't matter who's in there. They just want to hear the solid 'smack' of leather against flesh and see blood. That's why the promoters book a couple of dumb palookas who don't stand a chance of going anywhere against each other. It doesn't matter who wins the preliminary bouts because the crowd doesn't care. They're there for the main bout. Our job was to keep it going for at least six rounds and then take a dive. We had to string out the preliminary bouts until about nine forty-five. That way the main bout could get started on time at ten o'clock."

"Isn't there something wrong with that?"

"What's wrong with the main bout gettin' started on time? That's when it was supposed to start."

"I mean with fixing the preliminary bouts so that the fighters knew how many rounds it was going to go and who was supposed to win."

"So? What's your point?"

"Forget it. It's not important. How many years did your professional career last?"

"I started fightin' in the Wells Street Gym in Chicago in nineteen forty-nine. A promoter from Indianapolis picked me up in nineteen fifty-one and it was all up from there."

"What do you mean up?"

"I fought in Indy for a year then he traded me to a promoter in New York. I fought in Madison Square Garden for three years and got traded back to another promoter here in Chicago. I fought here for two years and in nineteen fifty-seven I got traded to a Jew promoter in Miami. I fought in Havana a couple of times before Castro took over and kicked the outfit out."

"How did you wind up in West Palm Beach?"

"The Jew got 'whacked' by the boys from New York for refusing to go along with their favorite boy in a bout on Miami Beach. I tried going free-lance for awhile then I found a black promoter out of Boca Raton who was trying to make a name for himself."

"What was his name?"

"I'd rather not say because he's real famous today. He had the strangest hairstyle I ever saw. It was piled on top of his head like a wild ass beehive."

"When did you stop fighting?"

"Haven't yet. I'll fight a pissed off wolverine at the drop of a hat," The old man shouted as he slid off the bar stool and took a pugilist's pose. "Wanna' go a couple of rounds with me?"

"Not on your life," Mack quickly responded as he shook his head. "I know when I've met my match."

"Come on," the old man egged Mack on as he thumbed the side of his nose with his left hand. "Try to hit me. I dare ya'. You've got at least twenty-five years on me and I can still whip your ass."

"I have no doubts whatsoever that you can and I don't need for you to prove it either. Why don't you slide back up here on the stool and tell me a little more about yourself?"

"Okay," the old boxer retorted as he dropped his fighting pose and slid up on the bar stool alongside Mack. "I've got a forty-two inch 'Louisville Slugger' under the bar for the hardheaded ones."

"What if the baseball bat doesn't do the trick?"

"I shoot 'em. My two best friends, *Smith & Wesson*, are also under the bar."

"Wow! What about the cops?"

"What about 'em? They know better than to mess with me or anyone else who hangs out in here. They'd wind up in cornfield in southern Illinois if they messed with me. I've got friends in this town that would put you in a wooden box just by me making a phone call."

"Rolf, you're a tough dude. Don't worry I'll pay my bar tab before I leave."

"You don't have a bar tab. Every thing is on the house. That was Guido's orders to me when he called to say that he was going to be late."

"I'll thank him if I see him tonight."

"You'll see him alright. He's on his way right now."

"How long will it take him to get here? I'm pooped and I have an early flight in the morning. I should hit the hay real soon."

"What time's your flight?"

"About nine o'clock."

"Are you flyin' out of O'Hare or Midway?"

"O'Hare."

"No problem. O'Hare's real close. You can be there in fifteen minutes tops. We close the bar at four in the morning so you have time for a couple hours of shuteye. Guido will make sure that you get to the airport in time to catch your plane."

"He doesn't have to take me to the airport. I have a rental car."

"I didn't say that Guido would take you to the airport. I said that he'd make sure that you got to the airport in time to catch your plane."

"Isn't that the same thing?"

"No even close. You really don't know who he is do you?"

"Sure I do. He's Guido Cameri. At least that's what he told me his name was. Is there something that I should know about him?"

"Maybe. If he feels it's important and that you need to know he'll tell ya'. Ready for another Bud? It's on the house."

"Sure. Why not?"

"It's on the way."

"Guido told me that you and him go back a long way."

"We go way back. We grew up together in the old Italian neighborhood."

"Where's that?"

"Arrigo Park. It's east of Ashland Avenue, west of Racine Avenue and north of Taylor Street."

"When did you stop fighting professionally in the ring?"

"Nineteen seventy-four. I got the crap beat out of me by a young German kid who was tryin' to make a name for himself and he used my head as a billboard. He hadn't figured out how the system worked yet. He was supposed to take the dive that night. "

"What happened?"

"He beat the crap out of me and wouldn't stop hittin' me in the head even when the ref tried to break it up. I suffered a concussion and spent six days in Rush Presbyterian Hospital. The docs said that I suffered drain bamage and couldn't focus my eyes well enough to see a punch comin' at me."

"Don't you mean brain damage?"

"That what I said wasn't it? Drain bamage! Maybe I can't see so good any more but I sure as hell can talk good English! What do you think I said?"

"Brain damage! You definitely said brain damage. Guido said that you worked for him at one time."

"One time! We worked together for more than twenty years! I started working for him when I got out of the hospital and I stayed with him through thick and thin until they sent him away to Joliet State Prison in nineteen ninety-five."

"What did he get sent away for?"

"The normal run of the mill crap. Extortion, embezzlement, black mail, runnin' a few numbers and broads plus Illinois State Sales Tax evasion. He got sent up for dumb ass state sales tax evasion!"

"What did he do?"

"It's not what he did. It's what he didn't do. He collected the seven percent Illinois sales tax from his clothing store outlet customer and forgot to pay it to the state."

"How could he forget something so simple?"

"He was selling hot stuff from the Merchandise Mart and only dealt in cash. He figured that no one would check him and somebody did. Somebody downtown in the Merchandise Mart fingered him."

"When did you start working for Guido?"

"When I stopped fightin' professionally in seventy-four."

"What kind of work did you do for him?"

"When he was in the insurance racket I sold policies for him during the week and collected the premiums every Friday afternoon."

"What kind of insurance did you sell? Life, health, homeowners, business liability?"

"It was protection insurance. If someone bought Guido's protection insurance we'd guarantee that nobody would torch the guy's place, break his kneecaps or beat up his wife and children."

"That's the old protection racket. It's called extortion and it's against the law."

"You're right, but we protected the guy's place and family."

"You protected him from yourself!"

"Naw. We protected him from everybody. Nobody, and I do mean nobody, would touch a place if they knew Guido had the insurance on the place. They knew better."

"How would they know?"

"We taped a photo of Guido in the front window."

"If he didn't pay then you burned his place down! Right?"

"Of course not! If we did that there'd be nothing to insure. That wouldn't be good business. I'd stop by Friday afternoon to collect the next week's insurance premium. If he didn't have the money I'd extend him until Monday and I'd warn him that his insurance policy didn't cover him, his business and his family for the weekend. Usually some unfortunate thing would happen to a member of his family."

"Give me an example."

"His daughter might be raped in an alley, his son might get in a street fight and get hurt real bad, or worse yet something bad might happen to his wife. Once the street punks knew the guy wasn't protected they'd move right in and work him over. We couldn't do nothin' because he didn't pay his insurance premium."

"Guido mentioned something about breaking kneecaps of people who didn't pay up."

"That was always a last resort and I got to do that. I was real good at it."

"How would you break someone's knee caps? Did you use a baseball bat or a tire iron?"

"Naw. They'd be too easy to see. I used a sapper."

"What's that?"

"They're easy to make. All you need is a six-inch piece of water hose, a six-inch piece of wooden dowel to slip inside the water hose for a handle and a two-ounce piece of lead that you can slip inside the business end of the zapper. I used car tire weights and wired them together."

Rolf stopped to take a deep drag of his nasty cigar, grinned and began again.

"I filled the water hose with rubber caulk and sealed off the end with a piece of twisted wire. I'd slip the wood handle inside my jacket sleeve and hold the lead end inside my palm. When I was ready to score I'd just open my fingers, the zapper slid down into my hand and with a flip of my wrist his kneecap was gone. No one ever saw a thing."

"That must have hurt!"

"It would put the guy right down on the floor. It worked real good on beefers in crowded elevators."

"What's a beefer?"

"A rat, a stool pigeon, a squealer, someone who'd sell you out for a buck or to deal a lighter sentence for himself by turnin' on you or anyone who needed to be taught a good lesson."

"How could you break someone's kneecap in a crowded elevator? Someone would see you do it."

"They wouldn't see me do it. I'd stand beside and to the left side of the mark and just as the elevator door started to open I'd zap him in the kneecap. He'd scream like a stuck pig and everyone's attention would be on him as he writhed in pain on the elevator floor."

Rolf stopped to take another deep drag of his nasty cigar, winked at Mack, grinned and began again.

"When I slipped out the open door I'd press the 'up' and 'close door' buttons and the passengers would be so preoccupied with the guy's screaming that they wouldn't notice. When the elevator reached the next floor and the passengers realized what happened I'd be out on the street and long gone. It was easy."

"Did you ever get caught?"

"No! If anyone said anything to me I'd pull back my jacket, let 'em get a good look at the shoulder holster under my left arm pit and smile. They always backed off."

"What did you do while Guido was in prison?"

"The same things I did when he was out. We still ran the insurance business just like we always did. I'd go down and see him every Monday and he'd tell me what he wanted done."

"Didn't the guards monitor your conversations?"

"Sure they did, but we had our own code. We talked about how many fish I caught the week before, if I won any prize money in the fishing tournament and if I found any new fishing holes over the weekend. It was easy."

"What did you do with the insurance money you collected?"

"Kept it in a steel box locked in the trunk that was welded to the car frame. It was safe."

"Didn't people know it was in the trunk?"

"Of course they did, but I kept my car in a locked garage and the street punks knew better than to even look at me, much less try to steal from me. I had other punks watchin' them."

"How long have you been running his place?"

"I took it over in eighty-five. The guy who owned it didn't pay his insurance premiums, had a real bad accident and his wife sold the place to me for a buck."

"What kind of accident did he have?"

"It was very sad. The cops found him hanging from a meat hook in a warehouse down on south Mannheim Road in Stone Park. Somebody had burned his feet off with a blowtorch and left him hanging there. The cops figured he wriggled around on that meat hook for three days."

"Why didn't he yell for help?"

"It's hard to yell when there's a tennis ball in your mouth."

"Oh. Do you own this place outright?"

"I have a couple of partners. Guido put in about twenty grand and so did Johnny Amorati. You met him at his going away party last night."

"Who carries your insurance?"

"I don't need any."

The Wolf Man came out from behind the bar, slid over to Rolf's left side, whispered something in his ear and slunk off toward the karaoke machine.

"Sorry, Mack. I have to take a phone call in the back. Wolf Man said that it was important. You hang out here and wait for Guido. He should be here anytime now. That Russian broad behind the bar will keep the Buds coming for you. Don't let her con you into giving her a tip by flashing her boobs at ya'. She's married to the Wolf Man and she works me for me. Anything you want to drink is covered."

"Thanks, Rolf."

"Don't thank me. Thank Guido when he gets here."

Rolf slipped off the barstool and tapped Mack on the right

shoulder as he headed for the tiny office tucked in behind the bar. The karaoke machine came to life and Wolf Man broke into the theme from the James Bond thriller *You Only Live Twice*.

Mack looked up just in time to see Wolf Man nod his head toward the front door and shake it from side to side. Mack understood his not so subtle message, and swung around on the bar stool toward the one-way glass.

Guido and his sidekick Rocco were in the hotel lobby and striding towards the lounge. Both men grinned from ear to ear as Rocco raised his right hand, blew on his knuckles and shook his hand as if he was in pain. Mack turned around to watch the amply endowed Russian bartender mix a Black Russian to go in a plastic glass.

Mack didn't hear the lounge door open but sensed that someone was behind him.

"Hey Mack. Wanna' buy a diamond for your sweetie back in Florida. I just got a shipment in from South Africa. A couple of airline pilots brought them in their luggage."

Mack didn't turn around when he responded. "Guido, I don't have a sweetie in Florida or anywhere else. But if I did I'd buy the biggest stone you have in a flash. No questions asked." Mack waited for Guido to make the next move.

"I'm glad that you wouldn't ask any questions because I wouldn't give you any answers anyway. How'd you know I was behind you?'

"The garlic gave you away when you whispered in my ear. You and Rocco must've stopped for a pizza on the way back."

"You're right! We stopped at the 'Sorrento Restaurant' right down the road on Mannheim. You're really good."

"Do you want me to tell you what part of Italy the garlic came from?"

"You can't do that? I'll bet you a hundred bucks you can't."

"Guido, you're on! The garlic came from a family-owned farm outside Palermo in northern Italy. Give me my hundred!" Mack swung around and held out his right hand with the open palm up."

"You're really good. Rocco, give him his hundred clams."

"Thank you Guido."

"How'd you do that?"

"Guess where the garlic came from?"

"I had dinner there last night and had a long conversation with the bartender. His mother's the cook and she uses old family recipes. She only uses garlic bulbs grown on her family's farm in Palermo. They fly a shipment in four times a year."

"You cheated! Give me my hundred bucks back!"

"I didn't cheat. You made a bet with me and lost fair and square. You should do your homework and know whom you're taking on before you make a bet. "

"I thought I did. But I didn't expect to find a ringer in my own bar."

"I thought this was Rolf's bar."

"He likes to think it is and I let him. That way I don't get hassled."

"How about Johnny Amorati? He told me that he has money invested in the place."

"Maybe he does and maybe he doesn't. He's going away for the next fifteen years so who cares? I don't."

"Is that fair to him?"

"So? What's fair? Where is it written in stone that life is supposed to be fair? There's no rules and the one who ends with the most stuff at the end wins. That's it. Period and the end of the story. Johnny loses."

"How about Rolf?"

"How about him?"

"If you take his bar he loses too."

"I'm not going to take his bar. I'm a convicted felon and I'm not allowed to own a bar, or have any direct financial interest in one, as a condition of my probation. If the state attorney even thought that I had anything to do with this place, he'd shut it down in a minute."

"That's why it's in Rolf's name!"

"Correct. However, my name's on the papers as Rolf's pre-need guardian in case something bad happens to him and he can't run the place anymore."

"Doesn't that revoke the terms of your probation?"

"No. My probation deal is that I can't own or have any

financial interest in a joint that serves booze. My name's not on the title or business license. I just come here once in awhile to check on Rolf."

"Don't you have an office in the back?"

"Kinda and kinda not."

"What does that mean?"

"My kid runs the short order food place for the bar. He makes a couple hundred bucks a week cookin' hamburgers and fries. It's all cash money so he's doin' alright.'

"Where's the kitchen?"

"Do you see the Dutch door over there past the end of the bar?"

"Yes."

"That's it. People can call down from their room and order room service or order right here in the bar. If you want to see a menu I'll tell the Russkie bar tender to bring one over here." Guido signaled for the bartender to come over.

"That's okay. I ate dinner already."

"She's here already. What do you want to drink?"

"Another Budweiser would be fine."

"Tanya, bring him another Bud. How do your boobs feel?"

"What do you mean how do my boobs feel?"

"Have you felt 'em since your surgery?"

"No. There're still sore."

"Pull up your blouse and I'll feel them for you."

"No way!"

"With the attitude I should put you on the street for twofers. We'd make a lot of cash."

"What do you mean twofers?"

"I mean that I'll sell your butt to two guys for fifty bucks. They'll get two pops at you for one low price. We'll make money in volume."

"You're a dirty old man!" The bartender snapped as she spun on her heels and stomped away.

"She doesn't know a real business opportunity when it hits her in the face. Where'd ya' go for dinner? Sorrento Garden again?"

"No. I met a friend who lives in Elgin at a place called The Assembly in Hoffman Estates for dinner."

"I know the joint! It's at the corner of Barrington Road and the south exit off the Northwest Toll Way. The outfit used to meet there back in the sixties and early seventies."

"Why would they meet there?"

"A lot of the guys from the Chicago outfit lived in Barrington and Inverness. And it was easy for the guys from Rockford and Milwaukee to find. What'd ya' have for dinner?"

"A Bionic Burger."

"That's the best thing they've got out there. They musta' sold thousands of those things."

"They are having a contest where customers fill out an entry form and guess how many they've sold since nineteen sixty-four."

"That's dumb!"

"Why?"

"If the IRS wants to audit them they'll have the records of how many they sold. The money in the cash register should match it. Then on the other hand there's the problem with the Illinois Sales tax."

"What problem is that?"

"In Illinois retailers are supposed to collect seven per cent sales tax on everything they sell and turn it over to the state every month. That's why I went to prison. I sold thousands of dollars worth of hot clothes from the Merchandise Mart and never charged sales tax. The state auditors came in one day on a routine audit checked my books and found out that I wasn't charging sales tax. I told 'em that all of the crap I was selling was used and I was told that sales tax didn't apply to used merchandise."

"It sounds logical to me. So, what happened?"

"They inventoried everything in the store, estimated my annual sales volume and computed sales taxes based on that estimate. I didn't use a cash register, didn't keep any paper records and I never deposited money in a bank. That's a sure way to get nailed. I tried to fight 'em in court, but it was a set up and I went down hard. I got ten years in Joliet, but I only served eight years. I can do eight years standin' on my head."

"Why only eight years?"

I got three month's good behavior credit on my sentence for

every year I kept my nose clean."

"You must have really behaved yourself in prison."

"I did in there. But I still ran my insurance business from inside. Rolf and Rocco kept things going for me while I was in the joint."

"Rolf mentioned that."

"What did he tell you?"

"Not much except that he kept your insurance business going for you while you were in prison."

"He didn't do it all by himself! Rocco was with him every minute and I told him what to do, when and how to do it!"

"That's exactly what he said. Almost word for word."

"Did he tell you that I was kidnapped by a Mexican drug outfit and held for a million bucks ransom in a moving van stashed in a warehouse on the south side? They wrapped my neck with rusty barbed wire and connected to a metal ring bolted in the side of the van. I lived like that for ten days!"

"No! He didn't mention it. Did someone pay the million bucks?"

"No! I fooled the Mexican who was watching me and escaped. He'd been torturing me by burning my feet with a blowtorch and I wouldn't talk. When he stopped I fell over on my side and pretended that I'd passed out. He panicked and went to get his boss."

"Why'd he panic?"

"They were torturing me to find out what I did with the million bucks I scammed them out of on a drug deal. If he killed me his boss would kill him because they'd never get the information out of me." When they came back his boss said *muerto* and drew his finger across his throat."

"*Muerto* means to kill in Spanish!"

"That's right. They were going to slit my throat because they thought I was almost dead anyway. But they made a big mistake."

"What kind of mistake?"

"The boss left and the other spic cut the chains on my legs and wrists with a bolt cutter. He didn't cut the barbed wire on my neck though. He left to get a water hose to wash me down with before he slit my throat."

"Why would he wash you down if he was going to kill you?"

"I'd been chained up in that van for ten days and had crapped and pissed all over myself. It really stank in there. The Mexicans believe that it's bad luck to kill someone who's dirty, so they clean them up first. Plus, he knew that he was going to have to drag my body out of the van by my feet and he didn't want to get himself dirty."

"So?"

"When he left I started bending the barbed wire with my fingers until it got hot and snapped. I jumped out of that van, with burned feet and buck ass naked as well and headed for an open door. When I hit the daylight I just kept running until I reached the next building. I ran inside and who do you suppose was in there?"

"The Mexican who was supposed to cut your throat?"

"No! The FBI! They had the place staked out and were going to raid it in fifteen minutes. I beat them to it, but they took the credit for finding where the Mexicans had me stashed and rescuing me. But that was okay."

"Why was it okay? You freed yourself and escaped."

"The Mexicans never got the million bucks and I told the FBI that I didn't know what the Mexicans were talkin' about. They believed me because they figured that nobody could take ten days of torture and not talk. But I did."

"So Guido, what did you do with the million bucks?"

"That's what the Mexicans kept asking me too. They dropped off a few kilos of cocaine in the trunk of a car and expected that I'd give 'em a million bucks. I never had a million bucks. It was a scam."

"What happened to the million bucks worth of cocaine they left in the car trunk?"

"That's the same question the Mexicans kept asking me and when I got loose the cops kept asking me the same thing for three days."

"Well?"

"Well what?"

"What did you do with the cocaine?"

"Never saw it and never had it. I don't deal in drugs. Hot diamonds, television sets that fall off the back of delivery trucks, watches, and antiques from Iraq I can handle, but not drugs."

"So, you were scamming the Mexicans and they were scamming you at the same time?"

"It looks that way. But I have a philosophy about scams."

"What is it?"

"You can't scam an honest man. Are you going to hang around for a while and listen to me and my boys sing karaoke tonight?"

"I don't know. I didn't get much sleep last night and I have to catch a plane out of O'Hare at a quarter after nine tomorrow morning. I can't miss my flight. I have to return my rental car and take their shuttle bus to O'Hare. I'll have to be there at least an hour before flight time in order to get through the security check. I'm going to have to leave the hotel no later than seven o'clock."

"Hang around for a while and enjoy yourself. For you everything's on the house. Order whatever you want. How about a broad? I can get you a young Russian girl that just turned sixteen last week. She's the bartender's sister. Have a good time and enjoy yourself. I'll make sure that you get to the airport in time for your flight even if I have to take you myself."

"What time is it?"

"A little bit after midnight. This place starts jumping about twelve-thirty when the shift changes at the Ford assembly plant in Melrose Park."

"I'll have another beer, watch you and your sons sing one song and then I'm going to bed."

"Okay. Sounds good. I'll get the bartender to set you up with a fresh Bud," Guido responded and nodded to the bar tender. She knowingly nodded back and reached into the beer cooler.

Wolf Man spotted Mack visiting with Guido and cranked up the volume on the instrumental version of the James Bond thriller *You Only Live Twice.*

Mack understood Wolf Man's message and realized that there was nothing he could do about it.

Chapter 17

"Mr. McCray! Please wake up and fasten your seat belt." The female flight attendant's soft voice cooed in Mack's left ear. "We are on our final approach to the West Palm Beach Airport."

"Huh? What?" Mack groaned as he attempted to sit up straight. Where am I?"

"You are on Delta flight nineteen forty-five to West Palm Beach. We'll be landing in West Palm Beach in just a few minutes. Please sit up and fasten your seat belt."

"How did I get here? I don't remember boarding the plane."

"The gate agent helped you board and you fell asleep before we closed the door. You must have been very tired. Your friend told the gate agent that you get airsick and took several pills to calm yourself down. That's what conked you out."

"What friend?"

"I don't know. I'm only repeating what the gate agent told me. Now be a good boy and fasten your seat belt."

"Okay."

"You'd better stuff that piece of paper back down into your shirt pocket before you lose it."

"What piece of paper?" Mack looked down and tried to focus his eyes on his shirt pocket.

"The pink piece of paper that's sticking out of your left shirt pocket. It might be a receipt, or something important." The flight attendant reached over and stuffed the paper down into in Mack's shirt pocket. "There. It should be okay now."

"Thank you," Mack managed to mutter.

"The flight attendant stood up and directed her attention to the passengers in the row ahead of Mack. "Please fasten your seat belts and raise your seats to a full upright position in preparation for our landing in West Palm Beach."

"Mon ami, did you sleep well?" Echoed a soft male voice with a distinct French accent from across the aisle. "Mon ami. Are you awake?"

Mack slowly swiveled his head to the left and felt his brain slide across the inside of his cranium. It came to a mushy stop just above his left ear.

"Mon ami, you've been sleeping like a baby for the past three hours. You must have had a wild time in Chicago last night."

"What makes you think that I had a wild time anywhere last night?" Mack managed to squeak out between his fuzz-covered teeth. "Were you there?"

"This matchbook cover fell out of your shirt pocket into the aisle when you slipped in your seat," the man replied as he reached across the narrow aisle and offered Mack a red matchbook. "It is from a karaoke bar on Grand Avenue in Chicago. Perhaps someone slipped into your pocket as a joke."

Mack reached for the matchbook with his left hand and held it out at arm's length so he could focus his bloodshot eyes on the cover.

'Karaoke with the Wolf Man' read the title. Mack flipped the cover open with his thumb. There were no matches and 'Maya' was scrawled in blue letters on the inside of the front cover.

"Did she leave you a phone number?" Inquired the Frenchman from across the aisle.

"No! And I don't know why this was in my pocket!"

"Mon ami, were you in the Wolf Man's karaoke bar last night?"

"Yes, maybe for a little while I suppose. I got there about ten-thirty, but I don't remember going to bed, or how I got here."

"Did you check any luggage?"

"I don't think so. I travel with just a canvas ditty bag. It should be in the overhead compartment."

"Mon ami, I saw the flight attendant place a tan bag up there. It must be yours."

"I sure hope so."

"Mon ami, did you get into a fight last night?"

"I don't think so. Why do you ask?"

"You have a bruise on the left side of your neck just above your shirt collar."

"That's not a bruise," offered the flight attendant with a wide smile. "It looks like a big old-fashioned hickey to me." She smiled as she turned around to give instructions to the passengers on the opposite side of the aisle. "I haven't seen one of those babies since junior high school."

Mack raised his left hand to the side of his neck. The skin felt warm to the touch.

"That's where it is mon ami. Right there! What did she mean when she said hickey? I have not heard that American word before. It appears to be a bruise."

"It means that some lucky female sucked on his neck to leave her mark to show everyone else that she was with him last night," offered the fight attendant from over her shoulder. "He's either dating a very young girl, or a very old toothless vampire."

"I don't know what you're talking about! I wasn't with anyone last night!"

"Didn't I hear you say just a minute ago that you don't remember how you got into bed last night, or how you got onto this flight?"

The flight attendant was enjoying the cat and mouse game.

"Perhaps you have a selective memory? Is Maya a pretty girl?"

"I don't know what you're talking about!"

"How about the name Maya that's printed inside that matchbook cover? Isn't that a girl's name?"

"Yes, but I don't see what that has to do with anything."

"Mon ami, the Maya were an Indian civilization in Mexico," offered the Frenchman.

"The Maya were in Guatemala," Mack retorted. "The Aztecs were in Mexico."

"Come on Mr. McCray," the flight attendant tittered. "Who's Maya?"

"I don't know!"

"Typical male selective memory syndrome. My first husband had it too."

"I don't have any problems with my memory. Maya's a young Pakistani hooker that hangs out in the parking lot of the motel I stayed at last night."

"Now the story is really getting interesting. How did you happen to wind up with that fresh hickey on your neck? Does she practice vampirism?"

"No! She's a nice girl who got stuck in a bad situation by her brother. He's making her pay off her passage into the United States by working as a hooker. Are you satisfied now?"

"Yep," the flight attendant responded with a wink as she turned and headed for her jump seat in the front of the aircraft. "Now it all makes sense," she offered over her left shoulder.

Mack reached into his shirt pocket, pulled out the pink piece of paper, glanced at it and stuffed back into his shirt pocket. It was an Enterprise Car Rental receipt.

"Mon ami, do you have a moment?" The dapper Frenchman attempted to get Mack's attention.

"I'm not your ami!" Mack swiveled in his seat so he could face the inquisitive Frenchman and his aching eyes almost focused and he scanned his questioner.

The man's medium length gray hair was a tad to long and reached over the collar of his shirt; he wore a thin mustache that was obviously tinted black because his hair was graying; soft, impish blue eyes sparkled beneath his busy gray eyebrows and a wide grin spread out below his mustache; his tweed jacket had seen better days and a brown hound's tooth hat, similar to those worn by in the infamous coach of the University of Alabama football coach Bear Bryant, rested across his knees. His light gray flannel slacks and brown penny loafers completed his ensemble. A white cotton shirt topped off by a purple bowtie peered out from inside his jacket. His long thin fingers, and professionally manicured fingernails, clearly indicated that he was a man of leisure who rarely, if ever, touched a tool with his bare hands.

"Look here Frenchy! I don't have any idea who you are and I don't care! Now why don't you sit your sorry French butt in your seat and shut up?"

"Mon ami, I am sorry if I bothered you. I just wanted to ask if you are familiar with Jensen Beach."

"I'm not your friend and why do you want to know about Jensen Beach?"

"Because I am staying at the Holiday Inn and I don't know how to find it."

"Jensen Beach is about thirty miles north of West Palm Beach. Is someone picking you up at the airport?"

"Yes. A driver from the Harbor Branch Oceanographic Institute is meeting me. Are you familiar with Harbor Branch?"

"Of course. They run marine research programs out of their facility north of Fort Pierce. Why are you going there?"

"I am from Paris, that's in France, and my area of expertise is cetaceans."

"Cetaceans? That's a genus of whales and dolphins isn't it?"

"That is not quite correct mon ami. Cetaceans are the family to which whales and dolphins belong, not the genus. I am here to study several toothed Atlantic dolphins that beached themselves on Jensen Beach Tuesday afternoon. I am staying at the Holiday Inn in Jensen Beach to be close to my work."

"Don't they have people at Harbor Branch who can do that?"

"Of course, but in France we have a very limited amount of knowledge about Atlantic pilot whales. The pod of dolphins that beached themselves on Jensen Beach is a very rare deepwater species that never come within fifty miles of the shoreline."

"What did they beach themselves?"

"That is exactly what I am going to try to determine. There could be many reasons including disease of their inner ears, or the pod followed a sick leader who preferred to run aground on the beach rather than drown at sea. Dolphins and whales are mammals that migrated from land to the water millions of years ago. They have an inner fear of drowning just like any other mammal. If they are very sick, or injured, and feel that they may drown they head for land where they originated."

"I thought that they just got lost or followed a sick leader onto the shore."

"Mon ami, there is no way that a cetacean could ever get lost at sea and accidentally beach itself! They have an internal navigation system and very accurate SONAR."

"How about ear mites. I read somewhere that ear mites drive them crazy an they run into shallow water to rub their ear holes on the dry beach sand to clean out the mites."

"No! Cetacean beachings have become very common around the world and we are attempting to determine the cause of each one through necropsies."

"Do you have any theories of your own?"

"I am keeping an open mind."

"You must have some ideas."

"Possibly, but they remain to be proved."

"Would you like to share some of them with me?"

"No! Mon ami, I do not know who you are. You might be a Russian spy,"

"Do I have a Russian accent?"

"No mon ami. However most Russian spies are recruited from American universities and have no accent."

My name's Mack McCray. I manage a small private marina in Port Salerno."

"It is nice to meet you Mr. McCray. My name is Francois Batteau and I am a cetacean researcher."

"Batteau? That name is very familiar. I've heard it somewhere before."

"Mon ami, have you studied cetaceans?"

"No, but I had an experience with dolphins in Hawaii several years ago."

"Where in Hawaii?

"Oahu. Actually it a secret base on an island in the middle of Kaneohe Bay."

"Coconut Island perhaps?"

"Exactly! How did you know that?"

"Mon ami, my brother Jacques ran a dolphin research program on Coconut Island for the American Navy in the nineteen sixties. He was attempting to develop a verbal method of communicating with dolphins. He drowned the same morning that the dolphins he trained were to be transferred to a marine park."

"Did he succeed?"

"In drowning? I think so – his body washed up on the beach."

"Not drowning! I meant did he succeed in verbally communicating with dolphins?"

"Yes. But the American Navy wanted him to do much more than communicate with the dolphins and he refused. Maybe that's why he was drowned."

"What do you mean by that?"

"By what, mon ami?"

"Why did you say he was drowned?"

"Because he could swim like a fish and once tried out for the French Olympic swim team."

"Maybe he was pulled under by the tidal current."

"Mon ami, if you spent any time at Kaneohe Bay you should know that there is very little tidal current there. It is almost land-locked."

"What do you think happened to him?"

"He refused to continue with the American Navy's Swimmer Nullification Project and was going to tell the media about it. Someone wanted him kept quiet."

"Who?"

"Mon ami, that is, as you Americans say it, the sixty-four thousand dollar question."

"Frenchy, what do you know about the American Navy's Swimmer Nullification Project?"

"Mon ami, my name is Francois not Frenchy!"

"I'm sorry. I forgot."

"Do not ever call me Frenchy again! Do you understand?"

"Yes. I won't call you Frenchy again."

"Everyone who reads a newspaper knows that the American Navy uses dolphins to protect its aircraft carriers and nuclear submarines when they dock in port."

"I've heard about the Navy using dolphins to locate undersea mines, but exactly what is the Swimmer Nullification Project? It sounds ominous."

"It is. Mon ami, it is common knowledge in the academic community that the American Navy transports Atlantic bottlenose dolphins from Florida to Hawaii and trains them at Coconut Island. Five fake seaplane hangers on the west side of the Marine Base on Mokapu Peninsula cover the dolphin pens."

"What do the dolphins do to swimmers?"

"A large needle, similar to the type used to fill up a basketball, or football, is attached to the dolphin's snout with a Velcro strap and a small cylinder of compressed carbon dioxide gas is attached to the needle. The dolphins are trained to approach a swimmer from behind, so they can't be seen, and stick them in their back with the needle. The swimmer finds the compressed carbon dioxide to be very unpleasant."

"Does it kill them?"

"Of course mon ami! They blow up and float to the surface very fast."

"*Ladies and gentlemen the aircraft is coming up to the gate,*" purred the flight attendant's throaty voice overt the cabin's almost unintelligible communications system. "*Please wait until the aircraft comes to a complete stop at the gate before you unfasten your seat belt and check around your seat areas for your personal belongings before deplaning.*"

"It's been very enlightening to have spoken with you," Mack offered as he unfastened his seat belt stood up. "I hope that you have a good time on Jensen Beach. The Holiday Inn is an excellent hotel."

"Mon ami, maybe I'll see you tomorrow? Do you ever come to the Holiday Inn?"

"Not recently," Mack said over his left shoulder as he stood up to join the single file line of anxious passengers shuffling towards the front of the aircraft. "It's about ten miles from where I live."

"I hope to see you again soon, mon ami," the Frenchman offered. "I like you very much."

"I like you too Frenchy," Mack responded as he stood up in the aisle, opened the overhead bin and reached for his canvas ditty bag. It wasn't there! A tan suede travel bag was the only bag there. "Hey Frenchy! I thought you told me that you saw the flight attendant put a canvas ditty bag up here!"

"Mon ami, I told you to call me Francois!"

"Whatever," Mack quipped. "Where's my ditty bag?"

"What is a ditty bag? I don't know the word ditty bag."

"Forget it Frenchy!" Mack barked as he turned to make his way down the aisle towards the front of the aircraft. "I'll check in the baggage claim area. They must've checked my bag."

"Mon ami, I told you to never call me Frenchy! My name is Francois!"

"Whatever you say Frenchy," Mack mumbled as he shook his head and walked away. "Whatever you say," Mack added over his shoulder.

Chapter
18

The concourse was packed with anxious travelers on their way to the main terminal to meet their waiting relatives and friends. Mack dodged in out of several elderly passengers doddering down the crowded concourse.

"Why would I check my ditty bag?" Mack thought to himself as he sidestepped a young girl, maybe all of seven years old, trailing a small pink suitcase equipped with pink plastic wheels. *"I always carry it onboard planes when I fly. This doesn't make any sense to me."*

Mack elected to take the short flight of seventeen stairs down from the concourse level to the baggage claim area because the escalator was packed. A dozen or so anxious limo drivers stood at the bottom of the stairs holding up white signs and sheets of paper emblazoned with the name of the party they were waiting for. Some of the signs were professionally prepared with the name of the client neatly printed in sharp block printed letters while other were hastily scrawled with a magic marker, in some cases what appeared to be a child's crayon.

Mack didn't see the name 'Batteau' on any of the signs and headed for the baggage claim area carousel. The alarm bell sounded announcing that the luggage from the most recent flight would be appearing from the baggage area immediately. Several anxious elderly women and their grandchildren jostled their way in front of the herd of waiting passengers that was five people deep in some places.

"Those old ladies probably have one or two bags each and it takes them plus their grandchildren to locate them," Mack though as he slowly shook his head. *"It would make it a lot easier if grandma could spot her own bags and drag them off the conveyor belt. The next thing I expect is that her son, or daughter, will both shove their way to the front of the line. But, at least I can see over them."*

Mack's thoughts appeared to be prophetic because a middle-aged bleached blonde clad in a blue spandex jumpsuit elbowed Mack in his left side and offered no apology as she shoved her way through the waiting passengers and headed for one of then elderly grandmothers and her two granddaughters.

"Mon ami, did you locate your bag?"

The voice came from behind Mack's left shoulder and he turned in that direction. It was Francois Batteau.

"I have my bags," the Frenchman offered.

"So? What do you want me to do?" Mack responded as he turned back towards the conveyor belt.

"Mon ami, I found your, what do you call it, ditty bag? It was in the overhead compartment in the row ahead of your seat. Would you like it?"

Mack swung around to face the Frenchman. He was holding Mack's canvas ditty bag at eye level.

"Of course I want it! Why didn't you tell me that it was there?"

"Mon ami, I told you that I saw the flight attendant place a tan bag in the overhead compartment above your seat. I did not say that it was your ditty bag."

"Are you going to hand it over or are you going to stand there all day?"

"It depends mon ami."

"It depends on what? It's my bag!"

"The driver from Harbor Branch did not show up."

"So, what do you expect me to do about it?"

"Will you consider giving me a ride to the Holiday Inn in Jensen Beach in exchange for your bag?"

"I don't have to give you a ride! That's my bag!"

"Your name is not on it. It might be my bag mon ami."

"Give me my bag, or I'll swat you across your pointed French head!"

"I don't think that I would do that if I were you."

The stern voice came from behind Mack's right shoulder and he turned his head to see who offered such a blatant challenge. It was a Palm Beach County Sheriff's deputy.

"We have laws in his county against assault," the wide-eyed, obviously agitated, overweight male officer added. "If you think that is your bag then let's all go over there in the corner and discuss the matter. If you can describe what is inside the bag I'll consider giving it to you. If you can't then it will be obvious to me that you made a mistake and I'll charge you with assault."

"You can't charge me with assault," Mack stammered. "I didn't hit him!"

"Under Florida Statute seven eight-four point zero one one you don't have to actually hit, or even touch someone. If you make a threat of physical violence, and you are capable of carrying out that threat, the verbal action constitutes assault. Do I make myself clear?"

"Yes sir."

"Excuse me *gendarme*," the Frenchman offered.

"What did you call me?" The deputy responded. "Did ya'all call me a germ?"

"No sir, I would not call you a microbe. I do not know how to say *gendarme* in English. Mr. McCray would you assist me please? My English is not very good."

"Frenchy, if I help you out of this do you promise to behave yourself and give me my ditty bag?"

"Of course mon ami. I was only trying to convince you to give me a ride to the Holiday Inn."

"If you need a ride to the Holiday Inn you can take a cab," the deputy offered. "It's only a mile or so down Belvedere Road from the airport."

"He's talking about the Holiday Inn in Jensen Beach," Mack responded. "He's from France and he's here to do some research on a pod of toothed Atlantic dolphins that beached themselves yesterday afternoon. I'll give him a ride because I'm going to Stuart any way and it's only another few miles up there."

"Then it is really your bag?"

"Yes sir."

"Then maybe I'll charge him with filing a false report. I don't like them foreigners anyway."

"He didn't file a report."

"He told me that was his bag."

"No, he didn't."

"Yes he did! I heard him as clear as a bell."

"Officer, why don't you forget the whole thing? I'll give him a ride to Jensen Beach, he'll give me my ditty bag and you can go back to chasing criminals."

"There aren't any criminals here in the airport, except that sneaky French guy. I don't like his attitude."

"If there aren't any criminals in the airport then why are you here?"

"It's kinda' like a training program. The department says that I have an attitude problem so they assigned me out here for thirty days. I'm supposed to be watching for terrorists and I don't like the way he looks. He might be a French terrorist. I think I should run him in on suspicion."

"On suspicion of what? He's a French scientist. He studies whales and dolphins. He's harmless."

"He talks funny and he called me a germ."

"He called you *gendarme*. That's French for policeman."

"I'm not a cop! I'm a Palm Beach County Sheriff's Deputy."

"He didn't know that. They don't have a word for sheriff's

deputy. They only have a word for policeman. Why don't you leave him alone?"

"Maybe I should run both of you in right now! You might be helping him!"

"Helping him do what? I'm just going to give him a ride to Jensen Beach."

"He might be planning on blowing up the Holiday Inn. Maybe he has a bomb in that ditty bag."

"There're only two pairs of dirty socks, two pairs of dirty jockey shorts and my shaving stuff in that bag. Besides the Holiday Inn in Jensen Beach is in Martin County and that's out of your jurisdiction."

"I suppose you're right on the jurisdiction part. Maybe I should take a look in that bag just be sure that there's no bomb in there."

"If you open it you might think that there's a stink bomb in there, but I'll guarantee you that there's no explosives in my bag. If there was it would have never made it though the security check point in Chicago."

"Chicago huh. That's where ya'll are from? I've got cousins up there somewhere."

"I'm from Stuart myself. I was in Chicago on business."

"How about him?"

"He got on the plane from a connecting flight that originated in Paris. He's cool."

"Are you vouchin' for him?"

"I suppose that I am. Can we go now?" It's a good hour's drive back to Stuart on I-95. It's six-fifteen and the peak of the afternoon rush hour."

"I suppose. Have a good day. If I hear anything about a terrorist plot at the Holiday Inn I'll be up there in a minute!"

"Jensen Beach is in Martin County. It's out of your jurisdiction."

"I forgot. Have a good trip back to Stuart." The embarrassed deputy spun on his heel and headed towards an elderly man wearing a white sari and a pink turban dragging a black storage box off the baggage conveyor belt."

"Can we go now mon ami?" The terrified Frenchman

whispered as he handed the tan canvas ditty bag to Mack.

"I suppose we can," Mack whispered back as he took his bag. "Frenchy, that guy didn't like you. He thinks that you are a terrorist."

"Mon ami, I am very scared. Will you please take me to Jensen Beach before he comes back for me? I think he is a Nazi."

"We don't have Nazi's here. We have to walk across the street to the parking lot to get my truck. There're a lot of *gendarmes* outside the terminal building. Stay close behind me, look only at the ground and they won't bother you. Don't look at them or they might suspect that you are a terrorist."

"Yes mon ami," the terrified Frenchman whispered under his breath. "I will do as you ask."

Chapter 19

"Mon ami, did you sleep well?"

The soft voice echoed in Mack's ear but it didn't compute. He rolled over onto his left side so that he faced the wall and covered his head with a pillow.

"Mon ami. It is time for you to get up." The voice was louder and Mack felt someone lightly touch him on his left shoulder. "It is time for you to get up and get to work. The Harbor Branch people are waiting for me in the lobby."

That got Mack's immediate attention. He threw the pillow against the wall and sat up. Bright beams of morning sunlight streamed though the light curtain fabric.

"Where the hell am I?" Mack shouted as he opened his eyes and attempted to get his bearings.

Two opened bottles of red wine set on the bedside nightstand. Another dead soldier leaned against the far corner of the room.

"Mon ami, you are in my hotel room. You were very tired when we arrived at the hotel last night."

"Why am I in your room? I don't remember getting here!"

"Of course you don't remember. You were very drunk last night when we left the hotel lounge."

"What was I doing in the hotel lounge? I offered to give you ride from the West Palm Beach airport to the Holiday Inn in Jensen Beach!"

"That's exactly what you did. We are in my room in the Holiday Inn. There is an excellent view of the beach from here."

"How did I get here?"

"You drove your truck. It's in the hotel parking lot."

"No! That's not what I meant! How did I get into your room?"

"You walked."

"How did I get in this bed? It's your bed isn't it?"

"Yes, it is my bed."

"Where did you sleep last night?"

"On the couch, of course. You snore like a pig rooting out truffles in the forest."

"What happened? Take me through every minute from the time we left the airport last night!"

"After the very bad experience with the American *gendarme* at the airport we very quietly walked across the road to the parking lot where you left your blue truck. We sat in line for many minutes waiting to pay for parking at the airport. You argued with the person at the gate where you paid your parking fee about the amount until she threatened to call the *gendarmes*. You left there very mad."

"Skip all that crap! What time did we get to the hotel?"

"Which hotel?"

"Here! What other hotel are you talking about?"

"The Holiday Inn in West Palm Beach. You stopped there before you got on the big highway. I think it is called I-95."

"Why would I stop at the Holiday Inn in West Palm Beach?"

"It was very strange to me. You said that you had to take a crap. What does the American word crap mean? It is new to me."

"It means to use the bathroom."

"Oh. You said that you had to stop at the Holiday Inn or you would crap in your pants."

"I understand. What happened after that?"

"You took a very long time and I was worried about you. I came into the hotel lobby and waited for you to finish."

"Skip all of that! Start at when we arrived here last night! I want to know how I got into your room and most importantly your bedroom!"

"You walked here from the hotel lounge."

"I know that you told me that! Why am I in your room and in your bed?"

"You were very drunk and in no condition to drive."

"How did I get drunk? I don't remember drinking anything."

"That is to be expected. Alcohol affects neural synopses in the brain and paralyzes short-term memory cells. It is quite normal for a person who consumes as much alcohol as you did in the hotel lounge last night. And you impressed everyone with your ability to sing."

"Sing what? I couldn't carry a tune in a gunny sack."

"You were singing karaoke and would not allow anyone else to use the microphone."

"I don't sing karaoke and never did!"

"You did last night. The bartender took pictures and said that he would leave them at the front desk for you to pick up when you left the hotel today."

"I don't remember anything! What time did we get to this hotel last night and why was I in the lounge drinking?"

"The traffic on the highway was very bad and there were several accidents. We got here about nine o'clock. I invited you in for a glass of wine, but you didn't stop there."

"What was I drinking?"

"You started with two glasses of Merlot, then it was beer and at the end you were drinking straight shots of tequila."

"What about all of these wine bottles? Who drank the wine?"

"We did. When you got back to the room last night you insisted that you needed wine to wash the taste of the tequila out of your mouth. You drank most of it. I only drank one glass."

"What time is it? I have to get out of here!"

"It is almost eight o'clock and I must leave also. The Harbor Branch people are waiting for me in the lobby. Would you mind waiting for fifteen minutes after I leave before you leave?"

"Why? I'm ready to leave now!"

"I don't want the Harbor Branch people to know that you spent the night in my room. It would be quite embarrassing for me if I had to explain it to them."

"Where are my clothes?"

"Mon ami, your pants, shirt and socks are in the living room where you left them. Your underwear is on the floor next to the hot tub. You left your ditty bag on the kitchenette counter. You should get it and brush your teeth before you leave. Your breath is absolutely horrid."

"How can you tell anything about my breath from over there? You're five feet away from me."

"Bad odors carry a long way. Would you consider coming back here and meeting for me for dinner about six o'clock? It will be my treat. Then perhaps you can show me around the area afterwards?"

"No!" Mack stood up beside the bed and he was naked as a jaybird. "Get your ass going so I can get my clothes on and get out of here!"

"Mon ami, aren't you going to wait for me to leave first? You might embarrass me."

"Quite frankly Frenchy, I don't give a rat's ass if I embarrass you or not. It's not my problem."

"Mon ami, I told you never to call me Frenchy," the Frenchman softly whispered as he slowly backed up and shook his right index finger in Mack's face from the safety of the bedroom doorway. "My name is Francois."

"Your name's crap!" Mack shouted as he lunged headfirst towards the Frenchman's finger. He missed and the panicked Frenchman dashed out the front door.

"I'll deal with you later," Mack muttered as he crawled across the carpeted floor towards his pants and shirt.

Chapter 20

Mack stopped at Denny's on U.S 1 just south of Monterey Road for breakfast and it was 9:27 A.M. when he pulled into the Port Sewall Marina parking lot.

Ralph was rocking back and forth in a wicker rocking chair on the front porch of the marina cottage. A 'boom' box sat on the wooden porch beside him, his eyes were closed and he was listening to Jimmy Buffet pound out *Maragaritaville*. Ralph didn't notice that Mack pulled his blue Ford F-150 pickup truck within three feet of his bare feet. Mack blew the truck's horn to get Ralph's undivided attention.

Ralph's eyes flew open and he leaped to his feet. "What the hell did you do that for?"

Ralph shouted in Mack's direction. "I wasn't sleeping on the job! I was listening to Jimmy Buffet. You should try listening to cultured music for a change. It'll expand your horizons."

Mack slipped out of the truck cab, slammed the door shut and reached the porch in two steps. "I'm certain that listening to *Maragaritaville* over and over again out of that symphonic orchestra quality instrument at full volume would expand my mental horizons. Exactly what job do you have over here?"

"I was watching the place for you while you were gone."

"Exactly what were you watching for?"

"I was scaring away the wild elephants so they wouldn't sneak in and eat the hibiscus bushes. Playing loud music to scare elephants away is an old African safari guide trick."

"I don't see any elephants and the hibiscus bushes look just fine to me."

"See! The system works. No elephants snuck in."

"Ralph, be serious. What are you doing over here so early in the morning? Did Joy throw you out of the house for messing around with those smelly armpit sweat sex pheromones again?"

"Naw. I thought that you were coming back last night and I waited for you. When you didn't show up I figured that something bad happened to you."

"What made you think I was coming back last night? I don't think that I gave you my itinerary or did I?"

"Naw. You didn't even tell me that you were going anywhere, but when I stopped over here Monday morning you were gone and the dog was hungry. Elmo said that he stopped by and had coffee with you about eight o'clock, but then you disappeared."

"Where's my dog?"

"He's over at the house and Joy's taking him shopping at Pet Smart this morning. Where have you been since Monday?"

"I had to make an unexpected trip out of town."

"Next time call me and tell that you're going and I'll come over and get your dog. You don't have to be secretive with me. I know that you do some weird stuff that you can't talk about."

"Thanks Ralph. I'll keep that in mind the next time. What made you think that I was coming home last night?"

"My cousin saw you at the West Palm Beach airport about five o'clock yesterday afternoon. He called me and told me that you were leaving with some weird guy that looked like a terrorist. He wanted to warn me about the guy in case you brought him here."

"How would your cousin know who I am?"

"He said that your name's on a security watch list and they keep tabs on you every time you fly in and out of the West Palm Beach Airport. Did you have a good time at the Holiday Inn last night?"

"What makes you think that I was at the Holiday Inn?"

"Your truck was parked in the parking lot."

"How do you know that?"

"My cousin told me."

"How could your cousin tell you that? He's in West Palm Beach!"

"Not that cousin. It was a different one. I have lots of cousins. My daddy had four brothers and three sisters. My cousins are everywhere. When my cousin in West Palm called and told me that you were giving that French terrorist guy a ride to the Holiday Inn in Jensen Beach I called my cousin up there, he works night security, and told him to keep on eye on you."

"What did he tell you?"

"He told me that you pulled in about nine o'clock and went to the lounge with that French guy. You both started in drinking wine. You switched to draft beer and the next thing he knew you were shooting down shots of tequila like they were bottled water."

"What else did he tell you?"

"He said that you're a damn good karaoke singer, but you hogged the microphone all night and no one else could get a shot at it."

"What else?"

"They threw you and the French guy out when they closed the place at two o'clock in the morning and he bought three bottles of red wine from the bar tender. He must've been planning a big party for later in his room. Did you guys have a couple of hookers? Come on Mack. You can tell me."

"No! There weren't any hookers. It was just him and me."

"Oh, that puts a different slant on things," Ralph responded as he thoughtfully stroked his chain with the fingers of his left hand. "Stop right there! Don't tell me any of the sordid details. I don't want to know any more."

"I'm sure you don't!" Mack shouted as he reached down, grabbed the legs of the rocking chair and jerked forward.

The chair flipped over backwards and Ralph rode it to the floor.

"Maybe this will give you a case of amnesia!" Mack wiped his hands on his pants, threw the cottage door open and stomped inside.

Ralph regained his footing and followed him inside.

"Mack, don't take it so seriously," Ralph pleaded as he walked behind Mack, but far enough away so that Mack couldn't reach him. "I won't tell anyone about your little secret."

Mack stopped in mid-stride and Ralph almost bumped into him.

"What little secret are you blabbering about?" Mack asked. "I don't have any little secrets!"

"Oh, you know," Ralph coughed slightly as he whispered and looked down at his feet.

"No! I don't know! Clear it up for me Ralph! Spit it out!"

"That you like guys," Ralph mumbled under his breath as he looked down at his feet. "No wonder Tina gets frustrated when she comes up here for the weekend."

"What? Are you nuts?"

"Didn't you spend the night in that French guy's room? My cousin saw you leaving about eight o'clock this morning and the French guy left first. My cousin said that the French guy was in a big hurry to get out of there."

"You bet he was. I'd killed him if I could've got my hands on his skinning ass!"

"Don't yell at me. It's not my fault that you're mad at him."

"I'm not yelling. I'm trying to make a point and I want you to clearly understand me."

"I know nothing," Ralph replied and put his left hand over his mouth to emphasis his sincerity. "Your secret's safe with me."

"What secret? I don't have any secrets!"

"Perhaps that was a poor choice of words. I never was any

good in English. I meant that I wasn't here this morning and I don't have a cousin who works at the Holiday Inn in Jensen Beach and he doesn't know anything either."

"That's better. Now what's been going on here since I left on Monday? Has Tina been calling?"

"She called Tuesday and told me that you didn't answer the phone. She asked me to check on you."

"What did you tell her?"

"I told her that the marina's phone is out of order."

"She won't buy that."

"She did. The phone really is out of order. Someone cut three feet out of the drop wire that comes off the telephone pole. Somebody didn't want you talking to anybody."

"Who did it?'

"Either a very tall guy, someone with a bucket truck or maybe a tree trimmer on a pole."

"Is it fixed yet?"

"Yep. The phone company ran a new drop wire on Wednesday. The phone works fine now."

"What did the repair guy say about it?"

"He couldn't figure out why somebody would cut three feet out of the drop wire if they just wanted to harass you. It was like they wanted to be sure that you couldn't splice it back together."

"Whatever. Did anything exciting happened around here while I was gone?"

"Just some more sub stuff," Ralph responded as put his hand over his mouth to stifle a yawn.

"What do you mean by some sub stuff?"

"While you were gone some of the charterboat captains spotted a black submarine on the surface out by Push Button Hill on Tuesday morning. When they tried to get close it filled up its ballast tubes and sank to the bottom. They tracked in on SONAR for a couple of hours while it cruised around."

"How long did they track it?"

"Until about eleven-thirty. They all pulled out when it came time for them to get back to the dock and drop off their noon charter parties."

"Whose sub was it?"

"Some of the charter captains think it's the ghost of a Nazi sub that was sunk off of the St. Lucie Inlet during WW II."

"I doubt that. It was probably a research sub from Harbor Branch or a Navy sub from the AUTEC Test Center in the Bahamas."

"Doesn't AUTEC work on anti-submarine warfare?"

"Usually."

"Why would an AUTEC sub be in so close to shore and up here? Don't they do most of their deep water testing stuff in the Turks and Caicos Islands?"

"That's true. How far out is Push Button Hill from the St. Lucie Inlet?"

"About ten miles. The LORAN coordinates of the center are 43055.6 and 61962.5 It's in five hundred feet of water."

"How deep is the water over it?"

"It comes up to within three hundred feet of the surface."

"That's more than enough water for even the largest nuclear sub. The distance from the keel to the top of their sail is about sixty feet."

"What do you think it was doing here?"

"I don't know. You might pass the story on to the media. They'll find out. What do you know about a dolphin stranding by the Holiday Inn on Jensen Beach this week?"

"That happened late Tuesday afternoon. The people at Harbor Branch said that the leader of the pod had a bad case of ear mites, ran up on the beach and the rest of them followed her. They all died. Those animals are just plain stupid! Why would all of them follow the leader up on the beach and die themselves? It doesn't make any sense to me."

"It doesn't make any sense to me either."

"The charterboat captains down at Sailfish Marina reported the sub to the Coast Guard station in Fort Pierce."

"What did the Coast Guard tell them?"

"They told them not to worry about it."

"Have any of the charterboat captains seen the sub since Tuesday?"

"Naw. They followed it on SONAR as it cruised around and settled down on the bottom on top of Push Button Hill in three hundred feet of water. One captain recorded it on graph paper."

"Did any of them notice anything unusual when they spotted the sub?"

"A couple of the captains said that their color video depth finders flashed red over the whole screen a couple of times, but settled down after that. They figured that the sub sent out an electronic countermeasure signal to screw up their SONAR so they couldn't track it. But they did anyway."

"Anything else?"

"Like what?"

"I don't know what. I'm just asking."

"There was a strange-looking purse seiner hanging just off the beach."

"Why did you call it strange-looking?"

"It didn't have any name painted on the bow, or any commercial numbers painted on the side. Why don't you stop down at Sailfish Marina and talk to the boys when they come in from their half-day trips. They can fill you in better than I can."

"I think I will," Mack responded as he led Ralph towards the front door. "Ralph, I have to take a shower and get cleaned up. I have a few things to do around here and then I'm going down to the Blake Library and do some research."

"What kind of research?"

"I'm going to look up your genealogy."

"What's that?"

"Your family history."

"Why would you want to do that?"

"I want to know how many cousins you have."

"I know all of them on my daddy's side. They're all boys. But if I tried to name off the ones on my mother's side I might miss a few. That side of the family breeds like swamp rats."

"That's what I figured." Mack gently shoved Ralph out onto the front porch. "Stop by later when you have more time to talk and take good care of my dog. Goodbye Ralph." Mack closed the front door and slipped the deadbolt closed.

"I doubt that Ralph even knows how many brothers and sisters he has," Mack chuckled under his breath as he shook his head from side to side and headed for the bathroom and a hot shower.

Chapter 21

Mack entered the Blake Library, turned to his left and headed for the reference desk. Janet, his stalwart friend, spotted him immediately and stood up to greet him. An impish grin spread across her face.

"So, Mr. McCray, where have you been this time? Back to Chicago to meet with some of your shadowy friends in some seedy bar?"

"Something like that and most of it's surreal at best. It's hard for even me to believe it and I was there!"

"I understand, or at least I think I do, but sometimes I wonder about you."

"What did you find out about the mask?"

"You won't believe it! I checked with the Smithsonian

Institution in Washington and this mask was discovered in nineteen sixty-six by an archaeologist from Yale during the excavation of the temple of *King Hanab Pakal* in the city of *Chich'en Itza* in *Pejen Province* in Guatemala. It was a funeral mask for an Olmec king who lived in the city of *El Mirador* in Guatemala."

Janet continued, "The Olmec civilization was pre-Mayan and disappeared in five fifty BC. There were thirteen Olmec kings and only eleven of their burial masks have been found. The masks are in museums and private collections all over the world."

"Why isn't this mask in a museum or private collection?"

"It was photographed, cataloged and placed in a locked collection box for shipment back to the Smithsonian. When the box was opened the mask was gone and a granite river rock was in its place. The mask hasn't been seen until now."

"Are you sure about all of that?"

"Here's a color photo of the mask directly out of the Smithsonian Olmec catalog," Janet responded as she handed Mack a white sheet of paper. "I pulled it off the Internet and printed it out for you."

"That's it!" Mack exclaimed. "That's the same mask that Carlos had behind the bar. Does the catalog say what type of stone it's made from?"

"It's carved out of green jadeite."

"That's it! The mask glowed green from the reflected light off the bar mirror. I have to find out how Octavio got it!"

"You can sell it for a small fortune. I checked Sotheby's website and they sold an Olmec stone mask similar to this for seventy-five thousand dollars two years ago."

"I can't sell it."

"Why not?"

"It's not mine. It belongs to a Guatemalan laborer in Indiantown. He claims that it's a family heirloom passed down for several generations. But there's a big problem."

"What kind of problem?"

"He's sitting behind bars in the Martin County Jail. Last week the owner of the Silver Saddle bar in Indiantown accepted the mask as partial payment of a bar tab. Saturday night the

Guatemalan came back to the bar, held a knife to the bartender's throat and demanded that he give him the mask back."

"What happened then?"

"The bartender pushed his emergency 'panic' button, Elmo showed up and arrested the Guatemalan for assault with a deadly weapon and attempted grand theft. His trial's scheduled for next week in front of Judge Greg Melton."

"What a story! Mr. McCray you truly live life on the edge."

"Now I understand."

"What do you understand Mr. McCray? I'm confused."

"The mask is Octavio's symbol of authority over the other Guatemalans in the labor camp. Without the mask he's nothing but chopped liver."

"Who is Octavio?"

"He's the Guatemalan who tried to steal the mask from the bar in Indiantown. I have to find it and get in back in his possession or the Guatemalans in Indiantown are apt to hurt someone."

"What do you mean by hurt someone?"

"The Maya believe that human blood sacrifices are necessary to cleanse evil spirits and bad omens away. The Guatemalans in Indiantown built an altar out of discarded wood sod pallets in the piney woods next to the Naked Lady Ranch on Martin Grade."

"How do you know that?"

"The bartender told me. He's scared half to death of them because he was the last person to have the mask in his possession. He figures that they might go after him and it might be too late to do anything about it."

"This is the twenty-first century! No culture practices human sacrifice. You're overreacting."

"I hope that you're correct. I have to get hold of Elmo and get back over to Indiantown!"

Mack turned, started to walk away from the reference desk, paused and came back to the reference desk like a scene from the television series *Baretta*.

"Janet, I just thought of something else."

"What else can I help you with?"

"Can you do some research for me on military and civilian mind control experiments?"

"Can you be more specific? I believe that the CIA conducted experiments with LSD in the nineteen-sixties."

"That's old news. I'm looking for civilian and military non-lethal warfare applications involving the use of electromagnetic wave transmissions to stimulate the human brain's Alpha waves above and below the earth's resonant frequency of seven point three Hertz. That means cycles per second."

"I hope all of that mumbo jumbo makes sense to you. I don't understand a word you said."

"Actually it is a simple concept that goes back into history for thousands of years. Have you ever seen people practicing meditation where they sit with their legs crossed and their palms facing upward as they hum?"

"Yes, and it always sounded more like a moan to me."

"They are humming the Hindu word *ohm* and attempting to bring their own brain's Alpha waves in alignment with the earth's resonant frequency of seven point three Hertz. Does that make sense to you now?"

"Of course. I'll check on the Internet. Stop by tomorrow and I'll let you know what I found,"

"Thanks." Mack started to turn away and paused. "Janet, there's one other small thing."

"What's that?"

"Can you run the names Guido Cameri, Rocco Pirelli, and Johnny Amorati through your computer data base? They live in Melrose Park, Illinois. That's a suburb of Chicago."

"I know where Melrose Park is! That's very close to Cicero where Al Capone's gang hung out. That's a very dangerous area. Where did you meet these guys?"

"In a seedy karaoke bar," Mack winked. "They gave me a ride to the airport yesterday."

"Were you in back Chicago stirring things up again?"

"Maybe." Mack winked at Janet with his right eye, gave her a thumb's up, turned and headed for the library lobby.

"*I wonder if that man knows if he is coming or going?*" Janet whispered under her breath to herself. "*One of these days I expect to read in the newspaper that he's disappeared from the face of the earth.*"

Chapter 22

Mack stopped for lunch at the Taste of Italy Italian restaurant in the Publix Shopping Center in Stuart. Afterwards he headed for Sailfish Marina in the Manatee Pocket.

It was 1:37 P.M. when he pulled out of the Publix parking lot and headed for US 1. He knew that the charterboat captains would be back from their half-day trips and be lounging around in the tackle shop telling fish stories. Each one would try to out do the other. Mack figured that they would be willing to provide some details about the submarine episode.

"I wonder if that weird French guy has any connection to the submarine sighting and the pilot whale stranding on Jensen Beach on Tuesday?" Mack tossed thoughts around in his head as he made the left turn off of Old Dixie Highway onto St. Lucie

Boulevard and headed for Sailfish Marina. *"Ben Brown told me something about some Navy experiments with EMP technology."*

When Mack pulled into an open space in the Sailfish Marina parking lot he noticed a white Ford Crown Victoria with a white U.S. Government license plate in the adjoining space.

"I wonder what the Feds are doing here?" He thought. *"Maybe it's Customs, or the DEA, doing some ground work for a drug bust. It's none of my concern and I'm going to keep my nose out of whatever it is."*

He shrugged his shoulders and headed for the tackle shop next to the boat brokerage office.

Three local captains lounging around the live bait tank under the porch eaves nodded at Mack in recognition, but didn't offer a salutation or verbal greeting. They acted as if they didn't know whom he was and could have cared less.

"Maybe I smell bad," Mack muttered under his breath as he nodded back.

One of the captains tilted his head up three times in the direction of the fuel dock and then turned his back to Mack.

"Now what?" Mack thought as he stopped and turned to face the wooden dock that extended 100-feet out into the dark, murky water of the Manatee Pocket.

Two men in long sleeved white shirts and ties were talking with two charterboat captains at the 'T' formed by two perpendicular piers at the end of the dock. The large red and white Citgo fuel sign over their heads glistened with reflected sunlight.

Both men frowned and one of them pointed towards the St. Lucie Inlet as if making a point. They shook their heads from side to side and shrugged their shoulders. The two men wearing long sleeved white shirts slowly shook their heads from side to side as the two charterboat captains slowly walked away from them in the direction of the tackle shop.

"Maybe those guys are DEA agents looking for an easy bust," Mack thought. *"The days of pulling in bales of 'square grouper' from mother ships offshore passed in the early 1980's. Whatever they're here for must have something to do with illegal Haitians coming in from the Bahamas."*

When the two nervous charterboat captains passed Mack on their way to the tackle shop one of them hissed under his breath.

"Mack, if you know what's good for you you'll hit the bricks and get out of here before Huey and Louie spot you. They're not taking 'no' for an answer."

Before Mack could respond, or ask a question, the two captains were out of earshot.

"*What the hell are they talking about? I haven't done anything,*" he thought.

"Mr. McCray! Stay right there please," echoed a deep authoritarian man's voice from the direction of the fuel dock. "We have a few questions we'd like to ask you."

Mack froze in place and turned slightly to his right so that he could see the fuel dock. The two men in long sleeved shirts were briskly walking in his direction. One of the men was black, stood at least 6 feet 6 inches tall and easily weighed 300 pounds. His shaven head made him resemble a black Mr. Clean.

Mack shook his head in disbelief as he mumbled under his breath.

"*That's Harold Bellefonte' from Jamaica. I haven't seen 'Slick Willie' since we pulled off that caper with the plastic sphinx statue a few weeks ago. I wonder what he's doing back here?*"

The other man was white, middle-aged, perhaps 6 feet tall and sported a black goatee and a full head of curly black hair.

"*I never saw that guy before,*" Mack thought. "*This must be serious business if Slick Willie has a partner.*"

It only took the two men a matter of seconds to reach Mack's side and the black man opened the conversation. "Mack, I'm sorry to bother you, but we have to ask you a few questions."

"That's fine Harold," Mack replied with a grin as he extended his open right hand. "Who's your buddy? I thought that you always worked alone."

"I'm sorry. I should have introduced him. Mack, this is John Cyr." The white man extended his right hand. "John's in south Florida on temporary assignment from Honolulu to observe our drug interdiction methods."

"It's nice to meet you Mr. McCray," the white man offered as he vigorously shook Mack's hand.

"Harold has told me a lot about you. I'm impressed."

"I hope that he didn't tell you everything," Mack offered as he winked at the black man. "Harold, you did hold a few things back from him didn't you?"

"Of course," he quipped as he winked at Mack.

"Harold, exactly what can I do for you? I've been out of town since Monday and I don't know anything about drug interdiction."

"That's not why we're here," the black man responded.

"If we were looking for drugs we'd be down here at night," the white man offered with a smug grin. "Everyone knows that the drug smugglers only work at night."

"Of course," Mack responded. "It would be much too obvious to bring a boat loaded with drugs through the inlet in the middle of the day when dozens of other boats are coming through at the same time."

"We know," the black man responded. "We went past your place yesterday and again early this morning. No one was there. Exactly when did you get back in town?"

"It's a long story."

"Didn't your plane arrive in West Palm Beach about six o'clock?"

"I got in town last night. Let's leave it at that."

"What do you know about a submarine that was spotted of the St. Lucie Inlet on Tuesday afternoon?" The black man asked.

"Nothing. I was in Chicago on Tuesday."

"What were you doing in Chicago?" The curly-haired white man spurted out as he prepared to make notes in his notebook.

"John, that's none of our business," the black man quipped.

"I was singing in a karaoke bar on Grand Avenue."

"What were you doing in a karaoke bar?" The white man asked with a gotcha' grin on his face.

"I was interviewing for a disc jockey's job."

"John, that's enough!" The black man stated. "Let's get back to basics."

"Mr. McCray, have you seen a weird-looking French guy wearing a thin black mustache?"

"No. Should I?"

"Maybe and maybe not. His name's Francois Batteau," the white man offered. "He's from France and he studies dolphins and whales."

"Most Frenchmen are from France," Mack offered. "Is there something unusual about that?"

"This one might be a foreigner."

"Most people from other countries are foreigners."

"That's not what I meant," the white man corrected himself as his face reddened. "I meant that he might be a foreign agent."

"Why would the French send such an obvious-looking spy to Stuart, Florida?"

"Mack, you know that the intelligence community believes in making things so obvious that they can't be seen," the black man offered. "The agency feels that this guy is up to something and they want us to find out what it is."

"He told me that he studies whale and dolphins."

"Aha!" The white man sputtered as he hastily scribbled in his notebook. "So, you do know him don't you?"

"He sat across the aisle from me on the flight from Atlanta to West Palm Beach."

"Mack, did he tell you why he's here?" The black man asked.

"He said that he was here to study a pod of dolphins that beached themselves north of the Holiday Inn on Tuesday. He told me that someone from Harbor Branch was supposed to pick him up at the airport and they didn't show up. I gave him a ride to the Holiday Inn from the airport."

"We checked with Harbor Branch and they don't know who he is!" The white man stated as he continued scribbling in his notebook. "There's no dolphins on the beach anymore. The Navy had a sea-going tug in the area and they sent it in to haul them away on Wednesday."

"Did they have a purse seiner out there too?"

"How do you know about the purse seiner?" The white man responded as he scribbled furiously.

"I saw it when the plane flew over Jensen Beach last night."

"That was a Navy research vessel," the black man responded. "They were in the area studying ocean bottom contours. It just looks like a purse seiner."

"Did the French guy say anything about the submarine?" The white man asked. His black, government-issued ballpoint pen was poised to take more notes.

"No. He only talked about the reasons why dolphins and whales beach themselves and mentioned that his brother did some work with dolphins on Coconut Island in Hawaii."

"I know exactly where Coconut Island is," detective John Cyr responded as he made notes. "It's in Kaneohe Bay on the west side of the marine base on Mokapu Peninsula. I used to go surfing over there when I was in high school."

"I know where it is too," Mack offered. "I've been there and I wasn't surfing."

"When were you there?"

"John, let's not go there," the black man responded. "I know when Mr. McCray was on Coconut Island and why he was there."

"How do you know that?"

"Sometimes you get on my nerves with your questions," The black man growled as he lightly tugged on the white man's left arm. "Let's go!"

"I'm not ready to go yet! I have more questions for him!"

"He's answered all of the questions that he needs answer for now." The black man's voice had dropped several octaves and came out almost as a soft growl. "I said let's go!"

"Why?" The white man whined. "I'm just getting warmed up."

"Because if you don't come with me right now I'm going to leave you here alone with him. You won't like that."

"Why not?"

"Because he'll turn your skinny ass inside out and feed it to the fishes before you can blink!"

"Hold on a minute! I'm coming!" The white man responded as he slowly tucked his pen in his jacket pocket and looked Mack directly in the eyes. "Mr. McCray, I advise you not to leave town. We may have some more questions for you."

"John, you must have a mouse in your pocket because I don't have any questions for him," the black man offered with a wink in Mack's direction as he turned and headed for the marina parking lot. "Are you coming with me or are you staying here?" he called over his right shoulder.

"I'm coming!" The white man responded as he stuffed his notepad in his shirt pocket. "Where're we going?"

"To the Holiday Inn on Jensen Beach," the black man shouted over his right shoulder. "If we find that French guy you can ask him questions until you're blue in the face."

"Can you speak French?" Mack asked.

"Why should I speak French?"

"He doesn't speak English."

"Crap! I know he's a spy now! I can feel it in my guts."

"I think it's your lunch," Mack offered. "You might want to stop at the rest rooms in Sandsprit Park before you leave. It's a long drive up to Jensen Beach."

"Thanks," the white man hitched up his pants and ran towards the parking lot and the white Ford Crown Victoria.

"You'd better hurry," Mack offered through clenched teeth. "I hope you crap in your hula skirt."

Mack turned and saw the two charterboat captains lounging around next the live bait tank. The older captain made a motion with his head indicating that Mack should join them. Mack obliged and headed for the live bait tank.

Push Button Hill

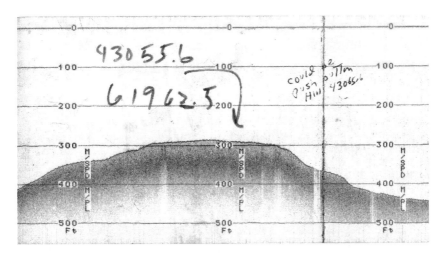

Chapter
23

Mack glanced at the marina parking lot out of the corner of his right eye without turning his head as he approached the tackle shop and the two captains lounging beside the live bait tank. The white Ford Crown Victoria was nowhere in sight.

"I'm glad that Slick got his temporary partner under control before he got in so deep that he couldn't get out," Mack thought as he sauntered towards the waiting captains. *"One more question in the wrong direction and that guy would have gone back to Hawaii in a box."*

"Hey Mack!" The older captain offered as he nodded his head to indicate that Mack should follow him around the corner of the building. "Captain Scott will watch the parking lot for us."

"Now what the hell is going on?" Mack thought as he stepped

onto the wooden porch, nodded his head at the younger captain and followed the older captain around the corner of the corrugated metal building. The west side of the building was shielded from the main road by several large yachts supported on metal stands. They were in the yard for bottom jobs and other maintenance functions.

When Mack came around the corner the waiting captain held the fingertips of his right hand against his lips as a signal for Mack not to talk.

"Don't ask me any questions, or say a word," he whispered. "Someone's been following me since Tuesday afternoon and my house was broken into last night while my wife and I were out to dinner at Shrimper's. Someone wants what I've got and it's not worth dying for."

"What is it?" Mack stammered.

"I told you not to talk! Just keep your mouth shut and listen. I'm only going to say this once! Do you understand?"

Mack nodded his head in acknowledgement of the order.

"I was fishing out on Push Button Hill Tuesday morning when that sub showed up. I figured that something was going on and took some digital photos of it and also the purse seiner that was hanging off the beach. I also recorded the sub on my graph recorder when it sat down on the bottom. I stashed the graph paper and the disk from the digital camera in a plastic freezer bag and taped it inside my hat. Bernie in the tackle shop will give it to you if you ask him for a blue baseball cap with the Sailfish Marina logo on it. Do you understand?"

Mack slowly nodded his head up and down.

"*Why does this guy want me to have this stuff? He's half scared to death.*" Mack thought. "*I don't want to be involved in whatever's going on.*"

"I don't care what you do with it, but get it away from here and don't tell anyone where you got it."

Mack slowly nodded his head up and down.

"I was in the Navy submarine service for four years and I spent some time over at the AUTEC Base in the Turks and Caicos Islands. I know that something big is going on and I don't want to be a part of it. If they know that I've got this stuff my life won't be worth a plugged nickel."

"*If he suspects that his life is in danger why is he giving it to me?*" Mack thought. "*I don't want it either.*"

"I know what you're thinking. You want to know why I'm giving the stuff to you. I saw several piot whales and a bunch of dolphins leaping out of the water like a sea monster was after them just before that sub surfaced. The purse seiner ran a catch boat with a net around them, but the pilot whales leaped right over the top of the net floats. All of the dolphins got caught and the purse seiner crew hauled them onboard."

"*This doesn't sound good,*" Mack thought. "*But now it all ties together. No wonder Slick and his buddy were down here.*"

"That big black guy and his dork buddy from Hawaii were putting pressure on me when you drove up. I told them that I didn't know anything and that I wasn't there. But, they had the Fort Pierce Coast Guard Station's radio log and an audiotape from Tuesday. I'm on the tape. The Hawaiian dork played it for me out of a digital pocket recorder."

"*This guy should learn to keep his mouth shut,*" Mack thought.

"The black guy told me that they know that I recorded the sub on graph paper because my voice is on the audio tape. They want the graph paper and digital camera. I gave them the camera, but the disk wasn't in it. I told them that the graph paper got wet and I threw it away yesterday. They spent twenty minutes going through the marina dumpster looking for it before they finally figured out that the city emptied the dumpster early this morning."

Mack couldn't restrain himself any longer.

"Why did you tell the Coast Guard that you recorded the sub and took pictures of it?' He asked.

"I was excited! I thought that it was a Russkie sub checking our coastline perimeter defenses."

"What do you expect me to do?"

"Everyone in town knows that you used to do secret government stuff. If it was a Russkie sub you're the only one in town that can get the material to the right people."

"I'm not involved any longer. I retired when I moved to Stuart in March."

"That doesn't matter. Everyone knows that you never get out of the mafia, or a government intelligence agency. Mack, you still have the contacts; you know who to get the stuff to and how to do it. I don't."

"I wasn't in the mafia!"

"I didn't say that you were. I also said government intelligence agency in the same sentence."

"I'll see what I can do."

"Thanks Mack. I'm counting on you. If anything happens to you because of this I'll feel guilty."

"Don't worry about it. Nothing will happen to me."

"What did those two yahoos want with you?"

"They wanted to know how to find Jensen Beach. I gave them directions."

"They'll be back."

"What makes you think that?"

"They didn't find what they were looking for. Mack, I've got to run. My mate's got the boat cleaned up and we have a three o'clock half-day trip." The captain raised his right hand in a stop gesture. "Wait here until I get halfway down the dock." The captain whispered. "They might be back already."

Mack nodded in acknowledgement, took a deep breath and slowly shook his head from side to side as he watched the captain confidently stride down the asphalt towards the floating dock.

"I'd better get down to the library and find out what Janet turned up on my Chicago karaoke bar buddies," Mack thought as he slipped around the corner of the building and headed for the marina tackle shop. *"I hope that Bernie knows which baseball cap I'm supposed to buy."*

Chapter 24

Mack pulled into the library parking lot at 3:52 P.M. and headed for the reference desk. Janet saw him coming and stood up to greet him.

"Why do you insist on continuously pushing the envelope," Janet blurted out as she shook her right index finger at Mack as a gesture of warning. "You've really done it this time buster."

"What are you talking about? I haven't done anything!"

"Do you recall those three people in Chicago that you asked me to check out for you?"

"Of course I do! I don't have Alzheimer's yet. I asked you to check out Guido Cameri, Rocco Pirelli and Johnny Amorati. What did you find out?"

"They are all mobsters! You're lucky that you came back in

one piece! They could have stuck you in the trunk of a car and left you at the airport if you said the wrong thing to them."

"I know that. So what? What did you find out about them?"

"You might not like what I found out."

"Why not?"

"It's very serious and you may not want to know in case you meet them again."

"Go ahead and tell me. I'll act surprised."

"That you know that Guido Cameri was a mobster?"

"Yes. He told me."

"He was the right hand man for the famous Chicago mobster Charlie Mangini who was murdered in his kitchen while he was cooking sausages for dinner. The murder was never solved."

"I know. Guido told me that the Federal agents protecting Mangini did it."

"What? Then he told you everything about himself?"

"Maybe. What else did you find out about him?"

"He was sent to prison several times for extortion, state sales tax evasion and a series of other crimes."

"I know. He told me."

"Did he also tell you that he was kidnapped by the Mexican mafia and held for a million dollars ransom in a moving truck stored in a vacant warehouse?"

"Yep. He told me. His stories all check out with what you told me. What about Rocco Pirelli?"

"He was Cameri's right hand man. He has spent time in prison for bank embezzlement, extortion, assault with a deadly weapon and theft. He was released from Illinois State Prison in Joliet a week ago after completing a seven year sentence for bank embezzlement."

"I know. He told me."

"Is there anything you don't know about these people?"

"Most likely. I don't know why they took a liking to me and which one of them took me to the airport Wednesday morning. What did you find out about Johnny Amorati?"

"He was the assistant chief of police in Stone Park and was convicted Monday for embezzlement of police department funds. He was sentenced to fifteen years in state prison. He reported to

Joliet State Prison on Thursday to begin serving his sentence."

"That's what he told me."

"Well now Mr. McCray! You seem to know just about everything. Why did you ask me to research them for you if you already knew all about them?"

"I was just verifying what they told me. I need information about someone else."

"Another Chicago mobster I suppose?"

"No. You might actually like this guy."

'Why should I like him?"

"He's French."

"*Oui! Oui!* What's this mystery man's name?"

"Francois Batteau. He's a French marine scientist and he specializes in the mysterious behavior of whales and dolphins that causes them to beach themselves and die."

"He should have been here to witness the dolphin grounding on Jensen Beach on Tuesday. Maybe he could have figured out why they did it. No one locally had any answers. They blamed it on ear mites."

"He's here. I met him on the flight from Atlanta to West Palm Beach and I gave him a ride from the airport to the Holiday Inn on Jensen Beach."

"Oh. Did he provide any insight as to why the dolphins beached themselves?"

"He said that the entire pod could have suffered inner ear infections that caused them to lose their orientation, or maybe a sick leader that led the pod ashore rather than drowning at sea. Whales and dolphins are mammals that migrated to the sea millions of years ago and they have a fear of drowning like any other mammal.'

"I see. Is there any other information that you can give me about Mr. Batteau to help me research him?"

"His brother Jacques worked at a top secret Navy research facility on Coconut Island on Oahu in Hawaii. He drowned while taking a morning swim by himself."

"That seems very unusual. Oahu is well known for the gentle surf conditions on its eastern side."

"How did you know what side of Oahu Coconut Island is on?"

"I went to Honolulu last year on vacation and I took a narrated bus tour around the island."

"I see. Would you research the faculties of all French universities that have a marine mammal program? The French guy said that he was from Paris and alluded that he was a university researcher."

"No problem. Is there anything else that I can help you with?"

"Did you find out anything about military or civilian experiments in electromagnetic wave transmission and mind control?"

"You only asked me about it this morning. I have more things to do all day than to just research off the wall things for you."

"I understand. I'll try to stop by tomorrow to check on your progress. Do you think that you can fit me into your busy schedule tomorrow?"

"Mr. McCray, don't be factious!" Janet reached for a wooden ruler that was strategically placed alongside her computer keyboard. "I strongly suggest that you find your way out of the library before I lambaste you across the knuckles with this ruler."

"I'm leaving," Mack mumbled as he turned and headed for the library exit. "I have things to do."

It was 4:27 P.M. when Mack pulled out of the library parking lot and turned south on Monterey Road. It was then that he realized that he forgot to ask Janet if she had found out anything more about the Olmec mask.

Chapter 25

Mack rounded the bend on Old St. Lucie Boulevard, Port Sewall Marina came into sight and he spotted Ralph and the Frenchman sitting in matching whicker rocking chairs on the front porch. Ralph waved at Mack and Francois gave him a mock French military salute.

"*What the hell's going on?*" Mack thought to himself as he pulled into a parking space in front of the marina cottage. "*What is that crazy Frenchman doing here?*"

When Mack slipped out of his truck Ralph gave him a hearty wave and a verbal salutation.

"Mack! It's about time you got back! Look who I found! Francois is going to spend the night right here in the cottage with you. He told me that you guys met on the flight from Atlanta to

West Palm Beach."

Ralph you have some explaining to do," Mack retorted as he stood in the pea gravel walkway leading to the wooden porch. "What's he doing here?"

"I told you. He's going to spend the night with you and I'm going to drive him to West Palm in the morning. His flight for Paris leaves at ten-thirty."

"Mon ami, I brought three bottles of red wine for you," the anxious Frenchman offered. Of course it is a Merlot, but unfortunately it is not from France; it is from California."

"How did you get here?" Mack addressed Francois.

"I met Monsieur Ralph on the beach and when I told him that you spent the night in my room he was kind enough to give me a ride back to your cottage."

"I was gathering sand fleas on the beach and Francois stopped to ask directions," Ralph proudly offered. "He was looking for the dolphins that got stranded on the beach Tuesday afternoon. They were gone because the Navy sent in a tug to pick them up and dispose of them at sea. We got to gabbing and he told me that he met you on the plane and needed a place to stay tonight."

"So I heard."

"I figured that because you knew each other that it would be okay by you."

"Ralph, you are in for a very big surprise. I think that Frenchy is attracted to male sex pheromones."

"Mon ami! I told you to never call me Frenchy! My name is Francois!"

"I'm sorry. I forgot."

"Mack, he knows all about the sub that was out on Push Button Hill on Tuesday and the purse seiner that was hanging around the beach."

"I do not know everything Monsieur Ralph. I simply know what I read in the newspaper this morning."

"Why are you leaving so soon?" Mack inquired as he leaned against the porch railing. "You just got here."

"Mon ami, there is no work for me to do because the whales are gone. But because we had such a good time together last night I welcomed the opportunity to see you again."

"Why didn't you take a cab to the West Palm Beach Airport?"

"The hotel called a cab for me and they told me that it could not be there for two hours. When it did not show up I decided to take a walk on the beach and that is when I met Monsieur Ralph."

"What time was that?"

"Mon ami, I think it was about two o'clock."

"Mack, we loaded up his suitcases and stuff about three-thirty and headed down this way. We've been waiting for you since four-thirty. We had five bottles of red wine when we got here and already killed two of them. Francois was getting ready to pop open another bottle when we saw you pulling into the marina."

"Did a couple of guys stop and see you at the Holiday Inn before you left?"

"No mon ami."

"Are you sure?"

"I am certain mon ami. What did these men look like? Maybe I saw them."

"One of them was a very big black man with a bald head and the other one was a white man with very curly hair."

"I saw two guys that sounds like them pull up just as we were leaving the hotel," Ralph offered. "They were driving a white Ford Crown Victoria."

"That was them."

"Who are they?"

"It's not important now, but it is important that Frenchy gets on his way to the airport. I can't afford for him to be seen here."

"Mon ami, please call me Francois!"

"Sorry, I forgot."

Mack turned his attention back to Ralph.

"Ralph, take him over to the Holiday Inn on US 1 in Stuart and drop him off. They'll call a limo service for him."

"Mon ami, I want to stay with you tonight," Francois pleaded as he reached for his wallet. "I will pay you for my lodging."

"Money isn't the issue Francois. It's your safety and mine. You'll be much better off, and much safer, if you spend the night in West Palm Beach. There's a very nice Holiday Inn on Belvedere Road and they have a van service that takes you right to the airport."

"Mon ami, I will miss you."

"I'll miss you too, but we'll both get over it in a few days."

"Francois, I guess we're lucky that we left your stuff in my truck," Ralph offered as he attempted to get out of the rocking chair. "Let's get going. I can drop you off and be back home in time for dinner."

"Ralph, where's my dog?"

"He's at home with Joy. They went shopping at Pet Smart this morning and she bought a whole bunch of dog toys for him. She wants to keep him for a couple more days. Is that okay?"

"No problem. Keep him over the weekend. I have a feeling that I'll be kept very busy when Tina shows up tomorrow afternoon."

"Great! Joy will be thrilled."

"I bet that my dog will too."

"Mon ami, would you like to write to me at my office at the University of Paris? I can write down the address for you."

"That's okay Frenchy. I'll pass."

Mack turned to face Ralph.

"Ralph, load him up and get him to the Holiday Inn in West Palm Beach. It's almost five-thirty and they probably have a six o'clock shuttle run to the West Palm Beach Airport."

"We're on the way," Ralph responded as he took Francois by the hand and physically pulled him out of the rocking chair. "Let's get going big boy. We don't have much time."

After Ralph's green pickup truck pulled out of the marina drive and was headed down Old St. Lucie Boulevard Mack turned and entered the marina cottage. The telephone rang as if on cue.

"Now who wants me?" Mack muttered. *"It'd better not be Slick! I don't need to catch any more grief over that French nut!"*

Chapter 26

Friday morning snuck up on Mack as a single sunbeam streamed through the eastern window and slowly crept along the hardwood floor and across his face. It's shimmering ray lightly danced on and off his closed eyelids. He brushed it away with his hand, but it always came back. Two empty bottles of California Merlot lay on the floor next to the lounge chair and a half full bottle rested on the clear glass, oval-shaped coffee table.

Mack didn't know what time it was and he didn't care. Tina called the night before and put him on notice that he would be at her mercy for the weekend. She wanted to go Indiantown and ordered him to have her sailboat ready to go when she arrived after lunch. Feeling despondent over Thursday's events, and what the future held for him, Mack finished the first bottle of Merlot by seven o'clock. The second bottle lasted until almost eight o'clock and he didn't make it halfway through the third bottle before he fell asleep in his chair. A blue baseball cap, emblazoned with a Sailfish Marina logo, sat on the coffee table beside the open bottle of Merlot.

"Hey Mack! Are you going to sleep all day?" Ralph's voice bellowed through the open screen door and reverberated throughout the cottage. "It's almost ten o'clock and it's time for you to get your lazy butt out of bed!"

Ralph burst through the screen door and Mack slowly opened his eyes.

"Ralph! What the hell do you want? I was sleeping like a baby."

"Didn't you go to bed last night?"

"What are you talking about?"

"Look at yourself. You're wearing the same clothes you had on yesterday afternoon when I left here to take that nutty French guy to the Holiday Inn."

"Did you get him there in time to catch the shuttle van to the West Palm Beach Airport?"

Mack forced his eyes to open and brushed away the dancing sunbeam.

"The last airport shuttle left the Holiday Inn at five o'clock. I wound up driving him down to West Palm Beach and after he checked into the airport Holiday Inn he insisted that I have dinner with him. I didn't get home until almost ten o'clock and Joy was pissed."

"You're lucky. If you had stayed any longer he would've had you singing karaoke in the lounge and you might have woke up this morning feeling completely compromised."

"What are you talking about? I had two glasses of wine and a steak dinner at his expense. He never said anything about singing karaoke."

"You were lucky."

"What are you talking about? Oh, I know. You partied with him at the Jensen Beach Holiday Inn and thought that I would too. No way José. I'm straight and proud of it."

"I didn't party with him. We had a few drinks in the lounge, I was tired and flaked out in his room."

"That's not what my cousin told me," Ralph chuckled as he grinned from ear to ear.

"Get out of here and leave me alone! I want to take a shower and get cleaned up."

"Tina called my house a few minutes ago and told me to get over here and check on you. She's been calling you all morning and all she gets is a busy signal. Did you leave the phone of the hook again?"

"I don't think so. She called me right after you left yesterday and told me to get her sailboat ready to go by noon today. She wants to take it over to Indiantown for the weekend."

"That musta' really pissed you off."

"Why do you say that?"

"You ripped the phone off the kitchen wall. It's hanging by the cord."

"I don't remember doing it."

"I don't doubt that after swilling down two and a half bottles of wine. How's your head?"

"It feels like a ripe cantaloupe. I need some coffee."

"You need a shower too. You smell like a goat!"

"I don't think that there was a goat in here last night."

"That was a figure of speech. You need a shower really bad. I'll go to the house, call Tina back and tell her that you're okay. Do you want to go to the Queen Conch for breakfast after you get cleaned up?"

"Sounds good to me," Mack stood up very slowly and placed his right hand on the side of his head. "I'll meet you there in a half hour."

"Roger," Ralph responded as he slipped out of the screen door, skipped off the front porch of the cottage and headed for his green pickup truck.

Mack headed for the bathroom and a hot shower.

Chapter 27

Mack urged Ralph to keep his mouth shut about his overnight stay with the mysterious Frenchman as they dined on amble portions of scrambled eggs, a generous slice of country ham topped with a pineapple ring and fried potatoes. But Ralph goaded Mack to the point that Mack told him to shut up and stomped out of the Queen Conch in feigned disgust. Once he was outside the restaurant Mack headed for the Blake Library.

He pulled into the library parking lot at 11:13 A.M. and headed for the reference desk. To his chagrin Janet wasn't there. Jack, a serious-looking young man, manned the position.

"Jack, where's Janet?" Mack demanded. "I need to see her!"

"She's in the back office working on inter-library loans. There's no one else back there. Just walk in and interrupt her. She won't care if it's you," Jack offered with a smug grin as he made a gesture towards the reference department office with a casual wave of his left hand without taking his eyes off of his computer screen. "She's been expecting you."

"Thanks," Mack mumbled as he headed for the reference department office.

Mack cautiously pulled the reference office door open. Janet was seated at her desk busily typing on her computer keyboard with a large stack of pink inter-library loan request slips neatly piled beside her. She was deeply engrossed in the seriousness of her task and didn't notice Mack as he slipped through the door and allowed it to quietly close behind him. He took full advantage of Janet's concentration and softly tiptoed to a position to her right, and slightly behind her cubicle, just out of range of her peripheral vision.

"Boo!" He whispered.

"Oh my God!" Janet exclaimed as she almost jumped out of her skin and turned to face him. "Mr. McCray! You should know better than to be sneaking around inside the reference office! There's a large sign on the door that clearly states that only library employees are allowed in here." She settled down in her chair, feigned mopping her bow and returned to her computer input task.

"Janet, I didn't mean to scare you," Mack replied with a semi-sheepish grin as he walked around to the side of Janet's cubicle. "Have you found out anything for me about the French guy I asked you about yesterday?"

"Maybe and maybe not." Janet didn't look up from her computer screen. "It depends upon whether or not you are going to act like a gentleman and behave yourself when you are in the library."

"I promise."

"You promise to do what you said."

"Exactly what was that?" Janet's eyes didn't stray from the computer monitor and her fingers flew across the keyboard as she entered one pink slip after another.

"To behave like a gentleman when I'm in the library," Mack offered as he looked down at the floor and slightly shuffled his feet to indicate nervousness. "I'll behave. I promise."

"Well, it is certainly about time that you did. Now what was it that I was supposed to be researching for you? I seem to have forgotten." Her fingers continued to fly across the keyboard and her eyes flashed with a spark of recognition of new newly found power. "We got very busy yesterday afternoon after you left."

"I asked you to check on a French marine scientist by the name of Francois Batteau. He specializes in the family of whales and dolphins."

"I have some bad news for you."

"What do you mean by bad news?" Mack squatted on his haunches next to Janet's cubicle. "Is he dead?"

"No he is not dead. He does not exist, or at least no one at the University of Paris seems to know who he is and Jacques Batteau did not have a brother. He was an only child and was born in southern California. I'm afraid that your guy is an absolute imposter. He sold you a bill of goods about himself."

"How do you know for certain? I e-mailed the director of faculty programs at the University of Paris. France does not currently have a marine mammal research program at any of their universities; however, they are interested in starting one. Does that satisfy your curiosity?"

"No! This guy was really French and he knew all about he Navy's marine mammal programs." Mack stood up as if to make the point. "How about double checking your sources?" "I know that this guy is for real."

"What's make you so certain that he's who and what he told you he is?"

"He speaks French and knows lots of stuff about whales and dolphins."

"Those are certainly finite qualifications. I'm impressed. Did he show you any identification such as his passport or driver's license?"

"Of course not!"

"Then I suggest that you were scammed," Janet's eyes returned to her computer monitor and her fingers began flying over the keyboard. "Mr. McCray, if you don't need anything else I must return to processing these requests for inter-library loans," she replied and her fingers never missed a stroke. "Doing your research for you put me behind in my work."

"What did you find out about military and civilians experiments in electromagnetic wave transmission and mind control?"

"Not much yet. However, the CIA and NSA have been conducting experiments with various transmission techniques designed for crowd control for many years."

"What have you got for me?"

"Nothing," Janet replied as she paused in her computer data input task and turned to face Mack. "I'm working this weekend and I'll have time to do some searching. Come back and see me Monday. That is if you can behave yourself." She returned to her mundane task and Mack thought he detected the trace of a smug smile on her normally stoic face.

"I'll behave," he mumbled under his breath and he turned to leave.

"What did you say Mr. McCray? I don't believe that I heard you clearly."

"I said that I promise to behave myself!" Mack barked. "Isn't that what you wanted?"

"Exactly! I'll expect to see you standing in front of the reference desk bright and early Monday morning." She never moved her eyes from her computer screen, or paused in her furious data input.

Mack slipped out of the reference department office and headed for the library entrance. Jack looked up from his computer monitor as Mack passed and nodded his head.

"I told you that she was expecting you," Jack glibly offered with a wide grin. "Did she fill you in on what she found out about that French guy? She spent a lot of time on it."

"She told me," Mack replied over his right shoulder without pausing in his step.

"*I'd better get my butt down to the marina and get Tina's boat ready to go or she'll have me for lunch when she gets here this afternoon,*" Mack thought to himself as he exited the library and headed for his truck.

It was 11:43 A.M.

Chapter 28

Mack wasn't in any hurry to get back to Port Sewall marina because he didn't expect Tina to arrive until well after lunch. It was almost an hour's drive from West Palm Beach to Stuart and Tina would certainly tidy up her office before she left for her condo in the Breakers to pack her bags for the weekend.

Mack decided to pull into Smokey's barbecue restaurant on US 1 for lunch. The place was packed and he didn't get back on the road for the marina until 1:52 P.M

He immediately knew that he was in trouble when he pulled into the Port Sewall Marina parking lot. Tina's silver-blue BMW Z 3 was already there. She was pacing up and down the length of the front porch and she didn't look even a little bit happy.

Mack decided to play it cool and act non-concerned. He gave

the truck's horn a soft 'beep beep' as he pulled into a parking space directly in front of the cottage porch. He opened the truck door and allowed the well-chewed wooden toothpick to drop from between his front teeth onto the pea gravel parking lot as he slid out of the cab.

"I certainly hope that you're planning on picking up that piece of refuse that you dumped onto the parking lot and disposing of it properly?" Tina barked from the porch. Her hands were placed on here hips in a 'show me' posture as if she was daring Mack to talk back to her. "Well?"

"Yep! I dropped this tiny toothpick by mistake and I'm certain that it added to the environmental refuse pollution problem," Mack mumbled almost under his breath as he bent over and picked up the masticated toothpick. "Where would you like me to put it?" He mumbled just loud enough for Tina to hear as he stood up and displayed the wooden trophy between his right thumb and forefinger.

"Bend over and stick it right up you butt!" She screamed as she waved both of her hands above her head. "Where do you think garbage belongs?"

"I'm not sure at this point," Mack mumbled under his breath. "In the garbage can," he sarcastically responded loud enough for her to hear clearly.

"What did you say?" She screamed as she stamped her right foot and headed in his general direction. "Are you making fun of me mister?"

"Of course not!" Mack replied as he made a sharp swivel hip fake to the right, which Tina bit on like a freshman high school cornerback, and dashed for the front door. He made it inside and slammed the door shut before she could regain her footing. "Never watch a runner's hips," he quipped through the door. "Always look at their knees because the body has to follow the motion of the knees."

"You won't have any knees left after I get my hands on you!" Tina screamed at the closed door. She realized that he hadn't thrown the dead bolt and was holding the door closed with his body weight expecting her to lunge at the door. Just as she reached the door he'd throw it open allowing her rush into the cottage and wind up in a heap on the wooden floor. "Why don't you make it easy for both of us and just give up? I'm going to win anyway."

"I don't think so," Mack replied under his breath, but loud enough so she could hear his comment.

"If you don't open that door I'm going to blow your house down! Then you'll really be sorry."

"I'm shaking in my boots."

"Mack, you'd better let her in," the soft-spoken male voice came from behind him. "She's really pissed off. I took care of her boat before she got here so you won't have to take her to Indiantown tonight."

Mack swung around and as he did he relaxed his position against the door. Ralph was sitting in one of the green recliners sipping a beer.

"You'd better let her in and make up with her, " Ralph offered as he took a deep swig of his beer. " She's mad as a hornet because you didn't have her boat ready to go when she got here."

"When did she get here? She wasn't supposed to be here until after lunch!"

"I dropped by the marina to check on her boat right after I left the Queen Conch this morning. I figured that you wouldn't have time to get her boat washed down and fueled up because of your trip back over the library. She pulled into the parking lot about noon. I had just finished washing down her boat and was on my way up the stairs when she pulled in."

"What did you do to her boat?"

"I fueled it up and washed it down with fresh water just like she expected you to do," Ralph replied with a slight smile as she took another a deep swig of his beer. "Plus, I tried to warm up the engine."

"What do you mean that you tried to warm up the engine?"

"I fixed it so it would turn over, but not start. You didn't really want to take her boat to Indiantown this afternoon did you? I figured that if she can't go by boat that she won't want to go and that gets you off the hook."

"Ralph! What did you do to her engine?" Mack realized that he had relaxed his position and swung his body back against the door. "Did you put sugar in the gas tank?'

"Naw. That screws up the engine permanently. I did something simple to it that you can fix in a minute whenever you want and be her hero."

"What exactly did you do?"

"I pulled out the lead from the ignition coil and slipped a piece of Teflon inside the top of the coil so the end of the coil wire can't make contact. No spark can reach the spark plugs. When you're ready all you have to do is pull out the piece of Teflon and the engine will kick over like a fuzzy gray kitten sipping warm milk out of a saucer."

"That's quite a visual description of a gasoline engine. Does Tina know what you did?"

"If she did she'd have the engine running and you'd be on your way to Indiantown. She came down and tried to start the engine so many times that she drained the battery dead as a doornail. I hooked up the trickle charger for her, but it'll take a couple of hours for the battery to build up enough amperage to turn the engine over. You're safe for tonight."

"She'll find a way," Mack responded as he pulled away from the door and allowed it to swing open just as Tina was making a running leap for it. Mack stepped in front of Tina and caught her in his arms as she sailed through the doorway. "I've gotcha' tiger!"

"You bastard!" She snarled through clenched teeth as she wriggled in his arms like a fish out of water. "I should've known that you'd do that. Let me go!" She ordered.

"Okey dokey," Mack replied as he relaxed his grip on her wriggling body and allowed her to slip through his arms and land in a pile on the floor. "Whatever you say ma'am."

"Mack, I think I'll be going now," Ralph offered as he set his empty beer can on the coffee table. "I get the feeling that you and Tina have some things to talk about. I'll catch up with you when you get back from Indiantown." Ralph stood up and headed for the front door.

"What makes you think that we're going to Indiantown?" Mack replied. "You said that Tina's boat engine wouldn't start."

"We're going to Indiantown this afternoon even if I have to

drag you behind your truck!" Tina screamed from her awkward position on the floor. "If you had been here to get my boat ready like I told you to do last night then the battery wouldn't be dead and we'd half way there by now."

"I'll see you Mack," Ralph shouted through the screen door from the front porch. Then he stepped into the parking lot and was gone from Mack's view.

"Mack! Help me up off the floor!" Tina barked as she extended her right arm as an indication that he was to take it and help her up form her sprawled position. "We're taking your truck to Indiantown and we're leaving right now."

"Why are we taking my truck? Your Beamer rides better."

"My engine's been running hot and I think my radiator's shot. That's why."

"Yes ma'am, I completely understand" Mack replied as he jerked Tina up and into a standing position. "Give me two minutes to throw some things into my ditty bag and I'll be ready to go."

"You don't have to pack anything, I already did it for you. Your precious ditty bag is packed and sitting right over there by the front door," Tina barked as she gestured towards two bags backed up against each other. "My bag's packed too. Throw it in your truck while I freshen up and be careful with it!" Tina ordered as she headed for the bathroom.

Mack shook his head, walked over and picked up the two bags

"*Why do I have such a bad feeing about this?*" He thought as he headed out the front door with a bag in each hand.

Chapter 29

Tina stayed strangely silent, as she slumped back against the straight-backed truck bench seat and stared out the passenger's side window all the way from Port Sewall Marina, down Kanner Highway until Mack crossed over Indiantown Avenue and turned south to make the loop onto Route 710. The sudden turn triggered the animosity that was built up in her psychic.

"Pull over there!" She barked as she pointed at the abandoned fruit stand on the side of the intersection. "We have something to talk about!"

"Why here?" Mack responded as he pulled into the loose gravel and slipped the transmission into 'Park'.

"Turn off the engine!"

"Why?"

"Because I said so!"

Mack obliged, stretched and slumped in his seat. "Now what did I do to piss you off?"

"What gives with the three open wine bottles in the cottage?" Tina demanded without deflecting her stare from the passenger's side window. "Just whom were you entertaining last night when I called you and told you to get my boat ready for today."

"What are you talking about?" Mack responded as he turned his head to face her. "I wasn't entertaining anybody. I was all by my lonesome and we both had a good time."

"Why were there three open wine bottles on the table?"

"I drank one, my lonesome drank one and we split the third bottle."

"Don't be a smart ass!" Tina snapped as she turned to face Mack with her arms folded across her chest. Her emerald-green eyes spit fire and chunks of brimstone large enough to kill a cow. "I know full well that you only drink Merlot when you are either real down in the dumps or entertaining someone of female persuasion."

"Just what makes you think that?"

"That's what you did to me back in March when you first got here."

"I didn't do anything to you. You were the one who showed up with the Merlot. How many wine glasses did you see on the coffee table?"

"I didn't count them."

"That's because there weren't any! My lonesome and me drank the rotgut straight out of the bottle. There's no reason to dirty a perfectly good wine glass unless you're trying to impress someone."

"You drank wine straight out of the bottle? That's gross and extremely uncouth!"

"So? I never said that I ever had any couth."

"Where were your scented candles and Indian incense burner?"

"What candles? I don't own an incense burner!"

"Isn't Maya an Indian name?"

"No! It's Pakistani! How did you know about Maya?"

Mack sat up straight and pointed at a wild turkey that crossed the road in front of them and slipped into the deep grass bordering the road.

"Did you see that hen turkey cross the road ahead of us?" He added in a futile attempt to change the subject.

"I'm looking at a big turkey right now!" Tina barked. "So, tell me Mr. McCray! Just who is Maya and what was she doing with you last night?"

"How did you know about her?"

"She wrote her name on the inside of this matchbook," Tina held up the red matchbook and flipped up the cover so that Mack could plainly see the name Maya. "Apparently she didn't want you to forget her, but she didn't leave you a phone number."

"She's a Pakistani hooker I met in Chicago. She's working off her passage. Her brother makes her work out of his hotel because he sponsored her to come into the country."

"Did she treat you well?" Tina grinned impishly as she fanned the open matchbook. "I understand that Indian women have to study a sex manual before they get married to ensure that they satisfy their husbands."

"I didn't mess around with her!'

"When were you in Chicago?"

"I left on Monday and came back Wednesday night."

"What were you doing there? You're supposed to be my marina manager and I would appreciate being notified in advance before you take off to meet a Pakistani hooker."

"I didn't go there to meet a Pakistani hooker! I went there to visit an old friend."

"I'll bet! If you came back Wednesday night why didn't you answer your telephone? I called you several times. I called Ralph in desperation and asked him to come over and check on you."

"Why did you call Ralph and ask him to check on me?" Mack sat up straight and stiffened in his seat. He had a feeling about where the interrogation was going next.

"I'm a big boy now!"

"Because I was worried about you! Where were you Wednesday night?"

"It's a long story and I'd rather not talk about it."

"Oh? I see. Maya left you for another man with more rupees in his wallet!"

"No! Maya is still in Chicago for all I know. She didn't come back here with me."

"Oh? She didn't? Then what's this?" Tina dangled a small silver pendant suspended from a silver chain in front of Mack's face. "I suppose that it found its way into your shirt pocket by accident."

"What is it?" Mack quipped. "I never saw that until just now."

It's a very unique charm carried by many Hindu women. Are you certain that your girlfriend is Pakistani?"

"That's what she told me."

"Pakistanis are Muslims. Perhaps in the throes of passion she forgot her religious conviction." Tina smiled smugly like the cat that just ate the proverbial canary. "You must have been very good to her."

"I didn't sleep with her!"

"I didn't say that you did."

"You certainly insinuated it!"

"Perhaps," Tina responded with a sly grin as she spun the pendant in a slow, ever widening circle in front of Mack's eyes. "Are you certain that she didn't tell you the meaning of this pendant. It is very rare and also very beautiful."

"No! And I don't care."

"You'd better care."

"Why?"

"She pledged herself to you by giving you her pendant."

"She didn't give it to me and I never saw it until you whipped it out in front of me."

"I found it in your shirt pocket when I tried to clean up the mess in your bedroom."

"Why were you going through my shirt pockets?"

"I was going to do you a favor by washing your dirty clothes. I always go through the pockets before washing shirts to be certain that there's nothing in them that'll clog up the washing machine filter. The corner of the room is not where you are supposed to store your dirty clothes. That's what the wicker hamper in your room is for."

"Is my interrogation over?" Mack reached for the ignition key.

"Not quite," Tina responded as she released the silver chain.

The pendant fell onto the truck seat.

"I want to be certain that you understand the importance of this pendant to that Pakistani girl."

"Why? She doesn't mean anything to me!"

"Because you mean something to her! I believe that she looks at you as being her salvation from a world of prostitution. She slipped this silver pendant into your pocket so that you would know that she expects you to come back to get her."

"Hogwash!"

"Then you really don't realize the importance of this pendant do you?"

"Guess I don't. Do you?"

"Yes! I most certainly do. It is a very sacred Hindu religious symbol called *Om*!

"So?"

"In our country a man gives a woman an engagement ring as a sign of his devotion and a promise of marriage. Often a Hindu woman gives her man an *Om* pendant as her pledge to him."

"So? It's only a piece of metal! I'll send it back to her."

"No! You will not send it back to her!"

"Why not? I have the hotel's address. Her brother runs the place. He'll give it to her."

"She'll be banished from the family if you reject her proposal. Your callous rejection of her devotion will bring disgrace to her family and they will have no choice but to stone her to death!"

"Tina, aren't you taking this charade just a little bit to far? How do you know all of this?"

"I studied Hinduism and several other Oriental religions when I was in college."

"Were you a pot-smoking flower child?"

"Yes! And don't make fun of me. I was able to get my mind and spirit in sync with Mother Earth through meditation."

"And pot-smoking helped?"

"It relaxes the mind."

"Did you sit on a blanket and chant your brains out?" Mack grinned and shook his head.

"I did not chant!" Tina spit out as she turned back towards the side window. "However, I did hum *Om* to myself to relax my mind and spirit," she mumbled softly.

"Can we go now?" Mack asked as he reached for the ignition key for the second time.

"No!" Tina barked as she swung around in the seat to face him. "You need to understand the seriousness of what you did and what the *Om* pendant means to Maya." Tina tenderly picked up the silver pendant from the truck seat relaxed her fierce glare. "Poor Maya," she whispered as he turned the pendant over and over between her fingers.

"I didn't do anything to her," Mack softly lamented as he gazed out of the truck's windshield. "It was all her doing. I'm innocent."

"So!" Tina screamed. "You did sleep with her! I knew it! I hope that her family looks you up and stones you to death! Better yet I hope they flay you alive from the inside out!"

"Hold it just a minute!" Mack vainly attempted to defend himself. "She snuck into my room after I went to bed. I don't remember a thing about it. She was in the bathroom brushing her hair when I woke up. She planned the whole thing."

"You sound like a typical man caught in an affair. Blame everything on the weak woman. Let's talk about the seriousness of what you did and the significance of the *Om* Pendant."

"Why? I don't really care."

"You'd better care when her family shows up to stone you for disgracing their daughter. Sit right there and don't move!" Tina shook her left index finger at Mack and waved the silver pendant in front of his eyes with her right hand. "Do you understand me?"

"Yes ma'am. I'm listening."

"The *Om*, or *Aum*, is the main symbol of Hinduism. Many religions believe that creation began with sound. For the Hindus and Buddhists, *Om* is the primordial sound, the very first breath of creation, the vibration of existence. The *Om* sign signifies God, Creation and the One-ness of all creation. Was your under developed Cretin mind able to absorb what I've said so far?"

"I think so," Mack softly mumbled as he shifted his position in the seat.

"What did you say mister?" Tina barked. "I didn't hear you!"

Mack jerked upright, looked straight ahead through the windshield and responded. "Ma'am. I said I think so, ma'am."

"That's better. Now pay close attention to what I'm about to say. It might save you hide if her family shows up at your front door with rocks in their hands."

"Ma'am! Yes ma'am. I'm listening ma'am!"

"That's much better. I like you change of attitude."

Tina softly patted Mack on the right knee with her left hand as she lightly fingered the silver pendant in her right.

"The *Om* symbol is a sacred symbol representing *Brahman*, the impersonal Absolute and the source of all manifest existence. *Brahman* is incomprehensible; so a symbol helps us to realize the Unknowable. *Om*, therefore, represents both the unmanifest and manifest aspects of God. *Aum* is said to be the essence of all mantras and ultimate reality. Do you understand now?"

"Ma'am. I suppose I do."

"I doubt it," Tina retorted with a frown and a shake of her head. "I hope that you are able to recall some of what I've said when her brother is flaying you alive. It might help."

Tina paused, turned her head towards Mack and punched him on the right thigh with her fist.

"Are you listening to what I'm saying?"

"Yes ma'am! I'm listening."

"Good. *Aum* represents all of the words that can be produced by the human vocal cords. *Aum* is the sound of the sun and the sound of light."

Tina's eyes closed and she rocked slowly back and forth in her seat before she spoke.

"*Aum* is the sound of assent, has an upward movement and uplifts the soul, as the sound of the divine eagle or falcon."

She slowly turned towards Mack without opening her eyes.

"Are you listening?"

"I'm listening," he whispered in hopes of not waking her from her trance.

His response snapped Tina out of her apparent meditative state and her eyes opened as she turned the pendant over in her hand.

"Look! There's a very significant symbol on the other side of the pendant."

"What's that ma'am?"

Mack's eyes didn't flicker and he continued to stare straight ahead at the center of the blacktop road.

"It's *Ganesh*! His ears and hands are beautifully reproduced! His arms are outstretched in a teaching position that one would expect to see in a human! I love it!"

"What's a *Ganesh*?"

"*Ganesh* is a Hindu God symbol and he is very important in the Hindu religion. That's all you need to know," Tina sharply quipped as she placed the *Om* pendant in her purse. "It's almost six o'clock. Let's get back on the road for Indiantown."

"Yes Ma'am. Why are we going to Indiantown?"

"Mr. McCray you can stop your feigned military grunt attitude. We are both adults, or at least I am. Let's go!"

"Okay," Mack grinned as he responded and reached for the ignition key. "But why?"

"Did you hear that Elmo arrested Octavio last Saturday night for attacking Carlos with a knife?"

"He stopped by Monday morning and told me. So what?"

"I think that I can help Octavio get out of this mess if I can get my hands on that mask."

"Why do you want the mask?"

"The mask is the only tangible evidence in the case, besides the statement that Carlos gave to Elmo that Octavio attacked him with a knife. Without the mask there's no evidence and no case for attempted grand theft because no one knows its value. It could be a fake and worth virtually nothing. Anything above five hundred bucks is grand theft. Anything below five hundred bucks is petty theft."

"That doesn't make any sense to me. What about the assault with a deadly weapon charge?"

"I think that I can convince Carlos to drop it."

"How?"

"He needs the Guatemalan and Mexican laborers' business to keep his doors open. If Octavio goes to jail Carlos loses his business. It's a matter of economics and justice has nothing to do with it. How much do you think the mask is worth?"

"I don't have any idea," Mack responded as he threw his hands up in the air. "It might be junk!"

"That's correct and for a charge of attempted grand theft to stick the object must be worth at least five hundred bucks! If there's no object to evaluate, then there's no case!"

"So, if you can talk Carlos out of the mask, then the case will fall apart for the lack of evidence."

"That's correct."

"Isn't that contrary to your role as a prosecutor?"

"No. This case is pure economics for Carlos and overrides the need for him to seek justice. Let's get on the road!"

Tina flipped her right hand towards the intersection of Indiantown Avenue and Route 710.

"It's almost six o'clock and I'm hungry."

"Ma'am! Yes ma'am!" Mack replied as he turned the ignition switch and started the truck engine.

"Shut up you jerk!"

"Yes ma'am."

Mack knew that it was going to be a very long weekend and one that he wouldn't soon forget.

"The Om is a sacred symbol representing Brahman, the impersonal Absolute and the source of all manifest existence."

Chapter 30

After Tina and Mack checked into the Seminole Inn, in separate rooms of course, they ate dinner and walked across Warfield Boulevard towards the Silver Saddle. It isn't difficult to locate the Silver Saddle because it's on the same street as the telephone company's microwave transmission tower and central office. It was 7:34 P.M.

"What makes you think that Carlos still has the mask?" Mack inquired in between dodging two sod trucks speeding down the street in opposite directions.

"I talked to Elmo this morning. Carlos refused to give it to him when he arrested Octavio Saturday night. I hope that it's still behind the bar."

"Why wouldn't Carlos give the mask to Elmo? It's evidence."

"That's true. But, Carlos may know the value of the mask and he might be negotiating to sell it to a museum, or a private collector. If he gives up the mask as evidence he'll never see it again."

"Do you think that the mask is valuable?"

"Only if it can be authenticated as genuine. If it's real it's worth about one-hundred thousand bucks to a museum and even more to a private collector."

"What makes you think that?" Mack asked. He was apprehensive about Tina's true motive for wanting the mask.

"I had my secretary do some checking on the Internet. The mask may be from a pre-Mayan civilization called Olmec that disappeared in five hundred BC. The Olmec didn't have a written language and wrote in hieroglyphs. A Spanish Jesuit priest destroyed all of the Olmec hieroglyphs."

"How did your secretary do all of that research without seeing the mask?"

"I took a photo of it with my digital camera when we were here."

"Yes, but you left your camera in your boat cabin when you went back to West Palm Beach. I stuck it in a kitchen drawer for safekeeping."

"What were you doing on my boat?"

"Cleaning it up. The cabin needed to be aired out. It was stuffy in there."

"I suppose that's okay as long as you didn't poke around in my personal things."

"I don't poke around in your stuff! How did you get a photo of the mask to your secretary?"

"My laptop is equipped with a satellite link and I e-mailed the photo to her before I took a nap. She e-mailed it to the Smithsonian and a few other places. She had all of the answers for me when I came into the office Friday morning."

"That's good thinking."

"I understand that you may have done a little snooping yourself."

"What do you mean?"

"The curator of the Mayan exhibit at the Smithsonian told her that someone from the Stuart Library system had e-mailed him the same photo."

"Maybe Carlos did it. Most people have digital cameras and the Martin County Library has a branch in Indiantown."

"Do they have a librarian named Janet?"

"I don't know. I've never been in the Indiantown Library."

"The Blake Library does."

"Does what?"

"They have a reference librarian named Janet. Does that ring any bells with you?"

"Nope. I'm not smart enough to use the library. I never did figure out the Dewey Decimal System."

"For some reason I don't quite believe you."

"Why don't you ask Carlos if he did it?"

"I can't imagine Carlos doing it. And if I did ask him, I'd be showing my hand. He doesn't need to know anything! I just want to get that mask away from him so Elmo can't use it as evidence in Octavio's trial."

"I understand completely," Mack replied as he stepped up onto the curb. "Your motive has nothing to do with the value of the mask. But, if you keep hollering at me everyone out here on the street will know about it and it won't take long for Carlos to find out."

"Okay already," Tina replied under her breath. "Keep your mouth shut when we go in and let me do all the talking. Carlos has known me for years, but he doesn't know you from Adam!"

"Yes ma'am. Do you happen to have an apple in your purse?"

He anticipated the 'round house right' coming and ducked as Tina's closed fist sailed harmlessly over his head.

"Don't telegraph your punches next time and you'll nail him good," Carlos hollered from the front door of the Silver Saddle. "Come on in and have a cool one. We have some things to talk about."

"You bet we do," Tina replied as she eyeballed the distance from Mack's head to her left hand. She calculated that her reach was about three inches too short unless she leaned into the punch. "I want to talk to you about Octavio," Tina added as she passed through the open door and headed for an empty booth in the back of the room.

"*Carmelita! Tres cervazas por favor,* " Carlos yelled Spanish instructions at the young Hispanic girl behind the wooden bar.

"I don't want a beer," Tina stated. "I'd prefer an *Absolut* vodka gimlet with an a lime slice if you don't mind."

"We ran out of vodka two days ago and my liquor distributor doesn't make a delivery until tomorrow. We are totally out of booze and wine. Beer is the best I can do."

"I guess that I don't have any choice. Is she the same girl that was here last week when we stopped in to see you? I believe you said that she's your niece?"

"Yes. Carmelita's mother is having some bad problems at home with her boyfriend and I let her move in here for a while. She tends bar for me to pay for her room and board."

"Is that all she does for you?" Mack asked with a sly wink.

"It had better be!" Tina barked. "She looks to be about fifteen years old."

"She's almost seventeen," Carlos added. "Hispanic women don't show their age until they're over forty and it's all downhill from there."

"Cut out that crap!" Tina barked as she gave Carlos a look that would melt steel. "You men don't get any better looking after forty either. You lose the hair on your head, grow hair in your ears and your potbellies hang over your belt like a slab of bacon on a smoker rack."

"Okay. I'm sorry. I didn't know that you were so sensitive. I apologize. Here comes Carmelita with our beers. Don't worry about paying. It's on the house.

After Carmelita served the three beers and had left the table Tina took charge of the conversation. "Carlos, why did you have Elmo arrest Octavio Saturday night?"

"He came at me with a kitchen knife and said he was going to cut my throat if I didn't give him that stupid stone mask. I didn't have any choice."

"Why didn't you just give him that mask and prevent the confrontation?" Mack asked

"He gave it to me as payment for his bar tab. It's mine now!"

"The last time we were here you told us that you thought it

was a fake," Tina barked. "If it's a fake it doesn't have any value."

"The Guats are afraid of it. As long as it stays up there behind the bar they stay quiet and behave themselves in here.

"I'll give you two hundred bucks for it!" Mack offered.

"What!" Tina screamed as she took a swing at Mack's head with her closed right fist and missed. "Keep out if this! It's between me and Carlos!"

"I thought that I'd bid up the stakes and make this more interesting," Mack replied from a crouched position out of Tina's reach. "You said that the mask's worthless and Carlos wanted to keep it. Don't you know that everything's for sale for a price. The price is the only thing at issue here."

"Shut up Mack!" Tina barked. "I'm handling this!"

"Tina, why do you want the mask so badly," Carlos asked. "What value does it have to you?"

"I feel sorry for Octavio and I don't want to see him go to jail."

"Even if I forget about him trying to steal the mask he's going to jail for attacking me with a knife."

"Not if you drop the charges," Tina cooed. "I might forget all about Carmelita if you do."

"Why should I?" Carlos barked. "You can't prove anything. She can't speak English."

"We have some very good interpreters at the courthouse," Tina replied with a grin. "I think that if she's offered a clean foster home with her own room and no harassment from you that she'll be willing to cooperate. I see charges for statutory rape and the violation of several Federal and state child labor laws. Are you willing to take that chance?"

"Okay! I'd give you the mask if I still had it."

"What do you mean if you still had it?" Tina asked with a shocked look on her face. "Where is it?"

"Didn't you notice when you came in that the mask wasn't behind the bar?"

"No. I didn't pay any attention."

"It disappeared Saturday night after Elmo left with the Guat in handcuffs. It was there when Elmo was wrestling with him and when I locked up for the night I noticed that it was gone. I don't have it. I'd give it to you if I did."

"Carlos, I don't think that I believe you!" Tina countered. "I'm not bluffing about pulling that girl out of here and charging you with statutory rape and violation of Federal and state child labor laws."

"That doesn't matter. She won't be here after this weekend."

"What do you mean by that?

"I sold her to another bar in Okeechobee. They need a young whore there."

"Carlos! You're going to jail and I'm going to throw away the key! You'll never get out!"

"Okay! You win as usual. I'll call Elmo tomorrow and tell him that I'm dropping the charges."

"It's too late for that. The case has already been filed and Octavio is scheduled to appear in court on Monday morning."

"What should I do?"

"You'll have to appear in court in person and tell the judge that it was a misunderstanding and that you don't wish to press assault or theft charges against Octavio."

"But what about Elmo? He saw the whole thing!"

"I'll take care of Elmo," Tina replied with a smug smile. "I don't think that he'll show up for court and the charges will be dropped because he is the only witness to the alleged assault."

"It isn't alleged!" Carlos stated vehemently. "He was going to cut my throat!"

"That's too bad. If he had cut your throat we wouldn't be having this conversation," Tina replied with a knowing smirk. "Let's get back to the mask! What did you do with it?"

"I've still got it," Carlos whimpered. "Don't worry. It's safe with me."

"I knew it!" Tina barked. "You lying *bastardo*! You were trying to con me. Where it is?"

"After Elmo left and the place cleared out I took the mask down from behind the bar, wrapped up in clean bar towels and packed it in an empty beer case. It's in the storeroom."

"Get it right now!" Tina barked as she stood up and pointed to the entrance to the back room.

"I'm going," Carlos, replied softly as he carefully slid his chair away from the table and stood up.

"*Uno momento por favor*," Carlos mumbled under his breath in Carmelita's direction.

"What does that mean?" Tina demanded. "Are those code words to tell Carmelita to hide the box?"

"He just said to wait a few minutes," Mack replied. "It wasn't code."

"Who asked you?"

"No one I suppose. I was just trying to help."

"Don't! I don't need any help. I can speak Spanish too. Didn't you hear me call him a *bastardo*?"

"I'm sorry. I didn't realize that you spoke Spanish fluently. I thought that perhaps, just perhaps, that you knew a few Spanish curse words like most *gringos*." Mack ducked below the table as Tina's right hand swept past the top of his head. "You missed again," he teasingly offered from under the edge of the table and immediately screamed as he fell off the chair onto the wooden floor.

"You didn't anticipate a foot in the crotch did you?" Tina whispered down to her writhing victim.

"Don't ever underestimate me and my willingness to wait until just the right moment to zap your smart ass!"

"I won't ever again," Mack managed to squeak between his spasms of pain. "I won't."

"You wimp. Shut up, get back in your chair and pretend that nothing happened. Carlos is coming."

Carlos approached the table with a Budweiser beer carton cradled in his arms and stopped in front of Tina. "Here it is," he bubbled as he extended the box in Tina's direction. You can have it. This thing's bad luck and almost got me killed."

"Just set it down on the table and open it up very carefully," Tina cautioned. "I'm superstitious."

"There's nothing in here except the mask," Carlos countered. "I put it in here myself."

"If Octavio was willing to cut your throat for it someone else may want it just as badly."

"Mr. McCray looks very bad. Is he sick?"

"He's not sick. He slipped off his chair and hurt himself. He'll be just fine."

Carlos pulled a towel-wrapped object out of the cardboard box and offered it to Tina. "Here you are Ms. Tina. I hope that you have an enjoyable time with your new toy."

Tina accepted the heavy object, set it down on the table and began to carefully unwrap the towel. A large, flat rock appeared when the last fold was rolled back.

"What kind of game are you playing Carlos?" Tina screamed as she pushed the rock and its towel wrapping off the table and onto the wooden floor. It landed with a muffled 'thud'.

"Oh no!" Carlos shouted. "Somebody stole the mask! I'm a dead man!"

"Carlos, are you trying to con me?" Tina cooed as she sharply tapped the tips of her manicured nails on the wooden table. "I can make this very nasty for you."

"No, Ms. Tina! I am not conning you! The mask was in this towel this morning when I checked the box. Someone came in here and took it when I was not watching! The Guats are going to kill me!"

"What makes you think that the Guatemalans are going to kill you? You didn't steal the mask."

"I was the last one to have it. They revere the mask as a God and they will sacrifice me like a goat!"

"What makes you think that," Mack softly inquired through spasms of groin pain.

"The Guats built a wooden altar out of sod pallets in the woods out on Martin Grade on a side road close to the entrance of the Naked Lady Ranch. It's right next to the pens where they hold cockfights. They're going to cut my throat and kill me," Carlos sobbed.

"How do you know about the altar?"

"Carmelita showed me when we went to cock fights on Sunday afternoon."

"She told me that it was for me if I lost, or sold the mask," Carlos sobbed. "The Guats require a blood sacrifice to satisfy their Gods."

"This is the twenty-first century and people don't sacrifice other humans to their gods," Tina countered. "If someone was missing in this area law enforcement personnel would know about it and take action to prosecute the people involved."

"Most of these people are illegal aliens and there's no record of them being here. If one of them disappears nobody says anything about it because they don't want to be next! I'm going to die tonight!" Carlos wailed.

"How about Carmelita?" Mack asked through his veil of pain. "Can't she help you?"

"She won't," Carlos wailed. "It's true Miss Tina. Everything you said is true. She isn't my niece."

"Who is she then," Tina inquired. "Where's her family?"

"I don't know. I bought her a month ago for two hundred bucks from a Mexican coyote who was passing through here with a semi-trailer full of illegals. He was selling them to the grove owners for three hundred each. I got a deal because she's too frail to work in the fields."

"We'll take Carmelita back to Stuart with us tomorrow and I'll see that she gets placed in a good foster home," Tina offered. "I'm pleased that you came clean about her Carlos, but where's the mask?"

"I don't know Ms. Tina. I don't know. Please believe me. I don't know," Carlos wailed as he sobbed like a child. "I don't know! I don't know!

"Okay Carlos, I believe you. You tell Carmelita to be at the Seminole Inn at eight o'clock tomorrow morning with her bags packed and ready to go. We're taking her back to Stuart with us."

"She has no belongings except for the clothes that I bought her."

"Have them packed in her suitcase along with her personal items."

"She doesn't have a suitcase."

"Do you?"

"Of course. I travel often."

"It's her suitcase now. Have her at the Seminole Inn at eight o'clock tomorrow morning."

"I will. You can count on me," Carlos whined as he bowed at the waist and reached down to kiss the back of Tina's right hand.

Tina pulled her hand away.

"You slime ball *bastardo*!" Tina screamed. "Don't you ever touch me!"

Carmelita had been watching the entire episode and slipped her head away from the doorframe of the back room before Carlos could see her.

"I'm sorry that I know you!" Tina snapped. "If the mask magically shows up between now and eight o'clock tomorrow morning bring it to the Seminole Inn when you bring Carmelita over. I would hate to read in the newspaper that you were a human sacrifice. Yuk!"

"Yes ma'am. I will look for it all night."

"*Asta mañana* Carlos," Mack offered as he stood up and headed for the door.

"*Asta mañana bastardo*, Tina countered over her shoulder as she headed for the door.

Chapter
31

Mack wasn't used to sleeping in on Saturday morning and today was no exception. He was out of bed, showered and in the dining room for breakfast when it opened at 6:30 A.M. Tina's instructions to Carlos the night before were to have Carmelita at the Seminole Inn at exactly eight o'clock.

After his third cup of coffee Mack glanced at his watch. It read 7:43 and he wondered about Tina and Carmelita.

"Where the hell can those two women be?" He thought to himself. *"I expected Tina to be down here for breakfast by seven-thirty. I'm packed and ready to go. Maybe she overslept, or Carlos sent someone over in the middle of the night to shut her up for good. He wasn't a happy camper last night when she was chewing his ass out over that girl. I'd better go upstairs and*

check on her."

Mack slid his chair away from the table and signaled to the waiter that he left payment in cash for his breakfast on the table. The waiter nodded an acknowledgment of Mack's signal.

Mack headed for the lobby, passed through the double French doors, turned to his right and headed up the narrow flight of stairs to the second floor. When he reached the top of the stairway he was surprised by what he saw. Carmelita was standing in the hallway, the door to Tina's room was open and the two women were talking. Fortunately for Mack, Carmelita's back faced the stairway and she didn't see him. Mack stepped back down so he could just barely see over the top of the stairs.

Carmelita held a newspaper-wrapped package in her outstretched hands and passed it through the doorway. Tina's hands became visible as she reached out and took the package out of her hands.

"*Gracias senorita*," Carmelita softly whispered as she nodded in head in appreciation of Tina's acceptance of the clandestine-looking package.

"*De nada*," Tina responded.

The door silently closed leaving Carmelita alone in the hallway. She turned towards the stairway and Mack was certain that she caught a glimpse of his face. He clumsily slipped backward down the narrow stairway, stumbled through the double French doors and back into the dining room. The surprised waiter looked up as Mack slumped down into the chair he had vacated just minutes earlier. Mack signaled to the waiter with his right index finger that he wanted a cup of coffee and the waiter nodded back his acknowledgement of the order. Mack looked to his right towards the double French doors and spotted Carmelita engaged in a whispered conversation with Tina in the lobby.

"*There goes the ball game*," Mack thought. "*I've been made and I'll have some heavy explaining to do about what was I doing up on the second floor.*"

It wouldn't be long before he found out exactly how much explaining he had to do. Tina was on her way through the double French doors and headed for Mack's table. She didn't look happy. Mack stood up, pulled a chair away from the table and nodded for her to sit down. She didn't.

"Okay buster!" Sparks flew out of Tina's emerald-green eyes as the venom-filled words roared out of her rapidly moving mouth. "Why were you sneaking around on the second floor a few minutes ago?"

"I wasn't sneaking around. You were late for breakfast and I went up to check on you. That's all."

"I didn't tell you that I would meet you down here for breakfast and I don't appreciate that you think that you have to check on me."

"I was worried about you. After what you said to Carlos last night I thought that maybe he sent a couple of his flunkies over here to shut you up."

"What made you think that? He's harmless."

"Don't you remember that you told him that you'd throw him in jail and throw away the key?"

"He knows that I was just joking. I'd never do that to Carlos. He's an old family friend."

"I think that he thought you were serious. What about the girl?"

"What about her?"

"It's almost eight o'clock. Is she packed and ready to go?"

"She's not going with us. She wants to stay here."

"What? Last night you made a big deal about taking her back to Stuart with us today."

"She came over to see me this morning and told me that she wants to stay here."

"But, Carlos told us that he sold her to another bar in Okeechobee!"

"That's another county and it's out of my jurisdiction. I can't do anything about it."

"Aren't you worried about her safety? He's going to sell her into prostitution!"

"He already did. It's a done deal and she's acceptable to it. That's why she came here early this morning to tell me about it. She's leaving for Okeechobee on the twelve-thirty bus."

"Can't you stop her?"

"Why should I? She isn't a United States citizen and people in her culture don't think that same way we do."

"Aren't you worried about what might happen to her?"

"Of course I am, but she's like the homeless animals in the dog pound."

"What do you mean by that? She's not an animal! She's a human being."

"You can't save every dog and cat in the dog pound. If you were to adopt everyone of them today and take them home with you the pound would be full again in a day or so."

"That's a pretty crappy analogy."

"It's the best one I have for this situation. Are you packed and ready to go?"

"Yes. My bag is in the truck."

"I'm ready too. My bag is in the lobby. You can pick it up on the way out."

"What about the mask?"

"What about it?"

"Did you pack it in your bag?"

"I don't have the damn mask! You were with me last night when Carlos tried to scam me. He's still got it stashed away somewhere. What makes you think that I have it?"

"I saw Carmelita give it to you when I came up the stairs."

"What?"

"I saw her hand you something wrapped in newspaper."

"That wasn't the mask!"

"What was it?"

"It was a package of her personal effects that she asked me to mail to her family in Mexico."

"Why would she do that?"

"She doesn't expect to ever return to Mexico and Carlos won't allow her out of his sight long enough for her to go to the post office."

"Oh. Did she say anything about the mask?"

"No. She was too scared to say much of anything. Did you see Carlos in the lobby?"

"No."

"She told me that he walked over here with her and was

waiting for her in the lobby."

"If he was there then he was invisible. I didn't see him."

"Let's take off and head for Stuart," Tina turned and headed for the French doors and the hotel lobby. "This trip was a bust."

"Why are you in such a hurry to get back to Stuart? We have all weekend."

"I'm going back to West Palm Beach and work on the cases that I'm going to prosecute next week," Tina barked over her shoulder. "Don't forget to pick up my bag on your way through the lobby."

Mack waved off the anxious waiter and dutifully followed Tina into lobby. He carefully tucked her bag under the tool bin in the pickup's bed and secured it in place with a pair of elastic cords.

After Tina had carefully stowed the newspaper-wrapped bundle under the front seat Mack switched on the ignition switch and started the truck's ancient engine. It snapped to life, the valves rattled slightly and it began to purr like a kitten once the lubricating oil reached the rocker arms.

"Which way do you want me to take back to Stuart?" Mack asked as he eased the truck out of the parking place and stopped at the parking lot entrance.

"Why are you asking me?" Tina snapped. "You're driving!"

"Because if I turned left and headed for Kanner Highway you'd ask me why I went that way and if I turned right you'd ask me the same thing,"

"Are you curious about the wooden altar that has Carlos all shook up?"

"No."

"I am. Take a right and head up Allpattah Road. We'll cut over on Martin Grade and go right by the Naked Lady Ranch. We should be able to see the altar from the road."

"So, you really believe that the Guats built an altar for human sacrifice out there?"

"It doesn't matter what I believe. I want to see it. Go!"

"Yes ma'am," Mack stated as he saluted Tina with his right hand and pulled out onto Allpattah Road and headed north. "We're on the way. The Naked Lady Ranch is our next stop."

Chapter 32

Mack pulled into Port Sewall Marina at 2:13 P.M.

The thirty-mile trip took longer than expected because Tina had insisted on getting out of the truck at the entrance to the Naked Lady Ranch and stomping around in the scrub pines bordering the vast pasture for almost half an hour. Afterwards she insisted on stopping for breakfast at the International House of Pancakes on US 1. There was a waiting list in front of them and they weren't seated and able to order until almost twelve-thirty.

"Here we are," Mack mumbled as he pulled into a parking space directly in front of the cottage. "Everyone out. Do you want me to help you with that package? It seems to be pretty heavy."

"No thank you!" Tina barked as she fumbled to pull the

newspaper-wrapped package out from under the seat. "I don't remember jamming it so far under the seat."

"You didn't," Mack softly mumbled under his breath as he held back a snicker.

"Then how did it get jammed so far back under here?'

"I guess that I did it." Mack reached towards the seat. "Do you want me to help you?"

"No! What did you mean when you said that you guessed you did it? Have you been snooping around?"

"I wasn't snooping. It slipped out when you got out of the truck to go into IHOP. I reached over and shoved it back under the seat. Your weight held it in place and when you got up the pressure on the seat was released and it slipped out. When you get out of the truck it should come right out."

"Did you unwrap it?"

"No. I just shoved it back under the seat. That package sure is heavy for that girl's personal belongings. Does she collect rocks?"

"She's Hispanic and I'm certain that she packed up all of her silver and stone jewelry."

"Oh. I thought it was a big rock." Mack paused for effect. "Or a stone mask," he grinned.

Tina couldn't swing at him because her right hand was wedged under the seat, but her blazing eyes told the story. If she could have turned him into stone she would have without a second thought.

"You just don't know when to quit do you?" She hissed. "These are Carmelita's personal effects."

Mack pretended that he didn't hear her, swung out of the truck cab onto the pea gravel parking lot and slammed the truck door behind him. He reached into the truck bed, loosened the elastic cords holding Tina's bag in place, lifted it up and placed it beside the driver's door of her BMW that was conveniently in the next parking place.

"Holler if you need help," Mack offered over his right shoulder as he stepped onto the front porch.

"I don't need your help. Just set my bag next to my car door."

"I already did."

Tina slipped out of the truck, rummaged around under the seat with her right hand and pulled out her newspaper-wrapped treasure. "See! I've got it! I didn't need your help."

"Good for you. I knew that you could do it all by yourself."

Tina slammed the truck door, walked to the front of her car, turned and faced the porch.

"I advise you to stay away from Indiantown," Tina stated. "Things are going to be very hot over there until Octavio's trial is over."

"I don't have any reason to go to Indiantown. Why should I?"

"Because you are always sticking your nose into places where it doesn't belong."

"Oh. I see. Was I the person who insisted on stomping around the Naked Lady Ranch looking for a sacrificial altar?"

"Shut up! I found it didn't I?"

"You found a pile of discarded sod pallets back in the woods. So what?"

"Couldn't you tell that someone stacked them in the shape of a pyramid? It's an altar and Carlos may well be in serious danger if Octavio is convicted and sent to jail."

"It looked to me that part of the top of the stack slipped off. It wasn't a pyramid."

"Believe whatever you want. You men are hardheaded! It's an altar!" Tina spun on her toes, opened the door of her Silver-blue BMW Z 3, tossed in her overnight bag and carefully placed the newspaper-wrapped package on the floor behind the driver's seat. "You'll stay away from Indiantown if you know what's good for you!" She shouted as she slammed the car door shut.

The dust from Tina's hasty exit had barely cleared away when Ralph's green pickup truck rounded the curve in front of Whiticar's Boat Works. He slammed into a parking space alongside Mack's truck, slipped out of the truck cab and sauntered towards the porch. He had a package in his right hand and an envelope in his left.

"Hey Mack!" Ralph hailed as he stepped onto the porch and headed for one of the rattan rocking chairs. "Did ya'll have a good time in Indiantown?"

"I had a lousy time and I have a lot of things to do around here now that she's gone. What brings you around here on a Saturday afternoon? Shouldn't you be out catching sand fleas?"

"I just came over here to give you your mail. You might be interested in what the retarded mailman left at my house for you." Ralph waved an envelope in Mack's direction. "I can't spend much time because I'm taking your dog sand flea huntin' this afternoon."

"What's with the package? It's not my birthday."

"That French guy that I took to the airport for you Thursday night was back in town. He stopped by in a cab a few minutes after you and Tina left for Indiantown. He said that he missed his plane was on his way back to the West Palm Beach Airport. He told me to give this to you personally. Ralph held a Border's bag out in Mack's direction. Ralph grinned as he spoke. "He must really like you a lot."

"I don't know what you're talking about," Mack responded as he lifted a flat, rectangular-shaped package about two inches thick, neatly wrapped with in colorful paper and topped with a massive red bow out of the bag. He slipped the clear plastic tape from the bottom and slipped out a book.

"It's a book," Mack offered. "I've already read it."

"What kind of book is it?" Ralph asked as he craned his neck to get a better look. "There's a wrecked boat on the cover! Is it a treasure hunting book?"

"According to the synopsis on the back cover it's about a top-secret Navy dolphin project in Hawaii."

Ralph reached over, gently pulled the book out of Mack's hands and looked at the author's bio on the inside of the back cover.

"This is the same guy who dropped off the package!" Ralph exclaimed as he pointed at the author's photograph. "Did you know that he wrote a book?"

"Let me see that!" Mack snatched the book out of Ralph's hands.

Mack was shocked to see the photo of the man he knew as Francois Batteau identified as Jacques Batteau in the author's biography and realized that he had to deflect Ralph's curiosity.

"The reason the guy in the photo looks like the guy who

dropped off the book is because he is his twin brother. This is the guy that I gave a lift up to the Holiday Inn a couple of days ago. He knows that I spent some time in Hawaii. It's no big deal."

"The title of the book is *Treasure Coast Archipelago*. What does Archipelago mean?"

"An Archipelago is a series of islands such as the Hawaiian Islands, the Bahamas or the Archipelago on the eastern side of Sewall's Point."

"Oh. Can I take it home and read it?"

'Of course you can. Just don't bend over the corners of the pages to mark your place."

"I won't. I promise."

"You said that the mailman dropped something off at your house for me? What is it?"

"It's a jury summons for Monday. You get to do your public duty," Ralph snickered as he held out the white envelope in Mack's direction. "I always get out of jury duty because I tell the attorneys that as far as I'm concerned if their client got arrested they're most likely guilty."

"That's not demonstrating very good public responsibility. You should look at jury duty as being a privilege and part of living in a democratic society."

"I'm not a Democrat!" Ralph emphatically stated. "I'm an Independent and the politicians have to cater to me in order to get my vote."

"I'm certain that they do. Let me have that thing so I can find out when I have to be there."

"I already opened it. You have to report to the Jury Room of the Martin County Courthouse at nine o'clock Monday morning."

"Thank you for protecting the integrity of the mail service. Is there anything else I should know?"

"I took that piece of Teflon out of the ignition coil on Tina's boat. It starts just fine now."

"You'd better be glad that she doesn't know what you did. She'd skin you alive and feed you to the cat snappers under the boathouse."

"She'd have to catch me first. I can run fast as the wind when I'm scared. She'd blame you anyway."

"Why would she blame me? You did it!"

"She'd think that you put me up to it."

"Thanks for nothing," Mack replied as he stuffed the jury summons into his shirt pocket.

"What are you going to do this afternoon?" Ralph asked as he looked up from the pages of the open book. "Do you want to go sand flea huntin' with me and your dog this afternoon?"

"No. I want to go by the Blake Library and check on a few things. Are you certain that he knows that he's my dog?"

"I think so. Every time we drive by here to see if you're home he has to get out and water the bushes. I'm sure that he remembers you. But he loves Joy."

"That figures. How about my cat?"

"I haven't seen him around here for a couple of days, but I did hear a big cat fight the other night. That might've been him because our neighbor's cat's in heat."

"If you see him tell him to get his butt home if he wants to eat."

"I don't think that he's very worried about eating. Joy fixed up a bed for him in the garage and she hand feeds him fancy cat food with a spoon twice a day. He eats better than I do."

"I don't doubt that a bit. Ralph I'm going in to get cleaned up and then I'm heading for the library."

"Okey dokey," Ralph replied as he stood up and headed for his truck. "I'm taking this book with me. It sounds real interesting."

"Enjoy yourself," Mack didn't wait for Ralph's reply and entered the cottage.

"*Now what am I going to do?*" Mack muttered. "*Wouldn't it be a kick in the head if I was selected for Octavio's jury? I'm going to fire up the boat and go fishing. I need some thinking time.*"

Chapter 33

Worried that he would be late for jury duty Mack left Port Sewall Marina at 7:45 A.M. and arrived at the Martin County Courthouse on East Ocean Boulevard at 8:05 A.M.

When he arrived at the courthouse all of the parking spaces in front of the courthouse were taken and Mack was forced to find a spot in the auxiliary parking lot behind the courthouse. He passed through the bored security guards at the entrance to the courthouse annex, took a left turn, walked down the hall and found the jury room.

A pot of freshly perked coffee surrounded by an assortment of donuts and bagels sat on a folding table in the western end of the room. Several prospective jurors who arrived ahead of him were reading a book or gazing out the windows and wondering what excuse they could give to get out of jury duty. No one, including Mack, wanted to be there, but it was a civic obligation. He took a seat in the front row, leaned back in the chair as best he could, closed his eyes and attempted to make sense of the events of the past several days.

Mack never made it to the library on Saturday afternoon or on Sunday. He went fishing Saturday afternoon on Sailfish Flats behind Boy Scout Island. He didn't try very hard and didn't catch anything, but he had time to think. Sunday he worked on minor maintenance projects around the marina. He replaced several cleats along the two finger docks, straightened out the mess in the boathouse, added shims to three of the wooden stairs leading down to the dock from the cottage, washed Tina's boat, filled the tank with fresh fuel and ran the engine in neutral for half an hour. Afterwards he drove to Sandsprit Park, parked his truck under a palm tree, walked down to the seawall and spent the rest of the afternoon watching the boats come in and out of the Manatee Pocket. He stopped at Shrimper's for dinner and drank three beers before going back to Port Sewall Marina. When he arrived at the marina he took the avocado green wall telephone mounted on the kitchen wall off the hook, wrapped the handset in a dishtowel and stuffed it in a drawer.

The jury room clerk interrupted Mack's daydreaming with a procedural announcement from her wooden lectern strategically placed directly in front of the seated prospective jurors.

"Ladies and gentlemen," she squeaked in her high female bravado. "May I have your attention please? It's eight forty-five and only thirty-nine of the forty-nine jurors we summoned have arrived. We will wait a few more minutes for the late arrivals before we send a sheriff's deputy to their home to check on them."

She pointed at the clipboard in her left hand and continued.

"One judge wants thirty-five jurors to choose from and those not chosen for his jury will be held over for the second trial."

A chorus of soft moans filled the room and the jury clerk held up her right hand to indicate silence.

"I understand how you feel, but because some of our Martin County residents have apparently decided not to fulfill their civic obligation to participate in the legal process guaranteed by the Constitution of the United States you must take up the slack.

Another, but much louder, chorus of soft moans filled the room. The jury clerk ignored them and pointed again at the clipboard in her left hand.

"Please come up to the table in the front of the room, pick up a clipboard and fill out the prospective juror questionnaire. The prosecuting and defense attorneys will use these questionnaires to determine if they want you on the jury. Please answer each question truthfully and write legibly. After you have filled out the questionnaire put the clipboard face down on the table in the back of the room,"

She pointed to a folding table nested between two bookcases filled with legal reference books.

"I thank you for your cooperation and understanding."

She didn't wait for questions, turned and went out the door.

The pool of thirty-nine prospective jurors was left to mutter their complaints to one another while they wrestled with seemingly innocuous questions as they filled out the juror questionnaire.

Three tardy prospective jurors, a man and two women, came into the room escorted by the jury clerk. Not pleased by their disregard of her self-important role in the legal system she directed them to her lectern and made them stand in front of her as indicated her displeasure with a gentle verbal chastisement and appropriate body language.

"I realize that each of you feel that you have a very good reason for reporting late for jury duty. However, I should report you to the judge. You could be charged with contempt of court." She tapped her clipboard with her right index finger for emphasis. "Because both judges are running a little behind on their dockets because of routine legal matters I'm going to cut you some slack. Go over there," the clerk demanded as she pointed at the table filled with clipboards. "Pick up a clipboard, fill out a prospective juror questionnaire and return it to me. Do you understand me?"

The three intimidated prospective jurors nodded their heads in unison and headed for the table.

The clerk tapped her pencil on the wooden podium to get the attention of the other prospective jurors who were chatting between themselves as they attempted to complete the juror questionnaire.

"Ladies and gentlemen. Please listen up!" She strained to be heard over the soft chatter. "I need your attention now!"

She lifted the base of the portable lectern and thumped it on the wooden floor. That got everyone's undivided attention.

"It's almost ten-thirty and the clerk of the court has advised me that one of the judges is ready to interview twenty prospective jurors. My assistant is passing out a red 'prospective juror' tag to each of you. It is in a plastic holder and you are required to wear it around your neck at all times. This is so that you will be recognized as a juror and no one will talk to you."

The room erupted in laugher.

"I don't see what's so funny about that," she quipped with a deep frown. "The tags are necessary because attorneys and witnesses might be around you. They don't want to say, or do anything, that might influence a juror. Do you all understand the seriousness of a trial? People's futures and freedom hang in the balance."

The room resounded with a single chorus of, "Yes ma'am!"

"Fine. I am going to read off the names of the twenty people chosen to go to the first courtroom. Line up single file at the door in the same order as you are called. The rest of you can leave if you promise to come back by one-thirty. Is that acceptable?"

The room resounded again with a single chorus of, "Yes ma'am!"

"I could hold you here in the courthouse, but you've all been very cooperative and I'll let you push it to one forty-five. Make certain that you're back here on time and don't get me in trouble with the judge! If you aren't back at one forty-five the bailiff will come looking for you and I will guarantee that you won't like that. Do you understand me?"

The room resounded for the third time with a single chorus of, "Yes ma'am!"

"Okay. Wait in your seats for me to call the names of the twenty prospective jurors that are going to the first courtroom.

Once they are lined up and out of the room the rest of you are free to leave. Wear your juror badges around your neck and be back here no later than one forty-five!"

The room resounded for the fourth time with a single chorus of, "Yes ma'am!"

While the bored clerk slowly read off the names of the twenty doomed souls Mack studied the jury pool. The forty-two people who showed up consisted of forty-one white men and women. A single black woman represented the minority population. Mack had taken time to interview the people sitting around him. Immediately to his right sat Elmo's ex-sister-in-law. The woman on his left was a legal secretary for an ambulance-chasing attorney and to her left sat a young female Florida State University graduate. She said that she was a controller for a local company and she was reviewing the month's preliminary financial reports. Mack congratulated her on being a Seminole and she apologized that her younger brother was a University of Florida Gator. Mack tactfully explained that there is hope for conversion and he could direct her to some FSU alumni who run a Gator reprogramming camp deep in the Everglades. She declined his offer.

Only one guy took advantage of the free coffee and bagels and gobbled them down like he hadn't had a meal in a week.

It was almost eleven o'clock before the twenty-two unfortunates were lined up and marched out of the room towards their unknown fate. Mack took advantage of the long lunch break and stopped by the library to see if Janet had any more information for him. Unfortunately the reference librarian on duty told him that Janet worked Sunday and Monday was her day off. Mack schlepped over to the Taste of Italy in the downtown Publix Shopping Center for the luncheon buffet. He made it back to the courthouse on time.

The names of the remaining twenty-two prospective jurors, including Mack, were called out and they formed a single line at the door. On command they marched like a column of Army ants down the hall, through the security station and across the open area into the courthouse wing. They took the elevator to the second floor and were marched into the courtroom.

Once the unhappy group was seated, and roll taken, the judge peered down at them over the top of his eyeglasses from his high perch behind the bench. The judge was slight of build, bald headed and wore a full white beard. He scowled and appeared irritated that his processing of legal paperwork had been interrupted by a gaggle of unhappy citizens who really didn't want to be in his courtroom. He didn't seem to be happy to be there either.

"Ladies and gentlemen," the judge announced in a soft southern drawl. "My name is Judge Greg Melton and I welcome you to my courtroom. I have a lot of paperwork to do and I am going to work on it while the attorneys ask you a few questions. Some of you will be selected as jurors and I only need six of you. The rest of you will be dismissed as soon as a jury is seated. Thank you for your attention and expected cooperation."

The judge gave a 'thumbs up' and went back to his pile of paperwork.

Mack looked around the courtroom to identify the participants. Four middle-aged overweight white male bailiffs were strategically positioned in the courtroom. The two deputies in the back of the courtroom watched the prospective jurors. Two deputies seated at a table in front of the courtroom two were engrossed in reading a newspaper.

The young female state attorney wore a rumpled blue suit that looked like it came out of a Wal-Mart dumpster. Her hair was a bedraggled mess. It begged for a hairbrush and five minutes of personal attention. The table in front of her was stacked with manila folders and she rummaged through them like an elephant looking for a peanut in a pile of straw. She seemed to be flustered as she approached the portable wooden lectern in front of the nervous potential jurors.

"We only need six of you," she nervously began repeating the judge's words. "Because we only need six of you, and there are ten of you in the front row, I'll only interview those sitting in the front row."

After interviewing the ten potential jurors in the first row she went on to the twelve seated in the second row. As they were interviewed people stated their reasons for not being able to sit on a jury. Some of them claimed they were going to lose money if they couldn't go to work, they were enrolled in school and couldn't miss class, they had to watch their kids, etc. The salty male defense attorney showed his frustrated at her indecision by shaking his head from side to side. She became very agitated when she realized that all twenty-two people in the jury pool in front of her had made up excuses for not being able to serve as a juror.

"A person's job, school and babysitting are not valid reasons to be excused," the prosecutor explained. "Some of us have gone through divorce," she said as she held her ringless left hand up in front of the potential jurors. "I understand the frustration of a single parent having to find someone to watch their children when they are on jury duty. However, it is not a valid reason to be excused. Serving on a jury is your civic obligation."

The first person in the second row was a deeply tanned, middle-aged man with obvious signs over overexposure to the sun. He spoke with a heavy southern accent.

"Sir, you have a very cute accent," she remarked. "I notice from the questionnaire that you live in Indiantown. Do know Deputy Elmo?"

"Yes I do and I was born in Indiantown."

"I'm from Alabama myself," she offered.

"I could tell by your cute accent," he quipped with a grin as he sat down.

The next prospect was a well-dressed man apparently in his middle forties. "I am divorced. My ex-wife goes to school on weekdays and I have to watch my eight-year old daughter," the divorced man offered. "Plus, I attend night classes at Indian River Community College and I have finals this week."

"I'm very sorry about your personal situation sir," the prosecutor responded. "And I understand the divorce and child care problem, however those are not valid reasons for you to be excused."

"I'm the accountant for a local company," the next nervous male candidate pleaded. "I have to get out the company's financial statements this week."

His excuse didn't cut the mustard either.

"I'm a critical care nurse," a middle-aged female offered. "I'm scheduled to work tonight and every night this week."

"I'm sorry. That is not a valid reason to be excused."

"I'm Deputy Elmo's divorced wife's sister," offered a soft-spoken female. "Does that count?"

"How do you get along with Deputy Elmo?"

"Fine I guess. I haven't seen him socially since he divorced my sister two years ago."

"Do you hold that against him?"

"Goodness no! Elmo's a good man. My sister's a slut. He did the right thing."

"Then I see no reason to disqualify you unless the defendant's counsel objects."

"No objection," the obviously disgusted defense counsel offered. "We'll take her."

"I realize that many of you live in Indiantown where the alleged incident occurred and know Deputy Elmo," the prosecutor remarked. "However, unless you are inclined to take Deputy Elmo's word over that of the defendant because of a personal relationship you will not be disqualified."

The next candidate, a bashful middle-aged female with mousy shoulder length brown hair, placed her hands in a prayer mode when she made her statement. "I'm not God and I cannot stand in judgment of another person. Only God can do that."

"You'll do just fine," the prosecutor responded. "Our laws are societies' laws, not God's."

"Ms. Prosecutor," Judge Melton called down from his lofty perch. "Please approach the bench."

The prosecutor looked over at the defense attorney and back at the judge.

"I only want to talk to you. Please approach the bench."

She picked her bottle of water off the table and took a long swig on her way to the judge's bench. She placed the cap on the bottle as she held it in front of her at the bench and her cheeks bulged with an obvious mouthful of water. The judge said nothing to her that Mack could hear.

After a few minutes of conversation with the judge the prosecutor returned to her table.

The judge rapped his gavel several times to get the group's attention before he spoke.

"Ladies and gentlemen the prosecutor has advised the court that she wishes to pursue a plea bargain with the defendant before final jury selection," he stated in a deep, authoritarian tone of voice, but still with the soft southern drawl. "Please leave my courtroom in single file and wait for the bailiff to call you back. If a plea bargain is not reached within fifteen minutes final jury selection will continue and the trial will begin at ten o'clock tomorrow morning in this courtroom. You are all excused for fifteen minutes. Please do not leave the courtroom."

Mack watched through the glass window in the courtroom door as the prosecutor attempted to make a plea deal while the prospective jurors were on break in the hallway. The defendant shook his head from side to side each time the prosecutor made a statement. She through up her hands and approached the judge's bench along with the defense attorney. It was obvious to Mack that a plea bargain was not reached and the trial would go on as scheduled. The bailiff came to the door and ordered the prospective jurors back inside the courtroom.

Mack glanced over at the defendant's table. A Hispanic male wearing a white shirt shook his head, looked at the ceiling and rolled his eyes at the all-white prospective jury panel in front of him. He started to cry and no doubt wished that he had taken a plea deal. The man looked like Octavio!

The judge came down from the bench, slowly walked to the back of courtroom and positioned himself behind the portable wooden lectern strategically placed directly in front of the nervous prospective jurors. He addressed the group in a soft, disarming county-boy voice with a definite southern drawl.

"Ya'll, I am very glad that you are in my courtroom today. Serving on a jury is a very important social responsibility and should not be taken lightly. Thank you for being considerate and I know that if you are chosen to be a juror in this trial that you will be fair and impartial."

Mack couldn't tell if his southern drawl was his normal speech pattern or simply a method to disarm the prospective jurors. They had to listen carefully to pick up each word and Mack was certain that he did it deliberately so that the audience had to listen carefully to hear what he had to say.

"There are four elements to a conviction and the state has to prove each one beyond a reasonable doubt," he stated. "Gosh I'm very sorry," he offered as his face reddened. "I seem to have temporarily forgotten what they are, but I'll cover them with the jury before they enter into deliberations. Thank you for your attention."

The judge gave a 'thumb's up' as he turned and walked back to the bench.

After the judge's speech the prospective jurors' attitudes changed from grousing to doing their civic duty and many changed their tune from what they had expressed in the prospective juror holding room. It might even be a fair trail.

The defense attorney and the prosecutor decided upon six of the ten prospective jurors seated in the front row. Mack and the rest of the relieved prospects were dismissed. Mack glanced at his watch on his way out of the courtroom. It was 2:47 P.M.

Chapter 34

The morning sun was streaking through the east windows of the tiny cottage when Ralph entered to wake Mack up and tell him that Tina wanted him on the telephone.

"Mack! Wake up!" Ralph bellowed as he entered the bedroom. "Tina's been calling my house and she wants to talk to you. She says that it's important."

"Tell her that my phone's broken," Mack responded without opening his eyes. "Tell her that I'll call her when it's fixed."

"She won't believe me. She thinks that you took it off the hook again."

"I did and she doesn't have any choice. I have a lot of things to do today and I don't need her on my butt."

"Are you going somewhere?"

"I have to do some research at the Blake Library." Mack rolled over and opened his eyes.

"What kind of research?"

"Archeological research."

"I didn't know that you are interested in archaeology. Did you know that Joy has a degree in Egyptology?"

"Yes, but I'm not interested in Egypt."

"Neither am I and that really ticks her off."

"Where's my dog?"

"When I left the house he was eating breakfast. Joy said she's taking him shopping to Pet Smart this morning. She said that he needs some new toys to play with."

"She's spoiling him rotten. That dog's never going to want to come home."

"That's what he told me."

"Ralph get out of here and go find something to do! I have to get cleaned up and over to the library."

"It's not quite eight o'clock and the library doesn't open until ten. Do you want to go to the Queen Conch and have breakfast?"

"No thanks. I'll pick up some coffee and a bagel at the Dunkin' Donuts on East Ocean."

"Okay. Suit yourself. I was going to buy."

"I appreciate the offer, but I have a lot of things on my mind."

"What happened with you and jury duty yesterday? Did you vote to hang the guy?"

"No. I was dismissed because I knew Elmo. He was the arresting officer in the case."

"What time did they cut you loose?"

"Two-thirty. I hung around to see what was going to happen."

"Why?"

"The judge wanted to go through a trial. Before the jury was selected, the judge directed the prosecutor to offer a plea bargain to the defendant and gave her fifteen minutes to get it. He sent the prospective jurors into the hall to wait."

"Did he take it?"

"No."

"Was Elmo there?"

"No and the judge dismissed the case for lack of evidence."

"Elmo's gonna' be pissed."

"That's his problem."

"What time did you get back here last night? I came by to check on you about nine-thirty and the place was dark."

"I pulled in a little bit after ten o'clock."

"You must've taken a side trip. It's only a ten minute drive from here to the courthouse."

"I was in Indiantown."

"What were you doing over there? Tina told you to stay away from Indiantown."

"I gave someone a ride and I'm not worried about Tina."

"Who?"

"The Guatemalan laborer that Elmo charged with aggravated assault and grand theft."

"Is he the one who pulled a knife on Carlos?"

"That's him."

"Elmo told me about that guy. He said that case was a slam-dunk. What about the aggravated assault charge?"

"Carlos called the clerk of the court during the lunch break and dropped the assault charge. The defense attorney didn't know about the call. That's why the judge was pushing for a plea bargain. All they had left to prosecute was the grand theft charge and Elmo didn't show up with any evidence."

"What did the guy try to steal?"

"Octavio didn't try to steal anything. He gave a carved stone mask to Carlos as payment for his bar tab and Carlos accepted it. A few days later Octavio told Carlos that he wanted the mask back because it was a family heirloom. When Carlos refused Octavio pulled a knife on him."

"If he pulled a knife why did Carlos drop the assault charge?"

"He needs the Hispanic laborers' business. If the guy had been convicted the Hispanics would stop coming into Carlos' place and he would go out of business."

"What happened to the mask?"

"No one knows. Carlos claims that it was stolen from his storeroom. The prosecutor only had a color photograph of it."

"Is it valuable?"

"No one knows. It could be twenty-five hundred years old, or a clever fake. If it were authenticated as genuine it would be worth as much as one hundred thousand bucks! However, if it's a fake it's worthless. The level for grand theft is a minimum value of three hundred bucks, but the judge couldn't substantiate grand theft charges because even if it was presented as evidence it hadn't been appraised."

"Where do you think it is?"

"Where what is?"

"The mask."

"I don't know."

"Do you want to go sand flea digging with me and your dog this morning?"

"No! I told you that I'm going to the library to do some research."

"What kind of research? Something about the mask?"

"Yes."

"Joy might be able to help you. She has a degree in Egyptology."

"You told me already. The mask is from Mexico, or Guatemala. That's a long way from Egypt."

"You'd better put your phone back on the hook before Tina drives up here and kicks your butt."

"I will. You'd better get going if you're going to catch any sand fleas before the tide starts coming back in."

"I'm on the way. Do you want me to bring your dog by to see you?"

"No. He might think that he lives here and want to stay. It sounds like he's having a great time at your place."

"Joy's is spoiling him worse than a red-headed stepchild."

"Tell him to have fun. I'll come over and pick him up when this mess is over."

"Okay. Suit yourself." Ralph turned and headed for the bedroom door. "Don't forget to put your telephone back on the hook. Tina's really pissed off at you."

"I will," Mack quipped as he gave Ralph a wave.

After Ralph left Mack dragged himself out of bed and headed for the bathroom.

Chapter 35

Just as Mack came out of the bedroom and headed for the kitchenette the phone rang as if it had ESP.

"*Damn!*" Mack muttered under his breath. "*Ralph put the phone back on the hook!*"

"Hello," Mack offered apprehensively.

"Where were you all day yesterday?" It was Tina!

"I had jury duty."

"Why didn't you tell me about it on Saturday?"

"Because I didn't know about it until Saturday night. The mailman delivered the jury summons to Ralph's house by mistake and he brought it over to me."

"Why didn't you call me?"

"I didn't think that it was important."

"Not important? Octavio's trial was set for Monday and you might have been selected as a juror. That wouldn't have been good."

"I was, but I was dismissed because I knew Elmo."

"What happened to Octavio? I was in court all day and by the time I got out the Martin County Clerk's office was closed."

"Carlos called in and dropped the aggravated assault charge and the grand theft charge was dropped for lack of evidence. The prosecutor needed the mask you swiped as evidence, plus there was no appraisal value determined for it so the judge couldn't accept a grand theft charge. The prosecutor only had a color photograph of it."

"I didn't swipe the damned mask!"

"Who did? It wasn't me."

"It wasn't me either and I don't appreciate your condescending tone. I'm an officer of the court."

"So what? Are you going to give the mask back to Carlos, or better yet to Octavio because it's his."

"I don't have it. What time were you dismissed?"

"About two-thirty."

"Where were you yesterday afternoon and last night? I tried calling you several times."

"I gave Octavio a ride back to Indiantown. I didn't get back here until after ten o'clock."

"Why did you go to Indiantown? I told you to stay away from there!"

"Octavio needed a ride and Elmo wouldn't take him back."

"Some of his people could've come and picked him up. The grove workers have a van."

"No one expected him to be released. Is there anything else you want to rag on me about? I have important things to do around here today."

"I suppose not. Is anyone else there with you?"

"Just the cat and he's pissed. He wants to be fed."

"How about your dog?"

"He's over at Ralph's and Joy's house. They've spoiled him rotten. Ralph said that he doesn't want to come back here."

"What makes him think that?"

"He says that's what my dog told him."

"Dogs can't talk to humans."

"Mine can." Mack pushed the telephone out to arm's length as he spoke. "Tina, are you still there? I can't hear you."

Satisfied that he had thoroughly frustrated Tina, Mack hung up the telephone, then quickly removed the handset from the bracket and placed the receiver on the kitchen counter. The telephone company's 'howler' began wailing and Mack wrapped the handset in a dishtowel to stifle the ear-piercing tone and stuffed it in a silverware drawer.

Mack turned towards the front door and spotted Elmo's patrol car pulling into the marina parking lot. Elmo parked directly in front of the cottage and tripped his siren to get Mack's attention. Mack ran out the front door and hollered at Elmo as he waved both hands in his direction.

"Cut that damn thing off!" Mack screamed. "What are you trying to prove?"

Elmo smiled, flipped off the siren, rolled down his car window and gestured for Mack to approach the car.

"Mornin' Mack," Elmo offered with a deadpan look on his face. "I've been meaning to catch up to you since that farce of a trial yesterday."

"Why?"

"I want to talk to you about why you, or Tina, stole that mask out of Carlos' place Friday night. You cost me a conviction and you have some explaining to do."

"I didn't steal the mask. Carlos went to look for it in his beer storeroom and it was gone. Somebody substituted a rock for it."

"He figures that the young Mexican girl switched the rock for the mask and gave it to you, or Tina."

"Let me assure you that she didn't give me anything, but I don't know about Tina. You'll have to ask her yourself."

"I already did. She said that she doesn't have it."

"Why didn't you show up at the trial?"

"Carlos called the clerk of the court and dropped the aggravated assault charge. Then because you or Tina swiped the mask I didn't have any evidence to support the attempted grand theft charge!" Elmo was shouting and his face had turned bright red. "I had that Guat nailed! It was a slam dunk."

"Elmo it wasn't a slam dunk. There wasn't any evidence of what he attempted to steal."

"The prosecutor had a color picture of it. That should've been good enough."

"Maybe. But, it hasn't been established if it's genuine, or a clever fake."

"It's real! I know it is!"

"He was just trying to get his property back. Certainly you realize that the threshold for grand theft is three hundred bucks and there wasn't any value established for the mask."

"Oh. I saw that Guat get into your truck outside the courthouse about four o'clock! Where did you take him?"

"Back to Indiantown. He needed a ride."

"Why did you do that?"

"Why not? He wasn't guilty. You dragged him over here and you should've taken him back."

"I only arrest them and take them to jail. It's not my job to take them home."

Elmo felt trapped and tried to change the subject.

"Did you hear about the nuclear sub that was spotted off of Push Button Hill by a couple of charterboat captains on Tuesday?"

"Yes. Ralph told me about it."

"What do you think it was doing out there?"

"How should I know?"

"I think you know something. What was it doing out there?"

"Submarine stuff. How's that?"

"Submarine stuff? What's that?"

"It's what submarines do best. It's better that you don't know anymore than that. You might get yourself into more trouble than you are now."

"What do you mean more trouble than I am in now? I'm not in any trouble. Am I?"

"The Guatemalans in Indiantown aren't very happy that you arrested their leader and threw him in jail. I'd stay away from there for awhile if I was you."

"Why? I'm the law over there. They wouldn't dare say

anything to me. Do you see the black stripe down the outside of my pants leg?"

"That stripe scares the hell out of them and they won't look me in the eye."

"They're afraid of the stripe?"

"Yep."

"Why would they be afraid of a stripe on your pants leg?"

"Because the Mexican *Federales* have back stripes on their pants too. They beat the hell out of people when they arrest them back in Mexico." Elmo puffed up his chest as he spoke. "They're afraid of me."

"Maybe they are. Did you know that the ancient Mayans believed in human sacrifice to cleanse away evil spirits and bad omens?"

"I read something about it in a book one time. Why?"

"You are definitely a bad omen to them. Did you know that someone built a wooden altar back in the woods off of Martin Grade close to the entrance to the Naked Lady Ranch?"

"That's no altar!

"Carlos thinks it is."

"I've been out here to check it out! It's just a pile of old wooden sod pallets."

"Believe whatever you wish."

"Mack, do you think that it's really an altar?"

"I'm not sure, but it certainly could be."

Feeling trapped Elmo tried to change the subject.

"Did you hear about the school of dolphins that beached themselves north of the Holiday Inn on Jensen Beach on Tuesday?"

"Yes. Ralph told me about it."

"Do you think the sub had anything to do with the beached dolphins?"

"No. Most likely they were infested with ear mites, came close to shore to rub their ear holes in the beach sand to get them out and got stranded when the tide when out. It happens quite often."

"Did you hear about the weird French guy that was staying at the Holiday Inn? He got some guy drunk and dragged him off to his room. I'm trying to find out who it was."

"No. I didn't."

"Oh. I thought you might know. Somebody told me that they thought they saw you singing karaoke in the lounge. I told them that you don't sing."

"It wasn't me. Elmo, do you ever listen to the car radio when you're in Indiantown?"

"Of course. I'm required to have my sheriff's department radio on all the time."

"I don't mean that radio. I mean your car's AM-FM radio. Do you ever listen to music?"

"I'm not supposed to, but every once in awhile I do. Why?"

"What station do you listen to when you're in Indiantown?"

"The local Hispanic station. I'm trying to learn Spanish, but those announcers talk to fast. Why?"

"Does the radio station's signal ever seem to fade in and out as you're driving?"

"All the time. It usually happens on the swing shift. Why?"

"Did you ever notice that the jukebox in the Silver Saddle seems to fade in and out?"

"I never noticed. I get in and out of there as fast as I can. Why?"

"Could there be a problem with the electric service over there? Maybe the power fluctuates?"

"Indiantown gets its electricity from the fossil fuel plant outside of town. I've heard that once in awhile they get some bad coal. I'll ask my cousin. He works there."

"Thanks."

"Mack, I've enjoyed our conversation, but it's a quarter to nine and I have to get going. I have a court appearance at nine o'clock. "I'll see you around."

Elmo rolled his window up, backed the car up, pulled out of the marina parking lot and headed for Old St. Lucie Boulevard. He gave two toots on the car horn on his way out.

Mack turned, shook his head and headed back into the cottage.

"Elmo knows more about that mask than he let's on," he thought. *"And why did he ask me if I knew about the submarine?"*

Chapter 36

At 10:32 A.M. Mack walked up to the Blake Library reference desk and tapped on the counter to get Janet's attention.

Janet looked up from her computer terminal and a broad smile crossed her face as she responds.

"What brings you in here today Mr. McCray? Are you looking for a wild adventure here in the library? We reference librarians lead a dull life you know."

"I came in to see you yesterday, but you were off."

"I worked on Sunday and yesterday was my day off. Don't you have jury duty this week?"

"I did. I got out of it."

"How did you do that?"

"Elmo was the arresting officer in the case, and the attorneys dismissed me because I knew him."

"What kind of trial was it?"

"It was the Guatemalan laborer from Indiantown that I told you about."

"The one who owns the mask?"

"Correct. However, his ownership is past tense. It's gone."

"Where did it go? Didn't you tell me that a bartender in Indiantown was holding it as payment for a bar bill?"

"He was, but it disappeared. Tina and I went over there Friday night to check on it. The bartender said that he packed it in a beer carton and hid it in his storage room for safekeeping. When he opened the box in front of us the mask was gone and a rock was in its place."

"That sounds like the same switch that was used when the mask was originally discovered."

"Exactly the same. But I think I know where it is."

"Do you think the bartender is lying?"

"Without a doubt he's lying about something, but I think someone switched the mask on him."

"What makes you think that?"

"Saturday morning a young Guatemalan girl showed up in the hallway outside of Tina's room in the Seminole Inn and passed her something heavy wrapped in newspaper. I'm certain that it was the mask."

"How do you know that she gave the package to Tina? Were you there?"

"I went upstairs to check on Tina because she was late for breakfast. When I got to the top of the stairs I saw the girl standing outside Tina's room and I saw her pass the package to Tina."

"Did you ask Tina about it?"

"Of course! She told me that the girl wanted her to mail her personal effects back to Mexico because she was being sold to a bar owner in Okeechobee."

"You can't sell people in this country! Slavery was abolished after the Civil War."

"You can if the person is an illegal immigrant and afraid of being arrested and sent to jail."

"She wouldn't go to jail if the INS caught her. The worse they would do would be to deport her back to Mexico."

"In her case it would be Guatemala and she doesn't know that. The people who hire the illegal Mexicans and Guatemalans keep them in line by telling them that the *Federales* will put them in prison for life if they're caught."

"There aren't any Mexican *Federales* in Florida."

"The illegal workers don't know that. They figure that anyone that carries a gun and wears a uniform with a black stripe down the outside of their pant legs is a *Federále* and out to get them."

"Don't most law enforcement personnel have a black stripe down their pants legs?"

"Yes and that's the point. The illegal immigrants don't look at a law enforcement officer as someone who will help them. They figure that they'll beat the hell out of them and take them to jail if they so much as look them in the eye."

"Oh. What's the status of Octavio's trial? That is his name isn't it?"

"Yes it is. You have an excellent memory."

"Not for much longer I'm afraid. It's slowly fading away. Is his trial going on today?"

"No. Judge Melton dropped the attempted grand theft charges yesterday afternoon for lack of evidence because the mask couldn't be produced. The prosecutor only had a photo of it."

"How do you know that if you were thrown out of the jury pool?"

"I went back in the courtroom after the jury was dismissed to observe the pre-trial motions. I thought I might be able to learn something. I'm taking notes for a book I might write someday."

"What about the assault charge for attacking the bartender?"

"The bartender called the clerk of the court while the jury selection process was going on and told her that he wasn't going to press charges. It's over. Octavio walked out of the courthouse a free man."

"How much do you know about him?"

"Who? Carlos or Octavio?"

"The Guatemalan laborer."

"Quite a bit. I gave him a ride back to Indiantown yesterday afternoon after the charges were dismissed. He told me his family history and the story of the mask. It ties in with what you found."

"Really? How did you communicate? Does he speak English?"

"His English is about as good as my Spanish, but we were able to understand each other."

"What did he tell you about the mask?"

"His grandfather was a digger at the excavation site when the mask was discovered. He's the person who took the mask out of the shipping crate and replaced it with a river stone."

"Wow! What a story!" Janet's face lit up as she spoke. "That matches what the curator at the Smithsonian told me."

"That's not all of it. He told me that the Guatemalans revere the temple sites as sacred and when an archeological excavation takes place the relatives of the person the temple is named for volunteer as laborers so they can rescue the family treasures and hide them from the archaeologists."

"Wow! Do the archaeologists have any idea that they're doing that?"

"I doubt it."

"Wow! What intrigue! It sounds like an *Indiana Jones* movie plot."

"It might just be closer than you may think. There's more."

"Really?"

"Really. His grandfather also told him that the tomb that contained the mask was his family's royal tomb. If what his grandfather told him is correct Octavio is descended from ancient Olmec Royalty."

"Really?"

"Really."

"Are you telling me that Octavio's bloodline is from ancient Olmec roots?"

"That's correct."

"Then it all fits!"

"What do you mean it all fits?"

"From what I found out in my research the mask is definitely Olmec and they pre-dated the Maya by almost eight hundred years. The Olmec left no written records except hieroglyphs that no one has been able to decipher to this very day and there is no Olmec Rosetta Stone."

"So what?"

"Without written records there is no way to prove or disprove family lineage."

"What's that?"

"A family tree so to speak."

"He has the Olmec mask that his grandfather gave him. Isn't that proof enough?"

"Of course not. Has the mask been appraised and authenticated by an expert?"

"I don't think so," Mack shrugged his shoulders. "It looks real to me."

"Of course it looks real and Mexico City has many factories that manufacture authentic-looking relics for sale to gullible tourists who want a bargain. It might be a fake."

"I don't think so. I believe Octavio's story."

"I'll admit that it's a great story and might even make an excellent movie plot, but before to get too excited I suggest that you have the mask appraised and authenticated by an expert. The Smithsonian might be willing to do it for you."

"Unfortunately I can't do that."

"Why not?"

"It's not my property, plus Tina has it. She probably sold it at the flea market over the weekend."

"Why don't you ask her about it?"

"I'd rather drink sulfuric acid and have my fingernails ripped out by decorative garden gnomes."

"That's rather silly isn't it? Garden gnomes are decorations. They aren't alive."

"Have you spent any time with garden gnomes at night?"

"Of course not!"

"They come to life at night and look for humans to kidnap and drag back to their caves."

"Mr. McCray, have you been drinking this early in the morning?"

"No. It's true. Just read some Norwegian folklore. It's well documented in the ancient literature!"

"I'll pass on that. Did you hear about the school of toothed dolphins that beached themselves on Jensen Beach, just north of the Holiday Inn, last week?"

"I was out of town, but Ralph mentioned it. So?"

"They showed it on television. It was pitiful to watch them squirming in the surf and calling out to one another. I cried when I saw it."

"It happens all of the time. It's a natural event caused by ear mites or infection."

"That's what the biologist from Harbor Branch said when the television reporter interviewed him. It's such a shame that they have to suffer that way. The French government sent their top dolphin researcher here to study the dolphin stranding."

"How do you know that?"

"I saw him interviewed on television. He has a cute little French mustache and a goatee."

"That doesn't hold any appeal for me."

"Did you hear about the Russian nuclear submarine that was spotted off the St. Lucie Inlet last week? Several charterboat captains spotted it and they chased it around for several hours."

"Ralph mentioned it."

"Do you think that the submarine had anything to do with the dolphin stranding?"

"No, and I don't think it was a Russian sub either."

"Why not? That's what the charterboat captains said on television."

"I didn't realize that our local charterboat captains were submarine experts. I doubt that anyone of them could differentiate a Russian Akula class nuclear attack subs from one of ours. Plus, the Russians wouldn't waste their resources spying on the St. Lucie Inlet. They didn't have very many subs left after the Cold War and they only have sixteen Akulas in service."

"How do you know that?"

"I read it somewhere."

"How many do we have?"

"Fifty-seven total. We have fifty of the original sixty-two in the Los Angeles class still in service and several of them will be decommissioned in the next five years. We only have three in the

Seawolf class out of the original twenty-nine scheduled to be built. And there are only four subs in the 'Virginia' class. We are only building one new nuclear attack sub every three years. The Chinese are far ahead of us."

"Why?"

"They have seventy-eight nuclear attack subs in service and build three new ones every year."

"How do you know all of this information?"

"I read a lot. Did you find out anything for me about the use of Alpha wave brain modification experiments for mind control via Extremely Low Frequency transmission?"

"Was I supposed too?"

"I asked you when I was in here last Thursday."

"I guess that I got busy and forgot. I did give you the information about those mafia guys you've been hanging around with in Chicago didn't I?"

"Yes and I appreciate it very much. But I really need some information about government experiments in Alpha brain wave modification techniques."

"Refresh my memory. I'll make a few notes this time so that I don't forget," Janet reached for a yellow pad and a ballpoint pen. "I told you earlier that my memory is going fast. I detest getting older."

"Why? You look just fine."

"I have so many wrinkles in my face and body that it would take a high pressure air hose up my butt to get them out."

"Let's not go there," Mack replied with a grin. "Just the thought makes a terrible visual."

"I know," Janet quipped with a sly smile. "I see them every time I climb out of the tub. Now exactly what did you want me to research for you?"

"Can you do some research for me on military and civilian mind control experiments?"

"Can you be more specific? The CIA conducted experiments with LSD in the nineteen-sixties."

"That's old news. I'm looking for civilian and military non-lethal warfare applications involving the use of Extremely Low Frequency electromagnetic wave transmissions to stimulate the human brain's Alpha waves above and below the earth's resonant frequency of eight point seven Hertz."

"Isn't Hertz a rental car company?"

"Yes, but in this application Hertz means cycles per second."

"Oh. I hope it all makes sense to you."

"Alpha brain wave modification is a concept that goes back into history for thousands of years. Have you seen people practicing meditation where they sit with their legs crossed and their palms facing upward as they hum?"

"It always sounded more like a moan to me."

"They are humming the Hindu word *Om* and attempting to bring their brain's Alpha waves in alignment with the earth's resonant frequency of seven point eight three Hertz. Does that make sense?"

"No, but I'll look it up on the Internet. Stop by tomorrow and I'll let you know what I found,"

"Thanks." Mack started to turn away and paused. "Oh Janet," he said with a pause for effect.

"Now what do you want?"

"I was just wondering about something else, but I'm certain that it's far out of your range."

"That sounds like a challenge to me," Janet retorted as she sat up straight and looked Mack directly in the eye. "Lay it on me big boy and I'll see what I can do. Nothing's out of my range to research."

"This may be a real stretch for you," Mack whispered. "But it's very important."

"I know what you're doing!" Janet grinned as she replied. "You're baiting me."

"I wouldn't do that."

"Yes you would! Now what is it?"

"What do you know about Hinduism?"

"A little bit. Ancient religions intrigue me and I took a lot of religion courses as electives in college."

"That was a long time ago wasn't it? Maybe you forgot a lot of stuff?"

"What do you want to know? I'm ready!"

"What is the symbolism of the *Om* symbol?"

"That's easy! Everyone with an ounce of brains knows that!"

"I must have been shorted in the brain department. Tell me and make me as smart as you are."

"I doubt that you could ever be as smart as I am, but I'll try. *Om*, or *Aum*, is of paramount importance in Hinduism and is a symbol representing *Brahman*, the impersonal *Absolute* and the source of all manifest existence. *Om* represents the un-manifest or *nirguna*, and the manifest or *saguna*, aspects of God. It pervades life and runs through our *prana*, that means breath. Now do you understand?"

"Of course! There's nothing about that not to understand."

"What is the significance of a Hindu girl giving a silver *Om* pendant to a man?"

"That's very important to a Hindu woman! That's her pledge of a lifetime commitment to him."

"What do you know about the Hindu God *Ganesha*? It's the one that looks like an elephant head on a human body."

"That's something I love to discuss. *Ganesha* is my favorite Hindu God."

"Why? It looks like an elephant with four human arms!"

"Don't be fooled by *Ganesha's* outward appearance. It's true that *Ganesha* has an elephantine countenance with a curved trunk and big ears, and a huge pot-bellied body of a human being. He is the Lord of success and destroyer of evils and obstacles. He is also worshipped as the god of education, knowledge, wisdom and wealth. *Ganesha* is one of the five prime Hindu deities whose idolatry is glorified as the *panchayatana puja*."

"Why does he look like an elephant with arms?"

"*Ganesha's* head symbolizes the *Atman*, the soul, which is the ultimate supreme reality of human existence. His human body signifies *Maya*, the earthly existence of human beings. The elephant head denotes wisdom and its trunk represents *Om*, the sound symbol of cosmic reality. In his upper right hand *Ganesha* holds a goad, which helps him propel mankind forward on the eternal path and remove obstacles from the way. The noose in *Ganesha's* left hand is a gentle implement to capture all difficulties faced by his subjects."

Janet sat up straight as she questioned her pupil.

"Now do you appreciate the role of *Ganesha* to Hindus?"

"I suppose. Is that all?"

"What else do you want to know?"

"Whatever you can tell me. I have an urge to understand Hinduism."

"Why?"

"It's a long story. I'll tell someday when I have time."

"Okay. Hang on. Here we go."

"Okay. Go slow because I'm a slow learner."

"The broken tusk that *Ganesha* holds like a pen in his lower right hand is a symbol of sacrifice, which he broke for writing the *Mahabharata*. The rosary in his left hand suggests that the pursuit of knowledge should be continuous. The *laddoo*, candy to you, he holds in his trunk indicates that one must discover the sweetness of the *Atman*. His fan-like elephant ears convey that he is all ears and listens to his petitioners. The snake wrapped around his waist represents energy. And he is humble enough to ride the lowest of creatures, a mouse."

Janet paused for effect and Mack pounced.

"Why does he have an elephant's head?" Mack asked.

The story goes like this. The goddess Parvati, while bathing, created a boy out of the dirt of her body and assigned him the task of guarding the entrance to her bathroom. When Shiva, her husband returned, he was surprised to find a stranger denying him access, and struck off the boy's head in rage. Parvati broke down in utter grief and to soothe her, Shiva sent out his squad of men to fetch the head of any sleeping being who was facing the north. The company found a sleeping elephant and brought back its severed head, which was then attached to the body of the boy. Shiva restored its life and bestowed that people worship him and invoke his name before undertaking any venture."

"This guy sounds like he'd be the top dog in a dogfight!"

"That's blasphemous and you should be ashamed of yourself!"

"I am. Please continue and I'm all ears."

"*Ganesha* is the destroyer of vanity, selfishness and pride."

"You could learn a lesson or two from his teachings."

"I will. I promise."

"*Ganesha* is the personification of the material universe in all its various magnificent manifestations. All Hindus worship *Ganesha* regardless of their sectarian belief. He is both the beginning of the religion and the meeting ground for all Hindus. "Janet shifted her position behind the reference desk to look Mack in the eye. "Did any of that make sense to you?"

"It was very interesting and I'm certain that it makes sense to you, but I have to leave now and do some research of my own."

"It's about time that you did some of your own work. What kind of research?"

"Fossil fuel electric generating power plants."

"Why would you want to know anything about them? The coal-burning plants generate terrible emissions and pollute the environment."

"I'm curious about why the power output fluctuates at night, makes electric lights flicker and radio stations' broadcast signal to fade in and out."

"I never noticed that at my house."

"That's because the electric power for this area is supplied by the nuclear power generating station on Hutchinson Island in St, Lucie County."

"That's what I thought. Then why are you interested in coal-burning power plants?"

"That's what they have in Indiantown."

"Oh. Have you taken up a new hobby?"

"No. I'm just curious," Mack winked as he replied, turned and headed for the door.

Chapter 37

Mack pulled his blue Ford F-150 pickup truck into a parking space at the Port Sewall Marina at 10:32 P.M. and switched off the truck's ignition. It had been a long day and he looked forward to crawling into bed, his wishes were not to be. He spotted Rat rocking back and forth in a wicker rocking chair on the front porch of the marina cottage.

"Crap! What the hell does Rat want at this time of night?" Mack questioned in his mind as he swung out of the truck cab and headed for the porch. *"I hope that he hasn't fallen in love with another goat."*

Rat didn't stand up to greet Mack and only lifted his right hand off the arm of the rocking chair in a slight wave of acknowledgement.

"Where've you been all night?" Rat questioned through his scruffy beard. "I've been waitin' for you since eight-thirty."

"I didn't realize that I had to provide you with a schedule of my activities," Mack responded with a grin as he swung into the rocking chair next to Rat's. "I haven't had to worry about bed check since I was in the military."

"I didn't mean that the way it came out," Rat offered. "It's just that I haven't seen you for a few days. I was worried about you."

"I'm over eighteen and I'm just fine."

"Elmo told me that you screwed him over on that Indiantown Guatemalan case."

"What are you talking about? I didn't have anything to do with it! I was passed over for jury duty and the judge dismissed the case for lack of evidence!"

"That's not the way Elmo sees it," Rat stammered. "He thinks that you are up to something."

"What makes him think that?"

"He saw you and the Guat leaving the courthouse together yesterday afternoon."

"I just gave him a ride back to Indiantown. He didn't have way to get back."

"Elmo thinks that you and the Guat are buddies."

"I don't care what Elmo thinks! I gave the poor guy a ride back to Indiantown because he didn't have any transportation. When did Elmo tell you this?"

"Late this afternoon just before dinner time. He stopped by Shepherd's Park while me and the boys was cookin' up some country stew using the stuff we picked up last night."

"Why would Elmo make a special trip over there to see you?"

"He'd been lookin' for you all day and thought that I might know where you went. Where was you all day anyway?"

"Elmo was here this morning. He left about eight-thirty to go to the courthouse."

"He got out of there about two o'clock. He wanted to talk to you about something and he told me that it was real important."

"I wasn't hiding from him. He could have found me. I went to the library about ten-thirty to see Janet and left there about eleven-thirty."

"Where'd you go after you left the library?"

"You are really full of questions tonight aren't you?"

"I suppose I am."

"I stopped at the Taste of Italy for lunch. Does that meet your approval?"

"You could've stopped by the boat and invited me. I like that place."

"I didn't have time. I had to go someplace."

"Where?"

'Why? Are you writing my personal travel diary?"

"No. I'm trying to fill in the blanks."

"I went to Indiantown. Are you satisfied now?"

"And you're just getting back here? That's only a thirty minute trip."

"Yes! I just got back! So what?"

"You don't have to get huffy with me. I'm just asking."

"The next thing you'll be asking me why I went to Indiantown!"

"That's right! What were you doing over there anyway? Have you got something going with some Guat? Some of them Guatemalan gals are real cuties."

"Of course not! I was checking out the Florida Power and Light fossil fuel power generating plant."

"Why would you want to do that? There's nothing special about it. They load coal in one end and set it on fire. The coal burns, generates heat, the heat makes water boil that turns a steam turbine and an electric generator. End of story."

"I have a new hobby. I'm studying power generating plants."

"Why?"

"They're very interesting. Did you know that the Indiantown power plant generates two and a half megawatts of electricity for every ton of coal it burns?'

"No, and I don't really care."

"It is a very efficient generating plant. It's one of the best in the country."

"Big deal. Why were you really over there? Were you messing around with the Mexican women?"

"No. I went over to visit the power plant."

"What time did you get over there?"

"About two o'clock. Why?"

"Because it's past ten-thirty. It only takes about a half hour to drive over there."

"I stayed late because I wanted to see how much light is emitted from the smoke stack."

"I can see that we're not getting anywhere with this conversation. Do you know about the nuclear attack sub that was spotted off the St. Lucie Inlet last week?"

"Ralph mentioned it."

"Some of the charterboat captains think it was a Russian nuclear-powered attack sub."

"I'm sure that they're right. The Russians have nothing better to do than spy on the St. Lucie Inlet."

"Don't make fun of it! Them Russians can be real sneaky! You never know what they're up to."

"I'm not making fun of the incident. It probably was a Russian sub. So what?"

"Maybe they were making a chart of this area."

"They don't have to make a chart. They can buy one at a marine supply store."

"Then what do you think the sub was doing here?"

"I have no idea. If I was to rationalize why I'd guess that they came up to practice taking manual terrestrial bearings with a pelorus, plotting their position on chart and comparing them to their satellite Global Positioning System reading."

"Oh. I guess that makes sense."

"It's the only explanation that does."

"Elmo thinks the sub was doin' some experiments with a secret sonar system that wiped out the dolphins that beached themselves on Jensen Beach last week."

"I suppose that could be true as well. But I don't care. I want to go to bed and get some sleep."

"If you're going to be so grumpy abut it then I'm goin' home. By the way, your cat's not here, but don't worry about him."

"Did you eat him?"

"No! He was here on the porch when I showed up and he was hungry. He bitched at me like a wife after two months of married bliss. I slipped inside your place, got a can of cat food out of the closet and fed him."

"Where is he now?"

"I don't know. After he finished the cat food he licked his butt and took off towards Ralph's house."

"He's probably after another handout."

"Where's your dog?"

"Ralph's had him over at his place for over a week. The dog thinks that he lives there."

"I suppose that Joy's spoiling him?"

"Ralph told me that she's treating him like a red-headed stepchild. Rat, I'm going to bed."

"Okay. I'll check back with you tomorrow. Elmo might be comin' by tomorrow to see you."

"I can't wait."

Rat didn't say a word as he slipped out of the rocking chair and disappeared into the darkness of the stairs leading down to the boat dock below.

Mack rose and entered the darkened cottage.

"I can't wait to see Elmo," he thought. *"I have a few questions for that boy."*

Chapter 38

It was 7:37 Wednesday morning and Elmo was waiting for Mack when he walked into the Queen Conch for breakfast.

Elmo invited Mack to sit with him in a booth in the back corner of the restaurant and after they had finished breakfast he began to grill Mack about going to Indiantown.

"Mack, what were you doing over in Indiantown yesterday afternoon?"

"How did you know that I was in Indiantown? Weren't you in court all day?"

"My cousin Albert told me. He saw you tooling it down Martin Grade in that old blue pickup truck of yours about one-thirty yesterday afternoon. He followed you."

"Who the hell is your cousin Albert?"

"He's a road deputy. He worked Indiantown for me yesterday because I was in court."

"Are you related to everyone in Martin County?"

"Most of the deputies and me are related. It's a family thing."

"Why did you send Rat down here last night to grill me?"

"I wanted to see if your story matched what Albert told me."

"Did it?"

"You spent about forty-five minutes poking through the piney woods and palmetto bushes at the entrance to the Naked Lady Ranch." Elmo paused and looked down at a small spiral ring notebook in his left hand. "You left the ranch at two-seventeen. "After that you stopped at the Florida Power and Light power plant. You left the power plant at three-twelve and went to the Hispanic radio station. While you were there you jawboned with Jack the station manager and Jose the station engineer. You left the radio station at four-sixteen."

"Your cousin didn't miss a thing, but he was two minutes off."

"What do you mean?" Elmo asked as he double-checked the hand-written entries in the notebook. "It's all right here in black and white. It clearly says four-sixteen."

"I left the radio station at four-eighteen."

"Oh," Elmo replied as he scratched out the entry in the notebook. "I'll make that change right now."

"Then what did I do?"

"You went to the company store and bought yourself a Honey Bun and a Dr. Pepper. You left the company store at four thirty-six."

"Then what" Mack attempted to recall his route in his mind. "I think I filled the truck up with gas at the Citgo station on the corner." Mack was attempting to cause doubt in Elmo's mind.

"No you didn't," Elmo stated as he ran his finger down the page of the notebook. "You filled up at the Shell Station. You pumped nine point four gallons of eighty-nine octane gasoline and you charged fifteen dollars and fifty-one cents on a Port Sewall Marina Shell credit card."

"I guess I forgot which station I stopped at," Mack meekly responded. "I would have sworn that it was a Citgo station."

"Good try Mack, but you don't win a prize. You pulled out of the gas station at four fifty-three. After that you drove out to the pepper fields and poked around the irrigation system pump house. The Hispanic foreman asked what you were doing and you told him that you worked for the Florida Department of Agriculture research station in Fort Pierce and were making a survey of pump sizes. Does that sound right to you?"

"It's pretty close. I told him that I was attempting to calculate the amount of water that is pumped out of the underground aquifer every day by agricultural interests. I asked him how many gallons a minute the water pump produced, how many times a day they ran the pump and the length of each watering cycle."

"Albert didn't write that down," Elmo quipped. "His Spanish isn't very good."

"What time did I leave the pepper field pump house?"

"Five thirty-seven."

"That's correct. I was getting pretty tired by then. What did I do after I left the pepper field?"

"You drove out to the orange grove about three miles north of Indiantown."

"What did I do there?"

"You told the grove foreman that you worked for the Florida Department of Agriculture research station in Fort Pierce and were making a survey of the orange trees in the immediate area for signs of citrus canker."

"What was the foreman's name?"

"Carlos."

"That's correct. He's been in this country for almost five years and he's an illegal immigrant. He's working out his transportation charges by working in the groves for three bucks an hour. He'll have it all paid off in five more years, if he stays healthy."

"Why did you ask me what his name was? Don't you remember?"

"Of course I do. I was just checking to see if your cousin missed any small detail."

"He didn't miss a thing. It's all right here in this notebook. I might be using it for evidence."

"Evidence of what?"

"Evidence of obstruction of justice charges against you."

"What?" Mack shouted. He paused before he spoke again because he sensed that he almost lost his cool. "Obstruction of justice for what?"

"I'm not sure yet, but I'm sure that you were up to something that I'll find out about later. I just want to make certain that I have all of the facts correct. Just in case I need to present them to a judge."

"Fine! I mistakenly thought that we were friends."

"We are, but I'm also a law enforcement officer and that comes before friendship," Elmo responded in a serious tone of voice as he ran his index finger down a page in the notebook. "Do you want to verify what you did after you left the orange grove?"

"Why not? If I'm going to be accused of something I'd better know where I was when I did it."

"What time did you leave the orange grove?"

"Six-thirty? I don't remember exactly."

"Six forty-seven to be exact. Then you stopped at the Seminole Inn for dinner."

"What did I have for dinner?"

"A New York strip steak cooked medium rare with a baked potato and green beans. You had a tossed salad with honey-mustard dressing on the side."

"What did I order to drink?"

"A glass of water with a slice of lemon. The server refilled your glass four times."

"What does the number of glasses of water that I drank with my dinner have to do with anything?"

"It's a small detail and in a serious case the devil is in the details."

"What serious case are you talking about?"

"I'm no sure yet, but I'm working on it. How much was your dinner bill?"

"Twenty-two bucks and fifty cents I think."

"How much did you leave for a tip?"

"Five bucks. I left a five dollar bill."

"How did you pay for your meal?"

"Cash."

"Did you ask the server for a receipt?"

"No."

"That's unfortunate and it shows that your memory is not very good. You might have a problem remembering details."

"What? My memory is just fine."

"The actual bill for your steak dinner was seventeen dollars and sixty-four cents without the five dollar tip. When you add in the tip the bill was twenty-two dollars and sixty-four cents."

"That's close to what I said!"

"Close only counts in tossing horse shoes and hand grenades."

'What time did you leave the Seminole Inn?"

"About a quarter to eight."

"Actually it was seven forty-eight."

"That's close to a quarter to eight!"

"Do you recall my analogy to tossing horse shoes and hand grenades?"

"Yes. I remember. What's your point?"

"Close doesn't count in either case. Where did you go next?"

"You seem to have everything written down in that stupid little notebook. I don't want to be wrong again. Why don't you tell me?"

"Don't you remember where you went next?"

"Of course I do. I stopped at the Silver Saddle across the street for a couple of beers."

"How did you get there?"

"I walked across the street."

"Where was your truck?"

"I left it in the Seminole Inn parking lot."

"Why did you do that?"

"It was easier to walk across the street than to start up the truck and drive over."

"Weren't you concerned that someone might steal your truck? Indiantown can be a dangerous place for a stranger. Especially at night."

"Why should I worry about someone stealing my truck? I took the keys with me."

"You forgot about the emergency key mounted under your left

front fender."

"No one knows that it's there."

"Albert found it. Someone could have used that spare key to borrow your truck, commit a serious crime and drop your truck back of at the Seminole Inn. You wouldn't suspect a thing."

"Did someone use my truck to commit a crime? Am I being framed for something I didn't do?"

"I can't either confirm or deny any investigation that may or may not be in progress."

"I don't like where this conversation seems to be going. Should I ask for an attorney?"

"No. If I thought for a minute that was necessary I'd read you your Miranda rights. I'm just asking you a few questions."

"If I'm accused of committing a crime then the answers I give can be used against me in court."

"That's correct, but I haven't asked you any specific questions relating to any alleged crime. I've just been asking you to account for your whereabouts yesterday afternoon and last night. What did you do at the Silver Saddle last night?"

"I had a couple of beers and left."

"Exactly how many beers did you have and over what time period?"

"I got there about eight o'clock and I left about ten."

"You walked in the front door at exactly seven fifty-three and you left at six minutes after ten."

"Okay. So what?"

"Exactly how many beers did you have in that two hour period?"

"Two or three. I don't recall exactly. You probably have a receipt anyway. Why don't you tell me?"

"You had five beers. They were all Buds in a bottle. Do you feel that your driving ability was impaired in any way when you left the Silver Saddle?"

"No! I'm six feet four and weigh two hundred and thirty pounds. Six beers have no effect on me!"

"What if you had been pulled over and ordered to take a field sobriety test?"

"What about it? I wasn't pulled over."

"Albert was going to and changed his mind. Would you have refused to take a field sobriety test?"

"Of course not! Elmo, where is this line of questioning leading?"

"You will know shortly. Do you recall striking any animals with your vehicle on the drive down Martin Grade back to Palm City?"

"No!"

"No what?"

"I didn't hit any animals with my truck!"

"Are you certain?"

"Yes!"

"What about that baby armadillo that you ran over exactly one quarter mile east of the entrance to the Naked Lady Ranch?"

"I don't recall hitting any armadillo."

"You did. Albert has it written down in black and white right here. You hit the armadillo at ten twelve and never slowed down or hit your brakes."

"Maybe that's because I didn't see it."

"Albert has it on video tape. He was right behind you."

"I didn't see anyone behind me when I was driving down Martin Grade."

"There goes your ability to remember again. Are you certain that your vision wasn't impaired after drinking six beers? That could have been a child."

"I was fine and a child wouldn't be on the road at ten o'clock at night!"

"A hitch hiker or a homeless person might have been."

"Do you recall talking to anyone while you were at the Silver Saddle?"

"No."

"While you were there you chatted in Spanish to the bar girl and tipped her ten bucks."

"How do you know that I tipped her ten bucks?"

"She gave it to Carlos."

"That ten bucks was for her! It was a tip for good service."

"Any money that passes in the Silver Saddle goes to Carlos. He has to pay the overhead."

"Elmo, what's this all about? What are you trying to prove?"

"You were a material witness in my case against that Guat and you blew it!"

"What do you mean I blew it? I wasn't picked for the jury."

"You talked Carlos into dropping the aggravated assault charge and took the mask so it couldn't be used as evidence for the attempted grand theft charge!"

"I don't know what you're talking about! I didn't do either one of those things!"

"When you and Tina were over there on Friday she tried to talk him into giving her the mask. When he wouldn't give it to her she came back and stole it!"

"That's not true!" Mack leaped to his feet and stared Elmo in the eye. "Tina asked him to produce the mask and he dragged a dusty beer carton out of the storage room. When he opened the box there was a rock inside. No mask! End of story."

"Carlos figures that it was an inside job," Deputy Elmo responded as he flipped several pages in the notebook and appeared to carefully study an entry. "He knows that Tina has the mask, but he doesn't want to accuse her of it."

"What are you talking about? Tina doesn't have the mask!"

"He figures that the Guatemalan girl that lives with him took it out of the beer carton when he was sleeping, hid it somewhere and snuck it over to Tina at the Seminole Inn on Saturday morning."

"What makes him think that?"

"He watched her walk across the street with a package wrapped in newspaper."

"That package was full of her personal belongings. She asked Tina to send her stuff back to Mexico because she figures that she's never going home. "Mack slid back down into his seat. "Carlos told her that he sold her to another bar in Okeechobee."

"He didn't sell her. He just told her that to keep her under control."

"What! Keep her under control for what?"

"She makes a lot of money for him. He's not about to let her go."

"What do you mean she makes a lot of money for him?"

"Those horny Guats line up for a shot at her on Friday night. He charges fifty bucks for fifteen minutes with her."

"What! He's pimping her?"

"Not exactly. She's working off her transportation expenses, plus room and board."

"What do you mean transportation expenses? She got here illegally."

"He paid ten thousand bucks for her. She has to work it off somehow and she can't do it by serving beer and washing dishes."

"He didn't pay ten thousand bucks for her. He got her for two hundred because the coyote knew that she was to small to work as a field hand."

"That's neither here or there. She owes him and she has to work for him until she pays off her debt to him. If she tries to leave before she pays off her debt he'll call the INS on her."

"That would be counterproductive. Why doesn't he just treat her right and pay her for the work she does? Then she would be happy and not want to leave."

"That's not the point," Elmo countered. "The fear of the INS and going to prison scares the hell out of the Guats and keeps them in line."

"The INS doesn't put illegal immigrants in prison. They just photograph them and send them back to where they came from."

"The Guats don't know that. It keeps them in line."

"That's a bunch of crap Elmo and you know it." Mack stood up. "Can I go now?"

"No! Sit back down," Elmo demanded. "There're a few more things I want to talk to you about."

"Like what?" Mack demanded as he sat back down. "Are you going to accuse me of murder?"

"No," Elmo answered softy. "Do you want to know where I was going with those questions?"

"I'm not sure. Is this a legal trap?"

"No. I was just trying to make a point."

"What kind of point? That I don't write down everything I do in a notebook like your cousin Alfred?"

"His name is Albert not Alfred and he'd be offended if you

called him Alfred."

"Oh. I'm sorry. Apologize to him for me if you feel it's necessary."

"Mack, I have a confession to make."

"Should I write it down or would it be better to get it on tape for use in court?"

"Neither one. My cousin didn't follow you around Indiantown yesterday. It was me in a plain car."

"What? Why?"

"I wanted to make a point and get your attention."

"You got my attention, but I don't get your point! What is it? That you can follow someone and not be seen?"

"No. I was trying to make the point that it's better for you if you leave the Guats in Indiantown alone and let them live their lives without interference from the outside. Everything has been working out just fine for years and everyone is happy. The Guats have a place to live and they're making more money than they did where they came from. It's a good system and you should leave it alone."

"They are being taken advantage of by the people who own the orange groves and fields."

"But look at it from their perspective. They have a job and a place to live. They're happy."

"I think that something's going on over there that's making them happy besides having a job and a place to live. I think that someone's using electronic mind control to keep them under control."

"What are you talking about?"

"Electronic mind control by the transmission of artificial Alpha brain waves at Extremely Low Frequencies directly into the fields, over their radios and through the electrical wiring in their houses!"

"Is that why you stopped at the FPL plant and the radio station?"

"Exactly! That's why I also stopped at the irrigation system pump houses. I wanted to locate the ELF transmission system and Alpha wave generator."

"I think you're nuts!"

"Did you ever notice that the radio station signal fades in and out and that the electric lights over there pulsate?"

"We already talked about that. My cousin told me that the coal they burn at the FPL plant fluctuates in moisture content and it doesn't burn at a steady rate. That causes the electric generators to fluctuate in their output and that's why the lights seem to flicker at night."

"They don't flicker! They pulsate! I took a frequency counter with me and measured the rate of pulsation at the power plant, the pump houses, the radio station and the Silver Saddle."

"What did you find out?"

"The pulsation rate varies between seven point eight three and eight point six Hertz."

"What does that mean in real words?"

"The resonant frequency of the earth as determined by Schumann's Resonance Theory is seven point eight three Hertz. If a person can get his, or her, brain's Alpha waves in sync with the earth's pulsation rate then he, or she, will feel very good."

"What's that mean? What's a Hertz? Don't they rent cars at the airport?"

"Hertz means pulses measured in cycles per second. Think about it this way. Standard one hundred ten volt alternating current is transmitted over power lines at sixty Hertz, or sixty cycles per second. Do you understand that?"

"I think so."

"Researchers found that if a person's Alpha brain waves are artificially stimulated to stabilize at eight point six Hertz their brain will be in a dreamlike, or Alpha state. They will be happy and not cause any problems. I think that is what's going on in Indiantown!"

"What does that mean in country boy English?"

"I think someone is using Extremely Low Frequency power transmission to deliver a signal at eight point six Hertz to the migrant laborers through the power lines, radio station and transmission lines buried alongside the irrigation pipes in the fields and groves."

"Why? They might electrocute someone?"

"There's no danger of electrocution, but there could be long term effects on a person's brain."

"Are you talking about brain washing like the Koreans did to our boys?"

"No. Brain washing is a psychological technique used to remove imbedded concepts and memories from a person's brain and replacing them with artificial concepts and memories generated by their handler. I'm talking about controlling a person's brain waves so they will never get upset or belligerent."

"How can they do that?"

"By transmitting artificial Alpha waves over the power lines, through the radio station and over the cables buried alongside the irrigation pipes in the fields and citrus groves. Doesn't the radio station pass out free radios tuned to only their station's frequency to the migrant workers?"

"Sure, but that's so they will listen to only their station."

"The CIA did the same thing in Laos. They dropped radios tuned to only one radio station frequency that was coincidently operated by the CIA and used to transmit ELF signals for mind control. That was an experiment in electronic brain washing!"

"Do you think that someone is trying to do that to the migrants in Indiantown?"

"I don't think they are trying to do it. I know that they are. I saw it and I measured it."

"Mack, you might be getting in over your head here."

"Is there any connection between the guy who owns the radio station and the people who run the migrant worker program?"

"They're brothers."

"Who owns the company store?"

"The brothers do and I think that Carlos has a piece of it."

"Was any of them in the military during the Viet Nam War?"

"The brother who owns the radio station was in the Air Force. He was in some kind of electronics field. That's why he started the radio station when he came home. His daddy was a cattle rancher up by Yee Haw Junction and he put up the cash for him to get started."

"Do you know what field of electronics he was in?"

"Is there such a thing as electronic counter measures? I think that what's he said he did."

"Bingo! Yes, there is! I think that we hit the mother lode."

"What do you mean?"

"Can you find out something and keep your mouth shut?"

"Sure. What do you want to know?"

"Last night, when I was driving back to Stuart on Martin Grade, I was tuned to the Hispanic station and the signal was fading in and out. Octavio told me that it was caused by power fluctuations from the Indiantown fossil-fuel plant when they burn cheap coal and mix it with sugar cane stalks."

"That's just about the same thing cousin told me."

Electric generating stations have voltage and current regulators that regulate their output. They might have a slight variation in the voltage output level, but not in the frequency. It's always at sixty cycles per second because our electric appliances are designed to work at only that frequency. There's something else is causing it and I'm going to find out what it is."

"What do you want me to do?"

"When I pulled off of Martin Grade at the power plant entrance I think I saw an antenna farm in a pepper field on the south side of the road. Can you run out there today and check it out for me?"

"An antenna farm? Are they growing antennas out here now?"

"They don't grow antennas. An antenna farm is a field where several types of antennas are erected to serve different purposes. Run out there and see if you can find some heavy wires mounted on big poles that form a diamond shape."

"What do you want me to do if I find them?"

"Take a picture of it and bring it back to me."

"What are you going to do while I'm out in Indiantown?"

"I'm going to the library and do some research. What are you going to do with that little note book?"

"I don't know."

"I do," Mack reached across the table and snatched the notebook from Elmo's hand. "I'll take care of it for you."

Mack stuffed the notebook into his own shirt pocket, stood up, turned and left the table.

Chapter 39

Mack waited patiently outside the main entrance of the Blake Library. When he left Elmo at the Queen Conch, Mack had forgotten that the library didn't open until ten o'clock.

When the library custodian finally managed to locate the correct key on his massive key ring he fumbled with the lock for what Mack felt as an eternity. Finally the doors opened. Mack brushed the custodian aside and raced towards the reference desk.

"Good morning Mr. McCray," Janet's soft voice oozed through a thick coating of ruby red lipstick and transparent lip-gloss. "How may I be of assistance to you this morning?"

"What's she doing wearing red lip gloss at her age??" Mack thought to himself as he tried to focus his attention on his mission. *"Maybe she has a hot date after work."*

"Did you find out anything for me about government experiments in mind control using ELF transmission?"

"I told you yesterday to come back this afternoon and I would try to have something for you," Janet responded with a sly smile. "We were very busy yesterday and you are not our only patron."

"I understand," Mack responded as he leaned over the counter and whispered in Janet's left ear. "This is very important to me. Is it very confidential material?"

"It is very sensitive," Janet whispered in response. "The library's computer system supervisor came to tell me that he was concerned because the library's computer system's internet firewall gave an indication that someone in the state of Virginia monitored my inquiry and tagged my computer's address."

"Did he know who it was?" Mack whispered.

"He said that it was a United States government agency and when he tried to break into their system his computer screen gave a security code warning and then his computer failed."

"Depending upon what key words you entered on Google You might be getting some visitors very soon," Mack whispered. "I should have warned you about the Echelon System."

"What's that?"

"It's a top-secret agency that the government won't even acknowledge exists. It's operated by the National Security Agency and their computers monitor Internet traffic including personal e-mails, web site visitations and Google inquiries. They have a list of key words that trigger investigations."

"That's what I used." Janet looked into Mack's eyes. "I always use Google when I'm doing research on the Internet. It's been very good to me. Do you think they'll come after me?"

"Do I think who will come after you?"

"The government! The men in black!"

"Maybe. You're a librarian and you don't have to divulge why you were looking for information and who asked you to do it."

"What if they torture me?" Janet whined as she whispered. "I can't stand pain and I vomit at the sight of blood."

She reached out for Mack's hand.

"Especially my own. I'll spill the beans if they torture me. I'll be so embarrassed if they force me to tell them that it was you."

"They don't use physical torture very often, except in very stubborn cases," Mack whispered as he patted the top of her left hand. "These days information is extracted via mental duress and the use of psychotic mind-numbing drugs. You might have a few nightmares afterwards, but they won't physically hurt you."

"Are you sure?" Tears welled up in the corners of Janet's eyes. "I'm afraid of pain."

"You might want to wear a lighter shade of lipstick?" Mack pointed at her lips with his right index finger. "Heavy lip gloss calls attention to you as possibly being a loose woman. Then they won't have any mercy. They'll have their way with you first."

"Oh no!" Janet blurted out as she stood up behind the counter. "I wore this because I wanted to look good for you when you came in today. I'll go in the back and wipe it off right now!"

"Hold it right there!"

Mack urged Janet to sit down by putting downward pressure on her hand.

"Don't be in such a big hurry," he added. "You look just fine. Anyway, if they do send someone down here to talk to you they can't be here until this afternoon. It takes a few hours for a plane to get here from Washington National Airport."

"Are you sure?"

"I'm sure. Now what did you find out?"

"I'm afraid to show it to you. If they find out, they'll torture me to get your name and then they'll torture you too."

"I'll take my chances. I probably know who they sent down."

"How would you know who they are?"

"Let's not talk about it here. I'll tell you someday."

"When?"

"Some day. What did you find out?"

"I'm scared," Janet, whined, as she cautiously looked around the library for any strange men in black trench coats. "I think they're watching us."

"Who do you think is watching us?"

"Them."

Janet nodded her head towards two middle-aged white men standing beside the copy machine on the other side of the room.

"They came in the library about five minutes after you did and they've been standing over there ever since."

"Have they made any copies?" Mack softly whispered.

Janet raised her head to respond.

"Don't look at them!" Mack cautioned.

"Why not" Janet lowered head as she responded. "I might be asked to recognize them in a police lineup after they torture me for information about you."

"They aren't NSA agents."

"What makes you so certain about that?"

"They aren't wearing black baseball caps and they're wearing deck shoes and no socks."

"So what?"

"NSA agents on assignment normally wear a plain black baseball cap to alert agents from other government agencies that they are in the area. Those guys are waiting for me to leave so they can come over here and hit on you."

"Why would they do that? No one ever hits on me."

"It's the lip gloss," Mack softly replied. 'It got my attention."

"I'll go in the back office and wipe it off," Janet softly whispered. "I didn't mean to turn anyone on."

"You can't help it. You're a natural male magnet. I feel the attraction every time I come in here."

"Shucks! You're just saying that to make me feel good."

"Did it?"

"Did it what?"

"Make you feel good?"

"Of course it did. Women like that kind of talk."

"Then I meant it. Did you find out anything about government experiments using ELF transmission for human mind control?"

"Yes. We'll have to whisper," Janet cautioned.

"Okay. Did you print any hard copies of the stuff for me?"

"Of course. They're in that brown envelope."

Janet motioned with a nod of her head to a large brown manila envelope tucked in corner of her desk.

"I'll slip the envelope to you when you leave, but I don't want those guys to see me doing it."

"They won't. I'll stand in front of you when you slip it to me."

"Are you ready? I'm going to talk low so they can't hear."

"Go for it."

"Government mind control experiments have been going on for a long time. Do you remember the LSD fiasco of the nineteen-fifties and sixties?"

"Of course. God bless Timothy O'Leary. A lot of potheads worship his memory."

"That's not what I'm talking about! There was an CIA experiment in New York City in nineteen fifty-three where they laced a poor unsuspecting guy's drinks with LSD and he jumped out of the window to the pavement ten floors below."

"He didn't jump."

"Do you mean that someone threw him out of the window?"

"I didn't say that. I just said that he didn't jump."

"Those two guys over by the copy machine are still watching us," Janet whispered as she nodded in the direction of the two seemingly interested spectators.

"They're not watching us. They're watching you and waiting for me to leave so they can try their nineteen fifties pickup lines on you."

"Do you think they're really that old?"

"I remember going to the fat guy's funeral last week. They must've dug him up again."

"That's gross!"

"Okay. Let's go! What else?"

"Keep your voice down in case they're listening to us."

"They won't be able to hear us unless they've got their hearing aids turned up the max."

"Cut it out! The skinny guy is kind of cute."

"Do you want me to go over and tell him that you want him?"

"Mr. McCray! Shame on you! That's crude!"

"It might just work if you play along and smile at him. I think he's interested."

"What makes you think that?"

"He's had his right hand in his pants for the last ten minutes."

"Mr. McCray! That's crude!"

"Okay. We've established that I'm crude and opinionated. Tell me what you found out."

"The CIA's clandestine experiments began under CIA

Director Allen Dulles in nineteen fifty-three when he authorized the MKULTRA Program. Most of the records related to the MKULTRA Program were destroyed by the CIA in nineteen seventy-two, but some of them made it to the public domain." Janet carefully looked around before she answered in a soft whisper. "I found them."

"Go on," Mack directed in a whisper. "Be more specific."

"The CIA's LSD experiments were often conducted on prisoners and patrons of brothels in the Washington, DC area set up and run by the CIA."

"Been there." Mack winked as he responded. "Done that."

"What! Mr. McCray! I'm ashamed of you!" Janet responded, but she forgot to whisper. "You, of all people, patronizing a house of ill repute! You should be ashamed."

"I am," Mack whispered. "Skip the LSD stuff. That's old news. I'm looking for recent stuff on the use of radio waves to transmit mind-altering signals to influence behavior."

"There's a lot of that." Janet's voice returned to a cautious whisper. "I found a nineteen sixty-three CIA Inspector General's report that aired all of the CIA's dirty laundry."

"Like what?"

"The report stated that MKULTRA was a program concerned with the research and development of chemical, biological and radiological materials capable of employment in clandestine operations to control human behavior."

"That's what I'm looking for," Mack whispered. "How detailed did the report get?"

"Very detailed," Janet whispered back. "I'll skip over the very early projects which were named 'Bluebird' and 'Artichoke' and start with the nineteen sixties with Project MK-DELTA that was done in conjunction with the Air Force's electronic warfare counter measures unit. They attempted electromagnetic subliminal programming of Air Force recruits by modulating Extremely Low Frequency signals through power lines, radio and television antennae, through mattress springs and even through a house's sixty Hertz wiring."

"I'm aware of that program."

"How? It was highly classified project."

"Let's just say I know about it."

"You were in the Air Force weren't you?"

"That's correct. From September fifteenth nineteen sixty to September fifteenth ninety sixty-four."

"What was your career field?"

"Let's just say that I spent some time in the electronics field."

"Oh," Janet sighed. "I won't ask you any more questions."

"Thank you."

"How about the Air Force's Project Phoenix? Do you know about that one?"

"Yes. It was conducted in nineteen eighty-three at Montauk, on Long Island. Keep going."

"Did you also know about the NSA project Trident?"

"Yes. NSA, in conjunction with FEMA, used black helicopters flying in columns of three across to beam out signals in the Ultra Frequency range as high as one hundred thousand watts to conduct experiments in human behavior control. They also flew over professional football stadiums on Sunday afternoons and recorded the roar of the crowd. That's old technology. What else did you find out?"

"Did you work on Project Trident too?"

"A little bit and I really liked the Japanese restaurant on Lake Montauk. Janet, what else did you learn?"

"How about the CIA's Project RF Media in nineteen ninety?"

"I was out of the loop by then," Mack whispered. "Tell me about it."

"The CIA used phase modulation over commercial radio and television stations to trigger behavioral desire in preparatory processing for mass electromagnetic control."

"No. The frequency is too high. What else?"

"The NSA and CIA sponsored a joint project in electronic programming in nineteen ninety that used ELF modulation over the national cellular telephone network. Unofficially they called it 'Wedding Bells' and its real name was Project Tower."

"Nope. Most of the population I'm interested in doesn't have cell phones. What else?"

"How about Project HAARP in Gakona, Alaska?"

"I heard something about it. Isn't that where the NSA and CIA are trying to influence the behavior patterns of the Eskimos by transmitting signals through long antennas buried in the ground?"

"That's it!" Janet exclaimed. "Do you want to hear about it?"

"No. What else?"

"The last CIA and NSA project I found was 'Project Clean Sweep'. It transmitted electromagnetic emotional Alpha brain wavelengths to crowds at football games and mass media outdoor events through helicopters that hovered over the crowd."

"Nope. That not the one I'm looking for either."

"I found the transcript of a U.S Senate hearing held on January twenty on the Air Force's 'Commando Solo' that uses low-flying aircraft to send subliminal radio frequency messages to manipulate the minds of foreign nations during their elections. It was used in Haiti and Bosnia."

"No. Did you see any projects that used large copper cables buried in the ground to transmit modulated ELF frequencies between six and nine Hertz?"

"The Navy conducted experiments using ELF waves using two antennas, each fourteen miles long, at Clam Lake, Wisconsin until nineteen seventy-six."

"That was for communicating with nuclear attack submarines," Mack responded with a smirk. "The Navy's code name for it was 'Sanguine.' Old news. How about the Russians?"

"The Russians kicked off a mind control experiment on July fourth nineteen seventy-six in the Ukraine with power generated by the Chernobyl nuclear plant."

"That's why the Russians built Chernobyl!" Mack responded. "What a slap in the face! That was the two hundredth birthday of the United States. That might be it! Tell me about it."

"The Russians transmitted a one hundred mega watt eleven Hertz signal through the ground and across the world. The U.S. Air Force identified five difference frequencies in the signal and the goal was to affect a change of consciousness in mankind."

"Those bastards!" Mack responded and he forgot to whisper.

The two men lounging next to the copy machine turned away and faced the wall.

"Nothing stops an ELF signal!" Mack continued. "It will go right though the earth and the ocean. The brain stops it long enough to cancel it out. What did they call it?"

"I couldn't locate a project name. But they have something called the Woodpecker transmitter system set up across Russia."

"What's that?"

"It's a series of radio transmitters placed two hundred miles apart across Russia that allow specific radio waves to be trailed to the geometric magnetic field in that area. They operate in the Low Frequency range and transmit a varying signal between one hundred fifty and one hundred seventy-five Hertz. The antenna is a series of three hundred foot-long copper wires buried in the ground in a spoke-like fashion that radiates outward from the base of the transmitter. Could that be what you are looking for?"

"Maybe. What do the Russians claim they use it for?"

"Weather control, but one scientist claims that they use it for population mind control."

"I'd be more inclined to believe the mind control function. They have to do something to keep their peasant population under control and prevent another revolution. Is that it?"

"That's it," Janet sighed as she nodded at the brown envelope on the corner of her desk. "Don't forget your envelope. I don't want anyone to see me passing it over to you."

"Maybe your two admirers over by the copy machine would like you to make them a copy too."

"It's too late to make fun of them," Janet blurted out as she covered her mouth with her hand. "They left right after you called them ignorant bastards. I think that you frightened them."

"I wasn't referring to them when I said that!" Mack retorted. "I was referring to the Russians."

"They didn't know that. They just hear you holler ignorant bastards and they left."

"I'm sorry Janet. I think that they were truly interested in talking to you and I screwed it up."

"Don't worry about it. The skinny one gave me a thumbs up' when he left." Janet quipped as she made a 'thumbs up' sign with her left hand. "If he's really interested he'll come back. They always do."

"Watch the lip gloss!" Mack cautioned. 'Don't lay it on too heavy or it'll make you look cheap."

"I might be easy, but I'm not cheap," Janet whispered under her breath. "Come up and see me some time big boy," she offered in a throaty, sensuous Mae West impression and winked at Mack.

"Maybe I will. Right now I have places to go and people to see." Mack replied with a wink as he turned, but he paused before he headed for the library exit door. "Oh Janet, I forgot to ask you something."

"What is it now Mr. McCray?"

"You mentioned something about a pod of dolphins that washed up on Jensen Beach last week."

"That's correct. I also told you about the cute French man who was in the library doing some research on our computers."

"I think that the dolphin stranding was caused by some new SONAR equipment that the Navy is testing offshore. Would you check it out for me?

"Of course I will. Would you like to give me some direction as to where I should begin?"

"Try the United States Navy's AUTEC website."

"What's that?"

"It's a top-secret submarine testing facility in the Bahamas."

"Here we go again!"

Mack pretended that he didn't hear her response as he turned and headed for the library lobby.

On his way through the lobby Mack noticed the skinny old man that got Janet's attention earlier when he was standing with his pal beside the copy machine. He was sitting in a chair across from the book check out desk and gave Mack a 'thumbs up' as he struggled to his feet with the aid of his aluminum cane.

Mack winked at the old man and gave him a 'thumbs up' as he headed for the exit. It was 11:27 A.M. and his stomach was growling.

Mack pulled out of the library parking lot, swung onto East Ocean Boulevard, turned left and decided to stop at the Sake House on the corner of Federal Highway and Kanner Highway and sample the Chinese buffet before he got on the road.

Chapter 40

Rat was waiting on the front porch of the Port Sewall Marina cottage when Mack pulled into a parking space at 9:37 P.M.

"What does he want at this time of night?" Mack thought as he swung out of the truck cab and headed for the front porch. *"I wonder if Elmo sent him over here again to milk me for information about what I found out in Indiantown?"*

"Howdy Mack," Rat offered from the security of the dark porch. "Ate dinner yet?"

Mack slipped into the empty wicker rocking chair on Rat's right side before he answered.

"Not yet. I just drove over from Indiantown and I didn't have time to pick up anything," Mack responded with hesitation. "What do you have in mind? Road killed coon or opossum?"

"Naw. I've got somethin' much better and it's almost fresh." Rat paused to take a big bite out of a sesame seed covered bun. "It's dolphin. I grilled it about an hour ago and brought down a couple of sandwiches for you. Want one? It's still warm. The aluminum foil holds in the heat."

"Sure. I love dolphin," Mack answered as he reached for the aluminum foil covered package in Rat's outstretched right hand.

"Take a bite and let me know what you think."

Mack unwrapped the sandwich, raised it to his mouth with anticipation and took a huge bite.

"What the hell is this," Mack sputtered as he spit the piece of sandwich out into his hand and looked at it carefully. "This isn't dolphin. It's some kind of meat. Is this road kill?"

"No! It's not road kill! It's really dolphin!" Rat vehemently stated as he took a large bite out of his own sandwich and began to chew. "I butchered it myself," he offered after he swallowed.

"I've never tasted dolphin like this! It doesn't taste like fish! What kind of meat is it?"

"It's dolphin. I swear." Rat took another bite of his sandwich and rolled his eyes with delight.

"Rat! This is not dolphin! It's some type of meat and it almost tastes like beef, but it's sweeter." Mack rewrapped the sandwich. "Did you butcher another manatee?"

"No! I butchered a dolphin." Rat took a bite of his sandwich.

"What do you mean you butchered a dolphin? Fishermen fillet dolphin. They don't butcher them."

"If it's a big dolphin you butcher them." Rat took a large bite of his sandwich and slowly shook his head from side to side to show his pleasure.

"The biggest dolphin I ever caught was a little bit over fifty pounds and I filleted it."

"This one was a lot bigger than fifty pounds." Rat stuffed the last portion of his sandwich into his bearded maw and reached his open right hand in Mack's direction. "Are you going to eat that?"

"No! You can have it," Mack cautiously responded as he handed the sandwich to Rat. "Tell me about this dolphin. Did you catch yourself or did you swipe it out a charterboat cooler when the mate wasn't looking?"

"I found it on the beach." Rat took a bite out of the sandwich and wiped his mouth with the back of his left hand and wiped his hands on his pants.

"Was it dead?"

"Naw. It was still alive. I slipped a rope over its tail and towed it back to Shepherd's Park."

"Why didn't you just pull it into your kayak? Would that have been a lot easier?"

"Naw, it was too big for that." Rat took another bite out of the sandwich.

"That must have been a big dolphin. Was it a bull or a cow?"

"I didn't turn it upside down to look."

"You don't turn a dolphin upside down to check its sex," Mack chuckled as he spoke. "Bull dolphins, that's the males, have a large squared off forehead."

Mack gestured with his hands to form a ninety-degree angle. "The cows have a rounded forehead. Which was it?"

"Neither one." Rat bent over and rummaged around in his backpack.

"What are you looking for?"

"Another sandwich. I thought that I brought three of them." Rat stuffed the empty backpack under his chair and turned to face Mack. "You told me that you like dolphin. I guess that I didn't cook it right for your taste."

"How did you cook it?"

"I sliced off a steak and threw it on the grill. I built a fire out of some mangrove trees. That's how we used to cook manatees in the good old days."

"What do you mean you cut off a steak? Fish have fillets not steaks."

"It wasn't a fish. It was a dolphin. That's what I've been trying to tell you for fifteen minutes."

"What! You killed a bottlenose dolphin and butchered it!" Mack stood up to make his point and waved his right index finger in Rat's face. "Killing a dolphin is a Federal offense and violation of the Federal Marine Mammal Protection Act! You could go to prison for that!"

"Don't shake your finger in my face like that! I'm not a child and I didn't kill it. It was already dead when I found it."

"Exactly where did you find it?"

"It was washed up on the sandbar on the east side of Clam Island."

"Did anyone see you towing it behind your kayak? You might have been reported!"

"Nobody saw me. I was out there all by myself."

"Where did you butcher it?"

"I pulled it around the north side of Clam Island and went into that little cove. Nobody saw me."

"What did you do with what was left after you butchered it?"

"I pulled it out to the channel between Clam Island and Sailfish Point. The tide was running out pretty hard and it sank to the bottom. The bull sharks found it right away. I doubt that anything's left of it except maybe the head."

"Rat, I'm worried about you. Killing a dolphin is a serious Federal offense!"

"I didn't kill it. It was already dead when I found it."

"It wasn't moving and had blood running out of its eyes and ears. Plus, a couple of small bull sharks had already eaten about half of it."

"Tell me about the blood coming out of its ears and eyes."

"It was red and there was a lot of it. That's what pulled in the bull sharks. I think it was alive and came through the inlet to find a safe place where it could rest up."

"Tell me about the dolphin's eyes. What did they look like?"

"They bulged out like someone with a thyroid problem."

"That's what I figured. How about its ear holes?"

"There was blood running out of them like it had been shot."

"I think that I understand now."

"Understand what?"

"What killed that dolphin? What did you do with the rest of the meat?"

"There wasn't much left after the homeless guys at Shepherd's Park got hold of it. They scarfed it down like they hadn't eaten in a month. I managed to get enough to make a couple of sandwiches for you."

"I appreciate your thoughts Rat. I really do, but I prefer the kind of dolphin that I'm used to eating."

"I understand," Rat replied. "I didn't mean to do anything wrong. It was already dead."

"That's okay. Whatever you do don't mention this to Elmo!"

"Why not?"

"He'll arrest you and charge you with violating the Federal Marine Mammal Protection Act."

"No he won't. He already knows about it."

"What? Why does he already know about it?"

"He was on water patrol today and came by Clam Island when I was butchering the dolphin."

"What did he say to you?"

"He told me to keep my mouth shut and he wouldn't tell anybody."

"Oh. Why would he do that?"

"I don't know, but he was real interested in where you were today. It was his idea to bring you a dolphin sandwich tonight."

"Why would Elmo be interested in where I was today? I saw him at the Queen Conch this morning when I stopped in for breakfast. He didn't say anything about it."

"He figures that you went back to Indiantown to snoop around, stir up the Guats and cause problems for him."

"I was in Indiantown all afternoon, but I didn't go over there to stir anyone up."

"Why did you go over there anyway?"

"Did Elmo tell you to ask me why I went to Indiantown?"

"Yep."

"Tell him that I went over there to talk the Guatemalans out of sacrificing his buddy Carlos."

"Isn't he the guy that runs the Silver Saddle?"

"That's him."

"Why would the Guats want to sacrifice him?"

"It's a long story, but it has to do with a two thousand year old carved jade mask that a Guatemalan laborer in Indiantown gave to Carlos as to hold as security against his bar tab."

"Elmo told me that Tina swiped the mask Friday night so it couldn't be used as evidence in the guy's trial."

"Tina didn't swipe the mask! That crooked bartender has it

stashed away some place. When this all blows over he's going to sell it for one hundred thousand bucks, or maybe more."

"Mack, what makes you think that the bartender has it?"

"When Tina asked to see it the mask he brought out a beer box with a stone in it. I know he has it!"

"Elmo figures that some young Guat girl that works in the bar stole it and gave it to Tina."

"I don't think so."

"What were you lookin' for over there today?"

"I wanted to check out the power output and distribution system of the Florida Power and Light fossil fuel plant."

"Why?"

"Power plants are my new hobby. Rat, did you know that burning one-ton of coal produces three megawatts of electricity?"

"Really? I always thought it was only two point five megawatts." Rat replied with an impish grin.

Before Mack could respond Rat slipped out of the rocking chair into the darkness lining the cottage and was gone.

"Rat! Don't you take off on me!" Mack exclaimed into the darkness. "I'm not done with you!"

There was no response, but Mack detected the sound of a paddle dipping into the water of North Lake.

"Elmo's desperate for information if he's counting on Rat to interrogate me," Mack thought. *"I think that he's more involved in this Indiantown fiasco than he wants me to know."*

Mack raised himself out of the rocking chair, stood erect, raised his arms over his head and stretched from head to toe. After a hearty yawn he headed for the cottage door.

It was 10:17 P.M. He felt a little nauseous and was ready to turn in for the night.

Chapter 41

Thursday arrived quietly. It was 9:12 A.M. and bright sunshine lit up the red crepe myrtle bushes lining the marina grounds.

Mack finished breakfast, fed the cat and was on his way out of the front door of the Port Sewall Marina cottage when he spotted Deputy Elmo's patrol car rounding the bend on Old St. Lucie Boulevard. Elmo wasn't hesitant about pulling into a parking space directly in front of the marina porch and held up his open right hand as a signal for Mack to stay put.

"I wonder what Elmo wants now?" Mack thought to himself. *"Maybe he wasn't satisfied with Rat's report of my whereabouts yesterday afternoon. I hope he makes it quick because I want to get to the library and find out if Janet got me some information on those Navy sub projects."*

Mack decided to present a good image, snapped to feigned attention, clicked the heels of his deck shoes together and threw Elmo a mock salute as he exited his car.

"What the hell did you do that for Mack?" Elmo bellowed as he shook his head from side to side. "Civilians don't salute law enforcement officers."

"I wasn't saluting you," Mack softly responded as he dropped his right hand to his side and grinned. "Something bit me over my right eye and I smashed a cockroach between my heels."

"I didn't figure you were," Elmo responded as he slid into a sitting position on the top step of the porch and signaled for Mack to join him. "How'd you like Rat's dolphin sandwich last night?"

"I didn't! Why didn't you pinch him for violating the Marine Mammal Safety Act?"

"He didn't kill the dolphin," Elmo chuckled as he shook his head from side to side. "It'd been dead for at least three days, maybe even more. I'd seen it two days before when a couple of pup bull sharks were dragging it around that sand bar over by Clam Island like it was a chew toy. It was pretty darn ripe then. I couldn't get closer to him than fifty feet."

"It's against Federal law to butcher a marine mammal!"

"I'm not familiar with the particulars of that law. Would you happen to have a copy handy so I can look it up?"

"Of course not!" Mack snapped back. "Go to the library and make yourself a copy. With all of the dolphins that we have in the Indian River Lagoon you should know the Marine Mammal Safety Act well enough to recite it verbatim."

"Are you telling me that I should memorize some dumb Federal law that I probably can't enforce anyway? I'm only a dumb county mountie. I can't enforce Federal laws."

"Yes you can!"

"No I can't!" Elmo snapped. "And that's the end of this conversation. Let's stop this small talk and get down to business. You know why I'm here."

"No, I don't know why you're here. Why don't you tell me?"

"Rat told me what you were doing in Indiantown yesterday."

"Exactly what was I doing in Indiantown yesterday?"

"You were sneaking around the power plant and a couple of

substations with a weird-looking gadget. After that you went by the radio station and visited with the station owner. And after that you went to Booker Park and spent about two hours with that Guat that should be cooling his heels in jail for trying to cut Carlos' throat! You got back here about nine-thirty."

"Rat gave you an accurate report. Did you check out what I asked you to do?"

"What was that?" Elmo responded with a quizzical 'gotcha' look on his face.

"The antenna farm! I asked you to look for it yesterday!"

"I forgot. I'll look today. What's it supposed to look like?"

"Forget it! I checked it out when I was there. There isn't one."

"Oh. I'm sorry."

"It's okay. Is there anything else you want to know?"

"Are you in a hurry to go somewhere? I was going to invite you down to the Queen Conch for breakfast."

"I already fixed my breakfast and yes I am in a bit of a rush."

"Are you going back to Indiantown? You've got them Guats stirred up enough already."

"No! I have some things to check on at the library."

"The library doesn't open until ten o'clock. It's not even nine-thirty. You've still got plenty of time."

"By the time I get there it will be ten o'clock."

"I think that you have something going with that librarian?"

"What librarian?"

"Janet."

"Why do you think that?"

"You spend a lot of time over there talking to her."

"She's a librarian. She answers people's questions."

Elmo decided to change the subject before he got in too deep.

"Did Tina call you this morning?"

"No! Why?"

"The next time she calls you tell her that she's on my crap list for stealing that mask."

"She didn't steal the mask!" Mack stated. "Carlos has it!"

"She screwed up my case against that Guat," Elmo shook his head as he responded. "Everybody's laughing at me. She made me look bad."

"Elmo, I'm telling you for the last time that she doesn't have the mask! Carlos does!"

"No he doesn't."

'What makes you so certain that he doesn't have it? Did you give him a lie detector test?"

"I asked him when I was over there yesterday. He told me that young Guat girl that he's been pluggin' took it out of the box in the beer storage room and swapped it for a rock. She wrapped the mask up in old newspaper, carried over to the Seminole Inn Saturday morning and gave it to Tina."

"I was there! She gave Tina some personal items to send back to her family in Guatemala."

"Believe me Mack. It was the mask. Tina told the girl to steal it for her so there wouldn't be any evidence against the Guat in Court on Monday."

"Elmo, even if the mask had been in the courtroom as evidence the judge would have still been forced to throw the case out of court."

"Why? I wrote up everything just right."

"No you didn't. You charged Octavio with Grand Theft and that requires a value of at least three hundred bucks. The mask was not authenticated as genuine, or appraised, and there was no value established for it. It might be real and then again it might be a cheap fake."

"That's not fair! Everyone knows that's it's genuine! That's why that Guat tried to steal it back!"

"Elmo, that's entirely possible, but look at it from the judge's point of view."

"I still feel cheated, but I'll catch him doing something else!" Elmo emphatically stated as he slammed his fist on the wooden step. "I'll get him!"

"Elmo, why did you send Rat down here last night to pump me for information?"

"I didn't send him down here!"

"He told me that you did."

"Okay! You caught me! But, I did it because was worried about you. You don't know how those Guats think over there. You might just disappear. How would you like that?"

"I'm not going to disappear. But, Carlos just might."

"What makes you think that?"

"Some of the Guatemalans are very unhappy with the way he treated Octavio and they want blood revenge to satisfy their god. They might take him out to that pile of sod pallets out on the Naked Lady Ranch and burn him alive to get revenge."

"Which ones?" Elmo stood up as he responded and patted the wooden baton hanging from a loop on his black leather utility belt. "I'll bust their heads open if they touch one hair on Carlos' head! He's my friend!"

"Take it easy Elmo. He'll be okay if he doesn't harass them."

"He doesn't harass them. I do! That's my job!"

"Yes, you are a definitely a very big part of the equation and I suggest that you cool it too."

"What can they do to me? I'm the law over there."

"Ever hear of a blowgun dart laced in *curari* poison? The poison causes paralysis of the lungs in less than one minute and there's no antidote."

"They wouldn't dare!"

"Don't be so sure about that. Some of them are very upset."

"What should I do?"

"Just try to be cool and show them some respect when you go into the Silver Saddle. Maybe you could learn how to say a few words in Spanish to impress them?"

"Like what?"

"How about good morning, good afternoon, good evening, how are you and thank you?"

"I couldn't learn all of that. I'm a country boy and I can just barely speak English."

"We know that, but Spanish is a very easy language to learn."

"Who's gonna' teach me?"

"Ask Carmelita. She'll help you."

"How can she help me? She can't even speak English?"

"She is very fluent in English and she might be willing to help you out with your pronunciation."

"What? She's just a bar hooker!"

"She has a Master's degree in Education from the University of Mexico. She was a high school teacher back in Guatemala."

"How do you know that?"

"She told me when I was at her house yesterday afternoon."

"What were you doing at her place? Were you messing around with her?"

"No, I wasn't messing around with her. I stopped to get her side of the story about the mask."

"What did she tell you?"

"She told me that Carlos switched the mask with a rock Friday afternoon when he heard that Tina and I were coming over to Indiantown."

"How did he know that you were coming?"

"Some little bird told him I guess. She didn't know who it was. But she was in the room when he got the telephone call."

"Oh. I guess I'd better get going if you want to get to the library on time."

"Elmo, there's no hurry. It's only a little bit after nine-thirty. I can make it there in ten minutes."

"Mack, Carlos is scared to death over being sacrificed. He knows about that pile of sod pallets out at the Naked Lady Ranch. Can you help him?"

"I've done what I can, but it's up to you and Carlos now. Just be cool and treat the Guatemalans with respect and allow them to maintain their personal dignity. They are proud people."

"Okay. We will. I'll tell Carlos when I'm there Friday night."

"You'd better get over there and tell him today! He doesn't have much time."

"Okay! I will."

"Elmo, tell me honestly, why didn't you bust Rat for carving up that dead dolphin? You know that it was against Federal law."

"I suppose I did, but he saved me a trip offshore."

"What do you mean by that?"

"I was supposed to find the dolphin, tow it about ten miles offshore and cut it loose."

"Why? The bull sharks and cat snappers would clean it up in a few days."

"The Navy wanted me to get rid of it. It was the only one they couldn't find when they were here last week doing their tests."

"What kind of tests?"

"They've been testing a new type of sonar equipment about thirty miles offshore and sometimes it affects dolphins. When they bust a pod of dolphins with the sonar the dolphins get disoriented and head for shore. The Navy has a purse seiner out of Port Canaveral under contract to gather them up and dispose of them offshore. That one got loose and made it through the inlet."

"Is that why several charterboat captains saw a submarine out by Push Button Hill last week?"

"Yep. The Navy had a couple of SEALs out looking for the dolphin and they tracked it through the inlet. They couldn't follow it into the shallow water by Sailfish Point and gave up."

"How did they get back to the sub?"

"I picked them up in my boat and ran them up the to SEAL Museum in Fort Pierce. The Navy picked them up later and flew them back out to the sub in a helicopter."

"You know more about that sub than you let on don't you?"

"I suppose."

"What kind of sonar are they testing?"

"I don't know. There're two Navy tests going on between Fort Pierce and West Palm Beach."

"What's the other one?"

"The Navy is testing a miniature submarine to look for mines on the bottom."

"So? What's unusual about that?"

"The sub's remotely controlled by a satellite and it tows a fish sixteen hundred feet, or more, behind it loaded with electronics and an orange laser."

"They usually employ that system with a helicopter. Why would they want to use a miniature sub?"

"The Navy figures that in time of war that the choppers would be shot down very fast."

"That makes sense. How're the tests going?"

"They're having problems with the steel tow cable kinking."

"They'll probably using a sheave with too small a throat for the cable. It should be at least twenty times the diameter of the cable. If the sheave is too small it will cause a wire cable to kink and develop fishhooks where it passes over the pulley."

"How do you know that?"

"You don't want to know and I can't tell you."

"I believe you."

"Elmo, why did you send Rat over here last night to pump me for information?"

"I thought that he might be able to find out something you wouldn't tell me."

"All you have to do is ask me yourself."

"Oh." Elmo blushed and shuffled his feet as he looked down at the ground. "I'm sorry."

"That's okay," Mack responded softly and patted Elmo on his right shoulder. "I'll overlook it this time, but don't ever try that covert stuff on me again. You're not very good at it and someone might get hurt. Do you understand what I'm telling you?"

"Yes sir."

"Good. It's almost a quarter to ten and I have to get going. The library opens at ten o'clock.

Are you going to Indiantown to brief Carlos today? I don't want him to get into any more trouble then he already is."

"I'm leaving right now," Elmo responded as he headed for his patrol car. "I'll be over there by ten-thirty and I'll tell him to be cool just like you told me."

"That's good," Mack offered as Elmo opened the car door. 'Don't tell him that I met with Carmelita and Octavio yesterday. He doesn't need to know everything just yet."

"I understand," Elmo softly responded as he gently closed the patrol car door.

After Elmo had left sped the marina parking lot and headed for Old St. Lucie Boulevard Mack couldn't help talking to himself.

"Elmo's just like a trained parrot," Mack said as he shook his head and headed for his pickup truck. *"He'll tell Carlos everything just like I want him to do. Carlos' butt is mine."*

Chapter
42

Mack sauntered into the Blake Library a few minutes after its ten o'clock opening and headed straight for the reference desk.

Janet was waiting for him with a big smile spread across her face. And opened the conversation when Mack was still ten feet away from her desk.

"Good morning Mr. McCray," she oozed in her best impression of Mae West's throaty drawl. "I think I have what you want this time." She winked at him as she cautiously scanned the library floor.

"What did you find out?" Mack gushed. He was completely unable to maintain a reasonable professional demeanor. "Did you find out what the Navy is doing outside the St. Lucie Inlet?"

"They're doing several things," Janet retorted with a slight lilt to her voice. "Which one do you want to know about the most?"

"What's affecting the dolphins and making them beach themselves?"

"You don't have a clue do you Mr. McCray?"

Janet was doing her best to play a cat and mouse game with him, but Mack refused to play along.

"I think that the Navy's testing a new high-powered sonar system that's blowing out the dolphins' ears and turning their brains into mush."

"That is a fairly accurate statement. It's called Low Frequency Active Sonar, or LFAS for short. The Navy developed it to detect and track quiet enemy submarines at long distance."

"Do you believe that?"

"That's what it said on the Navy's website."

"I asked if you believe what the Navy is saying not what they say on their website."

"Yes and no."

"What do you mean by yes and no?"

"I believe very little of what a government agency spews out in the way of information and even less if it is an arm of the military."

"That's one point we can agree on. Tell me what this LFAS Sonar is all about. Will it harm fish and marine mammals?"

"Most definitely, although the Navy claims that there is no scientific evidence that it does. Jacques told me that it is having a very detrimental effect on the ocean's population of marine mammal, mainly whales and dolphins."

"Jacques? Who's that?"

"Jacques is the French scientist from the University of Paris who came here to study the dolphin stranding on Jensen Beach last week."

"Oh. When did he tell you that?"

"Last night during dinner."

"What were you doing with him last night? He went back to France on Friday and Ralph took him to the airport."

"He missed his plane. The Paris Air Show started on Saturday and all of the flights to Paris are booked until this weekend."

"What were you doing with him?"

"We went out to dinner at Chez Paul, that's the quaint little French restaurant on the north side of the old Roosevelt Bridge. He's staying at the Jensen Beach Holiday Inn until Friday."

"I know where it is. What did you talk about?"

"His work with dolphins and whales mostly. It's a fascinating subject. His brother worked in a top-secret Navy dolphin project in Hawaii many years ago and unfortunately he drowned while out for a morning swim."

"I heard that. Did you talk about me?"

"Goodness no! Why would we spend time talking about you? He is much more interesting."

"Did he tell you why he was here?"

"He said that the French government is considering funding a dolphin research program at the University of Paris and asked him to develop a methodology for it."

"Did he have anything to say about the dolphin stranding on Jensen Beach last week?"

"There wasn't anything for him to see. By the time he got to the beach all of the dead and dying dolphins had been towed out to sea by a purse seiner."

"Does he have a theory about why they beached themselves?"

"He says that in most of the dolphin and whale strandings that he has studied that the animals' ears were shattered and their eyes bulged out of their sockets. He blames it on the Navy's testing of their new LFAS sonar system."

"Did he tell you where else he studied dolphin strandings?"

"The first place was on the island of Kauai in Hawaii about five years ago. It was mainly strandings of pilot whales. He said that the Navy admitted that they had been testing a new sonar system, but they hadn't violated the Federal Marine Mammal Protection Act."

"They always say that. Do you have any specifics on the Navy's new sonar system?"

"I have everything. Are you ready to absorb reams of technical information?"

"Go for it," Mack responded with a grin as he rested his elbows on the counter. "Just speak slowly so my feeble mind can stand a chance of absorbing some of it."

"Okay. Here we go," Janet slipped her reading glasses into a comfortable position on the bridge of her nose, shuffled a pile of papers in front of her and began. "Environmental activists have been fighting the Navy's use of their Towed Low Frequency Active Sonar Array for several years."

"Hold it a minute!" Mack barked. "What do you mean when you said towed?"

"The Navy tows a large barge equipped with gigantic underwater loudspeakers behind a ship when they are searching for submarines. Sometimes they tow the equipment behind another submarine."

"Could they use a satellite-controlled miniature submarine to do it?"

"I suppose they could, but understandably the amount of equipment that can be towed decreases proportionately with the size of the towing vessel."

"Of course they could tow a smaller version for close up warfare. Go ahead."

"Mr. McCray, are you certain that you can hold still long enough for me to talk?"

"Yes. I promise to keep my mouth shut and just listen."

"Very good," Janet softly responded as she repositioned her reading glasses on the bridge of her nose. " The power level of the LFAS Sonar is from an effective source level of two hundred and forty decibels, although the Navy claims that the conversion to water drops it to sixty-one point five.

"Wow! That's loud, " Mack offered. "That's three million times the power needed to blow out a human's eardrums."

"I thought that you were going to be quiet."

"I will. I won't say another word."

"That sound level is the equivalent of standing twenty feet away from a Saturn V rocket during a space shuttle launch." Janet paused for effect to see if Mack would offer a comment. He didn't so Janet continued. "Each underwater loudspeaker, the Navy calls them acoustic transmitting source projectors, can generate two hundred and fifteen decibels of sound all by itself. The sound pulse can approach one hundred and sixty decibels as far as one hundred miles away from the deploying vessel."

"How long do the pulses last?"

"I was coming to that!" Janet quipped. "I thought that you were going to be quiet?"

"I will from now on. I promise."

"Although scientific studies clearly indicate that whales avoid sounds at a level of one hundred and fifteen decibels the Navy asserts that it is safe to expose marine mammals to as much as one hundred and eighty decibels from LFAS."

Janet paused for effect and looked at Mack over the top of her glasses. She expected a reaction, but Mack placed the palm of his right hand over his mouth and shook his head slowly from side to side.

Janet continued, "A one hundred and eighty decibel tone is one million times louder than a one hundred twenty decibel tone."

"I know," Mack offered from under his hand. "It can cause hemorrhaging in the inner ears and brains of marine mammals."

"How do you know that?"

Janet stared at him over the rims of her glasses visually demanding him to explain why he interrupted her dissertation.

"The necropsies of beached whales and dolphins show hemorrhaging in their inner ears and brains."

"The Navy does not admit to that," she sternly offered. "Shall I continue?"

"Please," Mack softly responded from between his fingers.

"In July of two thousand and two the Navy asked the National Marine Fisheries Service to authorize a 'small take' of marine mammals by LFAS Sonar tests," Janet dryly offered with no show of empathy for the plight of the dolphins. "However, the specific upper limit number was not defined and the National Marine Fisheries Service exempted the Navy from the Federal Marine Mammal Protection Act. In two thousand and four the NMFS granted permission for the Navy to actively test LFAS Sonar for five years."

"I can't hold back any longer," Mack stated as he pulled his open hand away from his mouth. "Have there been any scientific studies of dolphins' and whales' reactions to the LFAS Sonar pulses?"

"Yes," Janet responded. "Observers in the immediate area where the Navy was testing LFAS in Hawaii documented that dolphins and whales leaped out of the water in sheer panic to avoid it."

"How long is a LFAS sonar sound pulse?"

"A single 'ping' for existing Navy submarine sonar equipment is one second in duration. However, with LFAS the length of the pulse can be from six seconds to as long as one hundred seconds."

"Wow! Mack responded. "That is an extremely long time for a marine mammal to be exposed to over one hundred decibels of sound. What is the frequency of the pulse?"

"The transmitted frequency varies between one hundred and five hundred Hertz."

"I don't believe for a minute that the Navy is using this new system to detect submarines."

"Why not?" Janet asked as she pushed her glasses almost to the tip of her nose and looked over the top of the lenses at Mack. "It all sounds good on their website."

"It sounds too good and it won't work to detect enemy submarines over long distances."

"Why not?"

"There're are a couple of reasons. Sonar, like radar, only works on a line of sight basis. Once the signal reaches the curvature of the earth it will disappear."

"How far is that?"

"Let me equate it to you on a visual basis. If you are standing on the beach you can only see about two and one half miles to the visual horizon. The higher up you are the farther you can see. If you are on a platform twenty feet high you can expect to see about five miles to the horizon."

"But a submarine is under the water and the distance would be much shorter!"

"That is correct, however, keep in mind that nuclear submarines operate to depths of five thousand feet and the measurement of the distance to the underwater horizon is based on how high above the bottom they are and the depth of the water."

"Oh."

"Why are they testing it so close to shore?"

"What makes you think that they are testing it close to shore?"

"Jacques told me that all of the stranded dolphins and whales that he has studied are species that normally live within twenty miles of the coast."

"Bingo!" Mack exclaimed. "There's another interesting factor that negates this system as method of detecting enemy submarines over long distances under water."

"What's that?"

"I thought that you'd never ask. Have you heard of the military's Stealth airplanes?"

"Aren't they made out of a material that's invisible to radar?"

"That's correct. Today's nuclear submarines are coated with the same material used on the Stealth airplanes to absorb sonar signals, plus a thick rubber coating to lessen noise intrusion."

"If the Navy isn't using it to detect enemy submarines over long distances what do you think they're using it for?"

"I have an idea that the LFAS sonar tests are a cover for a new type of under water acoustic weapon, but I'm not certain. What else did you find out?"

"According to one web site LFAS sonar has a range of up to one hundred and fifty miles and can track up to thirty six targets at a time."

"That doesn't make any sense either," Mack quipped.

"Why not," Janet responded. "It's right here in black and white." Janet tapped the pile of papers on her desk with her right index finger.

"Because the Russians only have sixteen submarines and they aren't going to deploy all of them to the same general area at the same time."

"How about the Chinese?"

"They had seventy-eight in service at last count and they are adding three more every year."

"Maybe the Navy is tracking China's submarines?"

"I don't think so."

"Why not?"

"Because the Chinese Navy is not going to deploy half of their nuclear attack submarines within a one hundred and fifty mile radius. Something else is going on."

"What do you think it is?"

"Tell me what else you found out," Mack responded as he stroked his chin with the finger of his right hand. "You might have the answer right in front of you. How long has the Navy been testing the LFAS sonar system?"

"They tested it twenty times in nineteen sixty-six before the Natural Resources Defense Council learned about it."

"How big is it?"

"The Navy has two versions. One of them is carried in a large surface barge that is towed by a Navy ship, plus they have a smaller system that can be towed behind a submerged submarine."

"That's it!" Mack exclaimed as he stood up straight.

"What is it?" Janet sheepishly asked as she pulled her glasses off and placed them on the desk.

"It's a big lie! LFAS isn't submarine detection sonar. It's an extremely high power acoustic sound system designed to destroy and neutralize an enemy sub's crew via Extremely Low Frequency transmissions. I'll bet that it was initially tested at the Navy's AUTEC underwater test center in the Turks and Caicos!"

"What does AUTEC mean?"

"Atlantic Undersea Test and Evaluation Center."

"Oh. Have you been there yourself?"

"A long time ago."

"I found out something else that you might be interested in hearing about."

"Shoot!" Mack responded.

"General Dynamics' Bath Iron Works in Bath, Maine is working on an acoustic-energy weapon for ship defense system that will disable an enemy ship's crew with sound," Janet read slowly and deliberately as if she couldn't believe what she was reading. "They mounted five acoustic projectors around the ship during their initial trials. Mr. McCray, this sounds like science fiction ray guns."

"Janet, believe me that it's real and it's not science fiction."

"How do you know that?"

"I might be able to tell you someday, but not now. SeaCo. was an early Navy contractor for their dolphin program and later changed their name to SAIC. They worked for years to design an acoustic weapon that would emulate the dolphin's ability to stun prey using acoustic energy in their echo location system."

"Dolphins can stun their prey? I thought they used their sonar system to locate food, not to kill it."

"Some bigger dolphins, called Bottlenose whales, do not have teeth and eat stunned prey exclusively."

"Wow! You should be teaching marine biology at a high school somewhere."

"I could teach at the university level. The concept of acoustic weapons is not new. The government experimented with high-energy acoustic pulses at the 'Non-Lethal Weapons Directorate' at the Quantico Marine Base in Virginia for several years. Funding was stopped and the project was moved to the Army's Picatinny Arsenal in New Jersey."

"Did they make it work?"

"Yes. The military has what they call a 'Directed Stick Radiator' that fires high-intensity sonic bullets up to fifteen feet. It inflicts severe inner ear pain and causes disorientation."

"It is very big?"

"No. One man can easily carry and fire it. It's encased in a polymer composite tube about forty inches long and two inches in diameter."

"Can you hear it if it's aimed at you?"

"No. The transmitted frequency, called infrasound, is less than twenty Hertz and well below the audible range of the human ear. The power level ranges between one hundred and twenty-five to one hundred and fifty decibels. However, tests have demonstrated that similar sounds that pass through water can tear cell wall structures; permanently damage nerves in the inner ear and can cause liquefaction of the bowels."

"Is that what is happening to the dolphins that strand themselves on shore?"

"I think so. They experience the same symptoms, but I have some research to do before I form a definite conclusion."

"What kind of research?"

"Very important research."

"Is there anything I can do to assist you?"

"I don't think so at this point," Mack responded as he tapped on the counter with his right index finger indicating an end to the conversation. He turned to leave and then turned back to face Janet. "There might be one small thing that you might be able to help me with, that is if you have time."

"I have time!" Janet enthusiastically spouted as she edged forward in her chair. "What is it?"

Mack leaned across the counter, cupped his right hand against Janet's left ear and whispered. "Find out if the University of Florida Agricultural Research Facility in Fort Pierce has any experiments going on in Indiantown."

"What kind of experiments?" Janet whispered back.

"Secret agricultural experiments in Indiantown," Mack softly whispered, in a covert tone. "Things they don't want the public to know about."

"Like what?"

"Secret stuff."

"What kind of secret stuff?" Janet whispered.

"I don't know," Mack replied. "That's why they call it secret stuff."

Mack winked at Janet with his right eye, turned and headed for the exit.

"*She has some contacts she doesn't talk about and if anyone can find out what's going on over there she can,*" Mack thought. "*Plus, she has the curiosity of a feline.*"

Chapter 43

"Mr. McCray! What a pleasant surprise that you came to see me," the nervous Frenchman mumbled through the slight opening in his hotel room door. "What can I do for you mon ami?"

"I told you before that I am not your friend!" Mack replied. "I want to talk to you about Janet."

"Who is this person Janet? Do I know her?"

"I would think so. You took her out to dinner at a fancy French restaurant last night."

"I did? Are you certain mon ami?"

"If you say mon ami one more time I'm going to jerk your silly head off and feed it to the bull sharks!"

Mack pushed on the door with his right shoulder, but the brass safety chain kept it from opening.

"What did you do to Janet last night? She told me that you took her out to dinner."

"Nothing. However, the woman I was with last night is not named Janet. Her name is Marilyn."

"Marilyn! Her name is Janet! She's one of the reference desk librarians at the Blake Library."

"That may be true mon ami, however the woman that was with me last night is called Marilyn."

"I suppose she told you that her last name is Monroe?"

"That is correct mon ami. Her name is Marilyn Monroe."

"You've been had Frenchy!" Mack grunted as he thrust his shoulder against the door. "Let me in! You and me are going to have a long talk!"

"I cannot allow that," the Frenchman responded as he also shoved his shoulder against the inside of the door. "You must leave immediately or I will call hotel security."

"I'm not leaving until we've had a face to face talk," Mack quipped as he shoved on the door.

"Mon ami, this is not a good time for me. I have company."

"What kind of company? I know it isn't Marilyn Monroe because I left her at the library about twenty minutes ago."

"It is a business associate and we are in the middle of very delicate negotiations," the Frenchman replied with a discernable hiss in his voice. "Please do not interfere."

"What kind of negotiations? Are you selling the Brooklyn Bridge or buying it?"

"I do not have to purchase the Brooklyn Bridge. I already own it. I purchased it three years ago when I was in New York City on a business trip. Mon ami, will you please leave now?"

"Not until you and I have a talk about what you're doing here and why you didn't take the plane back to France on Friday night. Ralph went to a lot of trouble to get you to the airport."

"I missed my flight by one hour and the remaining flights were booked solid with people going to Paris to attend the air show. I am scheduled to leave this Friday night on my original flight. Now will you please leave me alone?"

"No! Let me in, or come out here and talk to me, before I knock the door down and drag you out!"

"That is not necessary mon ami," the Frenchman responded in a soft whisper. "Please allow me a few minutes to become presentable and explain the situation to my business associate."

"It's almost noon! You should be presentable if you're in a business meeting!"

The Frenchman did not respond as he closed the door. Mack heard the brass deadbolt 'click' as it slid into place.

"What kind of game are you playing Frenchy?" Mack shouted at the door. There was no response.

"What the hell is that foreigner trying to pull off here?" Mack muttered under his breath as he leaned against the wall and shook his head. *"Why is he still hanging around?"*

Mack snapped his fingers. "I know what it is!" He said aloud just as the door to the Frenchman's room opened.

"You know what mon ami?" The Frenchman asked as he slipped out of the hotel room door and deftly closed it behind him before Mack could get a look inside.

"I know why you're here and why you're sniffing around Janet."

"I do not know any one named Janet mon ami," the Frenchman responded with a quizzical look on his face. "Perhaps you mean my friend Marilyn Monroe from the library?"

"Yes! I mean Marilyn Monroe!"

"What do you mean by sniffing around? I do not sniff around women. I simply inhale their beauty and aroma. It is much like entering a master chef's kitchen while he is preparing your meal. I allow the aroma to tease my senses and arouse my appetite."

"I'll bet!" Mack responded as the nervous Frenchman backed up against the wall. "Now spill it Frenchy!"

"Spill what mon ami?" The Frenchman's forehead crinkled as a body language sign of not understanding. "I do not have a bowl or soup or a glass of wine that I can spill for you."

"I know what you why you're here and I want to hear it from your own mouth," Mack shouted at the terrified Frenchman.

"I am here to study the reason for the dolphin strandings."

"You told Janet, I'm sorry Marilyn, that you are here to develop a dolphin research program for the University of Paris."

"That is true mon ami. That is why I am here. But allow me to assure you that I am leaving for Paris tomorrow night and I have no romantic intentions towards your friend Marilyn Monroe."

"Her name is Janet! What makes you think that her name is Marilyn Monroe?"

"She told me. She has been in many American movies."

"Frenchy, you have the charisma of a three day old road killed skunk and Marilyn Monroe wouldn't look at you twice!"

"What do you mean by road killed skunk? I am not familiar with the term."

"It is a very complimentary term. American women love to go to restaurants that serve road kill."

"Where can I find such a place?"

"Why?"

"Marilyn, also your friend Janet, and I are going out to dinner tonight and I would like to surprise her by taking her to a road kill restaurant."

"Try any of the local barbeque places," Mack responded with a grin. "Just tell them that you want the road kill special of the day. They'll know what to do."

"Do you have any particular road kill dinner selections that you recommend?"

"Try the road killed raccoon with giblet gravy and a side order of turkey nuts."

"What is giblet gravy?"

"Giblet gravy is a delicacy made from cooking the liver, heart and other organs together."

"Do turkey nuts grow on local trees?"

"Turkey nut trees come from the Erzurum Province of eastern Turkey. The Turks use them as a female aphrodisiac on their harem women. A local farmer planted a few trees on his place out by Yee Haw Junction in the nineteen fifties. They're usually served deep-fried and Marilyn loves them."

"I've heard of them. Is that all you want from me mon ami?" The Frenchman wiggled to get away from the wall. "May I go back to my business meeting now? My business associate is waiting for me."

"No!" Mack emphatically stated as leaned into the frightened Frenchman's face. "Where's your goatee?"

"What goatee mon ami? I am not wearing a goatee."

"The goatee you were wearing when you took Marilyn Monroe out to dinner last night!"

"Oh! That goatee? It is a fake. I bought it from a street vendor in New York City. Women like Frenchmen who wear goatees. I glue it on and take it off when I arrive back to my hotel."

"What were you doing in New York?"

"I go to New York often on business."

"Monkey business I bet. Like when you bought the Brooklyn Bridge."

"That was long ago, maybe ten years, on one of my first visits to the United States."

"A few minutes ago you told me that you bought the Brooklyn Bridge three years ago."

"I forgot. Now may I go?" The Frenchman hissed as he attempted to sidestep Mack's bulk.

"No! Not yet you little twerp! Do you work for the United Nations in New York?"

"What makes you ask that mon ami? It is a very unusual question for a fisherman."

"I'm a very unusual fisherman. Now answer the question!"

"I did not actually work for the United Nations. I was a liaison staff member for NATO."

"Were you assigned to NATO Headquarters in Brussels in nineteen eighty-five?"

"Yes. Why do you ask?"

"Because I met you at the NATO Undersea Research Center in La Spezia in northwestern Italy."

"That is correct mon ami," the Frenchman whispered.

Beads of sweat had broken out along his brow and ran down both sides of his face.

"That is very confidential information and I would appreciate it if you would not mention it to anyone else. I assume that you have satisfied your curiosity."

The nervous Frenchman squirmed to escape Mack's dominant body mass.

"May I go now?"

"No!" Mack responded as he leaned his bulk forward and

overshadowed the slightly built Frenchman. "You worked on the Low Frequency Active Sonar environmental adaptation research project! You aren't here to study dolphin strandings are you?"

"Yes I am mon ami," the very nervous Frenchman whispered. He was visibly agitated.

"You don't work for the French government and you aren't doing a feasibility study for a dolphin research program at the University of Paris are you?"

"That is partially correct. I do work for the French government and I am assigned to NATO."

"What about the dolphin project at the University of Paris?"

"There is none. May I go now?"

"No!" Mack responded. "Now tell me why you are really here or I'll break your scrawny neck and feed your fat head to the bull sharks!"

"NATO assigned me to study the effects of the American Navy's testing of broadband Low Frequency Active sonar on the littoral dolphin population along the Florida coastline."

"Why didn't they send an American researcher?"

"It was thought to be best that your American marine mammal researchers not be fully informed of the testing process for fear that they will become alarmed over the mass strandings of local populations of dolphins and whales. They will conclude that it is a natural event."

"That's just great! Don't tell them what you're doing and they won't be able to figure it out!"

"That is correct. May I go now?"

"No! Exactly what kinds of tests are going on here?"

"NATO's environmental adaptation studies are focused on research into Anti Submarine Warfare in using operations-friendly environmental sensing techniques supporting the requirement to optimally operate broadband Low Frequency Active Sonar in littoral waters."

"What does that mean in plain English?"

"The United States government supports NATO in conducting LFAS testing operations along your coastline to determine the obvious effects on the marine mammal population."

"What that means to me is that you are trying to determine

how many of our dolphins and whales will be killed, or maimed by LFAS tests."

"That is correct mon ami. May I go now? My business associate is waiting for me."

"No! That explains why some charterboat captains thought they saw a Russian sub out on Push Button Hill last week," Mack stated as he shook his head. "It was a Russian sub wasn't it?"

"It was a clone of a Russian Akula Class nuclear attack submarine used to insert realism in NATO training exercises."

"Why are these studies going here and at this particular time?"

"There was a serious incident at Pianosa Island on the southeast coast of Italy and NATO is no longer permitted to test LFAS within one hundred miles of the Italian coast."

"What kind of incident? How many dolphins were killed?"

"It was not dolphins that were killed."

"Then what was it?" Mack questioned. "Whales?"

"No. It was underwater divers and I do not wish to say anymore about it."

"That's just fine. NATO can't blow the eardrums out of Italian sponge divers, but our dolphins and whales are fair game. What about our divers?"

"There have been no reports of injuries to divers in Florida's littoral waters since the tests began."

"There have been several divers lost in the past few weeks. Most of them were never found."

"That is not related mon ami. Our LFAS tests are not conducted on weekends because of the possible effects on recreational divers."

"The divers that I'm aware of disappeared on weekdays."

"Simply coincidental and not related to our testing."

"I'll bet!" Mack emphatically stated. "What kind of subs are they using for the tests?"

"Spare generic nuclear attack submarines are utilized for offshore tests outside of ten miles from the coastline because recreational and commercial vessel operators may detect them if they operate in depths of less than six hundred feet. For littoral tests we utilize Global Positioning System controlled Remotely Operated Vehicles and small unmanned exploration submarines."

"Why?"

"NATO anti-submarine warfare studies indicate that small submarines and unmanned submersibles are very difficult to detect and provide a tactical advantage in littoral waters and choke points such as harbor entrances and designated Traffic Separation Schemes. The LFAS system provides immediate and definite all-weather detection and recognition of threat submarines and friendly submarines in shallow littoral waters."

"Plus, you can blow the sub crew's brains out and disable the submarine."

"I didn't say that mon ami."

"You didn't have to say it," Mack responded. "I figured it out all by myself. The LFAS testing is a cover for testing and training sub crews in the use of acoustic weapons. Why did that sub surface out by Push Button Hill last week? Was it in trouble?"

"No mon ami. It surfaced to draw attention away from the fishing boat that was attempting to capture the injured dolphins before they reached the beach."

"That makes sense! It was a decoy."

"May I go now?" The Frenchman was sweating profusely and balls of sweat rolled down his cheeks and dripped onto the front of his shirt. "My associate is waiting for me."

"Who do you have in there?" Mack emphatically stated as he stared the terrified Frenchman directly in the eyes. I cannot say specifically who it is but he is also a member of the NATO Scientific Committee of National Representatives as I am."

"What is that?"

"The Scientific Committee of National Representatives provides scientific guidance to the NATO Undersea Research Center and the Supreme Allied Commander Transformation."

"Is he an American?"

"Yes. May I go now?"

"Maybe," Mack softly responded. "Please give me his name before I'm forced to do something that you will regret."

"I cannot."

"If you don't tell me his name I'll break your neck, rip your head off and fed it to the bull sharks!"

"You can't threaten me!" The Frenchman wiggled and

attempted to evade Mack's bulk.

"That's a promise not a threat," Mack placed his hands around the terrified Frenchman's neck as added emphasis of his sincerity. "Give me his name."

"Doctor Sam Heaton! Please do not tell anyone that I gave you his name," the now profusely sweating Frenchman pleaded. "They will kill me."

"I won't," Mack replied as he dropped his hands from the man's neck. "Sam Heaton's an old friend of mine and we go back a long way. The last time I saw Sam he was living on a goat farm in Palm City. Tell him 'hello' for me when you go back in there."

"I will mon ami," the frazzled Frenchman rubbed his neck with both hands. "May I go now?"

"Yes," Mack responded as he stepped away and allowed the Frenchman some breathing room. "Take good care of Marilyn tonight or I'll break your neck!"

"I will mon ami. I promise."

"Frenchy, before I leave I have one more question for you."

"What is your question mon ami? I will try to answer it."

"Why does Marilyn Monroe think that your name is Jacques? When I met you on the airplane you told me that your name is Francois."

"Mon ami, you certainly know the answer to that question."

"I guess that I'm really stupid Frenchy because I don't."

"Mon ami, no man on the prowl for action gives a woman his real name."

The Frenchman winked, turned and opened the door.

"*Adieu*," he whispered as he slipped inside and closed the door behind him.

Mack turned and headed down the hall towards the lobby.

"*I remember hearing that the Navy was experimenting with a new weapons system on the Virginia class of nuclear attack submarines,*" Mack thought as he walked down the hall. "*I have to make some phone calls to some people in Norfolk when I get back to the marina.*"

Chapter 44

It took Mack almost an hour to get to the Blake Library from Jensen Beach because of the construction on the Stuart Causeway Bridge. Traffic was backed up because it was restricted to a single lane of traffic.

"*I have to warn Janet about that French guy before she makes a big mistake!*" Mack thought as he strode from the parking lot towards the library entrance. "*He's going to break her heart.*"

Mack entered the glass doors, turned left and headed for the reference desk. Janet wasn't there! Johanna was sitting behind the counter and she smiled as Mack approached.

"Good afternoon Mr. McCray," Johanna gushed. "How may I help you today?"

"Where's Janet!" Mack looked furtively around the library

floor and scanned the many computer terminals to his right. He didn't see Janet. "I need to talk to her!"

"She's off for the rest of the afternoon. Maybe I can help you with something?"

"Can you get hold of her? This is very important!"

"I don't think so. She's at the beauty shop getting her hair and nails done," Johanna offered. "She has a dinner date tonight with a real hot French guy from Paris."

"I know!" Mack replied. "That's why I need to see her. That guy's no good!"

"She doesn't think so. She spent a lot of time with him over the weekend. They got along real good. They went out to dinner at *Chez Paul* last night and she said that she had a good time."

"I bet she did! Do you know what beauty shop she's at? This is very important."

"I can't tell you that! It's personal information and we aren't permitted to give it out to library patrons."

"I'm not a library patron! I'm her friend and she may be in danger!"

"Rules are rules Mr. McCray and I must follow them. However, she left something here for you in case you came in this afternoon," Johanna replied as she reached for a small pile of papers held together with a paper clip. "They are articles about the generation of electric power at coal-burning power plants. Do you work for Florida Power and Light?"

"No! Electric power generating plants are my hobby!" Mack snapped back. 'Did she leave anything else?"

"Like what? I know that she was looking up something for you on her computer. I overheard her asking someone at the University of Florida Agricultural research Station in Fort Pierce about some experiments they are doing in the artificial stimulation of plant growth."

"I asked her to research that for me! What did she find out?"

"I don't see anything else out here for you," Johanna responded as she scanned the desk. "If she did it would have your name on it. Do you want me to go back to the office and look on her desk?"

"No! That's okay. I'll catch up with her tomorrow." Mack

replied. "Do you know where this French *gigolo* is taking her for dinner?"

"No. I don't. Mr. McCray, I don't mean to correct you, but *gigolo* is an Italian word for a young lover kept by an older woman. Jacques is older than Janet."

"I don't know the French word for slime ball. If she comes in, or calls, tell her that I said for her to be very careful around that French guy. He's up to no good."

"If I see her I'll tell her, but she really likes him a lot."

"Tell her to pull on his goatee."

"Why should she pull on his goatee? That would be rude."

"It'll come off. It's fake just like him. And tell her that his name is not Jacques, it's Francois."

"How do you know that?"

"He told me about an hour ago."

"Where did you see him?" Johanna asked. "Janet called his room at the Holiday Inn in Jensen Beach about noon and no one answered the telephone."

"He wasn't in his room at noon."

"How do you know that?"

"He was with me."

"What were you doing with him?"

"We were having a little heart to heart talk in the hall."

"What did you do to him?" Johanna asked as her mouth dropped into a concerned frown. "Is he okay?"

"I didn't do anything to the little wimp," Mack replied with a slight grin. "However, I told him that if he hurts Janet I'll rip his head off and feed it to the bull sharks."

"That wasn't a very nice thing to say."

"He's not a very nice person."

"He seemed very nice when he was in here talking with us."

"Johanna, do you like dolphins?'

"Of course! They're cute and very smart too."

"He kills them!"

"Oh no! I can't believe that! Jacques is a sweet man."

"Believe me he's a dolphin killer. Johanna, if you talk to Janet before she goes out to dinner with the little weasel tell her that he is going to surprise her."

"How do you know that?"

"He told me."

"Do you know what the surprise is?"

"Yes, but I can't tell you."

"Why not? I can keep a secret."

"Then it wouldn't be a secret would it?"

"I suppose not."

"If you do talk to her tell her not to eat the turkey nuts."

"Turkey nuts? What are they?"

"They grow on a tree in a remote region of the Erzurum Province in eastern Turkey. The Turks use them as a female aphrodisiac for their harem women. Some guy brought a few of the seeds back to Florida in the nineteen fifties and planted them in a field outside of Yee Haw Junction."

"Oh. Can you buy turkey nuts in a grocery store? I'd like to try them myself."

"It depends on the time of year. They have to be eaten fresh. You can usually find them around Thanksgiving and Christmas time. That's when they harvest the turkeys."

"Harvest the turkeys?" Johanna asked. "Don't you mean the nuts from the turkey trees?"

"Oops. That was a slip of the tongue. I meant turkey trees."

"What is the scientific name of the tree that turkey nuts grow on?"

"They're called turkey trees because they come from Turkey," Mack replied as he turned slightly to his left so Johanna couldn't see that he was repressing a sly grin. "I don't know their scientific name."

"I'll try to find it on the Internet," Johanna naively replied. "Do you want me to write the name down for you if I find it?"

"That's okay. I prefer to call them turkey trees," Mack responded while keeping his face turned away from Johanna. "Johanna, do you see those two old men over there by the copy machine?"

"Yes. They're in here every day."

"I think that the skinny one has the 'hots' for Janet."

"Maybe so. He spends a lot of time hanging around the reference desk when Janet's here," Johanna replied with a knowing look towards the aging duo. "He got really mad when Jacques starting coming by every day to take Janet to lunch."

"What! That French slime ball's been taking her to lunch too? Where does he take her?"

"They usually go to Carmella's."

"Where's that?"

"It's a little Italian restaurant on East Ocean Boulevard. You can walk there from here."

"Oh. Where's the beauty shop from here? Is it within walking distance too?"

"No. It's in the Harbor Bay Plaza in Sewall's Point."

"Thanks Johanna," Mack replied over his shoulder as he walked away. "I knew that you could keep a secret."

"You tricked me!" Johanna sternly replied in the direction of Mack's back. "That's not fair!"

"*All's fair in love and war,*" Mack mumbled under his breath. "*I wonder what idiot said that?*"

It was 2:42 P.M. according to the wall clock behind the check-out counter.

Chapter 45

Mack's trek to the Harbor Bay Plaza beauty shop was a dead end. Janet had already left when he go there.

He pulled into Port Sewall Marina at 3:46 P.M. and spotted Ralph digging in the flowerbeds in the northwest corner of the parking lot. He honked the truck's horn to get Ralph's attention.

Ralph waved, dropped the shovel and sauntered over to Mack's truck.

"Where've you been all day Mack?" Ralph posed the question knowing full well where he had been. "I haven't seen hide nor hair of you since Tuesday mornin'."

"I've been around the whole time," Mack replied with a forced smile as he dragged himself out of the truck cab, headed for the front porch and an empty woven rattan rocker. "You haven't been here at the right time to catch me."

"I thought that maybe a bunch of them hyped up Guats in Indiantown dragged you back into the woods for a blood sacrifice," Ralph countered as he eased himself into the other rocking chair and plopped his feet up on the porch railing.

"What makes you think that I've been over in Indiantown?"

"When I was over here Tuesday mornin' you told me that you took that Guat back to Indiantown Monday afternoon after the trial. Ya'll are such good buddies that I figured that you went back again to meet his wife and kids."

"That's a stupid thing to say!" Mack replied. "We aren't good buddies. I just felt sorry for him and gave him a ride back to Indiantown because he didn't have a way to get back."

"That isn't what Elmo said." Ralph grinned, pulled his feet away from the porch railing and sat up straight. "Elmo said that you and all the Guats over there in Indiantown are great buds."

"That's even stupider!" Mack exclaimed. "When did he tell you that crap?"

"This mornin' when we had breakfast together at the Queen Conch. He said that you went to Indiantown on Tuesday afternoon and didn't get back here until ten thirty that night."

"Did he tell you that I went back to Indiantown on Wednesday and didn't get back here until about nine-thirty last night?"

"He might have mentioned it in the conversation."

"Of course he did! Elmo sent Rat down here to milk me for information."

"Did Rat bring you a dolphin sandwich? He had a couple left over when he left my house and he told me that he was coming over here to give you one."

"Yes he did. He was here waiting for me when I pulled into the parking lot."

"Wasn't it the best dolphin you ever ate? I scarfed down two sandwiches and was going for a third one when he cut me off. He told me that the last two sandwiches were for you."

"Ralph, that wasn't the kind of dolphin you think it was."

"What do you mean? Rat said it was dolphin."

"Yes, it was dolphin all right. The same kind of dolphin that live under the boathouse."

"Do you mean the two dolphins from Hawaii, Kea and Puka?"

"That's correct and if you ate Rat's dolphin sandwiches you ate one of their relatives."

"What! Rat told me it was fresh dolphin! But it didn't taste like fish. It was more like blue fin tuna."

"Bingo! It was real dolphin. How does it feel to know that you ate Flipper?"

"Yuk!"

"Where did Rat tell you he got it?"

"He didn't. I assumed that he swiped it out of a charterboat fish box when the mate wasn't looking."

"Did you ever break the word assume down into three parts?"

"Let's not go there. Mack, tell me honestly. Where did Rat get the dolphin? It couldn't be roadkill!"

"Why not?"

"Dolphin swim in water. They don't cross roads."

"Rat found the dolphin washed up on a sandbar on the east side of Clam Island. It was dead and a couple of bull shark pups were tearing at it. The meat didn't need to be aged to tenderize it because the dolphin had been there for a couple of days."

"Yuk!" Ralph stood up, grabbed his abdomen, and leaned over the porch railing. "I'm going to barf!"

"It's a little late to barf. If you were going to get sick from eating that dolphin meat you'd done it within six hours of eating it. You'll be just fine. Just be careful when Rat offers you anything to eat."

"I will next time," Ralph replied as he sat back down in his wicker rocking chair. "Where were you all morning? I came over about ten o'clock to invite you fishing, but your truck was gone."

"Elmo was here about nine-fifteen to pump me for information. Did he send you over here to pump me for more?"

"Of course not! I just came over to see if you were okay and wanted to go snook fishin'."

"I appreciate your offer. But I have to run down to Sailfish Marina and talk to a couple of the charterboat captains when they come in at five o'clock."

"Who do you want to see down there?"

"Squeaky Murphy and his cousin Scratchy Briggs."

"Weren't those the two guys that were runnin' their mouths over the marine radio about seeing that Russian submarine out by Push Button Hill last week?"

"That's them."

"What do you want to see them about?"

"I want to verify a couple of things."

"Like what?"

"Just what they think they saw out there."

"Mack, be careful down there. Watch your back."

"Ralph, what are you talking about?"

"The Feds have had the place staked out since last week. They videotape everybody getting' on and off the charterboats."

"What makes you think that that the people doing the videotaping are Federal agents?"

"Mack, be serious! They're drivin' a white Ford Crown Victoria with government plates. That's the first hint. Duh!"

"Is one of them a big black guy with a shaved head?"

"Yep."

"That's Harold Bellefonte. He and I spent a night together in a West Palm Beach jail cell. What does the other one look like?"

"He's a skinny white guy, maybe six feet tall, has a lot of curly black hair and a goatee."

"That's John Cyr. He's a detective from the Honolulu Police Department. He's on temporary duty to observe the DEA's drug interdiction methods."

"That's strange."

"Ralph, why do you say that it's strange? Cross-training in very important for effective law enforcement."

"Would you run a load of drugs over from the Bahamas in the daytime if you saw two Federal agents video taping everybody who gets on and off a charterboat? Dude, it's a no brainer!"

"Did you call me dude?"

"Not really, it's a figure of speech. Everybody says it."

"Ralph, don't ever call me dude again or I'll shove a surfboard up your butt and you'll walk like a California surfing dude for a month afterwards. Understand?"

"Very clearly. What you want to see Squeaky Murphy and Scratchy Briggs about?"

"Ralph, that's really none of your business. Case closed. Don't ask me any more questions."

"Okay Mack! Don't get so testy about it."

"I'm not! I want to be certain that you understand."

"I understand. Can I go down to Sailfish Marina with you? I've known both of them boys for a long time."

"No! Have you seen anything strange going on outside the inlet since that sub showed up last week?"

"Nothin' except a little mini-sub that the boys spotted runnin' along the beach down by Peck's lake a couple of days ago."

"What kind of mini-sub? Did it have any markings on it?"

"No markings, but it had a number painted on the side up by the conning tower."

"What was the number?"

"Nobody thought to write it down. We were all so involved in tryin' to run it down that everybody forgot to do it."

"Another great example of great investigative potential. Did you catch it?"

"Nope! That little sucker was runnin' about thirty knots on the surface and my boat only does twenty knots runnin' at full bore."

"Didn't someone else have a faster boat than yours that could keep up with it?"

"Yes, old Stinky Fullerton got right up alongside of it and when his brother Odoriferous reached for it with the gaff it went under the surface and disappeared. I think somebody on shore was operating it by remote control and just messin' with us."

"It most likely was a tourist. Has the Russian submarine been seen again since last week?"

"Nope. Mack, what do you think that Russkie sub was doin' out on Push Button Hill?"

"I don't think it was a Russian sub."

"What do you think it was then? It looked like a Russian Akula class sub to me."

"Ralph, did you see the sub yourself, or did someone else tell you about that they saw?"

"I saw the pictures and one of the charterboat captains who was in the Navy identified it."

"Where did you see any photographs of an Akula class sub?"

"Down at Sailfish Marina. Squeaky Murphy took some shots of it with his digital camera and was showin' them around before the Feds took them away from him."

"When was that?"

"Monday afternoon when you were in court."

"Why didn't you tell me about it sooner?"

"Mack, you never asked me about the sub until now. I didn't think that it was important."

"It wasn't. Did the Feds interrogate Squeaky?"

"I don't know. I wasn't there when they nabbed him. Somebody told me about it."

"Who?"

"Elmo."

"How did Elmo know about it?"

"He was at the marina when the Feds busted Squeaky."

"That was good timing for Elmo. How did he know to be at the marina at that specific time?"

"I don't know."

"Ralph, did you just happen to mention to Elmo that you saw Squeaky's sub photographs?"

"I might have. I can't remember everything I say to people. My memory's not as good as it used to be just a few years ago."

"That's okay. I'll ask him about it when I see him."

"Mack! Don't say anything to Elmo about this. He'll think that I told you!"

"Ralph, you did tell me."

"I wasn't supposed to say anything about it to anybody!"

"Then I won't say anything to Elmo about it. Did that French guy say anything to you about why he was here when you drove him to airport last Friday night?"

"Nope."

"What did you talk about on the way to the airport?"

"Nothin' much."

"You can't spend forty-five minutes in a car with someone and not talk about something."

"He talked about dolphins and how sad it was that they got sick and washed up on the beach."

"Did he ask you about me?"

"He wanted to know how long you've been here and where you came from. That's all."

"What did you tell him?"

"I told him that you got here in March and that you came here form Chicago."

"Is that all?"

"Pretty much. Did I do something wrong? I don't want to get you in trouble!"

"Ralph, I seem to be able to get myself in trouble all by myself. Everything's just fine."

"Good!"

"What about my dog?"

"What about him? He's doing just fine. Joy took him dog toy shopping this mornin'."

"Does he remember where he lives?"

"I think so, but when you get him back he'll slip back into his normal routine."

"When do I get him back?"

"Mack, why don't you give Joy a few more days with him? She's bought a whole pantry full of dog food and dog treats."

"How about bringing him home Monday?"

"I'll tell Joy."

"Fine." Mack responded as he stood up. "Ralph, it's almost four thirty and I want to get down to Sailfish Marina and catch Squeaky and Scratchy when they come in from their charters."

"Okay Mack," Ralph replied as he stood up and stepped off the porch onto the pea gravel driveway. "I'll just go home."

"I don't see your truck in the parking lot," Mack noted. "Do you want me to give you a ride home?"

Ralph shrugged his shoulders in response, turned and began walking down the driveway towards Old St. Lucie Boulevard.

"Don't worry about me," Ralph muttered under his breath. "It's only a half-mile over there and I'll make it just fine."

"I'll see you later," Mack offered, but Ralph didn't respond.

Chapter
46

Mack parked his blue pickup truck in the parking lot next to the public launching ramps north of Sailfish Marina and walked down Old St. Lucie Boulevard to the marina driveway. He instantly spotted the white Ford Crown Victoria sporting the white U.S. Government license plate and took a detour around to the south side of the blue, corrugated steel boat storage building.

When Mack slipped out from behind the corner of the metal building he almost walked directly into the view of Federal Agent Harold Bellefonte and his Hawaiian partner John Cyr who had their video camera set up in the back of a white van and focused on the wooden pier leading down to the charterboat dock. They were so intent on videotaping the charterboat captains and their guests that they didn't catch sight of Mack out of their peripheral vision. Mack slowly backpedaled down the side of the building until he reached the door on the north side and slipped inside.

"Now what the hell am I going to do?" Mack thought as he walked down the open center of the gigantic storage building towards the marina office entrance. *"Those two bozos are taping everything that moves up and down that charterboat dock. I have to talk to Squeaky and Scratchy and tell them to keep their mouths shut before they get themselves into more trouble than they already are."*

Mack spotted Captain Squeaky Murphy walking down the dock towards the boat storage building and his brother Scratchy Briggs was two paces behind him. Both captains smiled when they came in range of the video camera, raised their right hand and gave the two agents huddled in the back of the white van a one-fingered salute.

"Now be careful boys, that's the way to really piss them off if you haven't done enough already," Mack muttered under his breath and he slowly shook his head from side to side. *"I'll be surprised if they don't leap out of that van and slap a pair of cuffs on both of them."*

Much to Mack's amazement the two men in the van ignored the obscene gesture and continued their mundane task of videotaping everyone walking down the dock. The two captains continued in a straight line and entered the boat storage building. Mack slid over behind a racked twenty-two foot Donzi sport fishing boat and waited for them to walk past him before he announced his presence.

"Hey Squeaky," Mack whispered as loud as he dared. "Come over here."

The intended targets of Mack's verbal invitation continued walking as if he wasn't there and he decided to try again in a much louder tone.

"Hey Squeaky!" Mack bellowed loud enough to be heard over the noise of the diesel-powered boatyard forklift. "Come here."

Both men froze in their tracks and swiveled their heads around in an attempt to locate the source of the voice. Mack remained hidden behind the Donzi because he didn't want to be seen by Harold Bellefonte and John Cyr.

"Who the hell are you and what do you want?" Squeaky Murphy managed to squeak out.

He suffered a blow to his larynx during a high school football game that damaged his vocal cords and earned him the handle of Squeaky.

"It's Mack McCray." Mack replied as he walked out from behind the boat and waved his arm so the two men could locate him. "Slip in here behind this Donzi so we can talk."

The two men obliged and Squeaky Murphy cautiously opened the conversation.

"Mack! Where have you been for the past week?" Captain Squeaky Murphy managed to hack out of his damaged larynx in several octaves. "Those two bastards and their video camera are driving our customers away! Can you run them out of here?"

"Why are they videotaping you and your customers?"

"They told us that it's a training exercise so they can practice using the video camera and recording equipment, but they've been doing it since last Wednesday! That's a lot of video training. My wife bought me a portable camera for my birthday and I had it up and running in thirty minutes."

"I don't believe that they're doing any training either," Captain Scratchy Briggs added. "I think they're videotaping our charter customers in order to blackmail them later."

"Why would they want to blackmail your clients," Mack asked. "In the first place they don't know who your customers are and second those guys are both law enforcement officers."

"A lot of our customers come here with their girlfriends and want to go out for a day of messing around," Captain Scratchy Briggs vehemently stated. "They don't care about fishing."

"But they don't know who they are," Mack offered. "They don't have their names or anything."

"Yes they do!" Captain Squeaky belted out. "The marina office makes a copy of their driver's license and makes them write down their next of kin's address and phone number in a notebook in case there's a serious accident while we're out on the charter."

"Oh, that's different Mack replied. "I wouldn't worry about it. Squeaky, I understand that you were showing people photographs of that submarine you spotted out by Push Button hill last week. Is that correct?"

"Yes. I have a few and I showed them to a few people. They were supposed to keep their mouths shut! Did Ralph tell you that I had the photographs?"

"Maybe he did, but didn't you give me the digital disk in that blue baseball cap that I bought?"

"Yes, I did, but I made a few prints the night before. That's what I was showing around."

"Do you still have them?"

"No! Your buddy Deputy Elmo ran his mouth to those two bozos out there in the trailer and they confiscated them."

"What did they say to you when they took them?"

"They told me that I never saw a submarine out on Push Button Hill and that it was a figment of my imagination," Captain Squeaky replied as best he could. "They wanted to know where the disk was and I told them that I threw it away. They didn't believe me."

"What did they do then?"

"They took my digital camera. Do you still have the disk at your place?"

"I think so," Mack replied. "I never did anything with the baseball cap when I got back to the marina. It should still be on the kitchenette table where I left it."

"Keep it in a safe place. I need proof of what I saw."

"What do you need proof for?"

"I called the *National Inquirer* and told them about the Russkie sub and they want to do a story about it. But, they're insisting that I give them some photos that they can publish."

"Squeaky, I wouldn't do that if I were you," Mack cautioned in a soft tone of voice.

"Why not? I know what I saw and I can prove it!"

"That's right!" Captain Scratchy Briggs added. "And he can prove it!"

"Squeaky, if you give the *National Inquirer* those photographs you might endanger yourself and compromise our national security," Mack cautioned.

"What do you mean compromise our national security?"

Captain Squeaky rasped. "I'm a Nam vet and I support our country all the way."

"I can't tell you everything about it, but the Navy was conducting some satellite submarine detection tests when you saw that sub surface out by Push Button Hill. It was one of ours."

"No it wasn't! Mack, I swear that it was a Russkie Akula class nuclear attack sub! Scratchy was in the Navy and he recognized it first thing."

"That's right Mack," Captain Scratchy added. "I was on a Navy destroyer and we had to memorize the silhouettes of all of our subs and the Russian's too. It was definitely an Akula class sub."

"It may have been a Russian submarine, but it was manned by United States sailors."

"How do you know that?"

"Just trust me. It was a captured Russian submarine that our Navy uses for training exercises."

"Why didn't somebody just come out and tell us?" Captain Squeaky barked. "We'd have kept our mouths shut about it."

"Because it might have compromised our national security," Mack cautioned. "Just keep your mouth shut about it, pretend that it didn't happen and you'll be okay."

"What about those two clowns out there in the van with the video camera?"

"What about them?"

"Why won't they just leave us alone?" Captain Scratchy pleaded. "We're Americans too!"

"Maybe one reason is that you keeping shooting birds at them. Do you suppose that thrills them?"

"No, I reckon not," Captain Squeaky, offered. "Should we go out there and apologize to them?"

"No!" Mack sharply quipped. "Leave them alone. Smile and wave at them when you see them."

"They might think that we like them!" Captain Scratchy insisted. "We don't!"

"You don't have to like them," Mack replied. "Just respect who they are and who they represent."

"What can they do to us if we don't," Captain Squeaky rasped.

"Anything they want, at any time they want, and no one will ever find your body."

"What!" Captain Scratchy screamed. "They can kill us if we don't like them?"

"I didn't say that," Mack replied. "They probably wouldn't touch you themselves, but they know people who will for the right price. They never found Jimmy Hoffa did they?"

"No, they didn't," mumbled Captain Squeaky.

"Point made and case closed," Mack responded. "Go home, take a hot shower and enjoy your life while you still have one."

"I'm out of here!" Captain Squeaky howled at two different octaves as he dashed out of the boat storage building towards the marina parking lot.

"Me too," echoed Captain Scratchy. "I'm right behind you brother! Don't slow down!"

"Why are some people such slow learners?" Mack mumbled at a barely audible level.

"Because they didn't have you as their teacher," rumbled a deep, demanding baritone voice from behind him.

Mack knew that it wasn't the voice of CNN!

Chapter
47

"Mr. McCray, we need to talk."

Mack started to swivel around to face his inquisitor.

"Don't turn around!" The deep voice rumbled. "You're better off that way."

"Why?" Mack responded as he returned to his original position. "I've met you before and I know what you look like."

"Maybe you do and then again maybe you don't," the baritone voice rumbled. "I'm not alone."

"Who did you bring with you this time? A couple of leg breakers from Chicago?"

"How'd he know," a raspy male voice, tinged with a heavy old-country Italian accent, echoed from behind the boat rack. The voice's owner was out of range of Mack's peripheral vision.

"Shut up Rocco," cracked an agitated male voice.

"Guido Cameri?" Mack responded. "Is that you?"

"No! It's not me!"

"Guido, now he knows it's you," the raspy male voice mumbled.

"Both of you shut up!" The owner of the deep baritone voice ordered. "Go sit in the car and wait for me. I need to speak with Mr. McCray alone."

"Yes sir," simultaneously echoed two male voices.

The boat storage building was eerily quiet except for the rasping of the soles of their shoes on the brushed concrete floor. The rasping grew softer and softer until it disappeared into the darkness at the far end of the massive building.

"Mr. McCray."

"Yes sir," Mack responded.

"We need to come to an understanding of what you do and don't know about this submarine business. Do you understand?"

"Yes sir. I understand. Exactly what don't I know?"

"First, let's determine what you do know, or perhaps think you know. What is your opinion of that little French dude?"

"Do you mean Francois?"

"You know full well that's who I mean. What do you think of him?"

"How do you mean that? I don't want to date him and I'd rather not see the little twerp again."

"How much do you know about him?"

"That's an excellent question," Mack responded as he started to turn around to get a glimpse of his conversation partner.

"Stop it right there or I'll turn the boys loose on you!" Rumbled the heavy baritone voice.

Mack paused before he responded.

"How can you turn them loose on me? You gave them a time out and sent them to the car."

"That was two of the four. Do you want to take a chance on the other two? The odds are not in your favor Mr. McCray."

"I think I'll pass this time," Mack replied. "I skipped lunch and my electrolytes are down."

"That's very wise. Let's get back to the original question."

"Now exactly what was that question?" Mack offered as a tongue in cheek comment that was meant to be funny. "I have a short memory span and can't concentrate when I'm under pressure."

"I asked you what you think of the French guy?"

"Oh, that guy. I think I said that I don't want to date him."

"Or, that you ever want to see him again. I remember. What do think about him as a person?"

"I think he's a little *gigolo* and a smart ass."

"What do you think of him professionally?"

"I don't know what he does? How am I supposed to know anything about his profession?"

"He works for us just like you did until a few months ago when you blew your cover."

"In what capacity?"

"He doesn't carry any hardware if that's what you mean. He's more of a white-collar book-smart type of agent," the deep baritone voice replied. "He uses his head to get things done not his brawn."

"He sticks his head in other people's business a lot."

"Are you talking about his fling with your librarian friend?"

"That and a few other things. He's a sneak."

"Maybe he is and that could be part of his training. Did you have any professional level discussions about what he does and why he's here?"

"When I met him on the plane last week he told me that he is associated with the University of Paris' marine mammal research program and was here to study the dolphins that strand themselves on the beaches along the east coast of Florida."

"The university of Paris does not have a marine mammal research program!"

"That's what I found out."

"What else did you find out?"

"He and I had a serious discussion at the Holiday Inn a few hours ago. He told me that he was a member of some high-flying NATO anti-submarine warfare testing program and he was here to determine the effects that the tests of acoustic weapons by submarines in shallow coastal waters had on marine mammals."

"That is very close to reality, but it's not a bingo."

"What do you mean?" Mack asked. "Did the little twerp lie to me?"

"Not exactly. He does work for NATO and he is studying the effects that acoustic underwater weapons are having on marine mammals, but that's not all. He works for us."

"In what capacity?"

"The marine biologist gig is his cover and we got him assigned to the NATO project."

"Why?" I don't understand."

"The agency does not have a good working relationship with the folks in the Pentagon and they're not willing to share any information about their weapons research and testing with us."

"That's nothing new, but the agency's always been involved in intelligence gathering not weapons research," Mack replied with a shrug of his shoulders. "Why now and where do I fit in?"

"Years ago the agency, NSA and Air Force put their best scientific minds together to research the effectiveness of Extremely Low Frequency signals on human behavior."

"I've heard something about that."

"Mr. McCray, don't try to play games with me," the deep baritone voice resonated with obvious irritation. "I've reviewed your file and I know exactly what projects you were involved with while you were in the Air Force including the development of electronic counter-measures. Let's stop playing mind games."

"Yes sir."

"Did he mention that the submarines are testing ELF wave transmission through acoustic transmitters?"

"Yes."

"Did he also give you the frequency range and power output level of the transmitters?"

"Yes sir," Mack replied. "Do you want me to quote them?"

"No. We already know them. Tell us what we don't know."

"How do I know what you don't know?"

"I just told you what we know. We need to know how much of our acoustic weapon technology the book-smart scientific nerds have given to NATO that could be passed on to the Russians."

"I think they have all of it based on what I heard."

"What do you mean?"

"Last Tuesday a Russian Akula class nuclear attack sub surfaced about ten miles offshore over a place the locals call Push Button Hill," Mack responded. "That was the same day a pod of dolphins washed up on Jensen Beach."

"We know about that. What else?"

"Apparently NATO was testing an acoustic weapon offshore that blew the eardrums and eyeballs out of those dolphins. The sub surfaced to pull the charterboats away from the dolphins while a purse seiner under contract to the Navy scooped up the dead and dying dolphins."

"We also know about that."

"The acoustic weapon is mounted inside the Akula sub! That's a Russian sub! They've got it!"

"Actually the sub only looks a Russian Akula class sub. It's one of our own Virginia class subs equipped with a facade outer shell to make its silhouette appear to be an Akula."

"Frenchy thinks that it's a real one!"

"That's what we want him and his book smart friends to think. Did he tell you why NATO chose this particular area to test their acoustic weapon?"

"Because of an accident with some divers near Pianosa Island on the southeast coast of Italy NATO is not permitted to test LFAS within one hundred miles of the Italian coast."

"That is also correct," rumbled the deep baritone voice. "It was a horrible accident."

"What exactly happened?" Mack asked.

"I'd rather not go into it. It wasn't an accident."

"What do you mean it wasn't an accident?"

"Some of our people were in the area monitoring the NATO tests. They got too close, someone got trigger-happy and they let go with a series of one hundred Hertz ten second bursts from an acoustic weapon mounted in the nose of a test sub. "

"Were you there?"

"No. My son was one of the observers. Let's go back to the French guy."

"Okay."

"He flipped over to the side of the radical environmentalists and is attempting to scuttle the LFAS sonar and acoustic weapon testing by feeding them detailed information on dolphin and whale incidental kills."

"Is that why the Navy had the purse seiner stationed just offshore on test day?"

"Exactly. Our folks in Paris alerted us that he was on the plane with you and we made certain that you would make contact with him. At the time we didn't realize just how well the two of you would get along."

"What are you talking about?" Mack spit out as he began to turn to face his inquisitor.

"Do not turn around Mr. McCray!" Ordered the deep baritone voice. "It would not be good for your health! Just relax."

Mack halted in mid-turn, wiped his forehead with the palm of his left hand before he spoke.

"Exactly what do you want from me?"

"Originally, when we sent you to Boston, we expected you to return with the details of the acoustic weapon under development by the Navy. However, since then we obtained that information from an inside source."

"Then what do you want?"

"Have you noticed anything strange about this French guy?"

"He can't make up his mind whether his name is Jacques or Francois and he wears a false goatee to impress women."

"Very good. He is one and the same."

"What?"

"Francois is Jacques and Jacques is Francois. There is only one person."

"Isn't Jacques the dolphin researcher that drowned at Coconut Island on Oahu a few years ago?"

"The one and the same. He changed his name to Francois and told people that he was Jacques twin brother, but he couldn't change his fingerprints. INTELPOL caught up with him when he applied for a position at the University of Paris. He pitched them on setting up a marine mammal research program."

"Why would he do that?"

"Marine mammals are the man's life. He developed a method of translating dolphin noises into a digital format that could be read by a computer and translated to English and vice versa. The man can talk to dolphins and they can talk back to him!"

"So, what's the problem?" Mack asked. "Dolphins aren't going to hurt anyone."

"That's what you think. The Navy has managed to train groups of four dolphins each to go on missions with SEAL teams, search out and destroy enemy swimmers. The latest version of the Virginia and Los Angles class of nuclear attack subs were redesigned to include a dolphin transportation pod. "

"What does that mean?"

"The *USS Jimmy Carter*, the third boat in the Seawolf class, was selected to be the test vehicle for the development, testing and evaluation of new techniques in submarine warfare. She was built with a wasp waist to provide room for the internal dolphin tank and remotely operated launch vehicle for the SEAL team."

"Wow! But what does this have to do with the French guy?"

"He's trying to sabotage the Navy's dolphin program by calling public and International attention to the incidental kill of dolphins and whales that occurs within the littoral testing area. He couldn't do it this time because only a few dolphins stranded themselves on the beach and they were gone the next day. That's why the purse seiner was stationed offshore. Its job was to coral the injured dolphins and carry them out to sea for disposal."

"Why did the sub surface out by Push Button Hill?" Mack cautiously inquired. "Was there something wrong with it?"

"No, there was noting wrong with it. It surfaced to get the nosey charterboat captains' attention so they wouldn't pick up on the SEAL team that the sub dispatched to locate one rogue dolphin that got away from the purse seiner."

"That must be the one Rat found behind Clam Island!"

"Who's Rat? Is he a human or an animal?"

"A little bit of both I suppose. He found a dead dolphin behind Clam Island and butchered it."

"That must be the one that got away from the SEAL team." The deep baritone voice lost some of its enthusiasm. "They followed it through the St. Lucie Inlet and lost track of it when it turned north into the shallow water of the St. Lucie River."

"That explains a lot!" Mack exclaimed. "Those are the guys

that Elmo picked up and took to Fort Pierce SEAL museum. I thought that he was pulling my leg."

"He wasn't pulling your leg. What did that Rat guy do with the dolphin?"

"He butchered it and split it with his homeless friends."

"What about the carcass?"

"Some bull sharks in the area took care of it."

"Did anyone see him butchering the dolphin? That's a serious Federal offense!"

"Only Elmo, and he told Rat that he couldn't enforce a Federal law. I think he felt sorry for Rat."

"I can only imagine how he must have felt. Mr. McCray you are released from your assignment regarding the Navy's 'Big Boomer' project effective immediately."

"Why? It was just getting interesting."

"We have all of the information that we need."

"What about the French guy?"

"The agency has no interest in him."

"He's leaving town tomorrow night."

"What makes you think that he's leaving town?"

"He told me today when I was grilling him at the Holiday Inn in Jensen Beach."

"Do you believe everything that someone tells you?"

"Not usually."

"Then I strongly suggest that you do not believe him and go about your normal business."

"Don't you want to find out what else he knows?"

"No. We have all of the information we need," the owner of the deep baritone voice responded. "Mr. McCray, it is time that we part company. I am needed elsewhere."

"But, . . . " Mack stammered as he started to turn around to face his inquisitor.

Chapter 48

"Mack! Wake up Mack!"

The anxious male voice registered in the back of Mack's foggy consciousness, but he could not drag himself into reality.

"Mack! Open your eyes!" The voice echoed through Mack's semi-consciousness. "You're not dead yet you ornery bastard!"

Mack's cognitive brain cells drifted somewhere between the axis of consciousness and the axis of death. His head throbbed in cadence with every beat of his heart and the sound of blood rushing through his carotid arteries beat a rushing tattoo through his ear canals. It felt so good that he was willing to continue drifting in mental limbo and not ever wake up.

"Mack! Get up now!" Roared a deep male voice beside his left ear. "If you don't wake up now you'll die right here."

Mack forced his heavy eyelids to open against their will. The room swirled around him and he felt like he was spinning in a centrifuge at 4 G's. His eyelids dropped down and he drifted back into the black nothingness of unconsciousness. It felt so good to be floating weightlessly in nothingness.

"Mack! Wake up before we lose you!" Roared the deep male voice. "Wake up now!"

Someone slapped Mack across the face with the palm of his hand and the sharp sting of pain quickly changed to numbness. He stirred, slowly opened his eyes and closed them again to block out the glare of the overhead lights mounted on the open steel beams of the boat storage building's iron roof trusses.

"Mack! You have to wake up! Roared the deep male voice. "It's okay. They're gone."

Mack felt a rush of adrenalin flow through his limbs that caused him to tremble from head to toe. He cautiously opened his eyes, blinked at the glare of the bright overhead lights and shook his head to rid it of cobwebs. At first his eyes did not focus until they locked onto a black face poised directly over his own. It was Federal agent Harold Bellefonte!

"Slick," Mack managed to stammer. "What are you doing here?"

"Saving your ass I suppose," the black man responded as he carefully raised Mack's throbbing head off the concrete floor. "You took quite a wallop on the back of your head and you may have a concussion."

"Who hit me?" Mack softly responded as he attempted to sit erect and fell back onto the concrete.

"Don't try to sit up! You might break a clot loose in your head," the black man cautioned. "I don't know who hit you, or with what. But, I suspect that it was a sapper because it didn't bust your skull wide open."

"Did you see anyone?" Mack whispered.

"No. One of the boatlift operators spotted you over here just before he closed the door for the night. We had packed up our video equipment and were pulling out of the parking lot when he flagged us down."

"Did he see anyone?"

"Nope. All of the charterboat captains had already left for the day. He was the last person here."

"What time is it?" Mack asked as he forced himself into a sitting position. "How long have I been here?"

"Right now it's a little past six-thirty," Slick replied. "I don't know how long you've been laying here, but John Cyr and I spotted you when you pulled into the marina about five o'clock."

"How could you see me? I slipped in behind you?"

"Our closed circuit peripheral cameras picked you up when you pulled into the parking lot. I figured that you were stopping by to tell us goodbye."

"Why should I do that?"

"We're done here. John has all the video tape that he needs to put together a training program when he gets back to Hawaii."

"Oh," Mack stammered. "I feel a lot better. Let me sit up straight."

"Okay, suit yourself. Don't blame me if your head busts wide open and your brains spill out onto the floor."

"I won't," Mack replied as he sat up straight and rubbed the back of his head with his right hand. "Ouch!"

"I told you that somebody smacked you on the back of the head. You have to learn to listen to me."

"Am I bleeding?"

"Not enough to make any difference. A sapper doesn't break the skin."

"Did you pick up anybody coming in and out of here on your video cameras?"

"We were taping the charterboat docks, not the boat storage building."

"That's not what I asked you," Mack snapped. "I asked if you picked up anyone coming in and out of here on your cameras, not your video taping equipment."

"I saw your buddies Squeaky Murphy and Scratchy Briggs leave about ten minutes after you came in. That's all."

"Did you see a stocky-built, white-haired guy around here?"

"No."

"How about a couple of rough-looking Italian guys who could have been in the cast of the *Godfather*?"

"Would that be *Godfather One* or *Godfather Two*?"

"Forget that I asked you anything," Mack quipped. "I think I can stand up now."

"Hang on," Slick replied as he slipped his left arm under Mack's shoulders. "Let me help you."

"Thanks."

"I'll get the other side," Detective John Cyr offered as he slid his right arm under Mack's left arm.

"Thanks," Mack replied as he rose to his feet. "I'll be okay after I get a chance to walk this off."

"Do you want to go to the hospital emergency room and have them look you over?" Slick offered. "We can drop you off."

"No thanks. I can drive myself."

"Suit yourself. All I can do is offer."

"I'm okay now. That really hurt!"

"I can imagine. You have a knot on the back of your head the side of a golf ball. You should go by the emergency room and get yourself checked out. You might have a serious concussion."

"I don't think so. My head's still throbbing, but my eyes are focused and I'm not dizzy."

"Bend down and let me look at your eyes," Slick ordered.

"Why?"

"Don't ask so many questions and just do it!"

Mack obliged and opened his eyes as wide as he could while Slick peered into them.

"Mack, I don't know how to tell you this, but your breath smells like the inside of a horse stall."

"What were you looking for in my eyes?"

"The signs of a concussion. You don't have one."

"How can you tell?"

"Your pupils are the same size."

"Oh. Thanks for your help guys. I'll be okay now."

"Mack, are you going to stop by the hospital and have yourself checked out," Slick inquired.

"Maybe. I think I'll get something to eat at Shrimper's first."

"You might collapse face down in the middle of your meal," Detective John Cyr cautioned. "Concussions can sneak up on you."

"I'll be fine. Why don't you guys take off? You must be on a time schedule."

"We have to get back to West Palm Beach and get this equipment checked in tonight," Slick replied. "John has an early flight out in the morning."

"Where's he staying?"

"The Holiday Inn on Belvedere."

"That's convenient," Mack replied. "You should have a good time tonight."

"What do you mean by that snide comment?" Detective John Cyr asked.

"It's Thursday night and Clematis Street rocks on Thursday night. I'm certain that Harold will see that you have a good time. Harold has a liberal expense account."

"Mack! I can't spend government funds on entertainment!" Slick countered. "You know better."

"It's never stopped you before Harold," Mack quipped over his shoulder as he headed for the back door of the boat storage building.

"Harold, what did he mean by that?" Detective John Cyr asked the large black man as he watched Mack schlep out the door and head towards the marina parking lot.

"I don't know," Harold Bellefonte replied. "He's just trying to play with your mind. He's very good at head games."

Chapter 49

Mack pulled into Shrimper's parking lot at 7:12 P.M. and found an open space next to the charterboat dock. He immediately spotted the short line of customers waiting for a table lounging on the inclined wooden ramp that led up to the restaurant's front entrance.

"*My heads hurts and I need a beer fix quick,*" Mack thought to himself as he walked up the ramp. "*I hope that they can seat me at the bar. I don't want to wait in line with these tourists.*"

Jenny, a very observant hostess, recognized Mack as a local fishing guide before he made it into the entrance and had a menu waiting for him when he arrived. She smiled as she made an excuse for the customers patiently waiting their turn to be seated in the crowded restaurant.

"Captain McCray is one of our most popular local fishing guides and he has a standing reservation for his regular table on Thursday nights," Jenny cooed in the direction of the restless line as she turned and motioned for Mack to follow her to the outside seating area.

"Please follow me Captain McCray," she stated loud enough for them to hear. "Your regular table is waiting and your party will be here soon."

"What do you mean my regular table is ready?" Mack whispered under his breath. "I don't come here every Thursday night and I don't have a standing reservation."

"You do tonight," she whispered back. "Someone called ahead and made a reservation for you."

"Who?"

"I don't know," the wispy-haired hostess whispered back as she gestured towards an open table for four next to the outside railing. "He spoke to our manager about five minutes before you came in."

"How did you know it was me?"

"Your name is embroidered over your right shirt pocket," she whispered back. "It wasn't difficult."

"Oh."

"Have a good dinner Captain McCray," she cooed loud enough for the patrons within ten feet of her to hear. "How many people are in your party tonight?"

"Only me," Mack whispered back. "Don't make such a big deal out of it."

"Three besides you. Very good," she replied. "I'll leave menus on the table for them and your server will be here in a moment to take your drink order."

"Wait a minute!" Mack exclaimed in a soft whisper. "No one else is showing up! Don't embarrass me!"

"It's just fine if they're a little bit late Captain McCray. We understand."

"What are you trying to do?" Mack whispered. "I told you that no one else is coming."

"Go with the flow and accept it," she retorted in a stern whisper. "I'm not allowed to seat a single customer at a table for four. Now be quiet and behave yourself. People are talking about you."

"What do you mean people are talking about me?"

"Look over there in the corner booth in the patio area," the hostess replied as she gestured with her right thumb. Then she bent over and whispered in Mack's left ear. "That couple apparently knows who you are."

Mack turned his head to the right so that he could see the patio area. His brain couldn't believe what his eyes saw. Janet and Francois sat cuddled together, on the same side of the table, in a corner booth. Janet turned her head away when Mack looked at her and Francois smiled and gave him a thumbs-up gesture. Mack slowly raised the middle finger of his right hand in response.

"What the hell are they doing here?" Mack hissed.

"They are having dinner just like you are Captain McCray," the hostess softly whispered. "I think that she's embarrassed to see you here and he seems to be showing off."

"I don't know either one of them!" Mack glibly stated. "They're mistaken."

"Captain McCray! Hold your voice down," she sternly remarked. "Everyone can hear you."

"I don't care! Can you find me another table?"

"No! This is the only table I have open and there's a waiting list. You're lucky that you got in."

"This is just great! Bring me a pitcher of draft Budweiser!"

"I'm not your server!" The young hostess arrogantly replied as she flipped her head to turn away and her ponytail flew across her face. "Please be patient. She'll be with you as soon as she can."

The hostess departed and Mack was left with his own thoughts and the stares of the diners at the surrounding tables.

He politely nodded in response and silently mouthed, "*I don't know those people.*"

His ignominy was suddenly expanded when the goateed Frenchman slid out from his seat beside Janet, stood up and headed across the open patio in Mack's direction. Janet cautiously smiled and politely waved at Mack.

"*Oh no!*" Mack thought. "*What does that little twerp want?*"

The suave Frenchman sidled up to Mack's table, turned so that his back was towards Janet so she could not see his face and offered a cautious greeting.

"Good evening Mr. McCray," he stated loud enough for

everyone within a radius of two tables to hear. "Thank you for your excellent dinner recommendation. However, we stopped at several local barbeque restaurants and could not locate turkey nuts on the menu. So, we came here for seafood."

Two female restaurant patrons at an adjoining table shook their heads and looked at one another with quizzical looks on their faces. Their male escorts shook their heads, looked at one another, and then up at the ceiling as if attempting to keep from laughing out loud.

"You are certainly welcome Francois, or is it Jacques tonight? You're wearing your goatee so you must be Jacques."

"Mon ami, my name is Jacques tonight as it has always been. You don't understand do you?"

"I understand that you're a bold-faced liar and a French *gigolo!*" Mack stood up and towered over the Frenchman. "If you do anything to hurt Janet I'll hunt you down, rip your head off and feed it to the bull sharks!"

The patrons at several adjoining tables slid their chairs away form the anticipated action.

"*Mon ami*, please calm down. I will do her no harm. Please allow me to explain myself."

"It had better be good!" Mack exclaimed as he pushed the Frenchman with his chest.

The pony-tailed hostess ran down from her perch above the open dining area and stood beside the un-intimidated Frenchman as she spoke directly at Mack.

"Captain McCray, I asked you nicely to behave yourself! If you don't sit down and act like a civilized human being I'll be forced to ask you to leave."

"Please sit down mon ami and allow me to explain," The Frenchman softly pleaded. "You do not frighten me, however, you are making several restaurant patrons very nervous with your ridiculous threats of violence."

The suave Frenchman directed his next remarks to the hostess, "Cheri, please bring every table in this area a bottle of Merlot to make up for the inconvenience and add the cost to my bill."

"Yes sir," she replied. "Does it have to be French Merlot? We only have California Napa Valley wines in the restaurant."

"That will be fine cheri," the Frenchman cooed as he kissed the top of her right hand. "Please add a twenty per cent tip for yourself."

"I'm the hostess and I don't get tips," She sternly replied. "Only the servers get tips."

"Cheri, I apologize because my English is not very good. Please add a twenty percent tip on the bill for yourself in addition to a twenty percent tip for each of the servers. Can you do that?"

"*Oui*! I can do that," she cooed. "*Merci beaucoup.*"

"You are most welcome. Cheri, please allow Mr. McCray and myself to have a brief conversation and apologize for us to any restaurant patrons that we may have inconvenienced."

"I will. Thank you for your generosity."

"You are very welcome," the Frenchman replied as he sat down in a chair on the opposite side of the table from Mack.

"Mr. McCray, we must talk and come to an understanding."

"What kind of understanding?"

"I have nothing except good intentions towards your friend Janet. We have much in common."

"Like what? She doesn't have two names and she certainly doesn't wear a fake goatee!"

"We are both single and enjoy each other's company."

"She's making a fool out of herself over you!"

"That is only your opinion mon ami. I will guarantee you that she is enjoying herself and will have much to talk about after I return to France tomorrow night."

"Why are you going to France?"

"Because I am French and I must prepare my proposal to the University of Paris for the initiation of a marine mammal research program at the University."

"Hold it right there, Frenchy! You already tried that story. You work for NATO and you were here spying on our Navy's submarine acoustic weapons tests."

"That is not entirely correct mon ami. I was here to study the effect that your Navy's acoustic weapons are having on the resident littoral dolphin population. I told you that."

"I suppose you did. Why are you using two different names? Is your name Jacques or Francois?"

"My given name is Jacques. In my other life I died and chose Francois as my new name."

"What do you mean your other life? Did you die and come back as a ghost to haunt me?"

"Mon ami, you truly do not understand do you?"

"I guess not. What's going on?"

"Did you read the book about dolphins that I gave to your friend Ralph to give to you?"

"No! I haven't had time and Ralph has the book."

"That book is about my first life as a dolphin researcher for the United State Navy on Coconut Island on the east coast of Oahu, Hawaii. I drowned and was forced to leave the island. I chose Francois as my second identity."

"You mean to tell me that you are living undercover? You are pretty darn obvious."

"Mon ami, I am not very good at keeping secrets and I must be with the dolphins. I am the only voice they have and I speak for them."

"You're either really serious about this or you're a nut case."

"What do you mean nut case? Is that like your famous American barbeque dish turkey nuts?"

"No! Why did you have to change your identity?"

"The American Navy ordered me to train dolphins to be watchdogs to hunt down and destroy enemy swimmers. I could not do that."

"What did the Navy call the program?"

"It was called the Swimmer Nullification Program and it is very secret."

"I'm sure that it is. So, what are you going to do now?"

"I am returning to Paris tomorrow night to develop a marine mammal program."

"What about your NATO job?"

"I'm done with NATO after this week. I saw for myself the effect that the LFAS sonar system and acoustic weapons have on littoral dolphins and whales. Now I must work to save them."

"Aren't you concerned that someone will come after you?"

"Why would anyone come after me? For what mon ami?"

"To shut you up!"

"No mon ami, I am not afraid. I died once and came back to fight for my dolphins."

"What about Janet?"

"I am going to ask her to come to Paris with me. I own a beautiful chalet in Marseilles."

"Do you think she will go with you?"

"I do not know mon ami, but it will not hurt to ask her," the Frenchman softly whispered as he stood up. "Please wish me luck."

"I will," Mack responded. "If she goes with you please take good care of her."

"I will mon ami," he responded as he turned and headed for his table and an anxious Janet.

"I'll miss her," Mack muttered under his breath as he shook his head and looked in Janet's direction.

Janet was busy rubbing the back of the Frenchman's neck and cooing in his ear. The Frenchman gave Mack a 'thumbs up' and a big smile.

"Captain McCray, what would you like to have for dinner?"

The female server's words brought Mack back to reality.

"I'll have the crunchy grouper sandwich with fries and tell the cook to hold the onion slice. I like it, but it doesn't like me. It gives me heartburn."

Chapter 50

Mack felt that something didn't seem right when he pulled into the parking lot of the Blake Library at 10:03 A.M.

The doors were open and library patrons were straggling through the double glass doors. However, he decided to sit in his truck for a few minutes and sip on his lukewarm cup of coffee in hopes of catching a glimpse of Janet on her way into the library.

After he finished dinner at Shrimper's the night before, Mack stopped off at Pirate's Cove Marina for a few beers with several of the charterboat captains who had stopped in earlier for a shot at the free finger food buffet and hadn't left for home. He didn't fall into bed until way past midnight and pulled the telephone receiver off the hook just in case Tina decided to call.

The cat woke him up at a little past eight o'clock and

demanded breakfast. Mack fed the cat and relaxed in a wicker rocking chair on the front porch of the marina cottage with a hot cup of coffee for almost a half hour before he decided to go inside, take a shower and get ready for the day's events.

It was Friday and Tina would be coming to Stuart for the weekend right after she shed her courtroom workload. He would like to avoid her today if at all possible, but she owned the marina and was his boss.

Without a doubt she would hound him into taking her to Indiantown in her boat, a trip he detested, unless he had a good excuse for not going. His excuse was simple enough and he made certain that her boat's engine wouldn't start.

A small piece of Teflon inserted between the output terminal of the ignition coil and the lead to the distributor cap guaranteed that no spark could reach the ignition points. Only an experienced mechanic would know to pull the coil wire of out the top of the distributor cap and attempt to draw an arc off of the engine block while the starter motor was engaged.

"Females don't know how to work on engines," Mack thought as he secured the piece of Teflon inside the ignition coil.

Mack waited in his truck for fifteen minutes and didn't see Janet enter the library. He had scanned the parking lot for her white Chevrolet Nova when he pulled in, but it wasn't there.

"Maybe she had car trouble," he thought.

He stretched, opened the truck door, shook the remaining drops of cold coffee onto the asphalt, sat the coffee cup into the plastic cup holder strategically mounted on the dashboard and exited the truck cab.

When Mack entered the library he nodded at the volunteer greeter seated at a card table, turned left and headed for the reference desk. Janet wasn't there, but Johanna was sitting behind the desk and she smiled when she saw him.

"Johanna, where's Janet?" Mack stammered when he was still ten feet away from the reference desk. "I need to see her!"

"Good morning Mr. McCray," Johanna quipped. "I'm afraid that you are out of luck today and you're stuck with me. What can I do for you?"

"Nothing! I need to talk to Janet!" Mack turned and headed for the back office located behind tall bookcases filled with hundreds of reference books. "Is she in the back office?"

"Don't waste your time! She's not coming in today."

Mack stopped in mid-stride, turned and faced Johanna.

"What do you mean she's not coming in today?"

"She called me about seven-thirty this morning and asked me to fill in for her. She's going out of town for the weekend and she'll be back on Monday."

"Where did she go?"

"I'm not permitted to release personal information about library employees."

"You can tell me! I'm a good friend of hers."

"Mr. McCray, I don't want to hurt your feelings, but you are a library patron just like everyone else. If Janet wanted you to know where she went she would have called you too."

"I need to know!" Mack stated as he leaned over the reference desk towards Johanna. "She might be in danger!"

"She went out of town with a friend. What kind of danger do you think she might be in?" Johanna asked sweetly. "She might be moonstruck, but I'm certain that she's not in any physical danger."

"What do you mean by moonstruck? She's not nuts!"

"She is certainly not nuts, but she might be in love."

"What? Are you crazy? She's not in love with anyone."

"I'm certain that Janet doesn't share all of her personal thoughts with you."

"I see her almost everyday! Who could she possibly think she's in love with? It's not that skinny old guy that's always hanging around the copy machine gawking at her is it?"

"Of course not! She has class and that old fart has as much sex appeal as a bag of dry dog food."

"Who else could it be? His fat friend with the gout?"

"No sir."

"Who?"

"Did you ever see the movie *The French Connection*?"

"No! What does that movie have to do with her?"

"Mr. McCray I gave you a very strong hint. Why don't you think about it?"

"*The French Connection?* Oh no! She didn't take off for France with that French weasel did she?"

"Mr. McCray, you are a very astute man and you figured it out. Now, if you don't have a need for any further research, may I tend to the needs of the other library patrons who are in line behind you?"

Mack turned around and saw that two elderly men and three equally aged women were in line behind him. They appeared to be irked at his lack of concern for their reference needs.

"I'm sorry," he stammered. "I didn't realize that anyone else was in line behind me."

"That's the way it is around here every day," Johanna offered.

"If Janet calls in will you tell her that I'm worried about her?" Mack responded.

"I doubt that she'll call in, but if she does I'll try to remember to mention your concern."

"Thank you," Mack replied as he turned, avoided eye contact with the now seven irritated people in line behind him and headed for the library exit.

"*That crazy broad is apt to disappear when that plane reaches France,*" Mack thought as he walked at a fast trot across the parking lot towards his truck. "*She knows too much about that French nut and what I've told her about the Navy's experiments with ELF for mind control, acoustic weapons and LFAS sonar. The French can market that information. I have to get to the West Palm Beach Airport and stop her before she gets on the plane.*"

Mack's overwhelming concern for Janet's safety was brought to an abrupt halt when Elmo pulled his patrol car in behind his truck and prevented him from backing out of the parking space.

"*What the hell does that goofball want?*" Mack hissed. "*I don't have time to fool around with him.*"

Elmo took his time getting out of his patrol car, slowly sidled up to the driver's side of Mack's truck and motioned for him to wind down the window with a twist of his wrist.

"Mornin' Mack," Elmo offered. "What brings you to the library so early this mornin'?"

"I had to check something," Mack responded. "What brings you around here?"

"I was checking on you. I stopped by the marina about a half hour ago and your truck was gone," Elmo replied with a slight grin. "I figured that you were up here checking up on who bopped you over the head in the boat storage building down at Sailfish Marina."

"How did you know about that? I didn't file a police report."

"That smart-mouthed detective from Hawaii stopped by the office to return the video equipment he borrowed from us and he filled the sergeant in on what happened."

"I suppose that if you know about it that everyone in town knows about it now?"

"Not everybody, but most folks heard about it" Elmo replied with an impish smile. "I mentioned it to the folks down at the Queen Conch when I stopped in for breakfast. They knew about it already."

"News travels fast in this town. Who told them?"

"The kid that runs the fork lift in the boat storage building works there as a cook on the nightshift."

"That's just great," Mack quipped. "Now I don't dare show my face in there anymore."

"It's okay. They feel sorry for you. You could've been seriously injured, or even killed."

"I wasn't."

"Do you have any idea who smacked you over the head?"

"No! Would it make any difference if I did?"

"If you knew who did it we could round them up and lock their butts up in jail."

"I don't know who did it, or even if someone did hit me. I might have hit my head on one of the metal boat storage racks when I walked in there."

"Why were you in there anyway? You keep your boat inside the marina boathouse."

"I stopped by Sailfish Marina to see Squeaky Murphy and Scratchy Briggs when they came back in from their charter."

"What did you want to see them about?"

"Why do you want to know?'

"If you hadn't noticed lately I'm a law enforcement officer and I'm checking out an assault."

"There wasn't a reported assault. I didn't file a report."

"You don't have to file a report in order for us to open an investigation into what happened to you."

"What? That doesn't make any sense!"

"Quite often crime victims, especially assault victims, are afraid to file a report with law enforcement for fear that their attacker will come back and take it out on them."

"Forget it Elmo! I hit my head on a metal boat rack."

"Why didn't you tell that to the detective from Hawaii when he helped you get up off the floor?"

"I was embarrassed. Now can I go? I have a lot of things to get done before Tina shows up this afternoon."

"You're too late for that."

"What do you mean by that?"

"She was just pulling into the Port Sewall Marina parking lot when I was leaving."

"Did you stop and talk to her?"

"Maybe, just for a little bit."

"What did you talk about?"

"That's kinda' between me and Tina isn't it?"

"Elmo! Don't try to play mind games with me! You'll lose! What did you talk about?"

"She took off from work today because she wants you to run her over to Indiantown in her boat for the weekend."

"I'm not going to do that!"

"She thinks you are."

"She has another thin coming. Her boat engine isn't running."

"Did Ralph forget to pull that little piece of Teflon out of her ignition coil?"

"How do you know about that?"

"He told me last week after you and Tina left for Indiantown in your truck."

"Does Ralph tell you everything?"

"No. If he did I'd know what you've been up to this week"

"Elmo, what makes you think that I've been up to anything?

"You're always up to somethin' that gets you into trouble," Elmo responded with a grin. "Mack, are you going to leave the Guats alone this weekend?"

"What Guats are you talking about?"

"Your buddies over there in Indiantown. You've got them all stirred up and Carlos is so scared about being sacrificed that he's been sleeping under his desk in the Silver Saddle."

"I didn't have anything to do with that. He brought it all on himself."

"Are you going to give Carlos the mask back? He wants to give it back to the Guat."

"I told you before that I don't have the mask!"

"Then if you don't have it Tina has it doesn't she? That Guat girl gave it to her Saturday mornin' when she was outside her room in the Seminole Inn!"

"I don't know what Tina has and what she doesn't have! You have to ask her yourself."

"I did when I saw her this mornin' at the marina."

"What did she tell you?"

"She said that you have it."

"I don't have it!"

"She said that she left it under the front seat of your truck when ya'll got back from Indiantown Saturday afternoon."

"No she didn't! She took it with her when she got out of the truck."

"There!" Elmo emphatically stated. " I caught you in a lie!"

"What are you talking about?"

"You just admitted that Tina had the mask stuffed under the front seat."

"I don't know if it was the mask or not! It was a package wrapped up in newspaper."

"Was it heavy?"

"I suppose so. So what?"

"It was the mask alright. I'm sure of it. Mind if I look under the front seat of your truck?"

"Of course I mind!" Mack replied. "What do you expect to find under there?"

"Evidence."

"What kind of evidence?"

"Evidence that you are an accessory to interfering in an formal investigation."

"What?" Mack yelled as he puffed up and sat up straight in his seat. "Elmo! Are you nuts?"

"I don't think so. Are you going to willingly allow me to look under the front seat of your truck or do you want me to call for backup?"

"Go ahead and knock yourself out," Mack responded as he reached across the bench seat and unlocked the passenger's door. "Keep in mind that Tina was sitting over there not me."

"The law clearly states that in absence of a passenger in the vehicle at the time of a search by a law enforcement officer that any contraband, illegal drugs or other illegal items found are the property of the vehicle driver."

"You won't find anything illegal under there!" Mack confidently stated.

Elmo didn't respond as he made his way around to the passenger's side of Mack's truck.

Chapter 51

Elmo's time-consuming search under the seat of Mack's truck for evidence of the jade mask only yielded a few scraps of newspaper. Much to his disappointment Elmo forced himself to apologize to Mack and left a little worse for wear.

After the futile search, and Elmo's embarrassed apology, Mack turned off his cell phone and drove out to Tiger Beach to watch flocks of screaming seagulls attack schools of glass minnows huddled in the surf for safety from rampaging bluefish. Mack realized that Tina was waiting for him at Port Sewall Marina and elected to bide for time. He wanted to delay the anticipated verbal confrontation and drive to Indiantown until the last possible moment. But, he couldn't put it off forever.

At 12:47 P.M. Mack pulled his truck into a parking space in

front of Carmella's Italian Restaurant on East Ocean Boulevard. He decided to stop there for lunch because Johanna told him the day before that the quirky Frenchman took Janet there for lunch several times during the week and he was hoping against hope that the couple would be there. They weren't.

The hostess seated Mack in a booth at the rear of the tiny dining room and he ordered the luncheon special of chicken Marsala, a side order of garlic knots and a glass of water. He dabbled with his food and took as long as he could in a futile effort to stall for time and put off the inevitable confrontation. He knew that Tina wasn't going to be pleased with him for at not being at the marina when she arrived and worse yet her boat engine won't start.

"*I hope that Elmo kept his mouth shut about the piece of Teflon in her boat's ignition coil*," Mack thought as he stirred what was left of the marsala sauce around his plate with a garlic knot. "*If she finds out that I stuck that Teflon in there she'll have my head on a silver platter.*"

Then he remembered that Elmo told him that Ralph sabotaged the ignition coil.

"*Elmo probably told her that Ralph did it and I'm home free if she finds it*," Mack chuckled under his breath. "*She'll rip Ralph's head off his shoulders and stuff it in a garbage bag.*"

"Excuse me sir," The young waitress asked. "Do you need a garbage bag for something?"

Mack snapped out of his self-serving fantasy when she spoke to him.

"No! I'm fine," he mumbled. "I was talking to myself about cleaning up my yard."

"Oh. If you're done with your lunch I'd appreciate it very much if you'd allow me to take your check up to the cashier," the waitress suggested. "It's almost two-thirty. The restaurant is closing and I'm checking out. We'll open again at five-thirty for dinner."

"What credit cards do you take?" Mack asked as he reached in his hip pocket for his wallet.

"We don't take credit cards. We only take cash."

"No problem. How much is my bill?"

"Seven dollars and forty-two cents." The young waitress squirmed slightly as she added, That's without a tip."

Mack tossed a well-worn ten-dollar bill on the table.

"This should take care of it," Mack replied as he stood up. "Keep the change."

"Thank you," she replied with a slight curtsey.

Mack pulled out of the restaurant parking lot, turned right onto East Ocean Boulevard. On his way back to Port Sewall Marina he stopped at the Ace Hardware store on Johnson Street and bought a roll of silver duct tape. After he left Ace Hardware he stopped at the Shell station on the corner of Colorado Avenue and Federal Highway and filled up the truck's gas tank with high octane.

"I know that I'll be driving that crazy woman to Indiantown and I might as well take the opportunity to run good gas through the fuel system," he thought as he gazed at the fast-changing digital numbers on the face of the gas pump that recorded the number of gallons pumped, the price per gallon and the total price of the sale. *"I know that she's going to stir up all kinds of hell when she gets over there."*

Mack took as much time as he could on the short drive back to Port Sewall. He took a side trip to Sandsprit Park and stopped at Sailfish Marina to chat with the forklift operator before he finally reconciled himself to his fate and headed for Old St. Lucie Boulevard and Port Sewall Marina.

"She's going to have my ass," he thought as he passed Whiticar's Boat Works and made the turn around the gentle bend in the road that led into Port Sewall Marina. It was 3:17 P.M.

Tina's silver-blue BMW Z 3 convertible was parked in front of the marina cottage. Tina was nowhere in sight, but a light blue leather overnight bag and matched cosmetic case sat on the front porch. An ominous-looking newspaper-wrapped package nestled between them.

"She's packed and ready to go to Indiantown," Mack thought. *"Maybe she'll change her mind about going after she rips my throat out."*

He pulled his truck into a parking space on the passenger's side of Tina's BMW, switched off the ignition and took a deep breath before he exited the truck cab. Before he took two steps

Tina walked out of the front door onto the porch to greet him. She wore fluorescent orange short shorts, a bright blue halter-top and a pair of orange tennis shoes. A wide smile crossed her face when she saw Mack.

"Hey there big boy!" Tina cooed. "I just got out of the shower. Where have you been all day?"

"Oh no!" Mack thought. "She's using reverse psychology to trap me! I'm a dead man."

Resolved to his fate, much as a downed Roman gladiator in the ancient stone coliseum, Mack hung his head as he mumbled what he knew was a futile response.

"I had a few things to do around town and I didn't expect you to be here until about five-thirty."

"That's fine," she responded with a slight shake of her head. "I know that you have a lot of man's stuff to do to keep this marina shipshape. Did you get everything done?"

Mack's basic instinct for survival told him to turn tail and run for the safety of his truck's steel cab, but his legs turned to stone and he couldn't move.

"I picked up a roll of silver duct tape at the Ace Hardware store on Johnson Street and filled up my truck with fresh gas. I figured that you might want to go to Indiantown tonight."

"Good thinking. You can never have enough duct tape. Did you pick up lunch somewhere?"

He knew that the guillotine was about to fall and he rubbed the back of his neck with right hand.

"I stopped at a little Italian place on East Ocean Boulevard next across from Walgreen's."

"Was it called Carmella's?"

"*She knows where I was all afternoon,*" Mack thought. "*Now she's baiting the trap.*"

"That's right," he cautiously replied expecting the verbal axe to fall. "It's a new place."

"I've heard about it. Several of the girls from the Martin County office go there for lunch a couple of times a week. What did you have for lunch?"

"*Here it comes,*" Mack thought. "*She already knows. One of her spies was there watching me.*"

He decided to test her source.

"I had spaghetti with a side order garlic knots."

"The next time you go there for lunch try the chicken Marsala," Tina smiled slyly and tossed her red hair with her right hand as she responded. "I hear that it's excellent."

"*She got me!*" Mack thought as he nervously rubbed the side of his face with his left hand. "*What can I say to get out of this?*"

"Mack, are you not feeling well?"

"I'm fine. Why?"

"You are sweating like an Iowa hog in the middle of July. Do you have a fever?"

"*She knows everything and she's just putting on the pressure to make me squirm and beg for mercy before she kills me,*" he thought. "*I'd better come up with something really good.*"

"My truck's air conditioner is acting up and I suppose that I'm a little fried."

"Why don't you go inside the cottage and take a shower while I fix you some ice tea?" Tina countered with a wide smile. "Do you like your iced tea sweetened or unsweetened?"

"*Oh no!*" Mack thought. "*She's going to poison me with something that tastes like sugar.*"

"Unsweetened. Too much sugar makes me hyper."

"That's perfect," Tina cooed. "I like my tea unsweetened too."

"*She's up to something really big this time,*" Mack thought. "*She's not going to let me get away.*"

"Do you want to go to Indiantown this afternoon?" Mack offered. "I see that your bags are on the front porch. I filled the truck up with high octane gas in case you wanted to go."

"*Please, if there is a god somewhere and you can hear me, help me out of this one and I promise to be good for the rest of my life and you can have my soul,*" he thought.

A similar plea to an unseen deity had worked for him when he was in the eighth grade and taken to the principal's office for spray-painting the male sex organs of an ornamental garden deer bright red.

"I was thinking about it and I wanted to take my boat over," Tina remarked. "I got here about nine-thirty this morning so we'd have plenty of time to make the trip and you were already gone. I tried to start the engine and get it warmed up. It turned over, but it wouldn't start. I guess I tried it too many times because the battery pooped out."

"That's unfortunate," Mack offered. 'Do you want me to check it out right now?"

"That's okay. It's fixed."

"*Oh no! She knows about the Teflon,*" Mack thought. "*I'd better plea for mercy.*"

"How did you fix it?" Mack asked. "I didn't know that you were mechanically inclined."

"I'm not. I was very fortunate because Ralph stopped by about noon and heard me cussing a blue streak all the way up here. He was a perfect gentleman and fixed it for me. He even connected the battery charger to a shore power outlet so the battery will be fully charged by tomorrow morning."

"What was wrong with the engine?"

Mack knew that he had taken the bait, hook, line and sinker, but it was too late to retract his leading question. He braced for the verbal assault.

"Silly me. There wasn't any thing wrong with the engine," Tina shyly replied with a sly smile. "I'm embarrassed about it. If I tell you what it was do you promise not to laugh at silly me?"

"*She knows!*" Mack thought as he glanced around for protective cover in case she had a pistol hidden in her halter-top. "*She's going to kill me after she's done playing with my head!*"

"I promise," Mack replied softly. He was ready to bolt for the safety of the steel truck cab.

"Ralph took the battery out of your boat and hooked it up to my engine with a set of jumper cables. This is so embarrassing. Are you sure that you want to hear this? I feel so stupid."

"*She's as stupid as a fox!*" Mack thought. "*She has me right where she wants me. I expect Ralph to jump out from behind a hibiscus bush with that piece of Teflon in his hand. I'd better fess up to it. Maybe she'll take it easy on me if I confess without further torture.*"

"Don't feel stupid," Mack offered. "Can I say something?"

"No. I'm the stupid one here and you are so smart. Let me explain."

"Oh no! Here comes the fatal blow!" Mack thought as he scanned the hibiscus bushes for a sign of Ralph's thinning red hair. *"He's around here somewhere and just waiting for his cue."*

"Ralph plugged some kind of wire back into the top of the ignition coil and the engine started right up," Tina cooed as she slightly tilted her head to the left and allowed her red locks to slip down the side of her neck. "You men are so smart when it comes to mechanical things."

"She got me!" Mack thought. *"I'd better confess and get this over with right now."*

"Ralph told me that it was all your idea. Why didn't you tell me about it?"

"I'm dead and they'll never find my body," Mack thought. *"She's set the trap and I stepped right into it. Here we go. Someone said that confession is good for the soul."*

"It was a great idea to keep someone from stealing my boat," Tina gushed as she waved her right hand towards the cottage door. "Mack, come in and get cleaned up. I'll have that iced tea ready to go when you get out of the shower."

"Two of us can play this mind game," Mack thought. *"I'll give her some of her own medicine."*

"What was a great idea?" Mack threw out as verbal bait expecting a verbal tirade in response.

"To install that piece of Teflon between the ignition coil and the distributor. A boat thief wouldn't think to look there if the engine didn't start. It was a brilliant idea! You should patent it."

"It's an easy thing to do," Mack replied with an air of confidence. "Anyone can do it."

"I don't think so," Tina softly replied as she stood ramrod straight and her emerald-green eyes turned to cold steel. "Only a sneaky person with an evil mind would think of such a dirty trick to avoid taking a relaxing boat trip to Indiantown!"

"I've been had!" Mack thought. "She's had her fun toying with me, now she's going to kill me."

"Mr. McCray! Listen to me!" Tina demanded. "Your ass is mine and you are going to pay, and pay and pay for that debacle!"

"Yes ma'am," Mack humbly replied. "I apologize for not

telling you about the piece of Teflon, but I did it to keep someone from stealing your boat. If a boat won't start up right away, a boat thief will usually give up."

"That really sounds good, but I don't believe a word of it! I think that you did it on purpose so you could get out of taking my boat to Indiantown today. But, I have news for you buster! I never intended on taking my boat to Indiantown today. We're driving and we're taking your moth-eaten truck!"

"I thought so! That's why I filled up the tank with high octane gas this afternoon."

"Don't try to pull the wool over my eyes buster! I deal with convicted felons all day that could charm the pants off of a nun if they had five minutes alone with them. You don't even come close."

"I'm not Catholic, so I wouldn't know how it's done. I've never tried it."

"Get your sorry butt inside and get yourself cleaned up," Tina barked. "I want to be Indiantown by five-thirty and it's almost four o'clock now. Hurry up and don't worry about packing anything. I threw your crap in a canvas ditty bag and it's hanging on the doorknob of the bathroom."

"Thanks for thinking of me," Mack softly responded.

"Don't get a swelled head over it! I wasn't thinking of you! I was thinking about Octavio and what we have to get done this weekend while we're over there."

"What are we going to be doing?" Mack replied as he slowly crept closer to the cottage door.

"We have to straighten out Carlos over this mask business and get Octavio's followers calmed down before they do something rash to Carlos and Elmo."

"What do you think they might do to them?"

"I already showed you the make-shift altar some of the Guatemalan men made out of sod pallets out by the Naked Lady Ranch. They're preparing to put it to use this weekend."

"What makes you think that pile of pallets is an altar? Somebody stacked those pallets up to get them out of the way."

"This week someone brought in a truckload of kindling and piled it around the base of the altar."

"Maybe it's for some local Klan initiation rites."

"I don't think so. The people who brought in the kindling were Guatemalans."

"So what? Most of the landscape and yard workers are Guatemalans. It was a convenient place for them to dump stuff and save a trip to the Martin County Landfill."

"Mack, aren't you worried about what might happen to Carlos if we don't get over to Indiantown and straighten out this mess?"

"No. It's not my mess."

"You'd better start worrying about it."

"Why?"

"Because some of the radical Guatemalans think that you have Octavio's jade mask," Tina quipped. "Your name is at the top of their barbeque list."

"I don't have the damn mask! You have it!" Mack replied as he pointed at the newspaper-wrapped package nestled between Tina's overnight bag and makeup case. "It's right over there."

"That's not the mask."

"It must be the mask. I saw the girl give it to you."

"The mask is not in that pile of newspapers," Tina sternly replied. "It's something else."

"Like what?" Mack demanded. "Dirty clothes!"

"I don't know. I haven't opened it," Tina coolly replied. "It's something very personal that belongs to Carmelita."

"Saturday you told me that it was her personal belongings that she asked you to mail back to her family in Mexico."

"I lied."

"What?" Mack asked. "Did you switch packages on her?"

"No! That's the same package she gave me on Saturday morning when you were spying on us from the top of the stairs. She saw you."

"What's in it?"

"I already told you that I don't know. I didn't open it. That would be a violation of her trust in me."

"Why would she trust you?"

"Because she knows that I am an attorney and an honest person. Do you want to know what she told me when she handed me the package?"

"I don't want to know," Mack replied. "It might be more information than I need."

"She told me that whatever is inside that package is very old and that I must protect it at all costs. I have to return it to her by six o'clock tonight or her life will be in extreme danger."

"What? Are the Guats going to barbeque her too? That sounds pretty far-fetched to me."

"It sounded a little out of the ballpark to me too at first, but after I listened to her for awhile I began to understand her."

"Understand what?" Mack asked. "That's she off her rocker? Too much *peyote* for her."

"She doesn't use drugs. She is a well educated woman."

"I know. She graduated from the University of Mexico with a Master's degree in Education," Mack quipped. "She was a high school teacher back in Guatemala."

"How do you know that?"

"She told me when I was in Indiantown on Wednesday."

"What were you doing in Indiantown on Wednesday?" Tina snapped.

"I went over to study Florida Power and Light's fossil fuel power generating station."

"Why?" Tina asked. "I really want to hear this."

"It's my new hobby. I was always fascinated by steam boilers and steam-powered turbines."

"Bull crap!" Tina barked in response. "You were sneaking around over there in the orange groves and bean fields. I heard all about it."

"From who?"

"It doesn't matter. You're damn lucky that someone didn't shoot you."

"Can I go take my shower now?" Mack asked as he slid closer to the cottage door. "I think that I really smell."

"Something about your story smells alright," Tina replied through her clenched teeth. "I'm going to find out what it is and then I'm going stake you out over a fire ant mound."

"Then I suppose that the unsweetened ice tea offer is out of the question?" Mack quipped as he slid through the doorway and dashed for the bathroom."

"You had better hire a food taster for the next six months!" Tina screamed after him. "Nothing that you ever put in your big mouth will be safe! Ever!"

Tina's comments were wasted because Mack had made it into the bathroom and locked the door.

Chapter 52

Tina stared silently out of the truck's passenger's side window as Mack drove down Kanner Highway on the way to Indiantown. Her silence made Mack nervous and he decided to tread on dangerous ground by opening the conversation.

"I'll give you a penny for your thoughts," Mack offered in Tina's direction.

She remained silent and began tapping the fingernails of her left hand on the vinyl truck seat.

"Don't wear out my seat," Mack threw out as a joke. "On my pay I can't afford seat covers."

There was no response from his apparently deaf-mute passenger and Tina maintained her silence until Mack passed the DuPuis Outdoor Recreation Area entrance.

"Is she pretty?" Tina coldly offered without moving her head away from the window.

"Is who pretty?" Mack countered pretending that he didn't know whom Tina meant.

"Maya, the Pakistani girl in Chicago," Tina countered without moving her head. "She must really love you."

"What are you talking about?"

"You know exactly what and whom I am talking about!" Tina spat out from her defensive position. "That poor girl pledged herself to you for life when she gave you her sacred *Om* pendant."

"I don't know what you're talking about," Mack offered as his meaningless defense. "She didn't pledge herself to me, or at least she didn't tell me about it. She slipped that silver thing in my pocket when I wasn't looking."

"What about the matchbook with her name on the inside cover?" Tina was prepared for her direct examination of the helpless perpetrator. "How did that find its way into your pocket?"

"I don't know," Mack softly offered.

"Speak up when you address me!" Tina ordered. "I'm not very pleased with you."

"What did I do now?" Mack had no idea of where her interrogation was leading.

"You stuck your big nose in where it doesn't belong," Tina spat out. Her eyes were apparently concentrating on counting the pine trees along the roadside as the truck sped past them at sixty-five miles per hour. "When will you ever learn?"

"*What do I say now?*" Mack thought to himself. "*If I answer at all I'll be wrong.*"

He decided to take a shot in the dark and took his foot off the accelerator when he replied so that she would think that he was concentrating on what she had said.

"I'm truly sorry if I said or did anything that offended you, or hurt your feelings."

"It has nothing to do with me!" Tina venomously spat out. "What about the girl?"

"Which one?" Mack didn't know if Tina was talking about the

young Pakistani hooker or the Guatemalan girl in Indiantown.

"Which one?" Tina screamed as she swiveled in her seat and stared at the side of his head. "So, there's more than one girl?"

"Are you talking about the girl in Chicago or the one in Indiantown?"

"Which one did you take advantage of?"

"Neither one," Mack nervously responded. He realized that he was getting in deeper and deeper.

"That's not what I understand!" Tina spat out her words in the manner of a spitting cobra directing its toxic venom in the eyes of its adversary. She was giving no quarter!

"Now what are you talking about?"

"Carlos told me that he saw you sneaking around over here on Tuesday and Wednesday. Did you go to her house?"

"Whose house?"

"Carmelita's!"

"She asked me to stop by for a few minutes on Tuesday afternoon and I did."

"Was anyone else home, or were you alone with her?"

"Her mother and brother were there the whole time."

"Oh," Tina softly responded. She was lost for words, but not for long. "How old is her brother?'

"I didn't ask him when he was born, but I'd guess that he's in his mid-thirties."

Tina elected to use a time-tested technique of an experienced prosecutor to confuse a witness. She changed the subject almost in mid-thought.

"Are you certain that Maya is from Pakistan?"

"What?" Mack responded. "I thought that we were talking about Carmelita!"

"Excuse me!" Tina snapped. "I'm asking the questions here and you're answering them! We are discussing both girls!"

"Oh."

"I asked if you were certain that Maya is from Pakistan. Pakistanis are Muslims and Indians are Hindu. The silver *Om* pendant is a Hindu religious symbol. She can't be a Pakistani."

"That's what she told me," Mack offered as he shrugged his shoulders to indicate his uncertainty.

"I think that she made it up," Tina quipped. "An Indian girl would be ashamed to admit that she's a prostitute."

"Whatever."

"Exactly what did you mean by that snide comment?"

"I think that I meant to say that I don't know and I don't care."

"That is really a chauvinistic attitude!" Tina quipped. "And I suppose that you don't care about what might happen to her because she pledged herself to you and you abandoned her?"

"*Oh no!*" Mack thought as his mind raced for a suitable response. It didn't find one!

"I didn't abandon her," Mack softly responded hoping that the positive remark would help to defuse Tina's wrath. "I had to catch my plane and come back here."

"That's abandonment pure and simple!"

"What?"

"She was expecting you to take her on the plane with you and you left her standing at the gate."

"I didn't see her at the gate! I don't even know how I got to the airport, or how I got on the plane."

"That certainly sounds like the actions of a responsible person," Tina sarcastically quipped as she turned her face back towards the truck window. "I'm very disappointed in you."

The trap was set and Mack was about to take the bait!

"What else could I do?" Mack offered. "I had to catch a plane and I was in no condition to know what was going on. She slipped that stuff in my pocket to make you jealous."

"Really?" Tina coldly asked as she slowly turned away from the window to face Mack. "Why would the poor girl ever want to make me jealous? Did you make her believe that we have something going on between us?"

"No!"

"She might be so distraught that she might kill herself," Tina sternly stated much like a disinterested schoolteacher lecturing an unmotivated classroom filled with bored students. She continued," "Or her family might stone her to death to avenge their loss of stature in the community."

"How can there be any loss of stature?" Mack offered. "The girl's a hooker! How much more stature can her family lose?"

"Prostitution is not looked upon as a shameful profession in many Hindu and Muslim communities," Tina sternly stated. "The family and community realize that a single girl must find a way to support herself and pay off her debt to her family."

"Oh," Mack responded. "I didn't know."

"Of course you didn't know! And you didn't take the time to find out either!"

"What do you want me to do about her?" Mack repentantly offered. "Should I fly back to Chicago and bring her back to the marina? She might be able to find a job in town."

"No! You dumb ass," Tina barked. "I don't need any Pakistani hooker hanging around my marina!"

"What?" Mack responded as he pulled off of Kanner Highway onto Warfield Boulevard and entered the city limits of Indiantown. "Didn't you just tell me that she pledged herself to me by giving me that sacred coin and that I'm responsible for what happens to her?"

"Did you eat dumb pills for breakfast this morning?"

"What did you mean by that?" Mack questioned as he pulled into the parking lot of the Seminole Inn and parked the truck in a vacant space under a blooming purple crepe myrtle tree.

"Are you totally naïve?" Tina asked as she opened the truck door and held it ajar with her right foot.

"What do you mean?" Mack offered as his defense. He hoped that she would accept an insanity plea. "I don't understand what you mean by naïve."

"Look buster! I don't give a rat's ass about the Pakistani hooker that you got yourself involved with and the last thing I want is for her to be hanging around my marina. I was trying to make a point."

"What was your point? I didn't get it."

"I can see that. I'll try to make it simple enough so that your mind can absorb it."

"Please," Mack countered expecting a violent verbal tirade to follow.

"I was pulling your chain the whole time," Tina replied as she successfully stifled the beginnings of a giggle. "I don't care about that girl and you shouldn't either. She was just looking for a soft touch and you fit the bill. She probably copied your address off of your driver's license. I'll bet that you'll be hearing from her very soon."

"Why do you think I'll be hearing from her?"

"She'll want money in exchange for returning your Social Security card, driver's license and whatever else she swiped out of your wallet when you were passed out in the hotel room."

"What makes you think that she has my driver's license and Social Security card?"

"I looked in your wallet while you were taking a shower," Tina quipped as she slipped out of the truck cab, grabbed her overnight bag, pulled the newspaper wrapped package from under the front seat and headed for the front entrance of the Seminole Inn.

"Why me?" Mack muttered under his breath as he glanced at his watch. It read 5:17.

Chapter 53

Mack and Tina sat together at a round table in a darkened back corner of the Silver Saddle and attempted to blend into the background. It was difficult because every patron in the bar except the two of them was Guatemalan.

The digital clock on the wall over the bar read 9:47. The multi-octave voice of Roy Orbison crooning *Pretty Woman* oozed out of the ancient jukebox and the dimmed overhead incandescent light bulbs slowly pulsated in time with the music. Tina decided to open the conversation.

"Did you notice that statute that looked like a dog smoking a pipe is gone?" Tina calmly inquired and nodded towards the bar.

"What are you talking about?"

"The last time we were in here there was a white stone statue on the back wall of the bar and I remarked that it looked like a dog smoking a pipe."

"I remember," Mack dryly replied as he sipped his beer. "So what?"

"I think that it might be important."

"What could be important about a statue of the dog smoking a pipe?" Mack attempted to show that he understood Tina's concern, but in reality he didn't care.

"I think that it ties in with the missing mask."

"You have the mask," Mack replied with a smug grin.

"I told you before that I don't have the damn mask!" Tina's curt reply reeked with indignation.

"Isn't it in the package that the Guatemalan girl gave you?" Mack teased as he raised his glass to his lips to take a deep swig of his beer.

"I don't know what's in the package. I didn't open it."

"Come on," Mack teased. "You know what's in the package."

"No I don't! I didn't open it."

"Why not?"

"Carmelita told me that it was some of her personal effects that she wanted me to mail to her family in Guatemala. It was none of my business."

"Why didn't you mail it like she asked you to do?"

"I forgot about it."

"Where's the package now?" Mack inquired.

"Carmelita picked it up at the hotel just before I met you for dinner in the hotel dining room."

"How did she know that you were here?"

"I called her when I got up to my room," Tina quipped.

"How did you get her telephone number?"

"She gave it to me when she gave me the package."

"What did she say when you told her that you didn't mail it?"

"She said that it was okay because there were some things inside it that she didn't mean to send."

"That makes sense I suppose," Mack replied as he raised his glass to take a deep swig of his beer. "Now what?"

"We have to put pressure on Carlos to return the mask to Octavio."

"What do you mean by we? Do you have a mouse in your pocket?"

"I mean both of us you dumbbell! He's a man and so are you. He'll listen to another man. You can influence him more that I can. I'm just a female."

"What do you expect me to do that you can't? You already threatened to revoke his liquor license and close the place down."

"I wouldn't do that to him."

"Why not?"

"He's a family friend and this is the only place that the migrant workers have to blow off steam."

"And to get clipped by a crooked bar owner with loaded dice," Mack inserted.

"Carlos wouldn't cheat anyone!" Tina asserted.

"Speak of the cheating devil," Mack replied as he nodded towards the bar. "Here he comes now."

Carlos cautiously approached the pair. A serving tray precariously balanced above his head in his left hand and bottle of Budweiser and a full martini glass wobbled from side to side as he walked towards the table. He gave Mack and Tina a broad smile as he set the tray down on the table.

"*Buenos noches*," Carlos offered as he set the martini glass in front of Tina. "An Absolut' vodka gimlet garnished with a lime slice for the lady and a bottle of Bud for the gentleman."

"Thank you," Tina replied as she reached for the martini glass. "I would have died of thirst in another five minutes."

"Thanks Carlos," Mack offered as he toasted Carlos with his empty beer glass.

"*De nada*," Carlos replied with a grin. "What brings the two of you over here tonight?"

"We came over to ask you what you did with the mask," Mack replied as he poured beer into his empty glass from the fresh bottle. "The trial's over and you won't get in trouble over it."

"I don't have the mask!" Carlos stated as he raised himself upward to a position like a soldier at attention. "You saw that it was gone the last time you were over here! Somebody swiped it and put a stone in the box where I kept it."

"The point is that you did have it and now you don't," Mack

stated as he took a deep swig of his beer. "You had the intention of keeping it and now you claim that someone stole it from you. Who do you suppose stole it?"

"I don't know!" Carlos defiantly croaked.

"Carlos, let's be serious about this," Mack offered. "How many people have access to your beer storage room?"

"Me, the Americano beer delivery man and Pedro," Carlos responded.

"Who's Pedro?" Mack asked as he poured the remaining beer into his empty glass.

"Senor, do you want another beer?" Carlos offered as he reached for the empty beer bottle.

"No!" Mack quipped. "Not right now. Who's Pedro?"

"He runs the card table and dice games for Carlos," Tina offered.

"I asked Carlos!" Mack snapped in response as his eyes narrowed to slits.

"Well! Excuse me for living!" Tina curtly replied. "Should I stop breathing too?"

"No, that won't be necessary," Mack softly replied. "I apologize for snapping at you."

"Apology tentatively accepted. Try being nice to Carlos. He's a family friend."

"I'll do my best to be nice. But you asked me to put pressure on him."

"I didn't tell you to interrogate him like a prisoner of war!" Tina snapped. "Be nice!"

"Yes ma'am, I'll try." Mack replied as he turned to face Carlos.

"Miss Tina, what do you want from me?" Carlos pleaded

"I want to know what you did with Octavio's jade mask," Tina replied. "It's worth a small fortune and you know it. Now cough it up!"

"Now who's not playing nice?" Mack quipped as he drained the remaining beer from his glass.

"Shut up and ask him questions!" Tina snapped at Mack.

"How can I shut up and ask him questions at the same time? I can only do one or the other."

"You know what I mean," Tina responded with a shake of her head.

"Carlos, tell me about that guy Pedro," Mack asked as he nodded towards the Hispanic man seated at the card table next to the pool table.

"What do you want to know about him?" Carlos responded with a quizzical look on his face. "He's my friend," he added.

"How long have you known him?"

"About two years. I gave him a job as a bartender after he got hurt falling off a ladder in the orange groves. He hurt his back and can't work anymore."

"How long has he been cheating people?" Mack asked with a limp smile.

"He doesn't cheat anyone!" Carlos stated. "He's honest."

"Without a doubt he is," Mack replied. "Why isn't he tending bar for you now?"

"Customers complained that he shorted them with their change and the register was always short after his shift. Because of his bad back he can't carry cases of beer and fill the coolers by himself."

"I see," Mack, offered. "Why was he always short?"

"He told me that he doesn't know how to count American money and he gets confused."

"So, that's why he's dealing cards. Doesn't he get confused there?"

"No. It is illegal to gamble with real money and we use colored chips. It is easy for him to understand the colors and the players place their bets in Spanish."

"I see. Does Pedro have access to the beer storeroom?"

"Yes, but he doesn't carry cases of beer out to the bar because of his bad back."

"Could Pedro have switched the mask for the stone?"

"No!"

"Why not?"

"He didn't know that the mask was in the storage room."

"Where did he think it was?"

"I don't understand," Carlos offered. "What do you mean senor?"

"You know exactly what I mean," Mack responded. "Did Pedro know that you hid the mask inside an empty beer carton and stashed it in the storeroom?"

"No. He did not know."

"Did he know that the mask was missing from behind the bar?"

"I do not know."

"Did he ask you about it?"

"No senor. He did not ask me."

"Why do you suppose he didn't ask you where it was?"

"I do not know senor," Carlos softly replied. "Do you want another beer?"

"After you tell me what you did with the mask," Mack emphatically stated. "Where is it?"

"I do not know senor."

"Carlos, who else could have stolen the mask?" Tina interjected. "If only you, Pedro and the beer delivery guy have access to the beer storage room it has to be one of you."

"I do not know Miss Tina. Maybe the Americano beer delivery man switched the boxes."

"Carlos, why do your lights pulsate in time with the jukebox?"

"What do you mean senor?"

"Look at the lights up there," Mack nodded towards the dimmed incandescent light bulbs strung from the open-beamed ceiling. "They are pulsating in time with the jukebox."

"I do not know senor," Carlos responded and shrugged his shoulders to emphasize his lack of understanding of the question. "I will call Florida Power and Light and ask them to check."

"That's a good idea," Mack replied.

"Carlos, where is Carmelita tonight?" Tina asked. "Is she sick?"

"No Miss Tina. She is not sick," Carlos responded with a sly grin. "She is entertaining a customer in the back."

"What do you mean by entertaining a customer?" Tina snapped as she stood up and stared into Carlos' eyes. "Explain what you meant!"

"This is payday and she makes extra money when a customer needs a senorita for company."

"What!" Tina grabbed Carlos by the front of his shirt and pulled his face close to hers. "Did you turn her into a prostitute?"

"I did nothing," Carlos offered in his defense. "She does what she wants when she is here."

"When did she start entertaining your filthy customers?"

"She started the first day she came here," Carlos. "She needed money to pay for her transportation here from Mexico."

"Who is she paying?"

"Me. I paid the coyote for her and she has to repay me."

"How much is she paying you?"

"One hundred American dollars each week on the principal. I paid ten thousand dollars for her."

"What?" Tina screamed. "The last time we were here you told me that you paid the coyote two hundred bucks for her because she was to small to work in the fields. She paid you back the first two weeks she was here!"

"I forgot the exact amount," Carlos countered. "She owes me for her clothes, her food and interest on my money," Carlos replied. "Please understand that I am a businessman," he pleaded.

"How much interest are you charging her?"

"Fifty American dollars per day."

"That's three hundred and fifty dollars a week!" Tina screamed. "That's more than you paid the Mexican coyote for her! You are a *bastardo*!"

"That also pays for her food and her clothes," Carlos offered as a futile defense. "She eats very much food."

"Tina, let go of his shirt," Mack interjected. "You aren't getting anywhere this way."

"Don't tell me what to do!" Tina snapped as her emerald-green eyes snapped like hot coals in a dying campfire. "I should break his neck!"

"That won't accomplish what we came here for will it?"

"I suppose not," Tina replied as she reluctantly released her grip on Carlo's shirt.

"We may not approve of what's going on here, but it's really none of our business."

"It's mine if he's running a house of prostitution! I'll close him down in a heartbeat!"

"That wouldn't accomplish anything. You told me earlier that he is a family friend and this is the only place that the migrant workers have to blow off steam." Mack attempted to apply Tina's own earlier argument against her. "If you close him down then the migrant workers will have no place to go. Do you want that?"

"I suppose not," Tina replied as she sat down in her chair.

"That's better," Mack positively replied as he turned to face Carlos.

"Carlos, I'd like another beer and bring the lady another Absolut' vodka gimlet."

"*Si senor*," Carlos softly responded as he began to turn away from the table.

"Hold it right there!" Tina interjected as she grabbed Carlos' left arm. "What did you do with that stone statue of the dog smoking a pipe that was on a shelf behind the bar?"

"*Que?*" Carlos asked, as he froze in midstep. "What dog statue?"

"It was on a shelf behind the bar when we were here last time!" Tina stated. "Now it's gone! What did you do with it?"

"Miss Tina, I do not understand," Carlos cautiously replied. "I do not remember any dog statue behind the bar. When did you see it?"

"The last time we were here. It was setting on the end of that shelf on the opposite end from where the mask was. I told you that it looked like a dog smoking a pipe."

"*Caramba!*" Carlos exclaimed. "Now I remember! That Guat girl that cleans up for me around here stuck it up there. She told me that it would bring me good luck."

"Where is it now?" Tina asked. "Did you hide it like you hid the mask?"

"No Miss Tina. I did not hide it," Carlos cautiously responded. He correctly figured that Tina wouldn't believe him no matter how he answered. "She took it back after the mask disappeared. You have to ask her where it is."

"I will, if she ever comes out of that back room."

"Why are you interested in that statue?" Carlos hesitantly replied. "It has no value."

"I think that it ties in with the missing mask," Tina responded.

"If we find the dog statue we'll find the mask."

"Do you wish to know what that statue is called in Spanish?" Carlos offered as possible retribution for his apparent lack of knowledge about the statue's whereabouts.

"Not really," Tina quipped. "Why should I care what it's called?"

"It might be important," Mack offered from his seat across the table. "It could offer a clue."

"Okay Carlos," Tina sighed as she responded. "What's it called?"

"The Guatemalans call it a *chacmool*," Carlos replied. "The girl told me that it brings good luck."

"What does *chacmool* mean in English?" Mack asked as he leaned forward on his elbows.

"I do not know senor," Carlos responded. "Maybe the girl can explain it to you later."

"Tell her to come over here to see us when she has some free time," Mack replied. "Now I'd like another beer and the lady would like a fresh vodka gimlet."

"*Si senor*, right away," Carlos offered as he turned away and headed towards the bar.

"Make it two vodka gimlets and make sure that it's Absolut' vodka!" Tina shouted at his back.

"Make it two Buds," Mack added. "Bring me a fresh frosted glass too!"

Chapter 54

Many strange things happened to Mack since he arrived at Port Sewell Marina in March, but none stranger than this.

A solitary shaft of sunlight squeezed its way through the tightly drawn window shade and danced its tantalizing dance across Mack's forehead like a teasing pixie.

He tried to ignore it, but the sharp pain in the right side of his face made him realize that he wasn't where he should have been. He slowly opened his right eye and as it began to focus he saw that the right side of his face was resting on stiff jute fiber floor mat. The sharp ends of the jute fibers pressed into this cheek and felt like the quills of a porcupine embedded in his flesh.

"Where the hell am I?" Mack asked himself. *"I can't be in jail. Jail cells don't have floor jute mats!"*

He didn't have to wait long for an answer. A sound similar to that of an Iowa hog rooting for bits of kibble in a feedlot echoed through the tiny room. The raucous sound came from somewhere directly above the edge of the bedspread.

At first Mack was taken back by the sheer magnitude of the sound, but then he paused and attempted to logically ascertain the source of the sound. He slowly opened his left eye, shading it with his left hand from the dancing beam of bright sunlight, raised his aching head up, supported it on his right elbow, and peered over the edge of the bed.

Tina lay sprawled, fully clothed, across the bed in a diagonal position. Her head pointed at the top right corner of the bed and her feet pointed at the lower left corner. Her mouth was agape and the raucous sound escaped with the expulsion of each breath.

"*How did we get here?*" Mack thought.

Pangs of panic flowed throughout his almost numb body.

"*What am I doing in her room? How am I going to get out of here alive?*"

Mack's questions were not answered. He was on his own to find a solution for his quandary. If Tina woke up and found him in her room there would be hell to pay and if she caught him attempting to escape he knew that he was a dead man! Mack decided to make a slow, but steady escape towards the door.

"*Where's the key for the door?*" He mentally asked himself because he didn't see a handle for a dead bolt lock. "*What if I need a key to open it? Then what am I going to do? I'm dead!*"

A loud rap on the door immediately answered his self-full filling prophecy.

"Room service," quipped a soft female voice with a slight Hispanic accent from the other side of the door. "It's ten-thirty and I need to clean your room."

"Wait a minute," Mack whispered. "I'll be right there."

His soft plea was answered by another loud rap on the door.

"It's ten-thirty!" Repeated the soft female voice from the other side of the door. "I need to clean your room!" The maid's tone was much firmer and very demanding.

"I'll be right there," Mack responded at an audible level. "I need a few more minutes."

"I understand," the maid responded. "It's Saturday morning and you like to sleep in a little. Miss Tina, you'd better see a doctor when you get home. Your voice sounds real hoarse."

"Okay, I will," Mack coughed as he responded.

"Who's there?" Tina shouted from the bed as she sat upright and stared down at Mack.

He attempted to roll himself into a ball and quietly slide under the bed, but he wouldn't fit.

"Mack! What are you doing in my room?"

"Sleeping I guess," he feebly croaked. "I woke up right here on the floor. Nothing happened!"

"That's usually the way it is with you isn't it?" Tina quipped as she pointed at the door with her left index finger. "Get out of my room and get yourself cleaned up! We have a lot of things to do today!"

"Yes ma'am," Mack squeaked. "I'm on my way. Nothing happened!"

"I know that! Get yourself cleaned up and meet me in the dining room at eleven-thirty!'

"I'll be there," he responded as he turned the brass doorknob and prayed that the door wasn't locked. Fortunately for Mack it wasn't locked and he escaped into the hall without a scratch. But his tribulations for the remainder of the day were far from over.

Chapter 55

Mack slipped into the Seminole Inn dining room at 11:15 A.M. and took a seat at a table facing the French entrance doors.

At the table to his immediate left sat three Power and Light linemen who appeared to be exhausted from working all night. At the table to his right two waitresses were busily folding linen dinner napkins while they chatted between themselves.

"Hey Dawn," a short brunette waitress called out to her tall redheaded compatriot across the table.

"What'cha want Terri?" The redheaded waitress responded. She didn't look up and kept on folding dinner napkins without missing a beat. "I'm listenin' to ya' gal."

"Did you hear about that big disturbance over at the Silver Saddle last night?"

"Naw. But, I suppose that you're going to tell me anyway. What happened?"

"I overheard a couple of Martin County Sheriff's Department Deputies at breakfast this mornin' talking about a bunch of Guatemalans that got drunk in there last night. The Guats dragged that sleazebag bar owner out of there by his ears."

"Did they string him up?"

"They didn't say what they did to him, but it wasn't good from what I understand."

"Terri, he's been cheatin' those Guats for years," Dawn responded. "My husband and a couple of his fishin' buddies stopped in there for a beer last week. He said that the owner and his Mexican buddy have been runnin' a crooked dice table for a couple of years."

"How'd he know that?"

"He watched the action at the dice table for over a half hour and the Guats never won."

"Dawn, did you hear about the big fire out on Martin Grade last night?"

"Nope," she responded and never missed a beat in folding napkins. "Tell me about it old gal."

"My husband's a volunteer fireman and he got called out at two-thirty this mornin'."

"Did some chicken farmer's house burn down?"

"Naw," Terri responded as she scooped up the stack of folded napkins in front of Dawn and placed them alongside her pile. "It was a pile of old sod pallets in the piney woods at the entrance to the Naked Lady Ranch."

"Did anybody get hurt?"

"Naw."

"Do they know how the fire got started? Was it lightening?"

"My hubby said that most of the crowd had already left by the time the fire trucks got there and about a half dozen drunk Guats were hanging around. He figured that they lost their paychecks at the dogfights and set the sod pallets on fire for the hell of it."

A soft metal bell sounded from the kitchen area and both waitresses left to pick up their orders.

Mack glanced up at the entrance door and saw a short, squat

baldheaded Florida Power and Light lineman standing at the entrance to the dining room. He seemed to looking for someone.

"Hey Jimbo," called out one of the seated Florida Power and Light linemen to the newcomer. "We're sittin' over here. We saved a seat for ya'."

"I see ya'," the burly, baldheaded lineman responded as he entered the dining room and headed for his seated buddies. After he took a seat and poured himself a cup of coffee he addressed the others.

"Where've you guys been all mornin?"

"We were down at the Naked Lady Ranch sinking some new poles and stringing up new feeder lines," answered a thin, bushy-haired lineman sitting directly across the table from the newcomer.

"How come? Don't the daytime line construction crews do that stuff?"

"Usually, but last night a bunch of drunk Guats started a fire in a pile of sod pallets that were right under the feeder line to the ranch."

"Did it cause much damage?"

"It cost FPL eight hours of double time for all three of us," replied the bushy-haired lineman. "We replaced two wooden poles and ran three hundred feet of new line."

"How long have you guys been in here?"

"About a half hour. We came in here to do our paperwork and grab some lunch."

"You guys were lucky," replied the burly, baldheaded lineman. "I had to replace a step-down transformer in substation number twelve all by myself."

"Why didn't you call dispatch for help? We'd come down and helped you out."

"It was no big deal. I've got a hydraulic lift on my truck and I snatched that old transformer out of there faster than a dentist can pull a baby tooth."

"What made you think that something was wrong with the transformer?"

"The owner of that Mexican bar called in complaining that his power was fluctuating."

"The engineer at the Hispanic radio station has been bitchin' about voltage spikes for a couple of weeks. I was called out here on that a couple of times myself and could never find anything wrong."

"Did you come out at night, or during the day?"

"Daytime. FPL won't pay for overtime for something like that."

"They did tonight. You wouldn't be able to find it during the day."

"Why not?"

"It's pretty complicated and it only happened at night."

"So?"

"Do you want me to tell you how I found it, or not?"

"Of course."

"The guy who runs the Mexican bar called in a trouble report last night that his lights were flickering on and off."

"What time was that?"

"I'd guess about ten o'clock because dispatch called me at home at ten-thirty and told me to get out here. I stopped in Palm City to pick up my truck and I got here about eleven-thirty."

"How'd you find the problem? I never could figure it out."

"The first thing I did when I got over here was to look for shorts in the drop line from our pole to his meter. The drop was okay. But, when I put my meter across the line at his meter I saw the voltage spikin' up and down just like a steady heartbeat."

"What was causin' it? Did he have a short in his inside wiring?"

"Naw. His inside wiring was okay. It was our problem."

"How'd you figure that out?"

"I traced the voltage spikes back to the substation step-down transformer."

"What was wrong with the step-down transformer?"

"It was arcing across the output terminals."

"Did anybody else call in a trouble report on it last night?"

"Naw. Only the guy who owns the Mexican bar."

"I wonder why somebody else didn't call it in? A lot of businesses are fed out of that substation."

"The arcing only happened after dark and it usually didn't

start until after nine o'clock. Most of the other businesses, except for the radio station, close at five o'clock so they wouldn't notice it. But, it didn't happen every night."

"What was causin' the arcing? Was there a crack in the transformer?"

"Naw. On real humid nights, when the temperature fell below the dew point, moisture built up on top of the transformer cap and the power arced right over it."

"Oh. How long did it take you to replace it?"

"After I found the problem I went back to the bar and told the owner that his power would be cut off for a couple of hours."

"What time was that?" Mack interjected across the space between the tables.

"Why do you want to know?" The burley lineman sharply quipped. "Do you work for FPL?"

"No. I was in that bar last night and I don't remember seeing you come in."

"I wouldn't expect that you would remember anything about last night."

"Why do you say that?"

"You were as drunk as a hoot owl and that broad you were with was passed out on the table."

"What time did you come into the bar?" Mack repeated. "It's very important."

"About one-thirty this mornin'."

"Did you see me leave the place?"

"Naw. I got done replacing the transformer about four-thirty and when I went back there to check if the problem was fixed the place was closed down. I don't imagine that those Guats wanted to sit around and drink beer in the dark."

"Did you check the drop line coming into the bar again?" Mack asked.

"Of course. I put my meter across the meter to check for voltage spikes."

"Were there any spikes?"

"Naw. When I fix things they stay fixed."

"Jimbo, if you got done at four-thirty this mornin' why are you just comin' in here for lunch?"

"Frank, I could ask you the same thing. What time did you boys get done replacing those two little wooden poles and stringin' that little three-hundred feet of wire?"

"We got done about a half hour ago. We couldn't do anything until daylight except cut off the power feed to keep those drunk Guats from bein' electrocuted. After we figured out what we needed we went to the pole yard in Palm City and picked up a couple of new poles. So, what took you so long to replace that sub-station transformer?"

"After I isolated the problem I drove back to Palm City and picked up a new transformer. I didn't get started on the job until about two-thirty."

"Did you see the fire at the Naked Lady Ranch when you came down Martin Grade?"

"Naw. I took Kanner Highway back to Stuart and cut up alternate seventy-six to the yard. I came back the same way."

"Didn't you see the red glow in the sky? It's only five miles from Kanner Highway to Martin Grade as the crow flies."

"Naw. I was paying attention to the road. There's been a lot of deer hit by cars on Kanner Highway at night and I didn't feel like messing up the front of my truck with deer guts."

"What you were really doin' was watchin' for deer a crossin' the road so you could go back later and 'pop' 'em out the window with a rifle."

"Maybe, and maybe not."

"So Jimbo, if you got done changin' that step-down transformer at four-thirty this mornin' why are you just comin' in here for lunch at eleven-thirty?"

"Dispatch sent me up to Okeechobee to check out a feeder line at a trailer park at Buckhead Ridge."

"Is that the trailer park on the north side of the road opposite Okee-Tantie State Park?"

"That's the one."

"How long did it take you to check out that feeder line?"

"About three hours."

"Doesn't a little red-headed, freckle-faced gal from Yee Haw Junction run the restaurant in the bait and tackle store right there next to the boat launchin' ramp?"

"Yep. She cooks a really mean country breakfast."

"The specs in Lake Okeechobee are runnin' ain't they?"

"Yep. I believe they are. Why?"

"How many specs have you got on ice in the cooler in the back of your truck?"

"A couple dozen. But, don't bother askin' for any because I filleted 'em out for dinner tonight!"

"*Things haven't changed a bit since I supervised a telephone company repair crew back in the seventies,*" Mack thought to himself. "*Maybe I'll run over there tomorrow morning and take a shot at those speckled perch myself.*"

His thoughts were short-lived because at that instant Tina appeared in the dining room doorway and signal for Mack to join her in the hotel lobby and she didn't look happy. Mack dropped a five-dollar bill on the table to pay for his coffee, stood up and headed for the hotel lobby.

"*Now what the hell's wrong with her?*" Mack thought as he ambled towards the doorway.

Chapter 56

"Mack! Get your butt over here," Tina hissed between her teeth as Mack approached the hotel lobby from the dining room. "We've got big problems."

"What kind of problems does she think we have?" Mack asked himself. *"I don't have any problems! I'm ready to got back to Stuart and get out of this mess. Her big mouth is causing all of her self-perceived problems and I don't want any part of them."*

"Yes ma'am," Mack replied as he stepped into the lobby. "What kind of problems do you think we have? Do you have a mouse in your pocket? I don't have any that I know of."

"You know full well what kind of problems we have," Tina hissed without moving her lips. "Carlos is missing. Some of the Guatemalans got drunk and kidnapped him last night."

"What makes you think that he was kidnapped?"

"Carmelita told me."

"When did you see her?"

"She came to see me after you left my room. She was waiting in the hall and saw you crawl out."

"I didn't see her."

"That's because you weren't looking and she was wearing a hotel maid's uniform," Tina hissed.

"Why was she wearing a maid's uniform?"

"She works weekends cleaning rooms to make a few extra bucks."

"That makes sense."

"Why did you call me out of the dining room? I haven't eaten anything since last night."

"I haven't either and you certainly won't starve to death," Tina hissed through her clenched teeth "We'll come back here for lunch after we make a road trip and look for Carlos's remains."

"What do you mean by look for Carlo's remains?" Mack exclaimed. "Is he dead?"

"Hold your voice down!" Tina ordered. "I think that the radical faction of the migrant workers sacrificed him last night."

"What makes you think that?" Mask asked. "He was okay the last time we saw him."

"Do you remember that Carlos told us about the sacrificial altar constructed out of wooden sod pallets out by the Naked Lady Ranch?" Tina hissed.

"That wasn't an altar!" Mack replied. "It was just a pile of old sod pallets."

"The Guatemalans had a big bonfire out there about two-thirty this morning and Carlos is missing."

"That doesn't mean anything," Mack replied. "They might have had a marshmallow roast."

"I don't think so," Tina quipped. "Do you remember what time we left the Silver Saddle last night?"

"No. I don't remember anything after we interrogated Carlos about the missing mask and I asked him what was causing the jukebox and overhead lights to fluctuate."

"The power company guy showed up about eleven-thirty to

check out Carlos' wiring in the Silver Saddle. He came back at one-thirty and told Carlos that he was going to turn off the power for a couple of hours."

"Where were we?" Mack innocently asked.

"You were passed out face-down on the table and I was dancing with Carlos."

"That's not the way I heard it a few minutes ago."

"What did you hear?" Tina snapped. "And from whom?"

"Those FPL guys in the dining room were talking about it a few minutes ago. The power fluctuations were caused by a defective step-down transformer at the sub-station that was arcing."

"What does that have to do with what time we left the Silver Saddle and your soused condition?"

"The FPL guy told me that when he stopped in the Silver Saddle to tell Carlos that he was cutting off the power that you were passed out face-down on the table."

"That's not true!" Tina snapped. "I never drink to the level of intoxication!"

"Do you remember how you got back to the hotel?"

"When the power went out two of Carmelita's friends assisted you across the street to the hotel. Unfortunately they dumped your flea-bitten carcass in my room."

"That explains a lot. What happened to Carlos?"

"Carmelita said that when she got back to the Silver Saddle two migrant workers that she didn't recognize accused Pedro of using loaded dice and dragged him outside. When Carlos objected someone hit him over the head from behind with a bottle and several men dragged him outside too."

"Then what did she say happened?"

"She said that the men loaded Carlos and Pedro in the back of a Toyota pickup truck and drove off."

"What direction did they go?"

"East like they were heading for Martin Grade and the Naked Lady Ranch!" Tina hissed through her clenched teeth as she looked around the lobby. "I think they sacrificed them on the altar and burned the pallets to hide the evidence. We need to find Carlos' ashes and give them a proper burial."

"The FPL guys said that the Guats set the pallets on fire because they lost their paychecks at the dogfights."

"Now you are being derogatory!" Tina hissed. "Refer to them as Guatemalans not as Guats!"

"Yes ma'am. The FPL guys said that the Guatemalans set the pallets on fire because they lost their paychecks at the dogfights."

"Dogfights are illegal in this county and Elmo stays on top of what's going on out here."

"If Elmo stays on top of what's going on out here then where was he last night when Carlos and his crooked pal were supposedly kidnapped?"

"He was working a drug interdiction case in Hobe Sound all night," Tina impatiently hissed. "I spoke to him a few minutes ago and he's going to meet us at the Naked Lady Ranch."

"Why?"

"So we can comb through the ashes and look for Carlos' body without interference from curious spectators. He's also bringing a crime investigation team with him."

"How can he bring a crime investigation team with him if there's no proof of a crime?"

"I called the sheriff at home and authorized it!" Tina hissed at slightly above an audible range. "Let's get going! I want to be there before Elmo shows up, " Tina hissed as she motioned towards the front door with her purse. "Try to act nonchalant."

"Yes ma'am," Mack replied. "I'm always nonchalant."

Chapter 57

Mack and Tina drove east on Martin Grade towards the entrance to the Naked Lady Ranch. When they were within one hundred yards of the entrance road to the ranch Mack spotted a Martin County Sheriff's Department's green and white patrol car.

"It looks like Elmo beat us here," Mack remarked to his anxious passenger. "How are you going to explain two roasted bodies to him?"

"I'm not, but why isn't the crime scene investigation van here too?" Tina hissed.

"I see a van on the other side of the entrance road down by the pile of pallets," Mack replied. "Maybe there're already going through the ashes."

Mack turned into the ranch gravel-covered access road, pulled up beside Elmo's patrol car and rolled down the driver's side window so he could talk to Elmo. Elmo did the same.

"It's a dry run Mack," Elmo chuckled. "There wasn't anybody burned up here last night."

"How do you know for certain?" Tina screamed across the seat towards the open window. "Carlos was kidnapped last night and some of the radical Guats had threatened to sacrifice him on that altar!"

"Now you are being derogatory," Mack offered. "You are supposed to refer to them as Guatemalans, not Guats."

"Shut up!" Tina screamed. "Elmo! Is that a crime scene investigation unit van down there by the sacrificial altar?"

"No!" Elmo replied with a grin. "It's a Martin County High School Alumni Booster's van. They're down there cleaning up their mess. They a held a pep rally and built a bonfire here last night to get the football team hyped up for today's game with Fort Pierce Central. The ranch foreman graduated from Martin County High School and his kid's the quarterback. He told the booster club that they could hold a pep rally here and build a bonfire if they cleaned it up. They collected sod pallets for about a month."

"What about Carlos?" Tina screamed out the window across Mack's rigid body. "He was kidnapped and thrown into the back of a Toyota pickup truck about two-thirty this morning by several Hispanic men."

"They brought him down here last night because he's one of the sponsors of the booster club," Elmo softly replied with a wide grin. "Carlos didn't want to leave the bar because he was so busy. So, they had an FPL guy cut off the power to the bar, kidnapped him and dragged him down here."

"What about Pedro?" Tina screamed. "He was kidnapped too!"

"Pedro's nephew plays defensive cornerback for Martin County and he was in on it."

"Where are they now?" Tina screamed. "I want to see Carlos and I want to see him now!"

"He should be having lunch at the Seminole Inn just about now," Elmo replied. "Carlos and Pedro spent the night there."

"Why?" Tina yelled through the truck window. "Carlos lives in the back of the Silver Saddle!"

"They got dropped off there about three-thirty this morning. They stayed at the Seminole Inn because the power was still turned off at the Silver Saddle and the air conditioning wasn't working."

"Who dropped them off?" Tina demanded.

"I did," Elmo snickered. "I was at the pep rally. I graduated from Martin County High School too."

"You told me that you were working a drug interdiction case in Hobe Sound last night!"

"I was, but it was all over by ten o'clock," Elmo replied. "The bad boys were caught red-handed with ten pounds of uncut cocaine in their boat and they're in the Martin County Jail."

"Elmo, I talked to a couple of FPL guys at the Seminole Inn a little while ago," Mack offered. "They told me that the fire was started by a bunch of drunk Guatemalans."

"About a dozen Guats showed up about three o'clock when the boosters were pulling out," Elmo added. "They'd been at the dogfights and were soused to the gills. I told them that they could stay if they'd watch the fire and make sure that it didn't spread. But, right after that an Indiantown Volunteer Fire Department truck showed up and the crew said they'd make sure that the fire was out. FPL's pissed because the fire took out two wooden power poles and some of the distribution line to the ranch house."

"The three FPL construction guys who got sent out on the job aren't pissed," Mack offered. "They got paid for eight hours of double time and they're as happy as clams."

"How do you know that?" Elmo inquired.

"I talked to them at the Seminole Inn before we came out here," Mack replied.

"Do they know that the Martin County High School Booster Club set the bonfire?"

"No. They think that the Guatemalans did it," Mack answered. "So does the Indiantown Volunteer Fire Department," Mack added with a smug grin.

"Good," Elmo whispered back. "I don't want the booster club guys to get in trouble over this."

"That sounds just like you self-centered, self-righteous hypocrites!" Tina screamed across Mack in Elmo's direction. "Blame everything bad on a minority group and take the credit for anything good!"

"Tina, take it easy," Mack offered. "Everything's okay and Carlos is alright. Let's go back to the Seminole Inn and have lunch. It'll make you feel better."

"The only thing that could make me feel better is if I can get my hands around Carlos' scrawny neck and slowly strangle him for sending me on this wild goose chase," Tina hissed as she seethed with emotion. "Let's go Mack!" She ordered. "Maybe we can catch him at the Seminole Inn!"

"Do you want me to follow you over there?' Deputy Elmo offered. "I don't have to be at the ball game until one o'clock."

"I don't think that it would be a good idea Elmo," Mack whispered across the narrow space between his truck and Elmo's patrol car. "You might have to arrest her for strangling Carlos."

"Do you want me to send somebody else over there?" Elmo asked. "Just to help keep the peace?"

"I think it's best if you just leave and go to the football game. Those Martin County Tigers might need your support."

"Mack, did I ever tell you that I played offensive guard on the nineteen seventy-six Martin County team? I was number seventy-two. I still have one of my jerseys at home."

"You just did. Congratulations."

"Do you want to see my football jersey? It still fits."

"Wear it the next time we have a manatee roast out on the sand bar by Clam Island."

"We can't have a manatee roast! Killing manatees is against the Marine Mammal Protection Act."

"I didn't say that we were going to kill a manatee. I said that we were going to roast one. There's a big difference between killing and roasting a manatee."

"Oh. I have to review the Florida Statutes on that one."

"Elmo, we're going back to the Seminole Inn for lunch. Good luck with your football game."

Mack didn't wait for a response, put the truck into 'reverse' and backed out onto Martin Grade.

"*Carlos, I hope that you're gone by the time we get there,*" Mack thought. "*If you're there it isn't going to be pretty.*"

Mack pointed the truck west towards Indiantown as Tina blankly stared out of the passenger side window in the direction of the still smoldering bonfire.

Chapter 58

Mack was amazed at Tina's stealth as she silently and almost motionlessly crept through the lobby of the Seminole Inn until she reached the half open set of double French doors leading into the dining room.

She reminded him of a female cheetah stalking a gazelle through the elephant grass of the Serengeti Plain waiting for the exact moment to strike her prey. The chase would last only a split second. The gazelle would not sense the cheetah's presence until her thin neck was broken. Her sightless eyes would slowly glaze over as the cheetah tightly grasped her throat and patiently squeeze until the trachea ruptured.

Tina's eyes did not blink, nor did she appear to Mack that she even breathed, as she positioned herself next to one of the half open French doors. Her emerald-green eyes moved slowly across the spacious dining room and froze when she spotted her prey!

Carlos and Pedro were seated three rows of tables from the entrance. Carlos' back was facing the entrance doors. Pedro was engrossed in following the hip movements of the tall, redheaded waitress and she allowed him to immerse himself in whatever male fantasy he was enjoying.

Suddenly Tina pounced and she was behind Carlos before he could turn around! He knew by the aroma of her signatory White Diamonds perfume that she was there and he took the initiative.

"Senorita Tina!" Carlos crooned in his best Hispanic accent. "Can you join us for lunch?" He added hoping to catch her off guard. He didn't!

"Carlos!" Tina began as she roughly kneaded the apex of his shoulders with her strong fingers. "You owe me an explanation!" She added as her fingers easily dug though his thin silk shirt into the tender flesh.

"That feels good Senorita Tina," Carlos uttered with a trace of anxiety. "Please don't stop."

"I won't until you explain your actions last night. If you lie to me I'll rip out your trapezius muscles and feed them to the pigs."

"Yes Senorita Tina," Carlos stuttered as her fingers dug deep into his tender trapezius muscles. "What do you want to know?"

"Where were you between one-thirty and three-thirty this morning?"

"I was at the Martin County Alumni Boosters Pep rally at the naked Lady Ranch."

"That's correct," Tina glibly quipped as she dug deeper into his trapezius muscles. "Why were you there?"

"I'm a member of the booster club and Pedro's nephew plays cornerback on the football team."

"Also correct," Tina softly responded as she squeezed both of his trapezius muscles between her thumbs and index fingers. "Why did you let Carmelita think that you were being kidnapped and might be sacrificed to some Mayan god?"

"I didn't tell her that I was being kidnapped!" Carlos exclaimed as Tina's probing fingers hit a tender spot and he squirmed in extreme pain.

"Carlos! Don't move, or do you want me to snap these muscles like a rubber band?"

"Okay, don't squeeze so hard," Carlos pleaded. "That hurts!"

"It's supposed to hurt," Tina added. "Why did you let Carmelita think that you were being kidnapped?"

"I didn't," Carlos pleaded in his defense. "Somebody hit me over the head with a bottle and I went out cold. I didn't tell her anything."

"You certainly let her think you were! Was the whole thing planned in advance?"

"No Senorita Tina!" Carlos stated. "I wanted to go to the pep rally with Pedro, but it was Friday night, we were busy and we couldn't afford to take off."

"What did you do with the jade mask?"

"I told you that I don't have it!" Carlos responded as he squired in pain.

"Where is it?"

"The girl took it!" Carlos tried to mask the pain with feigned enthusiasm.

Tina detected the pain in his voice and plucked both of his tender trapezius muscles simultaneously like a rock music bass viola player.

"Come on Carlos. You can do better than that," Tina teased as she gently patted his throbbing muscles with the tips of her fingers. "Carmelita doesn't have the mask. You do!"

"Why do you think that I have the mask?" Carlos whined as her sharp, probing fingers dug deeper into his aching trapezius muscles. "Senorita Tina, I showed you the rock in the box where I put the mask. Somebody switched it on me!"

"You switched it when you found out that we were coming to Indiantown to get it!"

"Senorita Tina, why do you want the mask? It has no value to you."

"I don't want it. I wanted it to keep it from being used as evidence against Octavio in his trial."

"The trial is over and nothing happened to him," Carlos whined as tears formed in the outside corners of his eyes. "You should be happy for him."

"I want you to give the mask back to Octavio," Tina urged. "It's his property and it has followed his family for many generations."

"I don't have it!" Carlos screamed as Tina pinched both of his trapezius muscles simultaneously.

"We can do this the easy way, or we can do it the hard way," Tina softly cooed. "Personally I like what we're doing here," she emphasized her statement by snapping the muscle strands.

Carlos responded by writhing in pain.

"Massaging you relaxes me and takes all of the tension out of my hands," she glibly added. "I could do this all day."

"Ouch!" Carlos bleated. "Senorita Tina, that hurts mucho!"

"Carlos, I know that you have the mask in a cardboard box hidden under your desk," Tina cooed in a soft southern drawl as she dug deeper into the sensitive muscle tissue.

"How do you know that?" Carlos moaned with pain and squirmed in his chair.

"Carmelita told me this morning when she cleaned my room and told me that you were kidnapped last night," Tina replied. "She was very worried about you," she added. "Shall we go over to the Silver Saddle together and get the mask right now?"

"Okay! You win!" Carlos shouted as his shoulders erupted with pain. "I give up."

"That's being a real smart boy," Tina quipped as she slammed both of her closed fists down on Carlos' sore trapezius muscles. "I was really beginning to enjoy this."

"What about Pedro?" Carlos whimpered.

"What about him?" Tina asked. "It's your bar. You should be able to open the door without him."

"Can he go home now? He knows nothing about the mask."

"Of course he can go home," Tina replied. "But he has to wait until we leave here and get to the Silver Saddle."

"Why?"

"Because I don't want him to get over there before we do and switch the mask for a rock like he did the last time."

"How do you know that he switched the mask for a rock?" Carlos asked. "He was in the storeroom when you were there and you didn't see him."

"Carmelita saw him make the switch," Tina quipped. "She's a very observant girl."

Tina relaxed her grip, patted Carlos on the right deltoid muscle and encouraged him to stand up.

Mack watched as Tina and Carlos walked through the dining room and headed for the hotel lobby. He wisely made no effort to intervene. He knew that Tina would have had him for lunch if he got in the way.

It was her party and he didn't want to dance with her!

Chapter 59

Carlos nervously unlocked the front door to the Silver Saddle and gestured for Tina and Mack to enter ahead of him. Tina declined his invitation with a negative nod of her head.

"Carlos, I'd prefer it if you go in first," Tina snapped. "I don't know what kind of booby traps you might have set up for us."

"Senorita Tina," Carlos whined. "I would do nothing to hurt you and Senor Mack. Please enter."

Tina cautiously slipped inside the dark room and groped for the light switch with her right hand. When she found it she flipped it up and the room magically came to life.

Dozens of empty beer bottles littered the sawdust covered wooden floor and shared the space with dozens of white paper plates encrusted with the remains of tortillas, empanadas and enchiladas. The smell of stale urine and beer oozed from the damp sawdust.

"Nice job of cleaning up last night," Tina offered. "Did you expect the cockroaches and ants to clean up for you?"

"No Senorita Tina," Carlos stammered. "I was not here at closing time and the girl was supposed to clean up and put things away."

"The FPL guy I met at the Seminole Inn told me that he didn't get the power back on until about four-thirty," Mack offered in Carlos' defense. "I doubt that she stayed up that late."

"Plus, she had to get up and get ready for work at the Seminole Inn this morning," Tina casually tossed in as an item of conversation to see if she could spike Carlos' interest.

Carlos didn't acknowledge Tina's sarcastic comment and hustled towards the doorway leading to the storage room.

"*Alto!*" Tina shouted."

Carlos stopped dead in his tracks. He slowly turned to face Tina and his face blanched white.

"Carlos, now just where do you think you were going so fast?" Tina barked.

"Senorita Tina, I was going to the beer storage room to get the mask for you," Carlos meekly offered.

"You know better than that," Tina responded as she stood with her hands on her hips. "You know full well that the mask is in a box tucked under your desk and your desk is in your office."

"I forgot," Carlos stammered. "I am very nervous."

"You should be," Mack interjected. "She's on the warpath and she wants your scalp."

Tina slowly turned from the hips upwards; keeping her feet firmly planted, and faced Mack. "I don't need your help Mr. McCray," she spat. "When I need your help, or your opinion, I'll ask for it. Do you understand me?"

"Yes ma'am, I understand," Mack replied. "It's your party," he added.

"What did you mean by that?"

"That you are in charge."

"Fine. I'm glad that we understand each other," Tina sharply quipped as she swung her upper torso in Carlos' direction.

"Senorita Tina, shall I go into my office and bring the box out to you?" Carlos stammered.

"I think not Carlos. Mr. McCray and I will both follow you into your office and watch you remove the box containing the mask from under your desk. Carlos, I sincerely hope, for your sake, that the mask is inside the box."

"It is there," Carlos offered. "I put it here myself after you left the last time."

"I knew that you had the mask all the time," Tina quipped. "You knew that it's worth thousands of dollars and you were going to sell it after Octavio went to prison for assaulting you."

"No Senorita Tina. I was not going to sell the mask. I was just keeping it for him." Carlos whined. "I don't trust the migrant workers because they would steal it from him."

"Carlos, I don't believe you!" Tina snapped. "Lets get in your office and dig out the mask!"

"Yes Senorita Tina," Carlos responded as he turned towards the doorway leading to his cluttered office. "Follow me."

Once the trio was inside Carlos' cramped office Tina gestured towards a wooden desk that appeared to have seen service in the Seminole Indian War.

Two empty *Corona* beer bottles, wedged in opposite corners of the bottom of the desk, served as replacement legs and a gaping hole the size of a basketball provided an air vent in the front. The side of a cardboard box, possibly eighteen inches square, was visible under the desk. Tina spotted it immediately.

"Carlos! I see the box," she barked. "Drag it out here and open it up. I want to be certain that we have the mask this time and not a stupid rock!"

"*Si* Senorita Tina," Carlos cautiously replied as he bent over from the waist, pulled the small box out from under the desk and offered it to Tina. "Here it is," he meekly offered.

"Set it down on your desk and open it," Tina ordered. "I don't want it blowing up in my face."

"Why would it blow up?" Carlos cautiously inquired. "It is not a bomb," he added.

"With everything I've been through over this I expect anything to happen. Now open it!"

"Yes Senorita Tina," Carlos replied as he placed the box on the desk and began unfolding the top flaps.

Tina leaned forward to get a look inside the box and saw an oblong shape wrapped in newspaper.

"Carlos, pull that thing out of there and unwrap it!" Tina ordered.

Carlos nodded in acknowledgement, placed both of his hands around the heavy object, slowly lifted it out of the box and placed it on the desk.

"Now unwrap it very carefully," Tina ordered. "And don't drop it! It's very valuable."

"*Si*, Senorita Tina," Carlos whined. "I will be very careful."

"It sure is," Mack mumbled under his breath and realized his error before his mouth closed.

"What sure is what?" Tina barked. "Explain yourself Mr. McCray!"

"The mask is very valuable," Mack offered in his defense. "It's the funeral mask of an Olmec king from central Guatemala, and it's more than twenty-five hundred years old."

"How do you know that?"

"I did some research at the Blake Library in Stuart."

"Who asked you to do that?"

"No one. I was curious and decided to check it out. It's worth one-hundred thousand bucks!"

"Who told you that?"

"Sotheby's in New York."

"Carlos, put the mask back in the box."

"But Senorita Tina . . .," Carlos attempted to make a comment, but Tina cut him off.

"Shut up and put the mask in the box! I'm taking it with me!"

Carlos frowned and shook his head from side to side and shrugged his shoulders. He willingly obliged because had not started to remove the newspaper wrapping from the heavy object.

"Tina wasn't the mask wrapped in a towel?" Mack offered.

"That's what this lying *bastardo* told us when we were here the last time," Tina quipped. "Don't you remember that a stone was wrapped in a towel? He wrapped the mask in newspaper to make it look like trash."

"That makes sense," Mack offered. "His idea was to make it look so obvious that it was trash that no would ever suspect that something valuable was inside the wadded up newspaper."

"He thinks that he's smart," Tina smiled as she replied. "That's why he's gotten away with a crooked dice table and a crooked dealer all these years. "But, he's not as smart as I am."

"I would imagine not," Mack offered. "You had him figured out all the time."

"That's right," Tina replied. "When Carmelita gave me the mask she told me that he wrapped it in newspaper to throw people off. He was even sleeping under his desk to keep anyone from stealing it."

"That's what Elmo told me too. When did you figure out that Carmelita gave you the mask instead of some personal effects to mail back to Guatemala for her?"

"I suspected it right away. I could tell by the weight of the package and the look on her face when she gave it so me. It was very heavy for its size."

"Why didn't you mail it back to Guatemala for her?"

"She never wanted me to mail it! She just wanted to keep it away from Carlos so that it couldn't be used as evidence in Octavio's trial."

"So, you willingly participated in withholding evidence? Isn't that a felony?"

"Not in this cause," Tina snapped in Mack's direction.

"Why not?"

"Technically I didn't actually know that the mask was inside the package."

"Didn't you just say that you knew it was the mask?"

"No. I said that I suspected it. Clean out your ears!"

"But you had to know that it was the mask!"

"No I didn't!" Tina snapped. "Let's go back to the Seminole Inn and have lunch. I'm starved."

Tina nodded at the cardboard box on Carlos' desk. "You carry it. It's too heavy for me."

"Yes ma'am," Mack replied. "I hope that I don't collapse for lack of food on my way across the street."

"You won't," Tina quipped as she headed for the front door.

Chapter 60

It is 1:47 P.M. and the Seminole Inn dining room is empty except for Mack and Tina who are finishing their brunch. Tina is pleased that she finally has the mask in her possession and keeps reassuring herself that it is under the table by tapping it with her right foot.

Mack appears to be disinterested in the whole matter, but engages Tina in conversation to stroke her ego and make her think that he cares.

"Tina," Mack asked between the last bite of his scrambled eggs and followed by a sip of water. "Now that you have the mask what are you going to do with it?"

"I'm going to give it back to Octavio," she hissed. "It belongs to him and it's an important symbol of his native history."

"Do you know where he lives?"

"He lives in the migrant quarters in Booker Park. I'll ask Carmelita how to contact him."

"How will you do that?"

"I'll ask her when she comes over to our table."

"What makes you think that she's coming over to our table?"

"Because she's walking through the dining room door right now."

Mack looked to his immediate left and spotted Carmelita heading for their table. She had replaced her maid's uniform with a pair of denim shorts, a yellow tank top and a pair of leather sandals. Mack noted that she was obviously not wearing a support bra.

"You'd better take her shopping this afternoon," Mack offered.

"Why?" Tina inquired. "She looks fine to me."

"She needs some instruction on how to buy a bra," he offered with a smirk and ducked to dodge an anticipated blow.

Tina ignored his comment and gestured at Carmelita for her to join them.

"Carmelita!" Tina offered as she rose from the table to greet her. "How nice of you to join us."

"I can't stay Senorita Tina," Carmelita offered as she furtively looked around the dining room.

"Why not?" Tina asked as she pulled the chair to her right away from the table to make room for Carmelita. "Please sit down and join us for lunch."

"Thank you for your graciousness, Senorita Tina, but I can not sit with you. I am a hotel employee and I am not permitted to mingle with the hotel guests."

"Bull crap!" Tina stated. "You're my guest and you can sit here if I invited you."

"I am sorry Senorita Tina, but I cannot stay. I must meet someone at two o'clock."

"Who could be more important than me and Senor McCray?" Tina inquired.

"It is not that you and Senor McCray are not important, but I have a very important meeting and I must ask you for a favor."

"Do you need a safe place to stay?" Tina asked. "You can stay at my condo in West Palm Beach as long as you wish," she added.

"I must have the box that Senor Carlos gave you this morning."

"Why?"

"Because I must return it to its owner," Carmelita replied. "I will be in big trouble if I do not return it to him this afternoon."

"Are you meeting Octavio to give him back the mask?"

"No Senorita Tina," Carmelita softly replied as she looked down at the floor. "It is someone else."

"Are you giving the mask back to that rat Carlos? Did he threaten you again?"

"No Senorita Tina, I am not meeting Senor Carlos. It is someone else."

"Who is it?" Tina asked as she threw her cloth napkin across the dining room for emphasis.

"I cannot say," Carmelita offered without taking her eyes away from the floor. "Senorita Tina, may I have the box, *por favor*?"

"Not until you tell me who you are meeting and why they want the mask!"

"It is not the mask they want. It is something much more important than the mask."

"Then why do you want the box?"

"Because the box does not hold the mask," Carmelita responded as she raised her head and cautiously scanned the dining room.

"You told me that Carlos kept the mask under his desk!"

"That is true Senorita Tina. The mask was in a box under his desk until Friday night."

"Isn't the mask in this box?" Tina queried as she tapped the box under the table with her right foot.

"No Senorita Tina. It is not."

"If the mask isn't in this box where is it?"

"The mask is safe."

"What's in the box? Did that bum Carlos switch the mask for a stone again?"

"No Senorita Tina, it is not a stone," Carmelita softly responded in a voice barely above a whisper.

"What is it?" Tina demanded as she pulled the box out from under the table.

"Didn't you recognize the wrapping?" Carmelita softly offered. "It is the same package that I gave you last week and that you returned to me yesterday afternoon. Didn't you look inside?"

"I never unwrapped it!" Tina stated. "Are you telling me that the mask isn't in this box?"

"Si, the mask is not inside the box. It is something that is much more valuable than the mask."

"What could be more valuable than the mask?" Mack interjected. "The mask is worth big bucks."

"Stay out of this conversation," Tina ordered, as sparks flew out of her emerald-green eyes.

"Yes ma'am," Mack responded as he switched his attention to a thirsty fly attempting to scale the inside of Tina's water glass. "I should have known better."

"Carmelita, I'm going to unwrap this package very slowly to give you time to explain why the mask is not inside. If it's a stone I am going to throw it across the dining room. Do you understand?"

"Si, I understand," Carmelita cautiously replied. "Please Senorita Tina, do not allow anyone else to see what is inside the package."

"Why not?" Tina responded as she lifted the newspaper-wrapped object out of the cardboard box began to remove the first of many layers of newspaper.

"Because the package contains a very powerful religious object that is sacred to our people."

"Like what?" Tina viciously inquired as she tossed the rumpled newspaper aside and began to remove the second layer. "Is it a cross, a statue of the Virgin Mary or a fertility god?"

"It is none of those things."

"What the hell!" Tina emphatically stated as she removed the last layer of newspaper. "It's the statue of the dog smoking a pipe," Tina added as she placed the carved stone object on the table.

"Senorita Tina," Carmelita attempted to interject.

"This is the stupidest-looking thing I've ever seen," Tina stated as she slowly rotated the stone statue around in a circle. "It's definitely a dog smoking a pipe and the dog's wearing pants."

"Senorita Tina, please do not make fun of the statue," Carmelita pleaded. "It is a very powerful religious symbol and harm could come to you."

"What is it?"

"It is called a *chacmool* and it is very old."

"What is it used for?" Tina asked as she continued to turn the statue in a slow circle.

"The pipe bowl would make a nice ashtray," Mack offered.

"Shut up!" Tina ordered. "Carmelita and I are having an intelligent conversation.

"Senorita Tina, the *chacmool* was used by Mayan priests for heart sacrifices."

"What!" Tina stuttered as she pushed the statue away. "You're pulling my leg."

"It is true Senorita Tina. The most important prisoners of war were sacrificed to the jaguar god by a team of four priests by holding the prisoner down on a stone altar and cutting out their heart. The bowl of the *chacmool* received the hearts of the victims."

"This ugly thing looks like a dog smoking a pipe."

"Senorita Tina, the reclining male figure is a feathered *Teotihacan* warrior sipping the blood of the victims to capture their strength."

"That's disgusting," Tina remarked as she looked away from the statue.

"I still think that it would make a good ashtray," Mack interjected. "What a story this thing could tell if it could talk."

"Shut up!" Tina responded with a glare that could turn stainless steel into molten metal.

"Senorita Tina, may I have the statue please?" Carmelita pleaded as she reached for the carved stone image. "*Por favor?*"

"Hold it!" Tina ordered. "Carmelita, why do you want this grotesque thing?"

"I must return it to the priest this afternoon."

"Why did you give it to me?"

"Senorita Tina, do you remember that I told you that the *chacmool* was used by Mayan priests for heart sacrifices?"

"Of course," Tina replied. "So what does that have to do with anything?"

"I gave the *chacmool* to you to protect Senor Carlos."

"Protect him from what?"

"I think that she's telling you that someone was planning on sacrificing Carlos and they couldn't do it unless they had this ugly thing."

"Senor Mack is correct. The priest must have the *chacmool* in order to properly perform a ritual sacrifice. I removed the *chacmool* from the bar after the mask disappeared and gave it to you so nothing would happen to Senor Carlos. When you returned it to me on Friday afternoon I hid it in this box in Carlos' office so that the priest could not harm him last night."

"Are you trying to tell us that someone was going to sacrifice Carlos' in some kind of pagan Mayan ceremony?" Tina asked with an arrogant smirk. "That's stupid!"

"Tina, don't you remember that Carlos' thought the Guats were going to sacrifice him on that pile of sod pallets out by the Naked Lady Ranch?" Mack offered. "He might have been right!"

"I told you that pile of pallets was an altar and you pooh poohed me about it!" Tina spat.

"I didn't take him seriously and in retrospect maybe I should have," Mack replied.

"Carmelita, why do you want the statue back right now?" Tina inquired as she traced her right index finger along the rim of the stone bowl. "Is someone planning on sacrificing Carlos tonight?"

"Senorita Tina, the high priest ordered me to return the *chacmool* to him this afternoon."

"Why would anyone want to do anything to you?"

"Because I prevented him from sacrificing Senor Carlos last night and he knows that I have the *chacmool*. I must return it to him today."

"Why does the priest want the statue today?" Tina inquired. "He had his shot at Carlos last night."

"He is going to make a blood sacrifice to the jaguar god tonight."

"Who is it this time?" Mack innocently asked. "Am I on the barbecue list?"

"No Senor Mack, it is not you."

"Then who is it?" Tina demanded. "We have to tell them so they can get away."

"It is me," Carmelita responded as she turned her head downward and blankly gazed at the floor. "I must make up for the loss of the priest's honor and to save our people."

"Why you?" Mack asked. "We'll take you back to Stuart and the priest can't get you there."

"Senor Mack, I volunteered," Carmelita softly responded without removing her gaze from the floor. "For me it is an honor. I shamed my people and caused many problems for you and Senorita Tina."

"What kind of problems did you cause us?" Tina asked as she reached for Carmelita's left hand, took it in her right hand and softly squeezed. "We're just fine and we had your best interests at heart."

"Senorita Tina, I got you involved when I gave you the *chacmool* to keep for me."

"That wasn't any big thing," Tina softly replied. "I brought it back yesterday afternoon."

"The priest knows that I took the *chacmool* and gave it to you. He was unable to perform the blood sacrifice last night and I am to blame."

"But you saved Carlos!" Tina exclaimed. "That must mean something!"

"Senor Carlos does not know that I saved his life and I do not want him to know. It is my turn to honor my people by being the blood sacrifice to the jaguar god."

"Tina, we have to stop this insanity!" Mack exclaimed. "Do you know somebody in Immigration that can get over here and round these people up before they hurt someone?"

"I'll make a few calls," Tina responded. "But keep in mind that it's Saturday afternoon and I'll probably just get their voice mail."

"How about Elmo?" Mack replied. "He might have some contacts!"

"I doubt it, but I'll try him at home," Tina responded. "Anything's worth a shot at this point."

"Carmelita, do you have the mask?" Mack asked.

"Not now Senor Mack," Carmelita softly replied with her eyes still focused on the floor.

"Carmelita, did you steal the mask from the bar?" Tina demanded.

"I do not steal Senorita Tina. The mask belongs to Octavio and Senor Carlos was going to sell it. I replaced it with the rock that you found in the cardboard beer box that Carlos gave you."

"Where's the mask now?" Mack asked. "Does Carlos still have it?"

"It is in a safe place," Carmelita replied. "Senor Carlos does not have it."

"Where is it?" Tina demanded.

"It is in a safe place Senorita Tina. That is all I can tell you," Carmelita responded with her gaze still focused on the floor. "May I have the *chacmool* now? *Por favor*?"

"If I let you take it, the priest will use you for a blood sacrifice," Tina responded. "I can't allow that to happen."

"But Senorita Tina, for me that it an honor," Carmelita softly pleaded with her eyes still focused on the floor.

"What will happen if you don't return the to *chacmool* to the priest today?" Mack inquired. "He can't do anything worse than cut your heart out and throw it in a Tupperware bowl."

"I will be flayed alive and the priest will wear my skin as he dances around the ceremonial fire."

"That doesn't sound very good," Mack replied. "We have to find a better alternative."

"How about if we take you back to Stuart and hide you at the marina?' Tina asked. "They won't be able to find you there."

"I will be forced to escape and return here for sacrifice," Carmelita responded. "It is my duty to my people for what I have done."

"Oh no!" Tina screamed. "You can't do that! We have to get you out of here."

"Carmelita," Mack carefully addressed the trembling woman. "You talk as if you know the priest. Do you?"

"Yes," she softly responded. "He is my brother."

"Octavio?" Mack exclaimed.

"Si Senor Mack," Carmelita responded as she raised her gaze from the drab floor and looked Mack directly in the eyes. "Octavio is my brother. You know that because you were at our home last week."

"Carmelita!" Tina interjected. "Are you telling us that Octavio is the priest that wanted to sacrifice Carlos?"

"Si Senorita Tina," the somber girl replied. "Senor Carlos shamed Octavio in front of his friends, took his mask from him and had Senor Elmo arrest him. He is very ashamed and must regain his honor through a blood sacrifice."

"Then he should take his revenge out on Carlos, not you!" Tina exclaimed.

"He can not do that Senorita Tina."

"Why not?" Mack interceded between the two women.

"Because I stole the *chacmool* and prevented him from sacrificing Senor Carlos last night. It is my fault and now I must pay my debt."

"But he's your brother!" Tina exclaimed. "How can he possibly hurt you?"

"It is my brother's duty to our people to reclaim his honor through a blood sacrifice and I have been chosen to replace Senor Carlos because I protected him from my brother. It is the way of my people and I am ready. I am not afraid."

"Where did your brother think the *chacmool* was?"

"It was my duty to protect the *chacmool* and that is why I removed it from the bar after Senor Carlos hid the mask. I told my brother that it was safe and hidden in the beer storeroom."

"So, when your brother went to get it last night there was a rock in the box?"

"That is correct Senorita Tina."

"No wonder he was pissed," Mack interjected. "He went to a lot of trouble to pile up those sod pallets and get the Guats riled up enough to drag Carlos and his buddy Pedro out to the Naked Lady Ranch. Why didn't they sacrifice Carlos last night?"

"Octavio couldn't find the *chacmool*," Carmelita explained. "When he opened the cardboard box he found only the rock."

Mack followed up with a seemingly logical question.

"What about the fire? Deputy Elmo told me that the Martin County Boosters Club found the pile of sod pallets at the Naked Lady Ranch and asked permission to hold a pep rally and bonfire there last night."

"That is true," the trembling girl responded. "The men who were supposed to protect the sacrificial altar had gone to the dogfights, gotten drunk and lost all of their money. When we got there the pallets were already on fire."

"If you were already there," Tina quipped, "Why didn't your brother sacrifice Carlos anyway?"

"The priest must have the *chacmool* when he performs a blood sacrifice. Octavio only had a rock," the nervous girl replied. "Plus, soon after we arrived at the Naked Lady Ranch the Indiantown Fire Department arrived to put out the fire. It was too late and there were too many outside people there."

"What can we do to make this all go away?" Tina asked.

"*Que*? I do not understand what you are asking," Carmelita replied.

"How can we help your brother regain his honor without sacrificing someone?" Tina responded. "If you give him back the mask and his stupid *chacmool* then he should be happy."

"He does not know that I have the mask and the *chacmool*," the girl replied. "I cannot give them both back to him."

"Why not?" Mack interjected. "If he gets his stuff back then he has nothing to complain about."

"He is a man and I am a woman," Carmelita sniffed as if she was trying to hold back a sob. "If he learns that I tricked him his pride will be destroyed and he will be required to satisfy the blood thirst of the jaguar god by hanging himself from a mahogany tree."

"Carmelita," Mack said. "It's not cast in stone."

"*Que*?"

"I think that Tina and I might be able to work things out with him if we can talk to him about it," Mack offered. "Where did you say you hid the mask?"

"It is upstairs on my maid's cart. It is wrapped in a towel in the bottom of my laundry bag."

"Why there?" Tina asked.

"No one looks in a hotel maid's dirty laundry bag," Carmelita sniffed.

"That makes sense," Mack offered. "Where is your laundry cart?"

"It is parked inside the storage room at the end of the hall."

"What time are you supposed to meet Octavio to give him the *chacmool*?"

"Three o'clock," she sniffed as a single tear ran down her right cheek and hung for a moment on her chin, as if it was undecided as what to do, before it rolled off and dashed into a soft 'splat' of nothingness on the carpet below.

"Where are you supposed to meet him?"

"Behind the Citgo station across the street from the Silver Saddle."

"Does Carlos know about this?"

"No senor."

"Tina, I'll run upstairs and locate the laundry cart if you sit here and keep Carmelita occupied."

"Okay," Tina dryly replied. "Then what?"

"We are going to meet Octavio behind the Citgo station at three o'clock. It's twenty minutes after two now and that should give us time to get our act together."

"What act?" Tina replied. "Do you have some kind of plan?"

"No! I'm going to play it by ear," Mack replied as he rose from the table. "When we get there just follow my lead and everything will be okay."

"Senor Mack, are you going to hurt my brother?" Carmelita asked between soft sobs.

"No Carmelita," Mack replied. "I won't hurt your brother any worse than he was going to hurt you," he added as he turned and headed for the dining room door and hotel lobby beyond.

Chapter
61

"*Buenas tardes*, senor Mack," whispered a soft male voice directly behind Mack's position alongside the Citgo station's air dispenser. "*Como esta usted?*"

Mack whirled around to face none other than Octavio himself who was leaning against the side of the building. Octavio was dressed in faded denim blue jeans, a denim shirt and a straw cowboy hat that had seen better days shaded his face from the fierce afternoon sun.

"*Muy bueno, gracias,*" Mack responded. "*Y usted?*"

"*Bueno,*" Octavio responded. "*Que pasa* senor Mack?"

"*De nada,*" Mack responded with a grin. "Octavio, your sister's not coming. I'm here in her place and we have to talk about last night."

"*Por que?*" Octavio quipped as he slumped against the concrete wall and began to pick an imaginary food particle between his front teeth with a wooden matchstick.

"Let's stop playing cat and mouse!" Mack stated. "I know that you think that you are a priest and have some kind of super powers over the rest of the migrant workers. I'm here to tell you that you don't!"

"Senor Mack, I do not know what you are talking about," Octavio replied as he stabbed at a food particle lodged in the slight gap between his front incisors. "I came here to buy a lottery ticket."

"I know better," Mack tersely replied. "You came here to collect the mask and *chacmool* from Carmelita so that you could regain your hold over the migrant workers. She's not coming."

"*Por que* she is not coming?" Octavio asked as he straightened up from his slumped position against the building wall. "She is my sister and she owes me."

"She doesn't owe you anything!" Mack exclaimed. "You're lucky that your sorry butt isn't still sitting in the Martin County Jail. She saved your ass!"

"What do you mean Senor Mack? I do not understand."

"Your sister stole the mask from Carlos and hid it in her hotel laundry cart so it couldn't be used as evidence against you in your trial. Then she hid the *chacmool* and gave it to Tina so that Carlos couldn't steal it too. He was going to sell both of them for much *dinero. Comprende?*"

"I understand Senor Mack. Where is the mask now?"

"I have it and I also have the *chacmool*. I'll give them to you if you agree to drop the idea of sacrificing your sister and Carlos."

"I was not going to sacrifice them!" Carlos emphatically stated. "I was just trying to scare them so they would return the mask and the *chacmool* to me. I did not know which one of them had them."

"That's a long story. Carlos thought that he had the mask, but he didn't. Your sister had it the entire time and Tina had the *chacmool* until Friday night when she brought it back and gave it to Carmelita."

"Will you give them to me now?"

"Not until you explain how you got them and why they are so important to you."

"How do I know that I can trust you?"

"You can't, but you have to take a chance on me if you ever want to see them again."

"*Caramba*! Senor Mack you give me no choice!"

"Octavio, I'm glad that you see it that way," Mack replied. "Shall we talk right here, or do you want to go somewhere else?"

"Here is fine. What do you want to know?"

"Tell me the truth about the mask. How did you get it and why did you offer to trade it to Carlos to pay off your bar bill?"

"I did not give it to him! I asked him to hold it as credit against my gambling debt until I got paid."

"Why would he say that it was payment for your bar bill?"

"He said that because gambling is not legal here and he knows that Pedro cheats us!"

"Where did you get the mask?"

"I told you when you drove me back to Indiantown after court. My great grandfather found it in nineteen sixty-six during the excavation of my family's pyramid in the city of *Chich'en Itza* in *Pejen Province* in Guatemala. It was a funeral mask for *King Hanab Pakal* who lived in *El Mirador*."

"Octavio, I think that there's a lot more to the story."

"What do you mean senor Mack?"

"You are *almenhen*. Your family was Mayan nobility."

"How do you know that word? It is from the ancient language of the Maya!"

"I did my homework. The black chickens that you gave to Carlos gave you away. Black chickens were pets of Chinese nobles and they were brought to Guatemala by Chinese sailors in fourteen twenty-one and given to Mayan nobles as symbols of their position."

"What else do you know about my family?"

"Your great grandfather was a Mayan priest and he discovered the mask so that the American archaeologists would stop looking for it. Then he stole it and hid it again. Your grandfather and your father were also both priests and so are you. The mask is a symbol of your authority."

"That is true. How did you find out?"

"Some basic library research, plus a color photograph of your mask was in a catalog."

"Did you tell anyone my secret?"

"No. My guess is that you came here to establish a form of civil government run by the migrant workers themselves and the mask is your symbol of authority to do so. I believe the Mayan word for a civil government is *ayuntamiento*."

"That is correct."

"Who sent you to Indiantown to set up a *ayuntamiento*?"

"A Catholic priest who served in this parish came to my village and described how poor the working conditions are in Indiantown for migrant workers. He was my visa sponsor."

"How about your sister Carmelita?"

"She was a school teacher in Guatemala. She came here to help me and to set up a Hispanic school for the children of the migrant workers. She is a very smart girl."

"She certainly is and your English has gotten much better in the last few minutes."

"Thank you. I am trying very hard to learn English."

"Octavio, tell me more about your family. What does your father do?"

"My father was a large landowner. He was killed by government soldiers on May twenty-ninth, nineteen seventy-eight during a government siege."

"Why?"

"A group of Mayan landowners, including my father, was protesting in the town of Panzos, in the province of Alta Veracruz, over the government's refusal to grant them land titles. More than one hundred men, women and children were killed that day. My mother, my sister and I fled to Mexico City to live with her sister."

"Were you and Carmelita raised in Mexico City?"

"Si."

"Did you both attend college in Mexico City?"

"Yes and no. Carmelita got her teaching degree from the University of Mexico."

"How about you?"

"I didn't know what I wanted to do with my life so I dabbled in history, political science and economics for my first two years at the University of Mexico."

"What did you do after that?"

"I applied for a student visa and was accepted at Arizona State University in Tempe."

"Did you finish and receive a degree?"

"Yes. I received my bachelor's in economics and applied for graduate school."

"Were you accepted?"

"Yes. I got my Master's Degree in political science."

"That explains a lot. Did you go back to Mexico City after graduation?"

"No. I moved to Los Angeles and got an internship at the Institute for Mexican Studies."

"How long did you stay there?"

"Two years."

"Then what? Did you get bored?"

"Sort of. I was invited to join to movement to organize the migrant workers in southern California."

"Did you?"

"Yes. I spent seven years working with Chavez in organizing the Mexican workers. My last position was Director of North American Field Operations."

"It sounds like you caught the eye of the right people."

"I was in the right place at the right time."

"What really brought you to Indiantown? I know that story about the priest coming to your village and anointing you as the savior of your people was a load of crap."

"The migrant workers here are destitute and under the control of the people who own the groves and vegetable farms. They also own the company store, the prices are double what they are in Stuart, and require the workers to cash their paychecks there. The workers have no way to get into Stuart and are essentially slave laborers. If they even whisper about complaining the big shots will threaten to call the INS on them and have them deported."

"What did you expect to do about it? The labor system has been working like this for many years."

"I was hoping to instill some ancient Mayan values of pride and self worth into the people so they would stand up for themselves against their bosses."

"Why did you masquerade as an itinerant laborer? Why didn't you just come out and tell them who you are and who you represent?"

"Most of these people are illegal immigrants and illiterate to boot. They wouldn't trust me if they knew I was a college graduate. They would think that I was a spy for the grove and field owners or the American government."

"I think that I understand. What's the real story behind the mask?"

"It is exactly as I told you. It is a sacred heirloom to my family. The workers know what it represents and it allowed me to have some influence over them without raising suspicions."

"Why did you give it to Carlos?"

"I wanted the men who come into the bar to see it and know that it was mine. It is a symbol of authority and power."

"What about the *chacmool*?"

"It also belongs to my family. It is a symbol of the blood sacrifices held by the Mayan priests to their gods. Only high-ranking nobles of the Mayans' captured enemies were allowed the privilege of having their hearts cut out and thrown into a *chacmool*."

"Why did Carmelita put it on the shelf in the Silver Saddle?"

"She thought that it would encourage the people to rally behind me, but they took it literally as symbol to prepare for a blood sacrifice. That's why they built the sacrificial altar out of sod pallets out at the Naked Lady Ranch. That was all real."

"So, that's why Carmelita took it down and gave it to Tina! She knew that they couldn't hold a blood sacrifice without the *chacmool*."

"That's right. They were ready to barbeque Carlos Friday night to avenge my honor."

"But they couldn't because they didn't have the *chacmool*," Mack replied with a smile. "Carlos had it hidden under his desk!"

"Yes, and he thought that it was the mask. He doesn't realize that his own greed saved his neck."

"Octavio, what are you going to do now?"

"I'm not certain, but I can't dissert my people. Someone has to fight for them because they are unable to fight for themselves."

"I agree. What are you going to do from here on out?"

"Unfortunately, although my work here is far from done, I can't remain in Indiantown any longer."

"Why not? You have established yourself as a leader among the migrant workers."

"I wish I could, but I'm a target because of all the ruckus. Plus, I have to get back to Los Angeles and prepare for a campaign in Napa Valley that kicks off the first of next month."

"What about Carmelita? Is she staying?"

"Of course not! I wouldn't leave her here at the mercy of that pig Carlos! She's going back to Los Angeles with me to get ready for the Napa Valley campaign."

"Who is going to take your place?" Mack asked. "These people need guidance and hope."

"They're already here. It will only take them a few days to get their feet wet, but they'll be up and running in a few days."

"What do you mean they? Is it another brother and sister team? Do I know them?"

"It wouldn't be fair to them and my people if I answer your questions. They require anonymity just like Carmelita and I had, that is until you and that big mouth Tina got involved."

"Oh."

"Now, if you don't mind, can I have my mask and the *chacmool* back? It's almost three-thirty. Carmelita and I have to catch a six o'clock flight to LA out of West Palm Beach."

"Carmelita has them. She's sitting in the Seminole Inn dining room with Tina."

"Gracias senor Mack," Octavio replied as he stretched, straightened his straw cowboy hat and began to walk away around the corner of the Citgo building. "*Hasta la vista,*" he added over his right shoulder.

Mack couldn't do anything except mumble, "*Hasta la vista*" as he watched Octavio disappear behind the Citgo station.

Chapter 62

It was a bright sunny Monday morning and Mack pulled into an open parking place at the Blake Library at 10:17 A.M. He anticipated that Janet had already returned from Paris.

"I didn't figure that she could stand that French guy for very long," he thought as he rumbled across the concrete patio towards the glass door.

To Mack's surprise, when he turned the corner in the lobby area, he spotted Johanna seated in Janet's normal position behind the reference desk. She smiled and waved when she saw him.

"Crap!" He mumbled under his breath. *"The old broad got hooked on that French phony's fake goatee and accent."*

"How can we help you this fine morning Mr. McCray?" Johanna bubbled.

"Janet was supposed to get me some information about the University of Florida's experimental project in the stimulation of plant root growth through the transmission of low frequency energy," Mack responded.

"I believe that she has what you asked for right here," Johanna responded as she reached for a manila file folder next to her computer keyboard. "She got it together for you before she left for Paris."

"Thank you," Mack stammered. "It should be very helpful," he added as he turned to leave.

"She told me that if you needed any more information that you should call the agricultural research station directly and ask for the project manager. Their telephone number is in the upper right hand corner of the first page."

"Thanks Johanna," Mack replied over his right shoulder. "I think that I have everything I need."

"Did you want to speak to her about it?"

Mack paused in mid-stride and slowly turned to face Johanna.

"How can I ask her? Do you have her telephone number at the University of Paris?"

"Of course not," Johanna replied with a slight smile. "She's in the back office gabbing about her wild weekend to everyone who will listen to her. Do you want me to get her for you?"

Mack didn't know whether to shout or play disinterested. He chose the latter.

"If you think that she has time to go over this stuff I'd appreciate it," Mack dryly replied.

"Of course she does!" Johanna stated. "She'll make time for you! You're her favorite customer," Johanna bubbled as she reached for the telephone. "I'll give her a call."

"Thanks. I'll wait over by the copy machines."

"Okay. I spoke to her and she said that she'll be right out."

Mack pretended that he didn't hear Johanna's last comment and strolled towards the copy machines.

"Mr. McCray! I'm back in town!"

Mack turned around to focus on the source of the voice. It was Janet and she was slowly hobbling towards the copy machines from the direction of the back office.

"*Her arthritis must be acting up,*" he thought. "*Or, maybe that French phony kept her busy walking around Paris all weekend.*"

"Mr. McCray," Janet gushed as she drew closer to him. "I have so much to tell you."

"I've already been to Paris," Mack defensively replied. "I even bought the Eiffel Tower once."

"It's not about Paris," Janet replied as she reached his side. "I never went, but don't tell the girls. They think that I ran off to Paris for the weekend with that French guy."

"What!" Mack exclaimed. "I distinctly remember Johanna telling me on Friday that you went to Paris for the weekend with that French gigolo!"

"I told her that I was going out of town for the weekend," Janet grinned as she softly replied. "If Johanna, and the rest of the librarians, want to think that I went to Paris with Jacques that's okay with me. I'll take the credit for a foreign conquest. It's fun."

"Where did you go? I was worried about you."

"I flew to Washington and spent the weekend with my sister. She works in the Pentagon. We spent the weekend prowling the back streets of Georgetown at night and spent Saturday in the Smithsonian."

"Why didn't you tell me where you were going when I saw you at Shrimper's Thursday night?"

"I was on a date."

"Where did you go after dinner?"

"That's very personal, but I'll guarantee that Francois had a good time."

"Wait a minute! You just called him Francois and before that you called him Jacques!"

"He's both and the same," Janet replied with a smile. "He's a twofer."

"What's a twofer?" Mack innocently asked.

"You get two men for the price of one."

"Oh. Why does he have two names?"

"He's Jacques and Francois. When he worked on a top-secret dolphin project in Hawaii his name was Jacques, but when he conveniently drowned during a morning swim, he went into the Federal Protection Program and changed his name to Francois."

"What do you mean by conveniently drowned?"

"The Navy was closing down the project and didn't want any witnesses. So, he drowned."

"I understand, I think," Mack replied. "I just feel left out."

"That's how I feel when you disappear for days at a time after asking me to research some wild thing for you," Janet replied. "Now, what's with this stupid electromagnetic energy plant root stimulation crap that you asked me to check out?"

"I've got the stuff right here. I'll look it over this afternoon."

"You didn't really need it did you?"

"Of course I did," Mack defensively replied. "That's why I asked you to look into it for me."

"When I spoke to Doctor Gary Diamond at the University of Florida Agricultural Research Station he told me that that he met you over in Indiantown last week and explained the entire project to you. Is that correct or not?"

"I guess so," Mack meekly replied. "We had a short conversation at one of the grove water pumping stations."

"According to him it was more like two hours," Janet sternly replied. "He told me that you asked about the effects of ELF transmission on plant root growth and that you were very interested in the frequency range and power output of their transmission system."

"That's correct. So what?"

"He said that he caught you rooting around some of the ELF transmission copper lines that are buried underground alongside the PVC water irrigation pipes."

"I wasn't rooting around! I was checking the power output level and frequency range."

"Why didn't you just ask them what they were for in the first place instead of concocting some wild story that the government and grove owners are trying to influence the behavior of the migrant workers through the transmission of ELF frequencies through underground transmission lines?"

"I didn't concoct any story about anything!" Mack exclaimed in his defense.

"The word was all over the intelligence community that you did," Janet softly replied. "Do you remember the two old men who were hanging round the copy machines one of the days when you were in here talking to me?"

"Of course I do. The skinny one was hitting on you and you enjoyed it."

"Nonsense! They are both retired CIA field agents and they were here checking up on you."

"What!" Mack exclaimed. "They didn't look like any field agents I ever saw."

"Are field agents supposed to look like field agents so that the bad guys can recognize them?"

"Of course not! Field agents are covert operatives."

"I rest my case," Janet whispered. "Be careful, I think that you're being watched right now."

"What? By whom?"

"Do you see those two ladies over there by the computer terminals?"

"Do you mean the old one in the walker and the other old one in a wheelchair?"

"That's the ones! They're retired NSA field agents."

"What makes you think that?" Mack asked. "They can't even walk by themselves."

"They told me and I believe them," Janet replied with a smug grin. "The one in the wheelchair used to mess around with President Kennedy when she was on White House security duty back in the early nineteen-sixties."

"She told you that?"

"Yep, and my sister verified it. She was a junior military attaché in the White House at the same time."

"I certainly believe that," Mack replied as he rubbed the right side of his face. "I assume that your sister and you had a good time running around Georgetown at night. Did she use her walker?"

"Excuse me!" Janet adamantly stated as she stood up on her tiptoes and tried to look Mack in the eye. "My sister had both hips replaced last year and she doesn't need a walker. She made it all the way through the Smithsonian without help."

"Why did you go to the Smithsonian if you and twinkle toes had Georgetown at your mercy?"

"That was really a snide comment wasn't it?" Janet remarked. "I went there for you."

"For me?"

"Yes for you. I went there to check on that silly mask that you are so worried about."

"Oh," Mack softly replied. "It's okay now. The mask is back with its owner."

"No it's not," Janet tersely replied. "The Smithsonian owns the mask and they would like to have it returned as soon as possible."

"What are you talking about?" Mack replied. "Octavio, the migrant worker from Guatemala, owns the mask. It is a family treasure that goes back in his family for hundreds of years."

"And his great grandfather stole it from the Smithsonian, didn't he?"

"He found it! He didn't steal it!" Mack retorted. "It was a family treasure and he saved it for the future generations of his family."

"He took it out of the shipping box and replaced it with a river stone. Isn't that what you told me?"

"Yes, but he did it to preserve the heirloom for his family. It never belonged to the Smithsonian."

"A Smithsonian archeologist found it, recorded it and registered it in nineteen sixty-six," Janet fumed. "Doesn't that clearly make it theirs?"

"Wasn't the archaeologist actually from Yale University?"

"Yes, but so what?" Janet asked. "What difference does that make?"

"If he wasn't a Smithsonian archaeologist the Smithsonian cannot lay claim to the mask."

"He was working for the Smithsonian!" Janet retorted as she glared at Mack. "It's theirs!"

"It's not theirs unless they can locate it and prove that it is the same one that the archaeologist from Yale found in nineteen sixty-six."

"They have measurements and color photographs!" Janet spit out. "I met personally with the director of the Olmec collection. I guarantee you that he can prove that it's the same mask!"

"I don't think so," Mack replied with a smug grin.

"Why not?" Janet demanded.

"They have to find it first."

"What did you do with it?"

"Nothing except give it back to its rightful owner."

"Isn't he in Indiantown?"

"Maybe he is and maybe he isn't," Mack teased. "He might be in Belle Glade, Fort Myers, Immokalee, Orlando, Ocala and maybe even back in Guatemala. They'll never find him."

"That's not fair!" Janet spit out as she stamped her right foot. "I was going to receive a finder's fee from the Smithsonian for locating the mask!"

"How much?"

"Ten thousand dollars!" Janet squirmed as she replied. "I was going to donate it to charity."

"I'll bet you were," Mack replied. "I hope that they didn't pay you in advance."

"They didn't give me the whole amount. They only gave me a small advance for my trouble."

"How much?"

"One thousand dollars."

"Check or cash?"

"Check."

"Have you cashed it yet?"

"No. I didn't get home until after ten o'clock last night," Janet replied. "The bank wasn't open."

"Then you have two choices."

"What two choices?"

"Cash the check and keep the money, or send it back."

"I must return the check because they are not going to find the mask if what you alluded to is true."

"That's the wrong decision," Mack quipped with a wink of his left eye.

"Why? I don't deserve the money."

"If the check was for your trouble they won't complain," Mack replied. "Plus, it's not worth their time or trouble to fly down here and take it back. Cash it, go to the Keys and have a fling."

"I never thought of it that way. I did go to a lot of trouble. How much does it cost to fly to Paris?"

"Less than a thousand bucks. Call a travel agent. They'll get you a cheap fare."

"I believe I will," Janet replied with a sly wink. "Thank you for your advice Mr. McCray."

"You are very welcome and there is no charge for my professional consulting," Mack quipped. "Now what's the skinny on the two old broads over there by the computer terminals?"

"They're both widows and on the make for a rich old geezer in their age group."

"I won't make the cut on either of those criteria," Mack replied. "See you around Janet."

"I'll watch for you Mr. McCray," Janet softly responded. "Please come in if you think we might be able to help you with any reference topics."

"I will," Mack replied.

He handed the file folder to Janet, turned and headed for the library exit. On his way out he glanced at the wall clock hanging in the lobby. It read 10:47 A.M. and he had a lot of things to do.

Epilogue

"Since war begins in the minds of men, it is in the minds of men that the defenses of peace must be constructed."

UNESCO Constitution

The 2500 year-old carved jadeite mask
was the death mask of an Olmec ruler.

Chacmools were used by ancient Mayan priests as repositories for the hearts of their sacrificed victims.

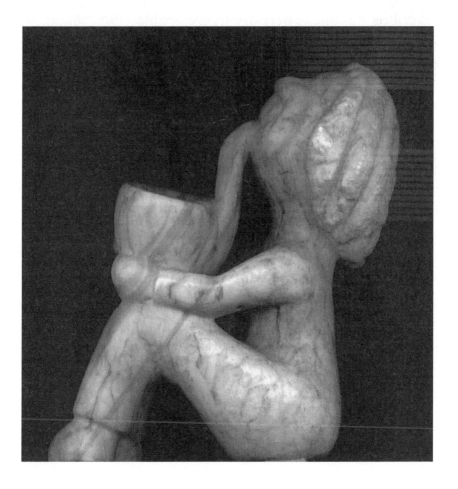

Acknowledgements

Where does one possibly begin to acknowledge and recognize the many people who assisted in bringing the saga of *JADE* to these printed pages?

I don't where to begin, and because I do not where to begin, I don't know where to end and I don't want to overlook anyone. There are many people who guided me, corrected me, chastised me, offered constructive criticism and tweaked the words, sentences, grammar and paragraphs until they made readable sense. It was a joint effort of almost epic proportions.

However, if you find something that you do not like, or maybe do not understand, or find an error in spelling, or questionable grammar such as a dangling participle, or hanging diphthong, please assign the responsibility for that snafu to me. I never understood those things.

Those many people who assisted me with research materials and provided hours of proof reading expertise are due more than I can ever repay, except to thank each of them for their efforts from the bottom of my heart.

Sincerely,

Paul

Paul McElroy is president of Charter Industry Services, Inc. headquartered in Stuart, Florida. The company specializes in conducting professional maritime training courses. He founded *Charter Industry* a trade journal for professionals in the marine charter industry in 1985. He has extensive writing experience in magazines and newspapers with more than 200 published articles to his credit.

Captain McElroy received his first United States Coast Guard license in 1983 and operated a sport fishing charter business in the Chicago area for several years. He currently holds a Merchant Marine Officer's MASTER - Near Coastal license He served in the United States Air Force, spent a two-year tour in the Far East and specialized in electronics. He speaks Japanese and Spanish.

Mr. McElroy received his Bachelor of Science Degree in Business Administration from Florida State University. Prior to joining the maritime industry he was an executive in the headquarters of a major telecommunications corporation. He lives in south Florida with his wife Michi, is a member of the Mystery Writers of America and the National Association of Maritime Educators. This is his sixth novel.

Contact him at: www.TreasureCoastMysteries.com